*About the Springfield Writers Group*

*Established in 2016, the Springfield Writers Group (SWG) is based in Brisbane, Australia. This group of emerging and established writers meet monthly over coffee and too many muffins to support each other's work and efforts towards becoming better writers. There is probably too much time spent laughing and enjoying each other's company, but we do get some work done as well. This anthology represents many months of work, learning, frustration, and joy.*

*Anyone wishing to contact the SWG can connect through the Queensland Writers Centre, who will forward information.*

# Elemental

Anthology of short stories
By members of the
Springfield Writers Group
Edited by Aiki Flinthart

*To all the authors out there – both published and aspiring – don't give up.*

*The SWG gratefully acknowledge the traditional owners – the Jagera, Yuggera and Ugarapul peoples of Ipswich and Springfield – as the keepers of ancient knowledge and whose cultures and customs continue to nurture this land. The SWG also pays respect to Elders – past, present and future.*

*Elemental* edited by Aiki Flinthart

Cover artwork by Croco Designs

Copyright © 2019 The Springfield Writers Group

All stories are original to this collection

A Cataloging-in-Publications entry for this title is available from the National Library of Australia.

ISBN-13: 978-0-9945928-4-2 (Trade Paperback)
ISBN-13: 978-0-9945928-3-5 (e-book)
Computing Advantages & Training P/L
PO Box 3388, Darra
QLD 4076, Australia

*Heartfelt thanks goes to all the authors in the Springfield Writers Group, for their enthusiasm, support, dedication and hard work. Also to our families, for their patience with our hiding away for hours on end as we tried desperately to scribble a few thousand words down. Thanks to Bookface bookstore, for hosting our monthly meetings and mainlining coffee for us.*

# Contents

# EARTH

# The Jig's Back Door

*A Hangman's Jig tale*

*DA Kelly*

'Are you certain we're heading the right way?' Sneath peered into the darkness. He waved his flaming torch back and forth, illuminating the cave walls. The roof was a jungle of tangled tree roots and low-hanging rock. Not a gem to be seen. Not a vein of gold gleamed in the torchlight. This treasure hunting was harder than he had planned. 'What's the map say?'

'Stupid thing is sulking,' Clutter said.

'Of all the maps in the world.' Sneath cuffed Clutter's pointy green ear. 'You had to steal that one.'

'Of all the goblins in the world, you had to be my brother.'

'Elder brother. Which makes me boss.'

'Then you hold the map.' Clutter thrust the ragged scroll into Sneath's chest. 'See if she likes you any better.'

'PMS,' Sneath said. 'Prissy Map Syndrome, that's what she's got.'

He unfurled the ancient vellum. The sketched landscape had changed since he'd last looked at it. There were no more forests and mountains dotted with towns. Now tunnels, underground streams and caverns sprawled across the map. Trouble was, when he tried to focus on a particular area, it faded and shimmered making it impossible to follow. He tried peering out of the corner of his eye, but the map was smarter than that. All it did was flash the words, *You are uglier than an ogre sucking a wasp!*

Forcing a smile, Sneath turned to Clutter and said, 'You just got to know how to talk to females.'

The map snorted, the sound emanating from the scorched vellum despite it having no mouth. 'Because you have so much experience.'

'If you weren't a scrap of old calf skin, you'd know what a terrific love-maker I am.'

'Thank the Mother Sky for small mercies,' the map said. 'And stop calling me The Map! I do have a name, you know.'

'Lemon-puss?' Clutter elbowed Sneath and grinned, his tiny, sharp teeth glowing gold in the torchlight.

'Amethyst,' the map said, with a haughty sniff. 'Amethyst Diaphany the Fourth.'

'You made that up!' Sneath scoffed.

'Either call me by my name or I stop guiding you.'

'Because you've been so extraordinarily helpful up until now,' Clutter said. 'You don't even have an X-marks-the-spot! I'm tempted to wipe my backside with you next time I—'

'Believe me,' the map said, 'I can make things a lot worse. Now, are you going to show me some respect, or will I roll up and shut up?'

The goblins looked at each other, shrugged and said, 'Amethyst Diaphany the Fourth it is, then.'

'But we're not going to spout that mouthful all the time,' Sneath said.

'Amethyst will do for now. And perhaps a bow here and there for good measure.'

'In your dreams!' Sneath sputtered. 'Why, if you didn't know where that magical Gem was hidden—'

'What was that?' Clutter spun on one boot heel, cocking his head to listen.

'Probably the witch,' Amethyst whispered. 'She's been hunting you since you stole me.'

'And you're just telling us this now?' Sneath said.

'I thought I'd lost her when we forded that river,' Amethyst said.

'You call being swept along by ice-cold rapids, fording a river?' Clutter muttered. 'Crawling out on a slimy finger of rock, shivering, half drowned—'

'Shhh!' Amethyst hissed. 'Douse the torch! Run forward seventeen steps, then turn right, drop to your knees and crawl until I tell you to stop.'

Distant footsteps echoed through the cave. The goblins didn't need further encouragement. Sneath kicked dirt over the flaming torch then shoved it in his backpack, the pitch-smeared end jutting over his shoulder. Never had darkness swooped over them so thick and so fast. Sneath darted through the black, counting as he ran. Clutter was a number behind, but that was typical. He'd probably knock himself out on a low hanging rock because he counted wrong. When Sneath reached seventeen he fell to his knees and scrambled along like a frightened crab. Amazingly, Clutter scuttled along just behind. Freezing, muddy puddles soaked Sneath's woollen trews, squelched between his fingers and splashed his sweaty face.

Amethyst, still grasped in Sneath's hand, coughed and spluttered. Who knew a map could cough? Sneath flapped Amethyst around, shaking her free of mud and water.

'Yes.' Amethyst wheezed. 'You definitely know how to treat a lady.'

'You get what you give,' Sneath said, puffing. 'How much further?'

'There's a deep ravine to your left, you can go that way if you like. Drop me before you hurtle down to Hell.'

'Oh, you are a rotten joke!'

'Birds of a feather,' Amethyst said.

'Would you both shut up!' Clutter whispered. 'Since when do witches wear hobnailed boots?'

Rhythmic, metal-on-rock steps echoed through the darkness. Stopped. Scraped as though the boot wearer turned on the spot. Probably listening.

'She must mean business!' Sneath scrunched up Amethyst and stuffed her down the front of his trews.

'Please! Kill me now!' Amethyst said, her voice muffled.

'Maybe I'll throw *you* down the ravine,' Sneath said as he crawled forward.

'It stinks in here!' Amethyst groaned. 'Have you never heard of soap?'

Voices drifted through the tunnel.

One deep, raspy and definitely male. 'They gotta be the worst thieves ever.'

The other voice was female, her tone nasty. 'Bright enough to steal from me.'

'Stop!' Amethyst shouted, making Sneath's squashy male bits vibrate. 'Make a slight right. No, your other right. Head into the passageway, but watch it. There's a bit of a drop at the far end, and there could be water at the bottom. The ogre won't fit through the passage. One less to deal with.'

'Ogre!' Sneath and Clutter spluttered together.

'You never said anything about an ogre!' Clutter said.

'My bad.' Amethyst, for once didn't sound glib or insulting, which caused Sneath's heart to flip-flop with fear.

'When we started hunting for the Lost Gem of Nerramai,' Sneath said. 'We never figured ogres would chase us. Still, once we find the Gem, we can level a mountain if we want.' He slithered along on his belly, the map squashing against his male-bits.

Amethyst didn't answer. Probably so impressed she was lost for words.

Sneath stretched his bony, green fingers forward through the mud, feeling for the supposed drop-off. Nothing but rock smoothed by goodness knows what. He felt up and around. The tunnel walls and roof were smooth as polished obsidian. His wiry hair stood on end. Something had worn the rock smooth and there was a good chance they were heading right for it.

Sneath rolled onto his side, tugged his trews open and said, 'You don't have a bit of fine-print stating *This way be monsters,* do you?'

'That will teach you not to read the instructions before you start,' Amethyst said.

'I didn't see any instructions!' Clutter crawled alongside Sneath and, fumbling in the dark, grabbed his brother's trews and whispered down them, 'You hid them from us, didn't you?'

'Do you mind?' Sneath clapped his hand over his crotch.

Amethyst didn't answer.

'Tunnel's not big enough for dragons,' Clutter said. 'So that's something.'

'You want the witch to catch us?' Sneath snapped at the map. 'You want to be locked up in that stinking old trunk again? Squashed among the mouldy boots and socks.'

Amethyst growled. 'She tortured me far worse than that.'

'Why?' both goblins asked.

'To force me to lead her to the Gem.'

'You have a choice?'

'It's complicated,' the map muttered.

'How can *we* be sure you're leading us to the Gem?' Clutter asked.

'You can't. Now come on,' Amethyst said. 'I hear the witch

likes goblin flambé. Crawl forward another few feet and you'll be at the drop-off. Hold your breath. Don't complain I didn't warn you.'

Grunting, Sneath patted his trews closed and crawled along the passage, his hands sliding forward so he wouldn't miss the drop-off. The ground vanished, then angled down in a slippery, putrid slide. Normally, Sneath would find the stench and whooshing sensation of careening down a slide of mud fun, but today was a rotten day, and all the excitement of adventuring had vanished in the dark. Clutter squealed and fumbled for Sneath, clutching his jacket with an iron grip.

They both tumbled through the air and plunged into an ice-cold lake. Sneath sucked in a shocked breath and a throat full of freezing water as he thrashed for the surface. Clutter flailed, grabbing for his brother, his nails gouging deep wounds in Sneath's face and neck. Coughing, Sneath fought to stay afloat, clambering onto whatever he could, which happened to be Clutter. Pain shot through his lower arm and he pulled away, his legs still peddling their way up his brother's thrashing body. Clutter disappeared from beneath him, leaving Sneath spluttering and flailing around in an awkward and rather ineffective form of swimming. In the dark, a few feet away, came a great gasp and a lot of splashing.

'Come any closer, Sneath.' Clutter coughed and wheezed. 'And I'll bite you again!'

Sneath sucked on his arm, tasting warm blood and torn flesh. Uncertain which way to swim, he reefed Amethyst from his trews, treading water while he held the map in the air. 'Which way now?'

'I am feeling wonderful, thanks for asking.' Amethyst shivered between Sneath's fingers.

'Come on, Amethyst!' Clutter said through chattering fangs. 'We are freezing here.'

'To your left there's an embankment,' Amethyst said with a sniff. 'It's the easiest way out of the lake. But there is a rather grumpy serpent eyeing you for supper from the shoreline.'

'What!' Both goblins squawked.

'Best you go right. There's a bit of a climb, but at least you won't end up gristle stuck between the serpent's teeth.'

'How do we know you're not leading us astray?' Sneath asked. 'For all we know, the other way will be worse.'

'Because you're my last hope.'

Sneath shoved the map between his fangs and headed right.

A soft splosh, flick and a splash drifted over to the swimming goblins.

*The serpent!* Sneath swam faster, his arms whirling like bony windmill blades. Clutter thrashed nearby. All smash and kick. Hopefully he was keeping pace.

Something cold and slimy slithered by Sneath, bumping him sideways. He yelped.

A great splash showered Sneath. Clutter howled from somewhere in the darkness above.

*Above?* Sneath squinted upward but could see nothing. *How did he get up there?*

A colossal splash was followed by a swollen wave that buffeted Sneath as the faintly-glowing serpent dove into the lake. Its sinuous body, ice cold and powerful skimmed past Sneath leaving a slimy trail on his arm. The serpent reared once more, it's snake-like whiskers slapping Sneath as it flicked its head. Clutter hollered high above once again then landed a few feet from Sneath, sinking underwater with the momentum of his fall. He shot to the surface, gasping and, from the speed and chaos of the splashes, Clutter swam like a wild thing.

Gummy lips clamped around Sneath's lower legs. Rubbery, wet whiskers drummed about his body. Sneath kicked and punched the serpent's snout. He reefed the torch from his sodden backpack, beating the serpent's head. Golden, implacable eyes glared at him from just below the surface. It bit the torch and tossed it aside. Sneath drew a small, steel blade from his belt and jabbed furiously in the darkness. The serpent thrashed. Sneath lurched free, surrounded by metallic-tasting water.

The brothers swam until they reached the shore—a greasy landing of rock and pebbles. Sneath crawled forward, groping for the cliff face. Rough stone grazed his hand. He thrust his dagger into its sheath and fumbled around for rock-holds. He began climbing. When he had managed a few feet, he glanced down looking for the orange glow of Clutter's eyes, but there was nothing to see. All he could hear was Clutter's puffing and the scuff of fingers and boots on rock. If only there was a speck of light. Just a chink would be enough to allow the goblins to see.

'Do you have an indilt wight?' Sneath asked Amethyst who was still clamped between his fangs.

'What?' Amethyst grumbled. 'You think I'm a multi-purpose tool?'

'You're 'agical. I's a logical westion.'

'Stop drooling on me!' Amethyst said. 'It's disgusting, and you're making my ink run.'

'You try talkin' to a shnooty map when i's a'tween your teess.'

'You try being stuffed in a mouth that smells like a sewer. I thought your crotch stunk! By the Sky Mother—'

'Oh, for da luv ov...' Sneath grabbed the map and shoved her back down his trews. 'Happier now?'

A smokey-red light lit the cavern, surging fog-like across the underground lake and up the cliff face where the two goblins clung like a pair of four legged spiders. The magical redfire, though low in power, stung Sneath's skin. He could taste sulphur and ash as though it had been painted on his tongue.

*Hope that's all the magic the old crone's got.* Sneath shot a look up, then down and across the lake. There knelt the witch and the ogre in the passageway's opening a few yards up the rock-face. The ogre's eyes reflected orange in the rusty light. Damn! He was a night-seer just like the goblins. He stood up and leaned out the hole, scanning the cavern. Though he was fully armoured in boiled leather and steel-plate, he was perhaps five feet tall. Made no sense. Ogre toddlers were taller than that.

'She's summoning redfire!' Clutter moaned. 'How are we going to outrun redfire?'

'From the taste of it, it's no real threat.'

'Hope that's her best trick, then.'

'There they are!' shouted the ogre, his gruff voice bouncing around the massive cavern in hollow echoes. He jumped into the lake and started swimming toward the goblins. With each stroke, the ogre grew, his arms bulging bigger and bigger muscles, his knobby head expanding like a bull's bladder blown full of hot air, his body spreading and lengthening until he was the height of a woolly mammoth.

'So much for redfire being her best trick.' Clutter climbed faster.

Sneath, thankful for the fiery, red light, scrambled upward, Clutter alongside him, his wide eyes glowing orange, his face dripping with sweat.

'Are you sure the gem is this way?' Sneath asked. 'Or are you just making us suffer for your own amusement?'

'Here's hoping, eh!' Amethyst chuckled; there was no mirth in the sound.

Erratic splashing floated up to the goblins. Sneath glanced down, expecting to see the ogre exiting the lake. But the ogre was frantically treading water, searching the darkness behind the him. He ducked beneath the blood-red water, popped to the surface, cursed and swam faster towards the cliff.

Ripples broke the lake's still surface. Slimy humps undulated then disappeared near the ogre. Sneath almost cheered the serpent on. He shot a look at the witch, still kneeling in the passageway. She watched on, her expression lost in the shadows, but Sneath could feel her hatred burning into his back.

The murky, red light she had conjured seared fire-bright, momentarily blinding the goblins before simmering back to a dull glow.

The serpent reared from the lake, its barbed, neck tentacles writhing. Water cascaded down its scaly body. It hissed, flicked its gold, shimmering gaze away from the ogre to focus on the witch. The serpent dived back into the water and swam towards the passageway.

'Good!' Clutter said between puffs. 'Get rid of the dangerous one first.'

'You don't think the ogre is a threat?' Sneath said. 'Because he's out of the water and a good few feet up the cliff.'

'He's heavy and awkward. Hopefully the rock won't hold him and he'll tumble like a turd into a cesspit.'

'You certainly know how to cheer up a goblin,' Sneath said.

'I do try.'

Sneath dragged himself onto the ledge. He fished Amethyst from his trews and lay there on his belly panting. Clutter flopped over the edge, huffing as he rolled onto his back. Sneath struggled up onto his hands and knees and peered over the ledge. The ogre, clinging to the cliff face, glared up at him. Hissing and splashing from the lake drew Sneath's attention.

'On all that's sacred!' He grabbed Clutter's shoulder. 'The witch is riding the serpent across the lake.'

'Crawl, you fools!' Amethyst said. 'To your right there's an overhang. Get under it while I see what lies ahead.'

'I'm more concerned about what lies behind!' Sneath scuttled beneath the overhang. He looked into Clutter's wide eyes. 'She's a Charmer! The witch is a Charmer!'

'She can't be a real powerful one or she would have bespelled us from the other side of the lake.'

'She charmed a serpent!' Sneath said.

'An oversized worm.' Amethyst scoffed. 'Not much of a challenge. Better not let her catch you both, eh?'

Grunting and scraping floated up the cliff, the sounds growing louder.

'Hurry!' Screamed the witch. It wasn't rage filling her voice. It was terror. 'Catch them before they get to the doors!'

'There's a tunnel at the far end of the overhang,' Amethyst said. 'To your right about ten feet away. Crawl along until you can't feel the rock wall. Don't bother feeling about when you get to the tunnel. It's wide enough to fit several mammoths side by side.'

'Where, exactly, are you leading us?' Sneath asked.

'To *The Hangman's Jig*.'

Sneath and Clutter gaped at one another, their eyes fire-gold in the dusky red gloom.

'The *Jig's* just a legend,' Sneath scoffed. 'Magical bloody bar where all the races drink and get along. As if. No such place. No gem is worth all this crud! If you don't stop this farting about and tell us what really lies ahead, we'll take our chances with the witch and that ogre. All we have to do is hand you over and—'

'Please?' Amethyst said. 'No!'

'We might be greedy, but we're not total fools.' Clutter crossed his arms. 'Are you leading us to the Lost Gem of Nerramai, or not?'

'There is a good chance you will find it at the end of that tunnel. In *The Hangman's Jig*. But you must outrun the witch first. She knows she can't go down there.'

'Why?' both brothers asked.

'She'll be tortured and killed.'

'See,' Sneath said to Clutter. 'Told you there was no place where magical folk all got along nice.'

Clutter glanced over his shoulder. 'Don't think we have a lot of choice.'

'And us?' Sneath eyed Amethyst warily. 'Will they torture and kill us? I'm not fond of being killed.'

'Not if you're as wily as I hope you are.'

'You have no idea,' Sneath muttered.

With that, the goblins scrambled beneath the overhang toward the tunnel.

The goblins' rapid footsteps echoed throughout the enormous passageway. Faint, empty things that died somewhere far above. Their whispered conversation lingered in the darkness as though the words flew about on wings.

'We should try and lure the witch down here,' Sneath said. 'Getting her tortured and dead will help us live.'

Clutter nodded. 'I like how you think.'

'How much further?' Sneath held Amethyst up in a futile effort to see directions.

'Not far,' Amethyst said. 'I should warn you. Once the doors open I'll turn into an ordinary map. You must tell Galrash that I am Amethyst Diaphany the Fourth. That you rescued me from Sangyll and that she's in the Serpents' Cavern. He'll know what to do.'

Heavy, iron-shod footfalls pounded along the tunnel behind. Something whistled overhead, thunking into the rock. Shards of stone rained down, scattering across the ground.

*Holy Sky Mother!* Sneath ran faster. *Rock-iron tipped arrows!*

The goblins hurtled along as fast as their short legs could go, with Amethyst flapping in Sneath's fist. The brothers slid to a halt in a haze of watery grey light at the end of the tunnel. Enormous bronze doors were embedded in the black rock wall before them, the tops lost in shadow. Intertwined floral patterns—green with age and dented and blackened in places—wove their way across the doors. Dim light shone through a lichen-and-tree-root-lashed hole, high in the stone roof, illuminating the platform on which the goblins stood. Deep gouges scored the earthen floor, and the surrounding rocks were scorched and melted into black glass.

The ogre roared. Loosed another arrow. It skimmed Clutter's head and rammed into the door. Clutter shrieked, clapping one hand to the bleeding wound.

Sneath put his shoulder to the great door and pushed, his boots scraping and slipping in the dirt. Clutter planted both hands against the bronze, adding his strength to his brother's. An arrow slammed into the door, barely missing Sneath's shoulder.

The doors swung open with a loud, rusty groan. Both goblins tumbled into a golden, hazy room the size of a small mountain. Sneath landed beside a pair of reindeer hide boots, their length lashed with rough leather thong. He gazed upward. And upward. A gnarly, bearded face stared down at him with amused disbelief.

*Troll!* Sneath surveyed the cavernous room. Looked like a tavern or maybe a brothel. It was difficult to tell from the view between the troll's legs. He wiggled to one side to get a better look. Smoke, heavy with the sweet smell of the drug, *Golden Brim* clouded *The Hangman's Jig.*

'There are dragons,' Clutter muttered. 'Maybe we should take our chances with the ogre?'

Great, winged serpents lounged here and there breathing plumes of fire into red-hot cauldrons. Spicy vapours rose from the iron kettles like silvery fog. The dragons sucked the drug in through their huge nostrils, their scales glimmering opalescent with pleasure.

'These dragons are flying so high they'll be lucky to see straight for a year,' Sneath said, his mind more on treasure and naked fairies than danger.

From somewhere at the rear of the cavern came warm, lusty laughs and naughty squeals. Cushions in iridescent aqua, blue and forest green scattered the stone-flagged floor, most of them occupied by under-dressed fairies and over-lusty trolls. A rolling bubble noise filled the shadows. From the sharp tang in the air, Sneath knew gurgle-pipes filled with pixie-dust were in high demand.

*Could be worse.* He offered the troll a weak smile and thrust out one, filthy hand. 'The name is Sneath. Happy to do business with you.'

'Not what I expected.' The troll scratched his warty chin.

'What are they selling?' a voice rumbled from somewhere deep within the brothel. It was a rich, hearty voice, male, and quite possibly the owner of *The Hangman's Jig.*

'From the looks of 'em,' the troll said. 'Nothing we want. Why else would they come in the back door?' He lifted thick brows and patted the huge doors. 'Didn't even know they worked.'

'Back door?' Sneath glared at the map, but she said nothing.

Footsteps clattered in the tunnel outside. Clutter whimpered, gingerly touching the wound on his head and staring at the blood.

The troll ripped an ogre's arrow from one of the bronze doors and looked it over, scowling. 'Rock-iron. Bone shaft.'

'What you got there?' asked a gravelly voice from beside the black-marble slabbed bar. 'That dinner? About time. I ordered ages ago.'

'Anyone feel like ogre for dinner?' the troll waved the arrow about.

'They's too puny to be ogres!' Gravelly Voice said. 'I picks bigger things out my teeths than them.'

Sneath dragged Clutter to his feet and shuffled further inside *The Hangman's Jig.* A shiver vibrated through Amethyst, into Sneath's hand, searing up his arm. He glanced down. She sagged, her images barely visible, her vellum brittle and scorched.

'Best shut the doors,' Sneath said, bowing and fluttering his hand in greeting. 'There is an angry ogre heading this way along with a rather nasty witch.'

'We're looking for someone known as Galrash,' Clutter announced. 'We have an important message.'

'Who's askin?' The troll poked Clutter in the chest, causing him to lurch backward.

Clutter rubbed his chest, wincing. 'As my brother said, before. His name is Sneath. I'm Clutter. Can you direct us to Galrash, please?'

'No one here by that name wants to meet you,' rumbled the voice from the brothel's shadows. A smouldering glow bloomed in the darkness for a moment, revealing one huge, emerald-green eye.

'But,' Sneath spluttered. 'We have a message from Ameth—'

Redfire flooded the darkness, streaming through the open doors, lapping the brothel's stone-flagged floor. The troll grinned, flashing a mouth of perfectly filed teeth. 'Deal with you both shortly.' He dragged Sneath and Clutter up by their soggy tunics and tossed them beneath a huge, ornately-carved table. Long, oak bench seats flanked the table. Luckily no one seemed to be seated on them.

'Ogre hunt! Who's with me?' the troll bellowed and thundered out the doorway. Hooting and hollering, four trolls followed, drawing great, shiny axes from the sheaths strapped to their armoured backs.

Whoops, howls and the clang of weapons rang through the tunnel. The redfire, pooling inside the brothel's doorway, flicked backward, surging towards the skirmish as though it was a living thing. For the first time in what seemed like ages, Sneath sucked in a deep breath.

*Safe.*

'I think we should live right next door to this place, Sneath,' Clutter said, his voice all sing-song with glee. 'Look, brother. Look at them dancing. All they're wearing are tiny flames and big smiles.'

Sneath turned his attention to a glossy black-stone stage in the centre of *The Hangman's Jig*. 'Ooh! I see what you mean!' Three fairies swayed and wiggled, tumbling through, over and around a vertical, glistening web that stretched the width of the stage. One fairy waved and blew the goblins a kiss that turned into a shower of flaming petals. The magical kiss danced across the smoky haze, seared bright and tinkled into nothing on the stone floor.

On a smaller stage, to the right of the bar, a wyvern the size of a large dog blew smoke rings from her nose and slithered through the hoops, her scaled body like molten gold.

'Why haven't we heard of this place?' Clutter glared at Sneath.

'We did,' Sneath said, 'But everyone made it sound too good to be true. Wonder if they did it on purpose to keep us out?'

Bellowing from the tunnel broke the goblins' dreamy thoughts. Sneath blinked and slapped himself across the cheek.

'Damn!' Sneath shook Clutter. 'Get a grip. The *Brim* is making us all gooey and easy pickings. We have a gem to find.'

'And we have to find Galrash,' Clutter said.

'We have to make sure they get that witch!' Sneath clutched Clutter's shoulder. 'We could distract her so the trolls can smash her one.'

'If there's one thing trolls do well, it's smashing.' Clutter crawled to edge of the table. He grinned, though his skin was sallow instead of his normal dusky-green. 'Oh!'

Sneath looked where Clutter pointed. Tacked upon a wood-panelled wall was a row of Wanted posters. A few depicted ogres, a couple were of fairies and at least half-a-dozen sported the snarling images of witches. One bore a striking resemblance to Sangyll, the witch.

The brothers shared a conspiring look, scrambled out from beneath the table and ran through the doorway.

'Sangyll the witch is down the tunnel!' Sneath shouted, waving his skinny arms, Amethyst flapping limply from one hand. As he pelted towards the fighting, he expected Amethyst to spout a sarcastic remark, or some un-helpful bit of advice. Nothing. She simply hung in his fist. Sneath felt a sharp pang in his gut. Whether it was sadness, fear or wind was debatable. The feeling didn't last long.

Redfire shot toward him, snaking up his body. Now the redfire was localised, it was far more potent. White-hot pain seared Sneath's body and he stumbled. His skin burned, but he didn't let the map go until Clutter snatched her free and darted to the edge of the tunnel. The redfire pounced, engulfing Clutter's wiry, little body. It surged upward, coiling around his arms. Then, just short of the hand that clutched Amethyst, the redfire stopped.

'You see that?' Clutter yelled to Sneath, his voice tight with pain.

'Yep.' Sneath shouted back. 'Seems ol' Sangyll is worried about redfiring Amethyst.'

'You thinking what I'm thinking?' Clutter gasped.

'We need to distract the witch with Amethyst.'

Hopefully the map wouldn't burn to cinders, because that would be unfortunate. The Lost Gem of Nerramai would be lost forever.

'Sangyll, over here!' Sneath screamed, grabbing Amethyst from his brother and waving her around.

'An extra pouch of silver to whoever kills the witch!' Clutter shouted to the trolls battling the gigantic ogre.

Sneath shot him an 'are you mad?' glance.

Three of the trolls grinned, hooted and left the bleeding ogre to their two friends. The ogre might be bigger than the trolls, but he had been no match for five of them.

Sneath flapped Amethyst about like a madman.

In the red light and squirming shadows, it was hard to tell if they were winning or losing.

Clutter ran past Sneath, a ferocious look on his blood-smeared face. He skidded to a stop ten feet from Sangyll and the three, circling trolls, grabbed up a stone and hurled it at her. He threw another, shouting, 'If you want this map, then you gotta go through me!'

Sneath raced up to his brother. 'Yeah! You gotta go through us. Walls of muscle we are. Warriors!' He muttered to Clutter, 'What are we doing? Are you mad?'

'Trying not to get killed.' Clutter pitched another stone, hitting Sangyll hard on the shoulder.

The witch screeched and threw herself between the snarling trolls at the goblins, bony fingers raking across their skin. Redfire oozed from Sangyll's body, engulfing the goblins, searing with magic.

Sneath hurled Amethyst clear.

The goblins howled, their tunics and trews scorched and smouldering. Blisters bubbled on their exposed skin as they rolled to the ground, both clinging to Sangyll like wild animals. As quickly as the fight started, it ended. A troll reefed Sangyll off the goblins and slung her against the tunnel wall. Her body slumped to the ground, unconscious. The redfire retreated into her, sucked away like a falling tide.

Sneath and Clutter collapsed, gasping and groaning. Clutter crawled over and flapped Amethyst triumphantly above his head, smiling weakly.

Two of the trolls stomped past the goblins, hauling a broken and bleeding ogre back to *The Hangman's Jig*. The remaining three trolls stomped down the tunnel. Sangyll sagged over one troll's shoulder, her face smeared in blood.

Sneath and Clutter staggered along behind, through the tavern's gaping doorway. Rich, spicy smoke clouded the fire-lit brothel.

'Give the little warriors an ale on me, Burdack,' called the troll carrying Sangyll.

At once, a bald gnome popped into view behind the bar.

Burdack, bedecked in green velvet and frothy lace cuffs and collar, sprang from what must have been a step ladder of some kind onto the bar. He trundled along the black-marble to a huge wooden barrel atop the end, adjusting his spectacles as he went. Burdack pushed the barrel's silver lever, pouring a couple of draughts into two huge pewter tankards.

'Service!' He shouted to no one in particular. One of the web-dancing fairies flew over, collected the drinks, and delivered them to the goblins.

Sneath smiled awkwardly, smoothed down his singed hair, and took a huge drink, the foam dribbling down his chin. Fruity with a bite of fire. Damn good stuff!

'Is it possible to talk to Galrash now?' Clutter leaned against a table leg, his tankard on the floor beside his blackened and burned trews.

A leathery rasping came from the shadows, and the huge emerald eye they had seen earlier fixed on the goblins. The brothel fell silent. As the eye rose higher, tinkling, clanking and jingling filled the hush. Then, a massive, scaled snout thrust towards Sneath and Clutter, swooping down so the dragon's maw was at eye level. More or less. The smell of sulphur, *Golden Brim's* spicy scent, and rotting flesh wafted over them.

'What could two spindly little entrees want so badly they'd go up against Sangyll and an ogre? And, then have the nerve to want an audience with the King of the Dragons.'

'Well, your Most High Royalness.' Sneath bowed, wincing with the pain of his burns.

'You assume I am the King?'

'You have the bearing of a leader.' Clutter bobbed his head, hissing between his teeth with discomfort.

'And of royal blood,' Sneath added with another painful bow.

'And you both have the villainous tongues of goblins.'

'A little harsh, all things considered,' Sneath said. 'But I will give you that one.'

The dragon laughed, a rich rumble that blew the goblins halfway across the brothel's stone-flagged floor. They staggered back to the dragon.

'We are here to deliver a message to Galrash. Either you are he, or you are not.' Clutter wavered on his feet. 'We're tired, injured and we have come a terribly long way.'

'You are brave,' the dragon said. 'I will give you that. Perhaps a tad ignorant but, for goblins, you stack up nicely. I'll tell you what. You tell me your message and I will make sure Galrash receives it.'

'Not good enough,' Sneath said through clenched teeth, his body searing with pain.

The whole brothel erupted with guffaws, hoots and hollers.

'Seems like we'll be getting goblins for supper,' barked a troll. 'Crispy cooked and stuffed with stupid.'

The dragon held up one taloned foreleg for silence. 'All right, I can respect courage. Despite the rude flavour. I am Galrash.'

'How can we be sure?' Sneath eyed the dragon shrewdly.

'Just tell me the information and be done with it,' the dragon growled. 'I weary of this game.' He swivelled his head and blew a gout of flame at the unconscious Sangyll who hung by her wrists from a pair of iron manacles beneath her Wanted poster. The remaining posters blackened, curled and floated to the floor like smouldering moths.

The goblins gazed at Sangyll, her ragged dress alive with flame, her skin charred and crackling. They looked at one another, mouths gaping.

'We have come into possession of a map,' Clutter blurted. 'Not just any map I must add. A magical map that's supposed to lead to the Lost Gem of Nerramai.'

Sneath snatched the limp map from his brother's hand and

unfurled it for all to see. Trolls, dragons, fairies and Burdack the barkeep crowded around to see. Sneath had never felt so small and vulnerable.

'And,' Sneath added, 'the map talks.'

'That scrap of skin? You can't even make out the markings!' A troll snorted, grabbing for Amethyst.

Sneath might be small but he was quick despite his injuries. 'She talked until we got in here. She said that we must talk to Galrash and tell him that she is actually Amethyst Diaphany the Fourth. And she was taken by Sangyll.'

'Sangyll tortured her and everything trying to make her reveal the location of the Lost Gem of Nerramai.'

'And did she reveal this information?' Galrash stared at the goblins intently. 'Answer me!'

'No!' Sneath squeaked. He tried his best smile. 'She remained strong.'

'As she would,' Galrash said proudly. He glowered at the crowd. 'Move aside or burn.'

Everyone scrambled back from the dragon leaving the goblins alone in the dragon's shadow. Galrash rose on his haunches and roared. The goblins clamped their hands over their ears, cowering beneath the dragon's mighty bronze body.

'Place the map down and move,' ordered the dragon. 'Long since we have gazed upon Amethyst, the heart, the power of we dragons. Never knowing where she had gone. If she lived.'

Sneath placed Amethyst on the stone-flagged floor, smoothed out her edges and gave a her a little pat of reassurance. The goblins backed away to stand with the trolls pressed against the brothel walls. And waited.

Galrash roared once more. The cavern rumbled. Dust and stones tumbled from the unseen ceiling, crashing into the flagstones. The mighty dragon breathed a soft feather of flame over Amethyst.

'No!' Clutter shouted in shock and stepped forward. A troll grabbed him, dragging him back.

Garash ignored the crowd and sent another tongue of flame across the map. It curled. Writhed. And started to swell, surging upward, outward. The old vellum shimmered in the firelight and burning witch. It changed form, growing legs, wings and a towering body, pushing tables and benches aside as it grew.

'Amethyst!' Sneath said, his eyes wide with awe. 'Look at you!'

There, beside Galrash, where the map had sat, towered a resplendent, golden dragon. Galrash bowed low. 'We have searched for centuries, my queen. For you. And for the Gem of Nerramai.'

'I don't doubt it,' Amethyst placed a taloned fore-leg on Galrash's shoulder.

'What happened, my Queen?' Galrash asked.

'Sangyll's mother found me while I lay brooding. You know how distracted I get. The foolish witch knew nothing—thought I had already laid. She tortured me, but I refused to talk, so she turned me into the map hoping I would lead her to my Nerramai.'

'And you did not, my brave queen.'

Sneath jumped up, arms flapping with excitement. It all made sense! 'You couldn't lead her to the Gem of Nerramai because you hadn't laid it when she cast her spell.'

'The Gem is an egg?' Clutter frowned. 'We went through all this for an egg?'

'An egg from a queen dragon.' Sneath looked pointedly at Amethyst. 'I think, all things considered, that we deserve a handsome reward. A chest of jewels. Or gold? Nothing wrong with gold. Though I do prefer jewels.'

'Don't even think of asking for the Gem of Nerramai!' Amethyst pointed a huge talon at the goblins. 'I'd never entrust my daughter to you pair.'

'How about we allow you to live?' Galrash lowered his head and eyed them shrewdly.

Sneath groaned. 'But after all we suffered. The insults, the pain, the fear, the—'

'What about what you put me through?' Amethyst said with a snort. 'I've seen and felt things that are seared into my memory for all eternity.'

'And it is because of us, Your Highness,' Clutter said. 'You will live out your long years as a dragon and not some mouldy bit of vellum.'

'Well spoken.' Galrash called to the tavern keeper, 'Burdack, tend the wounds of these two rascals.'

'How about the key to your strongroom?' Sneath glanced around, thinking fast. 'A few measly gems, or pearls—'

'No!' Amethyst said.

Galrash chuckled, a deep throaty sound that rumbled through Sneath's chest. 'When you two are healed you may take whatever you can carry out of here in one trip.'

'Er,' Clutter put up his hand, 'do we have to carry it out the way we came in? Could be a bit tricky.'

Sneath glared at Amethyst. 'Why *did* we go that way. I hear there's a front door.'

The huge golden dragon drew herself up and sucked a deep breath, her eyes blazing.

Sneath shuffled a few steps back, dragging Clutter with him. 'Forget it. Doesn't matter. Everyone's happy. We'll just get on with picking out our reward, shall we?'

After a long pause, Amethyst released the breath and her eyes narrowed. 'If you must know, it's because the front door is spelled against goblins. Pesky little creatures you are. Believe me, I'd have preferred that way, too. Especially if it saved me sniffing your crotch!'

Galrash snorted a laugh, which he turned into a cough when his queen glared.

'And,' Amethyst continued, 'once you gather your reward, the back door will be sealed as well. You'll only get one trip to the *Jig*, so make the most of it.'

Sneath elbowed Clutter. 'I'm going to start a rigid exercise regime. Bulk up my muscles and my stamina.'

'I like how you think, brother.'

The End of Another Sneath and Clutter Adventure.

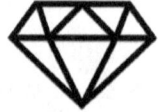

# In Every Reign a Little Life must Fall

*Aiki Flinthart*

'Just how many pieces of blood-chert do you need, kiddo?' Barrik hefted the red rock in his meaty hand. He raised the chert into a beam of sunlight that filtered through the oddity-shop's grimy window. Dust glittered and swirled like fairy-sprinklings in the musty air. The chert, with its veins of quartz, looked exactly like petrified steak. I shuddered.

'As many as it takes,' I replied. 'Just store it with the others.' I hung my cloak over one arm and tossed a silver queenshead at him to pay for storage and silence. He caught the coin and ran a dirty thumbnail around the edge.

'Fair enough.' His black eyes flicked my way again.

'How much do I have now?'

Barrik placed the stone on his brass scales and added a number to a leather-bound journal on the counter. 'Eighty-nine point eight kilos. But only nineteen point eight of that's here. You took the rest away last month.'

'Crap.' I swiped a hand over my short hair. One hundred grams. I'd miscounted. Including the one hanging under my shirt, between my breasts, I was short by one piece.

A man's weight rested uneasily on my shoulders. A kingdom's fate, too. There was no-one else to save Rosa or the stupid, ill-fated Reizend. Just me.

'Y'know, with your hair dyed dark,' Barrik mused, 'anyone ever tell you, you look a bit like—'

My dagger vibrated in the timber post next to his head. He gulped. I sauntered up and retrieved it.

'No,' I said. 'At least, not twice.'

'Sorry. Why do you want this stuff, anyway?' He dropped the stone into a leather sack and stowed it beneath the counter. 'Trying to corner the market in blood-chert?'

'Nope.' My dagger slipped into a boot. 'Just got a customer who likes rocks.'

When I looked up again, Barrik had a small crossbow pointed at my head and a smirk on his jowly face.

'Seriously?' I sighed. 'How long have you known me, Barrik? You really think I'd swindle you?'

'Oh, six years.' His finger tightened on the trigger. 'You were about fifteen when you first came in with that sweet little sister of yours. Fair warmed my heart how she looked up to you. Remember how she begged you to buy that old book for your mam's birthday. Never could say 'no' to her, could you?'

'Tell me about it,' I muttered.

He pointed at the sack of rocks. 'Then you started all this.'

'And?'

'And I hear things. How you lie and cheat to get them. Pretty light-fingered, too. Just surprised you haven't killed anyone, yet.' He shook his head and sighed, like a disappointed father.

'Don't tempt me.' I glowered. 'What do you want?'

He shrugged. 'Well, I figure you've done all the hard work. 'Bout time you cut me in on the action. Someone must want these bad if you're willing to give up five years for rocks.'

I held up my left hand and waggled the little finger with its missing end-joint. 'See this? Blood-sacrifice to the Goddess just to be able to track them down.' My cloak-sleeve fell back, exposing a forearm scarred with dozens of fine white lines. 'And these. One for each piece. You prepared to make a sacrifice?' The lump of stone in the invisible spider-silk bag around my throat warmed, anticipating a blood-rite, as it did when I neared a fresh piece of chert.

'Maybe. If the money's worth it.' He glanced dubiously at my arm and shuffled his feet. 'Got a kid to feed now, see? Shop's not earning enough. That damned demonic dwarf Frodo...Freddo—'

'Friedenzwerg,' I said.

'—is running Ebene for the Princess and he's just raised the taxes again.' Barrik grimaced sheepishly. 'We all gotta make some sacrifices, the wife says.'

'Yeah, she would.' His wife was one of the best-dressed women in Ebenton.

His eyes narrowed, finger curling around the crossbow trigger.

'Fine! I'll cut you a deal.' I draped my much-patched brown cloak over my shoulders. The cloak was old; a birth-gift from the Elf-king no less. The candytuft-flower clasp was a little stiff. 'Ever heard of the cloak of ignorance?'

The caterpillar-brows over Barrik's eyes crawled closer together. 'Always thought that was some kind of...thingy...metaphor for not going to school.'

'Not so much.' I finally got the clasp shut, flipped up the hood, and waited.

He glanced down at the crossbow in his hand then peered suspiciously around the shop. I remained still. His eyes slid off me and swept the jumble of dusty furniture and shelves full of honest-to-Goddess antique cursed spoons and djinn-inhabited bronze teapots. He shrugged and released the string-tension on the bow then tucked it under the counter.

I slipped around behind him, careful not to brush against a teetering stack of faux-ancient tomes. A large hunk of amethyst on a shelf over his head ought to be about right. I plucked it off the shelf. Force and timing had to be perfect. Didn't want to kill him. The amethyst hit his head exactly square and Barrik folded like a bad souffle to the scuffed wooden floor. I dropped the crystal. He ought to think it had fallen on him.

I prodded him with a toe. Years of trust and business and the big oaf decides to screw me over because his wench of a wife has expensive tastes. I was tempted to empty his till, but the mention of his kid held my hand. Kids shouldn't have to suffer from their parent's stupid decisions. Family is supposed to look after each other.

I hefted the sack of blood-chert over my shoulder. There wasn't much else of value in the store. Or, at least, nothing I valued. But, out of habit, I cast an expert eye over the display cabinet. A glitter attracted my attention. I slipped a deft hand between Barrik's patchy fae-wards and extracted the figurine. A small stone fox carved from rust-red sparkling sandstone. My sister's favourite animal. I tucked it into a pocket. Not quite what I'd hoped to bring her, but she'd like it.

As I turned toward the back door, light reflected off something in the shopfront. Above a cabinet stuffed with pink-cheeked dancing faun ceramics. Squeezed between a stuffed ogre head and a rusting 'magic' sword. A tarnished silver hand mirror.

I swore.

'You daft frog-kisser!' I kicked the unconscious Barrik in his well-padded ribs. 'A mirror? You deserve to get rolled.' There was nothing I could do now. I flipped a rude hand-signal at the speckled glass and stalked out the back door.

'You're looking glum tonight, love.' Barb's gravelly voice interrupted my personal stormcloud of doom. She slid a fresh tankard along the bar and half-heartedly wiped along behind it with a stained pink cloth. A smear of something infectious spread across the scarred timber.

'Ever have one of those days where you wonder if it's all worth it, Barb?' I scrubbed at my scalp and sipped the dark ale. Five bloody years and, just when I thought I was done, there was one more bloody piece of bloody stone to find.

But Barrik was right: my sister looked up to me; needed me. I'd never been able to refuse her. That's why I'd chosen this path when I could have spent the last five years drinking wine and eating quail eggs. Telling servants what to do. Dancing sedately. Bathing regularly.

The longer I was away, the harder it was to remember exactly how she'd talked me into it.

'Worth it?' Barb chuckled, her expansive fake bosom almost jiggling out of her once-red dress. 'I wonder that every time the tax-collector comes, or some drunk shoves a hand up me skirt, love. So, yeah, every day.' She flicked at a slow-moving fly, which fell and drowned happily in a puddle of beer. 'But I've worked my arse off to build this place so I'd have something to leave the kids. Think they're grateful?'

'Er...' I raised my brows. 'Yes?'

'Nope. Don't care a bit.' The waving towel flew dangerously close to glassware and swirled smoke puffing from the fireplace. 'Just off doing whatever they want, on my money.'

'Doesn't that bug you?' I didn't really care, but her chatter saved me thinking about my own dilemma.

She scratched at the five-o'clock shadow along her square jaw and snorted. 'Nah. So long as they're happy. It's what family does, innit? Sometimes you give up what you want so yer kids can have what they want. Otherwise, what's the point? Besides, things're gonna get better in Ebene, they say.'

'Really? How?' I slurped another mouthful, savouring the rich malty flavour. Whatever else she did, Barb made a damned fine beer.

'Well,' Barb said, pondering, 'apparently now the princess is up and about, we might not have to go to war with Tal after all.'

I coughed. 'Princess Rosa is…er…up and about?'

Barb grinned, showing the polished, white-oak teeth she'd bought last year. 'We all thought she was dead or in the deepest palace dungeon and that's why the dwarf-demon, Friede…Fredden—'

'Friedenzwerg,' I said wearily.

'—was running Ebene. Turns out she was just pining for her lost prince. She snapped out of it the day Tal started marching. Now she's doing the right thing by Ebene, poor lass.'

After staring morosely into my drink for a few more seconds, I sat up. 'Hang on! What right thing by Ebene? And why were we going to war with Tal?'

Barb lifted her plucked brows. 'You have been off in the boondocks awhile, haven't you, love? Prince Lastig of Tal finally demanded compensation for the loss of his brother. Thinks we murdered Prince Reizend. Said Queen Ivy sacrificed him in some dark magic ritual that backfired and killed the Queen and Princess Helli as well.'

I suppressed a gasp and covered my shock by drinking deeply.

Barb dismissed the rumour with a noise of amusement, then leaned close and whispered. *'Everyone* knows it's no co-incidence the Crown Prince of Tal and the Crown Princess of our royal family disappeared at the same time. It's obvious: Reizend preferred Helli to Rosa and they ran away.'

I choked, spraying beer across the counter.

Barb wiped the mess. 'Laugh if you like. But it explains why Rosa went into a decline and wouldn't marry Lastig instead. Kept him on a string for *five* years! Can't blame him for finally getting sick of it and declaring war.' She sniffed.

'Are you saying Rosa's agreed to marry Lastig? To stop the war?'

'Looks that way. Lastig's on is way here to the palace. Wedding's in a week. Bit of a rush-job, if you ask me. Poor Princess Rosa. Duty over love. The things we women do for our families, huh?' Barb gave the counter a few more wipes then swayed off and poured drinks for a boisterous group of travelling actors. One motley-clad jongleur slid his hand up her leg. She casually punched him and he keeled over, unconscious.

I groaned and dropped my head onto my forearm, heedless of the beer soaking my sleeve. Five goddamned years. So close! I'd condemned Rosa to five years of imprisonment while I chased bloody rocks, all for nothing. There was no way I could find the last piece in a week. I'd let her down. And I'd written a letter four months ago to say I was coming back with the last piece. How was I supposed to tell her I'd fucked up?

I wrenched at the amulet around my neck and achieved nothing but a deep score in my skin. Of course it wouldn't come off. Not until I'd found every bloody piece. Wouldn't even let me cross Ebene's borders with my head still attached.

A hearty guffaw from the actors interrupted my self-flagellation. I swilled beer and gazed at the amateurish portrait hanging on the wall behind the bar. The artist had captured Rosa's enormous blue eyes and hopeful naivete exactly, even if her head was weirdly oversized. In her dark hair nestled her birth gift from the Elf-king: the wine-red carnation brooch. Rosa always wore it even though it wasn't magical, like my cloak.

Beneath her image hung a smaller one—of Reizend, Crown Prince of Tal. His blond, brooding intelligence made a perfect foil for her sweetness. As long as he was happy with beauty and goodness, and didn't place too much value on brains, they'd make the ideal monarchs for Tal.

Wait! Maybe that was why she'd made a reappearance and agreed to marry. Yes! That was it. She hadn't given up on me or Reizend. She knew I was coming. This agreement to marry fusspot Lastig must be a ploy; a tactic to delay Lastig until I showed up with Reizend, his brother.

But Rosa was expecting me to come back with the full ninety kilos. I only had eighty-nine point nine. And there was no time to find the last piece. Still, there was enough rock to maybe convince Lastig to hold off for a while. He'd have to be told the truth, though. And that would fall to me, even though it was Queen Ivy's fault. Hers and Friedenzwerg's. But I was the only one left to fix this mess and I hadn't sacrificed five years of my life to fail now. There had to be a way. Rosa was depending on me.

The clinking bag went back over my shoulder. I clasped the cloak together and flipped up the hood. Everyone ignored me as I left.


Getting into a fortified hill palace isn't as hard as one might think. At least, not if one grew up roaming the palace halls and testing the security by trying to sneak out. I'd managed to escape several times. Even taken Rosa with me into Ebenton, to Barrik's shop, when we needed to find unique birthday gifts for our mother.

In a way, this whole mad situation was my fault. If I'd never let Rosa talk me into buying that blasted grimoire, our mother wouldn't have learned the spells that set everything in motion. Still, no-one had forced Queen Ivy show off to Rosa and Reizend by saying the summoning spell. Or the scattering one. Mother always had been a bit reckless.

Barefoot, I splashed up a freezing stream at the base of the hill and parted a fall of vines screening a cave. Inside, I flipped open a brite-lite, stolen from a mage, and played its uneasy green glow across the dripping walls. A narrow, hand-hewn path clung to the wall above the stream. I clambered up and tugged my boots back onto numb feet. The lockpicks under the innersole of my right boot had shifted. I swore, pulled the shoe off, readjusted the picks to a comfortable position then shoved my foot back in.

By the time I climbed up to the palace's lowest levels, twenty kilos of stone weighed fifty and the cold air burned in my throat. I paused outside the secret entrance, panting. Pathetic. How was I supposed to carry ninety kilos of stone to the upper levels? Well, I'd solve that later. For now, I'd offload this bag with the rest and see what was going on abovestairs. If Rosa was panicking about Lastig she'd be pretty happy to see me.

I just needed to speak to her in private without alerting anyone to my presence.


A few minutes later, lighter by nineteen point eight kilos, I eased open the door to the great hall with one hand. With the other hand I struggled to close the candytuft-flower cloak clasp.

'Ah! There you are.' A cheerful, rough voice greeted me from waist-height.

I looked down.

Friedenzwerg flashed a broad grin and swept a bow. His large head ended up around my knees and the temptation was almost irresistible. With an ominous clank of metal, seven palace guards stepped into formation around him. The leader eyed me significantly, fingers white on his sword-hilt.

I finished doing up the clasp and muttered something rude. Too slow with the cloak. But maybe it wasn't too late.

'Freddy,' I said. 'Always a pleasure. Been awhile. Killed anyone recently?' I smiled sweetly.

His grin became fixed and his dark eyes narrowed.

'Not since you left,' he returned, his smile malicious and filled with more sharp teeth than I remembered. One hand strayed to the red silk bag he wore on a thong around his neck.

I glared. 'Well, I'll be leaving again. Just came to chat with Rosa.'

'Oh,' he said coolly, 'I think you'll be staying for a week at least.'

'Really?' I folded my arms and raised one brow. 'And what if I don't want to stay?'

Friedenzwerg spread his thick-fingered hands. 'We'll just have to change your mind. After all, you have a wedding to attend.'

'Not if I can help it,' I shot back, then cursed myself for showing my hand too early. Time to redirect. I needed to get past Friedenzwerg, see Rosa, and then see Lastig of Tal. Convince them to put off the wedding and the war until I found that last stone.

I eyed Friedenzwerg. His purple and gold puffy-sleeved doublet and pants made him look as broad as he was tall. The small horn-buds poking through his slick dark hair were ridiculous. Getting past him shouldn't be hard.

'Freddy, have you heard of a cloak of ignorance?'

'Do you mean the metaphor—'

'Not so much.' I flipped the hood up.

'—or the actual cloak of ignorance?' The dwarf continued. 'As in the magical item which, if named and touched, becomes visible to the namer.' He poked me in the ribs with a finger. 'Oh, look. There you are.'

I swore and yanked the hood down.

Friedenzwerg chuckled. 'Did you forget that I'm a Summoned One? I saw the magic aura before you even put the hood up. You'll have to do something a little more impressive to outthink me, Princess Helli.'

'Helli!' Rosa's voice lilted down the hall. She glided toward us, hands outstretched, blue chiffon floating behind her. Her soft lips parted in a delighted smile. The red carnation brooch glittered in her long, dark hair.

The guards stepped aside and she grabbed my hands. Her blue eyes gazed beseechingly into mine. My heart melted. I'd missed her unquestioning faith; her belief I could fix anything. I believed it myself when she looked at me like that.

'You're back. I'm so glad.' She kissed my cheek. 'Just in time to rescue me from my folly. Like you always do. Thank you.'

I curled a lip at Friedenzwerg and smiled at my sister. 'Of course. We'll stop this ridiculous wedding, I'll bring Reizend back, and everything will be fine.'

Rosa's eyes widened. Her rosebud lips fell open. 'Reizend? Oh, no. The wedding must go on. Once you marry Lastig, this mess will all be put to rights.'

'What? Once *I* marry...' I dropped her hands. 'By the Goddess, Rosa, what are you talking about?'

Friedenzwerg flinched. 'I'll thank you not to invoke Her name in my presence. Rosa, I think we'd best explain this in a less public place.'

Rosa blushed and caught his hand to her cheek. 'Of course, dearest. You're right.' She took my fingers and pulled me toward a parlour nearby. 'Come, Helli.'

Stunned, I could only follow.


'Let me get this straight,' I said, scraping my hair into an unruly mess. Rosa reclined on a gilded daybed, with her blue dress draped elegantly, looking at home amongst the velvet drapes and sombre portraits of our ancestors. Friedenzwerg relaxed on a chair beside her, one stumpy leg crossed over the other, smiling in unholy amusement at me.

I glared at Rosa. 'I gave up my position here as Queen for the last five years, trying to find a way to reunite you and Reizend. And now you're telling me I wasted my time because you've fallen in love with…with…' I pointed at Friedenzwerg.

Rosa beamed and nodded. 'I knew you'd understand, dearest. Freddy's been ever such a support. I was so miserable with Mother and you gone, and no hope of marrying Reizend. And running a country is much harder than I thought. It all seemed too much.' She lifted anxious eyes. 'I'm just not *you,* Helli. I have no head for business. Freddy does, though. He looks after me so well.'

'But…but…' I paced the room, clutching my head. 'I wrote. I came back every year as often as I could. You never said…I scoured the damned kingdom for your sake!' I flung my arms wide. 'And he's a *demon!* Are you telling me you prefer a demon dwarf to Reizend? Remember him? Tall, intelligent, handsome…tall. The next king of Tal?'

'But Reizend's gone,' Rosa said simply, 'and Lastig's such a fussy bore.'

I gaped. 'But you're fine if *I* marry Lastig?'

'You once said a Crown Princess must never expect to marry for love. I'm sure you'll grow to like him.' Her mouth drooped. 'But I just couldn't. Not now I've come to love Freddy. You do understand, don't you?

Nothing emerged from my open mouth.

'Oh. You don't. You're angry at me.' Rosa burst into tears and buried her face in her arms. The sound of her sobs wrenched at my heart. Maybe she really was in love.

'Oh, Goddess.' I covered my eyes for a moment. 'Rosa, you know I want you to be happy. You're my sister. But are you sure Freddy doesn't have you under a spell?'

'Demon magic, remember?' Friedenzwerg held up his hands, palms out, and cocked his head. 'Curses, yes. Love spells, no. What can I say? The kid has a way about her. I just can't say 'no' to her.'

Rosa raised her head and sniffed, sapphire eyes drowned in

sparkling tears.

I sighed, unable to resist the hope in her expression. 'Maybe we can work something out.'

Smiles wreathed her face. She leapt to her feet and threw her arms around me. 'Oh, thank you. You're the best sister, ever.' She sat down, hands clasped on her knees, gazing at me in the eager way she had when I agreed to do something crazy for her.

'So,' I said, pacing back and forth. 'Where would you go? I mean, he is a demon. It's not like many places will welcome him. Don't get me wrong,' I added when her face fell. 'You're welcome to stay here, but the people of Ebene are...well... less than thrilled by his leadership so far.'

'That's silly,' Rosa said stoutly. 'He's doing a splendid job. His magic gets me anything I want. It can do the same for them. Of course we'll stay here. You'll marry Lastig, go to Tal and be Queen Consort. I'll rule here with Freddy. We already are, so it makes sense, really. Why upset things?'

I sank on to a chair and stared at her. Could she really be that naïve and selfish? Had she always been and I too gullible and blinded by her adoration to see it? Once upon a time, her logic would have seemed perfectly sane. Perhaps five years on the road had changed me more than I thought.

'What about my happiness?' I said. 'What about what I want?'

Rosa sent me a mournful look. 'I know. It's so unfair. But remember the story you told me—about when I was born and the Elf-king gave me this?' She touched the carnation brooch in her hair.

'I know, I know.' I dropped my head into my hands. 'The Elf-king was annoyed because you cried so much. I said I'd do anything to make you happy. But to be fair...I was only five. And you were crying a lot. Screaming, really.'

There was a long, hopeful silence.

'What about Reizend?' I managed, swallowing a lump in my

throat. 'When I bring him back, he's going to be a little…irritated that he's lost his bride and his country in one hit, don't you think?'

Rosa smiled serenely and squeezed Freddy's hand. 'That's easy. Just don't bring him back. After all, without all the pieces he can't be restored, can he?'

'I supp—' I sat up straight. 'Wait, how did you know I don't have all the pieces?'

She flushed and glanced at Friedenzwerg. Her free hand crept to her throat and her gaze flickered down.
Friedenzwerg harrumphed, glaring at her. She started. The pink in her cheeks deepened. There was a long, awkward silence. I thrust a hand into my pocket, fingering the little sandstone fox I'd intended gifting to Rosa. Perhaps the animal was a better symbol than I'd realised. Perhaps we'd both changed and my little sister wasn't so little any more. Perhaps…I looked at her…I'd never been able to refuse her before for a good reason.

'The mirror.' I said, deliberately switching my attention to Friedenzwerg. 'You saw me talking to Barrik in the shop. That's how you knew about the chert, isn't it? About the cloak, too. Dammit!'

'Yes!' Friedenzwerg said. 'Yes, the mirror. That's how.' He shrugged. 'And since you couldn't find that last piece, I guess we'll just have to leave poor Reizend to his rest and move on.'

'Uh huh,' I said, eyeing him with distaste. 'Not sure being Scattered into a hundred pieces of blood-chert counts as rest, actually.'

The dwarf raised his hands, palms out. 'Don't put that on me. It was your mother's spell that went awry, not mine.'

I jabbed a finger at him. 'You deflected it so the casting hit Reizend.'

'Not intentionally,' he said, pious.

'You lying little—' I rose and took a step toward him.

Rosa leapt to her feet, as pale as she had been flushed.

'Don't hurt him!' She wrung her hands. 'You wouldn't make me so unhappy. Please, Helli?'

'It's no use, darling. She just doesn't understand.' Friedenzwerg stood.

'Oh, yes I bloody-well do,' I muttered.

'Guards!' Friedenzwerg yelled.

I withdrew my hand from my pocket and leapt at him. We tumbled to the cold marble floor in a tangle of arms, scrabbling for a hold, throwing wild punches that barely connected. Rosa shrieked at me to stop. I could have stabbed him, but that wasn't my aim. Demons couldn't be killed by steel, anyway. He opened his mouth. I jammed a forearm into it to prevent a spellcast. He bit, his sharp little teeth breaking skin. I yelped and kicked at his stomach. The dwarf choked a cough and released me.

The door burst open and his men hauled me upright. Blood dripped down my arm, making my clenched fingers slippery.

Friedenzwerg wiped his mouth and glared. 'Take her away. Maybe some time in the dungeon will change her mind.'

'No! Not the dungeon.' I tried to wrench free but his men held me firm. 'Anything but that.' I cast a pleading look at my sister.

'Oh, dear. I'm so sorry.' Rosa sniffed and dabbed her eyes. 'I feel awful. Please agree? Even Lastig's better than the dungeon for the rest of your life.'

I bit my lip, hesitated then raised my chin and glared at them defiantly.

'No.'

Rosa's eyes widened. Her lips fell open. 'No?' she whispered. 'But you *can't* say no.' Her fingers fluttered to her hair.

'Watch me.' I smiled. 'No.'

'Take her.' Friedenzwerg dismissed me with a languid wave and a cool look.

The palace only had one, large cell. We'd never really had need for dungeons. No one used it. Well, almost no-one.

The guards took my dagger, patted me down for other weapons, and shoved me into the darkness. They left and closed the door with an ominous clang.

I rattled the bars a few times and yelled obscenities to make sure no-one would come. Then I hurried to the darkest corner and began tipping out bags of chert onto the floor. When I had the whole lot in one pile I opened the brite-lite I'd left there with the bags. By its green glow I smeared blood from my arm onto the piece of chert in the bag around my throat. The chain unlocked and the rock fell to join the others.

I opened my hand and let fall the final piece. The piece I'd lifted from the red silk bag around Friedenzwerd's neck and replaced with the little fox sculpture during our scuffle.

I spoke the words the Goddess' priestess had given me so many years before. The words to undo the Scattering spell.

A flash of blood-purple light seared my eyes and swirled around the pile of stones. The chert rattled and jumped, merging, twisting and morphing into a vaguely-human outline. With one final, soft explosion of light, the spell finished.

Reizend stood before me, blinking and swaying on his feet. He looked a little older, but still wore the same ridiculous blue silk and lace formal outfit from five years before.

'Hey.' I lifted a hand.

He squinted and peered at me before inspecting his surroundings.

'Helli?' He patted his head as though testing to make sure it was attached. 'What happened? Why are we in a dungeon? What happened to your hair? And your arm? Where's Rosa?'

I sat down to take my boot off. 'It's a long story.' The lockpicks fell into my hand. 'I'll tell you on the way to Tal.'

'Tal?' His brows snapped together. 'Why Tal? Are we in Ebene? I'm here to marry Rosa. Last I remember was being in Queen Ivy's room and that dwarf demon appearing.'

'Ya,' I said, working on the door lock. 'Like I said. Long story. We're heading toward Tal to intercept your brother.' I straightened and pushed open the door.

'Lastig?' Reizend hurried to my side. 'What's he got to do with this?'

'He's got an army I need to borrow. I want my kingdom back. Here.' I handed him the cloak.

He accepted but stood there holding it, staring at me blankly. 'Isn't this your birth-gift from the Elf-king? It is looking a little ratty, but don't you want it?'

'Not so much.' I flashed him a mirthless grin. 'I've worn it too long already.'

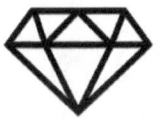

# Strange Topaz Sheep

*Lynne Lumsden Green*

'Hello, missus. My name's Rod,' said a rust-smeared man. 'I hear you like strange sheep. You looking for new stock?' He pointed to a rusty ute, loaded with a trio of wooden crates in the tray.

'Yeah,' I said. 'But I'm not a missus. My name is Una Schäfer. I breed boutique sheep for hobby farmers who want pretty animals for spinning wool.' I have unusual stock; black, white, and piebald breeds—which spinners love.

I would never get rich by breeding boutique sheep, but I like them, and I was looking for a lifestyle rather than a cash cow. You've heard of crazy cat ladies? Well, I was a silly sheep person. I wasn't what you'd call famous, but word gets around.

I was at the stock sales looking for something different. I didn't hold much hope for the animals in rusty-guy's crates, but there was always the off-chance I could get a lucky break. I walked over to the ute.

From between the slats, slot-pupil eyes stared at me with a mixture of despair and derangement—which is the normal expression of a sheep alone in a small box. Sheep don't work well alone. One animal stamped its feet and butted the wall of its crate;

I'd put money on that one being a ram. The other two shifted their feet restlessly, but there wasn't enough room in their crates for them to pace.

'What do you think?' asked Rod, which came out as 'Whaddy ya think?' Ah, the charm of the Australian Strine dialect; it never faded.

'Can't tell. Can we get them out of these travelling crates for a look?'

'No go, missus—um, Una,' said Rod, as he shook his head. With his mottled red skin, he looked as rusty and dilapidated as his ute; so much so I expected him to rattle. 'It's too much trouble penning them again.'

I wasn't going to buy anything from him, sight unseen. I turned away.

'Wait. I can give you a good deal. These are special animals,' he insisted.

'I'm not buying your sheep without inspecting them,' I said, 'particularly if they are something special.'

'Two hundred a head.' Rod's voice turned shrill. He slapped his hand down on his fender, shaking loose several flakes of rust. 'S'bargain at that price.'

'No sale,' I replied.

'Five hundred for the lot!'

'If they're so special, you might find another buyer. But no see, no sale.'

'Four hundred!'

I shook my head. 'Look, you're doing yourself no favours bringing down the price. Are they stolen? You trying to unload them before the law catches up with you? Or have you neglected them, and they're sick and you want to make some quick cash before they die? Pack it in. I won't report you, *this time*, but I'm not buying your sheep, either.'

'Jeez, you've got it all wrong,' he whined. 'Like I said, once the buggers are free, it's bloody impossible to get them back into their boxes.'

Ah, now I had him pegged. He was an amateur, some city guy who had bought a weekender, and played at being a farmer. His authentic farm ute had misled me.

I decided to take pity on him. And my curiosity was piqued. 'Tell you what. Unbox the quietest one, and I promise I'll crate it up again, whether I buy it or not.'

He didn't look relieved, but resigned. 'Okay. I'll get the ewe lamb out.'

I don't know what I was expecting; probably a wild chamois or some other species of goat. People made that mistake a lot, confusing goats with sheep—particularly with white angora goats. Goats tended to be more independent, curious, and agile than sheep, which certainly could make them difficult to pen. I preferred sheep for that very reason. I didn't even use a dog with my beasts, because they were so tame that I could halter lead them anywhere. All I had to do was shake a bucket to catch them.

Rod opened one end of the crate by sliding boards up. The wrong end. The animal faced the other way and she couldn't turn around in the crate. He tried to coax her out, but the poor thing didn't know what to do. I could tell she was getting more and more distressed from the frantic tattoo of her hooves.

'Do you want me to give it a go?' I asked.

'Please, missus. If you'd be so kind.'

I jumped up onto the tray of the ute, grabbed one of the sheep's back legs, and dragged her out of the crate. The lamb bleated a protest, but didn't struggle too much; animals can sense the touch of a confident handler. She just needed to know she could safely back up.

As promised, the ewe lamb was a strange-looking animal. For

starters, it was bright orange colour. The only way a sheep can be orange is if the wool is dyed. Normally, sheep's wool is white, brown, or black. I pulled the animal's fleece apart to see if the colour was just on top; a natural stain from red or orange soil. The orange colour went all the way to the roots. The staple had a nice crimp and seemed a good quality, but I would be the first to admit that I wasn't a professional wool classer.

When I sniffed my fingers, they were greasy with lanolin, but didn't smell like lanolin, more like lavender and something sweet and nutty—macadamias maybe. Had he shampooed the animals, trying to remove the orange colour? Was it some medicinal concoction? The ewe appeared to be healthy.

The wool was thick with dust and other contaminants, so maybe not a shampoo, then. My lanolin-sticky fingers were covered with gritty, glittering flecks. Mica? Or had the animal been sprinkled with glitter at some point?

The ewe's eyes were the normal tan of an ordinary sheep. It was a tall, rangy beast, but I had no idea if that was a trait of its breed or just her own individual variation. Some sheep get skittish when handled, but not this beast. If anything, she acted like it was sedated. Listless? Again, I wondered if the animals were unwell.

Still, there was no such thing as topaz-coloured sheep.

'Haha. Cute joke. You got me,' I snarked, irritated at the time wasted with this prank. 'I'll pop her back in the crate and be on my way.'

'What? Wait? No joke, missus. What you see is what you get,' said the man. He wrung his hands.

'An orange sheep? Come on. I admire the dye job, but I'm not falling for it.' I grabbed the ewe by the wool of her butt and shoulders and backed her into the crate. She went calmly; I don't know why her owner thought she was so difficult to pen. I slid the boards back in.

The ewe lamb made a small noise of protest. Everyone thinks sheep go 'baa', but their normal sound is more like a shrill 'mear-ah-ah-ah'. This was more of a deep, throaty 'gagarrrr', as if the animal wasn't too worried.

'I promise you I never touched any dye to those animals,' said Rod, 'nor the ones I have at home.'

'What? You've got more of these jokers? That's an awful lot of trouble for a lark.'

'Like I said, I'm on the up and up,' explained the man. 'I'm not a farmer by trade. I'm a roadworker. I was looking for a small herd of sheep, as a prezzie for the wife. She spins and knits, and we've got a bit of land, and I thought a herd of sheep could keep the grass down … as a bonus, that kind of thing. One of the agricultural research places was shutting down due to funding cuts.' He jerked his thumb over his shoulder, roughly in the direction of beyond the black stump. 'Picked up their experimental flock for a song.' He looked at the back of his ute, his expression unreadable. 'But I had no bloody idea how hard they'd be to look after. My word, no, not a bit. Dunno how farmers manage.'

I didn't need much imagination to know what happened. I'd put good money on his bit of land not being big enough to support one sheep, let alone a whole flock. The animals would have stripped his patch, maybe even eaten all his garden plants. He probably hadn't counted on spending money on feeding them.

Goodness knows what his wife had to say about the orange wool. Whatever had the scientists done to get that result? The wife might have liked the colour, but shearing is an expensive skill and needs proper equipment. She might have coped with cutting the wool from one sheep with scissors, but not clipping a whole flock. Once Rod had discovered how much it would cost to hire someone to shear his animals, on top of the cost of feeding them, he must have crated up these three and brought them to the stock sales. He was likely trying to recoup his costs.

'So, how many more animals do you own?' I asked.

'Five. Eight all up.'

'I'll buy them for what you paid,' I said. I was more worried about the animals now I knew their story. Orange or not, I didn't like the idea of this nelly harming the flock through ignorance. After all, I could always sell them on, to a petting zoo if nothing else. Kids would enjoy the novelty of orange sheep, though I suspected the colour would fade once I put them on a normal diet.

'Really?' said the man, with dawning hope.

'Yes. After all, you told me yourself you picked them up for a song.'

I put the flock of orange sheep in a paddock near the house, so I could keep an eye on them while they settled in. In a new environment, sheep are nervous and hyperaware. I wanted to make sure my new flock didn't suffer from too much stress.

Their fleeces resembled sunflowers in the sunlight; attractive when framed by green grass and blue skies. I handled them every day to get them used to human interaction, leading them on a halter, bucket feeding, and brushing their fleeces. The younger animals could spring exceptionally high when excited or startled. Generally, they were friendly and well behaved. The more I handled the animals, the more I realised Rod was an amateur who didn't know sheep.

After brushing them, I was always covered in glittery flecks. I looked like a Seventies disco queen—not that I minded. Who doesn't like an extra bit of sparkle in their life? The flecks didn't look like scurf—basically sheep dandruff. And the flecks certainly didn't have the greasy feel of suint, a build-up of lanolin. It was something of a mild mystery.

What flummoxed me was their breed. I figured the easiest way to fix that was find out from the scientists who worked with them. It turned out a Professor Jason Aeolia had been in charge of the ovine research department in the closed facility. However, he now worked in Argentina. No one had his exact address. I sent him a letter via the Australian embassy and hoped for the best.

While I waited for his reply, I developed a fondness for the little herd. My flock of strange orange sheep slipped effortlessly into being pets. My heart melted when they hastened to greet me at their paddock gate.


Two months after I had contacted the embassy, I received a reply from Professor Aeolia. He did mention the flock, asking after their wellbeing. Better, he gave me contact details for his research assistant, Crispin Crius. I sent Mr Crius an email.

The next day, I was in the birthing pen with one of my topaz-orange sheep. She had already given birth to an ewe lamb, but she was having twins. Any doubts I had about their colour being a dye vanished when I saw the dear, sweet apricot lambkin. I couldn't wait to safely deliver her sibling.

'Hello? Hello? Anyone here?'

As I was up to my elbow in ewe, I refrained from shouting an answer. I didn't want to startle the momma while I tried to straighten out her baby. The unborn twin had one leg twisted back and I was gently moving it forward.

A man walked past, still calling out, but he didn't glance into the pen. He had a crisp black beard, curling black hair and a Roman nose... a perfected version of Adrian Grenier. Or a god. I nearly forgot what I was doing, but managed to murmur, 'Hey.'

He jumped at the sound of my voice and turned. His dimples deepened. 'Oh, hi! Are you Ùna Schäfer?'

'Yes. And who might you be?'

'I'm Doctor Chris Crius. You emailed me asking about the Aries flock. I can see you know the animals pretty well.' He smiled, flashing an engaging amount of even, white teeth. 'Would you like some help?'

'I have it under control.'

At that moment, I managed to get the wayward limb straightened. I pulled my arm out, and the lamb followed. She took her first breath and bleated. Her mother struggled to her feet, turned, and shouldered me out of the way, eager to lick her babies dry.

I was grinning like an idiot and kneeling in the filth with my arm covered in blood and mucus and straw sticking out of my hair and clothes. Yet I didn't care that I was a mess in front of this delicious morsel of manhood.

My twin lambs were healthy and alive, and enchanting.

'I can see that the flock is in good hands,' said Doctor Crius, from behind my shoulder.

'You called them Aires? Like Airedale terriers? They're a British breed?' I grabbed one of the old towels I kept in the birthing pen, and attempted to wipe away the blood and muck. All I did was spread it around.

'No. Aries, like the zodiac sign. The winged ram that became the original golden fleece. They're from the Western side of the Black Sea, Georgia to be exact,' explained Doctor Crius. He gazed down at the lambs with a doting expression. 'Dr Aeolia imported them specially. He's from that area, himself.'

'So, is their orangey colour natural?'

'Yes. It is unique to their variety.' The corners of his eyes crinkled as he smiled. 'But, hey. You probably want to clean up. This new mum probably wants some privacy. Shall I come back at a better time?'

'No, no. It'll only take me a mo to tidy up. Can I offer you a cup of tea or coffee while you wait, Doctor Crius?' I did not want to let this gentleman wander off without getting more details about my flock.

'If you want, I can make us the cuppas,' he replied. 'Just point me at your kitchen. And please, call me Chris.'

Dear me. House-trained *and* attractive *and* knowledgeable about sheep? He had to taken. I snuck a look at his left hand. No ring, not that that meant so much these days.

I hurried into the bathroom and groaned at my reflection in the mirror. So classy. I changed my clothes, managed to remove the muck with a washcloth, and brushed the straw and shit out of my hair. Looking like a civilised human being, and—better yet—feeling like one, I joined Chris in my kitchen. We sat at my grandmother's huge, scarred wooden table, sipping milky-sweet tea made just the way I liked it, and munching homemade chocolate-chip biscuits.

The morning light slanted in through the windows, catching in the curls of Chris' hair and making his eyes look very blue. I pretended my heart wasn't beating nineteen-to-the-dozen, and fought to keep my focus on sheep. Normally, I wasn't such a fool around guys; I had little time for socialising. But Chris Crius pushed all my buttons.

I took a swallow of tea. 'What can you tell me about my flock of Aries sheep?'

'Well, what *can* I tell you? You obviously know how to care for them. I've never seen them looking so well,' replied Chris. He glanced out the window to the paddock that held the flock, sprinkled over the grass like clumps of wildflowers.

'What research were they used for? Big pharma stuff?' It still worried me, the thought of those little sweeties being used for experiments. I loathed testing on animals.

'No, nothing like that.' Chris stared into the distance then shrugged. 'Dr Aeolia had some very strange ideas about breeding sheep for more than just meat and wool. He never told me exactly what he was doing. We were just breeding the Aries to his specifications and sending away DNA for testing. I wasn't surprised when they cut our funding. Jason disappeared to Argentina without a word.' He hesitated. 'He did take an esky of frozen embryos, though. Always wondered why he cared more about them than the sheep. My job was caring for the flock while I worked on my own thesis. I like animals better than test tubes.'

'So you were their main carer? Why does their fleece get so dirty? Do they suffer from a type of flaky suint?' I asked. I still brushed a lot of shiny yellow grit out of my animals, daily. The ground where I tended them was beginning to sparkle in the sun.

'Dirty? Have they been taking dust baths?'

'No. But their wool seems to attract a lot of specks of mica or something. Is it a type of scurf? First time I brushed them, I thought someone had been playing silly buggers with glitter.'

Chris tapped his chin with the tips of his fingers, looking perplexed. 'Jason used to ask me to brush the flock regularly, but they were kept indoors in pens. No dirt. Just straw and straw dust.'

'I can get you a sample, if you like. I always brush them in the same place. The grit is all over the ground.'

'Okay. Just take me to where the magic happens.'

We drained our cups.

As I led Chris into the paddock, the flock looked up with interest. I wasn't carrying a bucket, but they wandered in our direction anyway. Chris was pleased to see them.

'It's great to see them looking content. It was nerve-wracking to wonder where they would end up. I was worried a butcher might buy them,' he told me. 'I had no say in the auction. And I live in a townhouse, so I couldn't even buy one as a pet.'

I shuddered at the thought of my flock converted into mutton.

The animals were close enough to pat. I buried my fingers into the poll of the nearest animal and she leant against my legs. As I scratched the sheep's scalp, I asked, 'Were they advertised as a heritage breed?'

'Nope. The company contracted to sell up the facility weren't used to handling stock, just scientific equipment. I'm surprised you went to the auction, really.'

'I wasn't the one who bought them. They spent a few months with a hobby farmer who had no idea.'

Chris laughed, causing two of the flock to bound away. They didn't go far, and quickly returned. All the flock enjoyed being patted, cuddled, or scratched.

'Well, this is it,' I said, pointing. We were standing next to the fence. The ground wasn't bare of grass, but the constant use had created a minor bald spot where the soil showed through. In the sunshine, the dirt sparkled like a disco ball.

Chris crouched down to inspect it. 'Wow. So shiny!'

He pinched some of the glitter between his finger and studied it closely. 'It isn't mica. You know, if I didn't know any better, I'd say this was gold dust. I do a bit of fossicking, for fun.'

'Who would be insane enough to sprinkle sheep with gold dust?'

Chris looked thoughtful. 'No one, but sheepskins were used as a method of filtering gold in previous eras. Maybe this was a breed developed to be efficient gold filters?'

'Look. That might not even be gold.' I scuffed at the ground with my toe. That was a lot, if it really was gold.

'True. You should get it tested.'

'Oh my,' I said, stunned. 'If it is, where could the gold be coming from?'

'We kept the flock in environmentally-controlled pens, and they were fed expensive supplements, and you keep them on grass. Maybe the change in diet?' suggested Chris. He patted two of the sheep. The others were getting jealous and kept trying to butt their way forward.

I switched to scratching the poll of one of the jealous animals.

'My pasture is high in forbs. Do herbs take up gold? Maybe that helped?'

'No idea. Botany's not my area of expertise. Could be. That would be closest to their natural diet. And the breed does come from Georgia's gold-mining district.' Chris inspected underneath his fingernails and dug out gold-coloured grit. He looked down at the sparkling ground.

'This must be what Jason was hoping for. Sheep that can secrete heavy metals would be an enormous benefit to the environment.' Chris' eyes lit up, causing my heart to thud harder.

'But gold isn't toxic, is it? Not like lead or mercury,' I asked.

'No, not on its own.'

'Will this affect their health?'

Chris looked down at the flock, who were still struggling to get their share of attention. 'They look healthy enough to me. Healthy and happy.' He grinned, and added, 'You always get the best cream from contented cows.'

I grinned back. 'I guess these animals really do have a heart of gold.'

Chris chuckled. We both liked punning. Win!

Then realisation struck. If news got out about my flock, they might become a target for greedy capitalists. 'Gold is a more valuable commodity than wool. Farming for gold is easier and cheaper than mining.'

Our eyes met and we both looked back down at the sheep.

'Who was funding your research?' I asked.

'Mainly the government and a couple of private companies. We were an agricultural research centre, and this current bunch aren't really into supporting scientific research. That's why Jason headed overseas.'

'So,' I said slowly, petting one of the ewes, 'This discovery would get you funding, wouldn't it?'

Chris straightened. That dazzling smile flashed, and he shook his head. 'Maybe. But this is such a small herd that they aren't a viable concern against our current mining industries. The amount of gold they produce isn't in commercial quantities. I doubt I could get any funding for the environmental aspect of their abilities ... not at the moment.' He hadn't stopped patting the animals. 'But I'd like to see how they get on, if you don't mind. Maybe visit you...them a couple times a week? Just for research purposes, I mean.'

'Deal.' I stuck out my hand and we shook on it.

I was still grinning like a loon when one of the ewes butted me behind the knees and knocked me over. Chris helped me back to my feet. I was now covered in glittering dirt.

'You are probably wearing the most expensive work clothes in Australia,' said Chris. 'And you make them look good.'

I decided then that—even without the gold—the strange sheep were my best buy ever.

# They Labour in Vain who Build It

*Psalm 127:1*

*Jo Seysener*

'Pigboy, it's M8te. You up?' Mole8 released the button. Waited. He tried again. Maybe he had timed it wrong, and Molehouse7 was asleep, or out in their tunnels.

'Yo.' It was a phrase from an ancient comic book—the only book left in the molehouse. 'Yo? Pigboy? You there?' Odd. Pigboy always manned the radio between his nap cycles, while his family dug the tunnels, hunted for water, or tended the fungus gardens.

M8te was the name Pigboy had given him years ago when he first worked the radio and Sita moved into the tunnels. Pigboy was the only person Mole8 had spoken to outside of his own molehouse for years. Now, Pigboy was the only person Mole8 spoke to at all.

'Pigboy? You there, mate?' Mole8 stifled a giggle at his own joke. There was a long pause. Mole8 kicked the vine his potato radio grew from to distract himself. Fear burrowed in his belly, wriggling like a knot of worms. 'Pigboy?'

Surely there was nothing wrong at Pigboy's end; it must be him. Mole8 checked his connections but they were all fine. He tried to raise his friend again. And again. The transceiver sat silent. So did Mole8.

He bit his lip and stared about the room, picking out the empty strands of his net pack, lying loose across the dirt floor. In his head he tallied the cans and bottles of water hiding at the back of the cupboard. There weren't many. He would have to leave his molehouse soon. This morning he'd decided to tell Pigboy he was coming.

Mole8 studied the molehouse, seeing it fresh for the first time. The dome shaped rooms his grandfather had dug and lined with concrete. The ventilation tube, going who-knew-where. The storage cupboards that used to hold thousands of tins, bottles of water and batteries. The comforting closeness of the space. Warm. Safe. Familiar.

He closed his eyes, just holding panic at bay. But he was almost out of food. And he'd been alone for so long, now. He would have to risk the journey through the tunnels to Pigboy's. A direction he hadn't ventured in since...

He shook his head to clear it. He picked up the transmitter, tried Pigboy once more, then put it gently back down. He sat there awhile, with the transmitter under his hand, hoping the fluttering sickness in his stomach would go away. It didn't, so he swallowed and nodded.

Crouching over his net pack, he collected strands and knotted them together. The contents of the cupboard filled it too quickly. Thirty-seven cans, twenty small bottles. The work came quickly after so much practice.

His meagre food supply was stashed safely at the top of the pack, along with his comic book, wrapped carefully in canvas; a small spade, tools and scrap for tunnel repairs loaded beneath. He hoisted the net onto his back, straining beneath the weight of cans and scrap metal. More crap than scrap, really.

He took one last, long breath, patted the curving wall, flicked on his torch, and walked out of his molehouse.

Mole8 counted his steps as he travelled, watching his boots kick up little puffs of dust. This first section would be easy, nothing in his way for the first one hundred and eighty-eight steps. He knew them well.

At one hundred and sixty-nine steps from the molehouse where he'd spent his whole life, Mole8 halted. He hated this section. His skin prickled, little hairs rising on his arms through a paste of sweat and dirt. Stomach knotting, he forced his feet onward. Sweat beaded in the nape of his neck and ran down his back, dampening his shirt. His breath came fast.

Step, step. His breath hitched.

*Step.*

Here the earth was soft. Walls smoothed in three places. He'd used up a lot of his water cementing those walls, evening out the slurry, pressing hard as it dried. Packing the earth that had killed them over their heavy bodies.

He placed his hand over one of the small handprints in the tunnel wall, covering it completely. His hand was much larger now. His vision swam. He didn't have enough fluid to spare, crying over something gone. Useless. A cramp began in his stomach, travelling to his heart. He forced back bile pooling in his throat.

Three perfectly-rounded pebbles were set into the wall, one for each of them. Mole8 touched each one, sighing as the tears flowed anyway. Somehow, touching them was important.

At the final grave he paused, unsure what to do next. Should he speak to them, say goodbye? No words filled his mouth, though he tried to think of something respectful. A thank you to the earth, for keeping his family safe, here-but-gone? Or should he rage and scream for taking them from him? They were one with the earth, now. Free from fear.

The earth took what she wanted, gave when she could, protected and punished, cradled and killed. Moles lived that way. He knew that, but it didn't make losing them easier.

He tried to recall feeling Dad's arms around him, his musky scent. But the image of his father's face blurred, fading. He let out a hollow breath. Holding up both hands, he flattened them on the wall separating him from his father's body. He bowed his head, forehead touching the hardened earth, and whispered a word.

After a quiet moment he stepped back and moved on.

Twenty-six easy steps later he stopped. This was the furthest he had ever been on this side of Molehouse8. Dad never expected him to go further. The thought niggled. The other families had been this way. They'd left just after he was born. Mum never talked about them, but they had left belongings behind. A few scraps of their lives. Sita had drawn pictures in the dirt of a little girl. He couldn't remember her name.

He glanced back over his shoulder, into darkness. His last chance to turn back to safety. No. There was nothing left, now.

His stomach rumbled. Mole8 reached for a can. He'd forgotten to eat in his rush to get to Pigboy. He flicked open the ring-pull—gently, so as not to end up with the little ring in one dirty fist and an unopened can in the other.

How was Pigboy doing? What could have gone wrong for Pigboy not to answer his call? For *anyone*? Silence from a molehouse...Mole8 shook his head.

He dipped his fingers in and came up with his regular: beans. One of his few reading words. Granny Mills had taught him and his sister—*no, I won't think of Sita right now*. But the thoughts came anyway. Dark hair curling about her neck, her smell—cleanest of them all when she cuddled him. A cold shiver raced across his back. Sita had been a great digger. Now she was pressed into the wall of one of her own tunnels, covered by a smattering of dirt and a round pebble. His breath hitched.

*Eat the beans.*

One finger, then another.

*Eat the beans.*

Another and another. Faster, until his fingers struck the bottom of the tin with a dull thud. Mole8 dripped a little water into the can, swirling it to collect the sauce. Nothing goes to waste—Granny Mills used to say it constantly. Annoyingly.

He grimaced. She was gone, too, into the earth's belly years before. He shoved the empty can into the net. Time to go forward. Mole8 trudged another few hundred steps, counting each one as it took him further from home. Far enough for now. Must be close to a nap cycle.

He curled into a ball on the tunnel floor. Wriggling to get comfy, Mole8 felt for his tool belt and cursed. He had forgotten it. That would have been useful. But he wasn't turning back. Persistence was the key. That's what Mum had said. He tried the word out on his tongue and tripped over it a few times. Finally, he had the flow of it. Then he remembered he needed to save his fluids and stopped.

Fourteen tins of mostly unknown vegetables later, Mole8 was two thousand, seven hundred and eighty-four paces into the next tunnel. He had fixed walls, dug through cave ins, and was completely covered in dirt. That wasn't unusual.

What *had* been odd was the size of one of the cave-ins. Dad had said it was a small cave-in that took up most of the tunnel. Beyond it was the tunnel leading to Molehouse7. With a little excavation, it should have been easy to go around. Instead, Mole8 found a path around the cave-in where it piled high to the roof. Mostly on one side. On the other side a path had been dug into the side of the tunnel.

The excavations looked old but the tunnel beyond was newer. Fresh. Maybe Dad hadn't been down this way and someone from the other end had done the work? Pigboy's people, maybe?

If the path had been made by Pigboy's molehouse, then they must be close. He had to keep going. Keep moving forward. To Pigboy, to Molehouse7. Never backward, no matter how much he wanted to.

Persistence.

Granny Mills had another way of saying it. KBO. *Keep Buggering On.* Mole8 liked that word. Bugger. It worked best when he stubbed his toes. Which was a lot. Granny Mills said KBO was what the famous Mr Churchill used to say, during the last world war, before the Big War.

The Big War had a name, but she refused to say it. Or talk about it. But she would talk about the Second World War. Her grandad had fought in it, Mole8's Great-Great-Granddad. Mole8 didn't know what a war was, or what being famous meant.

Perhaps Mr. Churchill had been a Superhero, flying through the night, rescuing people from the bad guys. That's what important people did in his comic book, after all.

The comic was his favourite thing, besides batteries for his torch. He liked the image on the cover: a tall man with big arms and a flapping cape. Mole8 flexed his arms like the superhero, but his lanky muscles were only good for pulling scrap from the earth, not for rescuing people. Mr Churchill must have had big arms, too, and a cape. That would be good—a cape. Then he'd look like a hero when he rescued Pigboy.

He paused in his walking and swallowed hard. Pigboy had to be alright. He would be there. The radio would be broken, that was all. Pigboy and his family would be waiting, safe in their Molehouse. And wouldn't they be surprised to see Mole8? Smiling, he resumed walking.

The beam from his torch flashed forward. Here the tunnel widened out. The high roof was only packed dirt—*no wonder Dad warned me not to come along this way, with no roof support*—and opened into a small cavern. A wall of solid earth reflected torchlight back at him.

He frowned. The tunnel to Molehouse7 was supposed to be a straight line after the last cave-in site. Mole8 stepped into the small room, turning in a semi-circle. The light showed solid surface until he was almost all the way around, where it disappeared into blackness.

A tunnel bored into the earth, back the way he had come, at a slight angle to the right. A similar tunnel turned off to the left. He must have missed it with the first sweep. It led more in the general direction of Molehouse7 than the one to his right.

Worry niggled. Surely Dad wouldn't have given him such different directions? Maybe his memory was wrong. Yes, that must be it. Molehouse7 had to be this way. Soon, he'd find Pigboy and they'd laugh about how dumb he was.

Shrugging his pack deeper down his back, he headed into the left tunnel. Several spots in the walls appeared to be patched. Some recent, others crumbling, older looking. One even of cement. There hadn't been the parts to mix cement for a long time. At least, not in his section of the Molehouse Network. Dad had told him how to make it up, should he ever chance across the right mix.

The tunnel curved, turning back on itself. Mole8's chest tightened. Bugger! Maybe he had taken the wrong turn. What if he was lost? Would he never get to see Pigboy? Maybe he would wander alone in the darkness, until his legs gave out.

He kicked at a small pile of loose dirt. Pebbles rattled off the wall with tiny echoing ticks of sound. Should he return to the cavern? Have a look at the other tunnel? This one had felt right, but perhaps he had made a mistake.

Wait. That first cave-in site; the way the path wound around the heap of debris; the newer looking tunnel beyond. His gut clenched.

Could the cave-in have blocked the path to Molehouse7? But no, surely he would have been told if they changed the tunnels in that direction? Dad would have told him. Unless...

Unless someone else had changed the tunnels, when Dad was no longer there to maintain them. Pigboy knew about the cave-in, his family's fate. The thought of someone—*his friend, perhaps*—being so close, but not visiting Molehouse8 made his chest hurt. Could they have come in while he was digging in the other tunnels? No. He knew no one had been in his molehouse.

Alone. Always alone.

He filled his cheeks with air and puffed them out. Torn nails scratched his scalp, dislodging sweat-soaked clumps of dirt. He would keep going in this direction. His chosen path. He snorted. Dirt and snot shot out of his nostrils. Like he got to *choose* anything. He didn't choose to be born here. Didn't choose for the earth to swallow his family. Didn't choose to be alone.

Well, now he *was* choosing. He'd go this way and he'd find Pigboy. Nothing would stop him. Nothing! He kicked another pebble, walking quickly, making more ground than his entire journey so far.

The roof section here was crisscrossed with hairline fractures. Shudders ran up his spine, so he studied the walls instead. Jumbled bits of rubble and wood poked through. His neck itched, and he scratched until it was sore.

The tunnel curved away from where he thought Molehouse7 was. He should turn back. Not only were these tunnels old, he wasn't even heading in Pigboy's direction anymore. He'd made the wrong choice.

He turned back, breathing easier. He'd go back to the first cave in and dig around. He should have just enough tins to get him there.

A stone turned underfoot and he tripped, sprawling face first over a mound of debris. His torch fell from his hand, flickered and dimmed. Something snapped. The ties of his netting let go, scattering supplies over the tunnel floor. He groaned, hearing cans tumble over the floor, bouncing and grumbling. They rolled and were still.

He lay in the half-light for a moment, his chest heaving, heat boiling up from his guts until it poured out his mouth in a scream that scraped his throat raw. The echoes mocked him, sounding like people that weren't there.

The rage didn't leave and the scream came again. He rose to his feet and kicked at the uncaring wall. Screamed and kicked and kicked again until dirt showered his foot and dust hung heavy in the air.

The echoes sounded like the earth grumbling and mumbling. Like Granny Mills had when she was annoyed. Mole8 stopped, his cheeks hot and breath short. The grumbling continued, growing louder. He choked and dropped to his knees, patting the ground as though he could soothe the earth. Dirt fell on his head. He rolled onto his back, staring at the ceiling of the tunnel.

His skin prickled and the urge to run hit him hard, yet he stayed frozen, watching the thin cracks grow bigger. Dirt trickled down, dusting his face. Mole8 smashed his lips shut against the dirt. More fell from the roof of the tunnel and he accidentally sucked in a great breath. He coughed as more dirt fell on him. He couldn't close his eyes. If these were to be his last moments, he would see every second.

'I'm sorry!' he whispered. 'I'm sorry.'

Cracks danced across the roof of the tunnel, mica shining in the torchlight like the mobile of tin cans that used to hang over his bed. Chunks of dirt and rock poured down, covering the torch, blanketing him, leaving him in darkness; as a mother prepares her child for sleep.

Mole8 didn't know how long he lay there, trying not to choke on the fine dust floating in the air. It was still, hot. Lips clamped shut. Would he suffocate? With dirty fists, he rubbed his eyes, blinking to clear them. He felt about for the torch in darkness. Panic bloomed. Where was it? Nothing was possible without it. He could be groping about in unknown tunnels forever.

His breath wheezed. Scrabbling fingers found the edges of what felt like his net, and he clung to it like a safety blanket. He rolled onto his stomach, pulling. It was too heavy and wouldn't budge. He scraped away dirt. His fingertips hit cold metal, fumbled for the switch. There! Light again. *Breathe.* His heart slowed. He should be used to the dark. But it was different when he had no choice.

Mole8 swung the light towards the tunnel. His heart sank. There was no path back to Pigboy, or his Molehouse. A mound of rubble filled the tunnel top to bottom. He would never be able to dig through.

At least he wasn't dead, buried beneath the mass of dirt. He looked at his net. A few strands lay exposed, along with several broken cans and burst waterbottles. Small tears and frayed edges appeared in the netting. There would be no quick repair job. He took stock of the bent and battered metal, burst cans oozing a sludgy mix of rusty browns and dull greens, seasoned with a sprinkling of dirt.

His sight blurred, darkening at the edges. Dizzy, he hung his head below his knees. How much farther was it to Molehouse7? Doubt punched him in the gut. Too many questions.

He stuck a finger in the goopy food staining the tunnel floor. No point in wasting it. He shovelled the mess into his mouth, picking out larger clots of earth before he swallowed them. For the first time he could remember, he gorged himself. He ate until only a muddy puddle remained. Weariness overcame him. He switched off the torch and slept where he lay.

Mole8 awoke, flicked on the torch and stared at a dirt roof. It didn't bother him at first, until he couldn't find the edge of his bed. He sighed. The cave-in. The broken net. Still surprised he wasn't buried, he checked the wall blocking his way back, just in case he'd imagined it.

Nope.

He rolled his neck and shoulders, working out cramps which felt like pebbles rubbing against each other, and began knotting the loose strands of the net back together.

He was halfway through his repair job—the net and contents much smaller after he had dragged them from beneath the mound—when he realised there was something missing. He picked over the scrap, counting cans on one hand.

Where was it? *There*.

A curled page poked out from the dirt pile. But only a page, crumpled and torn. Frantic, he scrabbled at the dirt, freeing another can and scattering rubble around him. But there were no more pages. They were gone, buried beneath the earth like his family.

Mole8 sighed, a small whimper in the silence. He stared down at the images in his lap, the crumpled superhero squashed onto a building. He smoothed the tattered paper out. The colours weren't so vivid now, dulled with a layer of dirt.

Tears tracked down his cheeks, creating muddy splotches on that last, precious page. No. Mustn't waste water. With the utmost care, he undid his shirt and slipped the paper beneath it, between the singlet and Dad's shirt on top. He didn't want his sweat to wreck the comic. He buttoned the shirt back up, pressing a hand over his chest. He could feel the little thumps of his heart through the thin material. He picked up his pack and moved on.

Forward. It was the only direction left to travel.

He didn't bother to wipe the tears from his face.

Each step felt heavier than the last.

How long since other people had come this way? Which way

had they gone? Would he find their remains along the path, uncovered and left for whichever rat-like animals lived here? If there were any animals at all. Mole8 grimaced. He was used to geckoes hanging from the ceiling, clicking and chattering. Giant roaches crawling over his face at nap time. But it had been a long time since he had seen any of those.

If he didn't find food…dare he hope for a rat? He had no way of cooking it. He shuddered. There were some things that even a lone Mole didn't want to face.

A short distance from the rubble mound, the tunnel divided. He took the right hand one, hoping the tunnel would curve around, towards Pigboy. A little later the tunnel did curve—and even in the right direction. Mole8 let out a happy whoop. The sound echoed down the empty tunnel. He picked up his pace and managed to extract a can from the pack without sitting down. His first ever walking meal.

Smiling, he strode along the curving tunnel for a few dozen steps, then halted. Yet another junction. Again, he took the right hand one. Another divide in the tunnels, then another.

Too many. The map in his head twisted and it felt like he'd turned away from Molehouse7.

He stopped and leaned against the wall, not wanting to sit, but sliding down onto his pack anyway. Weary arms fell to his lap and slipped off. His hand brushed the hard-packed floor. There was little loose earth here, no pebbles to speak of.

The walls were smooth and evenly rounded, as though a great boulder had rolled through and cleanly taken all the insides of the tunnel with it. Granny Mills said the first tunnels were built with huge machines that chewed through the earth. Until they ran out of fuel.

How big the machines must have been. It was hard to picture something huge enough to carve out a tunnel this size. He rubbed the smooth surface of the walls. Much better than any digger could have made, especially with the gentle slope of the floor.

His tired eyes drooped; head nodding. Jerking upright, he ran his fingers along the floor again. Must keep going. Must find Pigboy.

Wait. The *slope* of the floor? No. Please, no. He fumbled in his pack for the tool he needed—a level, his father had called it—a short piece of clear, rubbery hose, filled with a mix of fluids.

Nothing. *Tell me I haven't lost that, too!* His fingers closed on the small piece of plastic. A little bubble of air floated on top. When placed on a flat surface, it was supposed to sit in the centre.

Mole8 carefully laid it on the ground, holding his breath. The bubble wobbled in the centre for a moment and he breathed out. Then it slid to one end of the hose.

His stomach plummeted. Uphill. He had been travelling uphill. He groaned and would have fallen if he hadn't already been squatting down. The ground seemed to sway. It would only take a small rise and he would miss Molehouse7 altogether. He could be sitting right on top of it and not even know.

Again, the urge to backtrack hit him. Too many turns and choices. Yet no choice at all, really. He had to go on. With the greatest of efforts, he hauled himself up.

*Trudging.*

Mole8 walked back the way he had come, pausing to measure the incline at intervals. After a time, he reached a place where the tunnel flattened out and the tiny bubble stayed in the centre of the hose.

He was over halfway back to the cave-in that had almost smothered him. Assuming he'd remembered the turns right. Little hairs stood up on his arms in a shiver that wracked him head to toe. For just a moment he couldn't breathe, as though the earth squeezed him too tight, suffocating him.

He shook his head. The feeling eased and he breathed again.

Drawn to one side of the tunnel wall, he paused, staring in the direction he associated with Molehouse7. Here the walls of the tunnel were patched in sections with an assortment of materials from different generations.

He poked a callused finger into a bare section of wall. Silt—where an underground river may have once run. A good place to dig. Easy. He snorted a short laugh. There might even be water.

Cheered somewhat at the thought of work—*something useful*—Mole8 fell into his natural rhythm. Scrabbling out silt, raising little mounds off to the side of the entrance to his new tunnel. This new path would lead him to Pigboy. Definitely. Tiny steps forward, checking his progress was level. KBO. He was going to make it now; he knew it.

*Dig. Remove. Repeat.*

*Dig.* Remembering scratching out a cave-in long ago.

*Remove.* Scraping the dirt away, uncovering white-blue flesh. Carving out the ledges, mixing precious water with the dirt. Sliding the bodies along each ledge, stacking one alongside the other. Packing the dirt in over their still forms, marking each with a treasure pressed into the setting mud.

*Repeat.*

Every so often he stopped, out of breath. Opened another can.

*Repeat.*

*Repeat.*

Dust filled his nose and mouth. He tried to swallow but choked. Unable to focus on anything but the next part of his process. Not wanting to. Tired. So, so tired, but digging, digging. Getting to Pigboy. Soon. His wish come true.

Soft vibrations rumbled beneath his feet and shook the loose dirt around him. His flashlight flickered and went out. Cursing, he dredged out the last two batteries by touch. Stacked the little cylinders. Light flooded the tunnel he had dug. How far had he dug, now? He hadn't counted his steps.

He paused in retrieving the spade. More vibrations beneath his feet; in the walls. He should be afraid of another cave in, but he didn't care anymore. He could only think about digging. Nothing else mattered.

So he stood, waiting.

When the tunnel didn't cave in, Mole8 resumed digging. The vibrations became loud, bouncing from wall to wall. He frowned. Not a cave-in? Each step brought him closer to the source. Perhaps some great living thing, slumbering in the dark?

More likely it was Molehouse 7. Maybe they'd found one of the huge digging machines. Mole8 dug until, with a *tonk,* the spade hit something solid. He scrabbled dirt away, filling the tunnel behind him with his excavations. The surface of this *thing* was cool, and slightly rounded.

The area began to open out, soil loosened and fell away into a natural cavity next to the object. A shape emerged; a big tube, maybe? Metallic, and new—well, newer than any metal he had seen. The object must be huge. Made of some sort of alloy. The hardest material he had ever come across. Even banging with his fist resulted in only the smallest of sounds.

Eyes closed, he pressed his face against the surface. Cool and smooth. Only moments ago, shovelling dirt and dust he'd felt like an old man, muscles aching, bone tired. Now he had made a discovery. He was the comic book hero, defeating bad guys and saving the world. But there were no bad guys, and only him in the world.

Mole8 brushed dirt from the surface of the object. Markings emerged. Letters painted white stood out against the shiny metal. N-A-S-A. He knew those letters, they were all in BEANS. But they meant nothing. He whispered the word through cracked lips. No word he'd heard.

Maybe it was a giant can of some new sort of beans. He snorted a laugh. Nearly all his supplies were gone. A giant can of beans would be just the thing. Now to find a door—or a giant pull-ring. He grinned.

He dug further around the side, past the NASA sign. There was a small patch of colour—blue, white and red in a sort of squashed square. He swiped at the top of the picture. It looked old, plastic peeling at the edges. A tiny piece flaked into his hand. He brushed it away and touched a bump below it.

The soft earth flowed through his fingers. A green glow filtered through the soil. The bump became a rectangle sticking out from the metal. Not a part of the tube, something joined to it.

Dad had said never to dig down. Mole8 ignored that advice. Curiosity drove him. The thrum of the vibrations seemed almost *warmer* here. Had he been digging deeper and not realised? He was so tired, but he wanted to solve this mystery before his next sleep.

This must be why Molehouse 7 hadn't answered. They were all too busy with this machine-thing. Wouldn't Pigboy be surprised?

Using the bottom of his shirt to wipe the box, Mole8 stared. A word was written on it. Only it was a word he couldn't read. He knew it started with an 'E', but the rest made no sense at all. A funny, sideways cross, a stripe with a dot on top, and another cross, standing up. He added the first letter to create a word. E-X-I-T. What did *that* mean? A gap beneath the box underlined it then curved down, disappearing below the soil line.

Mole8 sat with his back against the metal, warmed somewhat in that patch from his body heat. The vibrations thrummed like a heartbeat. He switched the torch off. The light below him cast a green glow.

He moved around, making first his shoes green, then his hands. Would the light shine through his feet? He took his shoes off and pressed his feet to the glow. It did! His toes were a weird pinkish-brown colour inside. He grinned.

He continued to play with the light, the first he'd seen that wasn't from a handheld device. He sat down on it. *The sun shines out of my ass,* Granny Mills used to say. He giggled. A high-pitched sound. It echoed around the blunt-ended cavern. Giggled, and giggled. And giggled.

After a while he subsided to hiccups. Mole8 was tired. He closed his eyes and slid sideways. The air felt thicker, heavier. His new tunnel had no ventilation, unlike the older ones his father had monitored all his life; his father before that. Mole8 sighed and coughed, just a little.

He tried to make himself comfortable, fidgeting about on the ground. Something dug into his back. Fumbling around, his hand struck the last can secured in his net-pack. Limbs heavy, he shrugged, freeing the pack. All that remained was the spade, a small, almost circular piece of metal, and his can.

He leaned back against the cylinder, the contents of his pack in his hands. It was funny such a huge object didn't take up the space, or make him feel small. It felt like company. There were probably people inside. A colony working and living together.

Or maybe they were trapped inside the container, and he, the Superhero, was there to rescue them. To save them and bring them to a new world.

What would the new world look like? Would it have skyscrapers and sunny skies, like the comic? Would there be bad guys and heroes? Would there be moles like him living beneath the ground, holding up the foundations? He smiled, drowsy.

He didn't want to be Mole8 anymore. He wanted a real name, like his parents and sister had, or Granny Mills. A superhero's name. Dad had given him a title—the last Mole in Molehouse8. He sighed. Even Pigboy had a name.

His chest ached and his throat tightened. He wasn't going to get to see Pigboy. He had called Mole8 something else, called him

M8te. Much better. Now he had a new name. He could be M8te. M8te to everyone in his new family, just there on the other side of this great metal slab.

Soon they would come out and find him. Pigboy and the others. He would send out a search party from his molehouse, looking for him. M8te wanted to leave a message for him, so they would know who he was, even if he was sleeping.

Propped on one elbow, he stretched for the remnants of his pack. The little disc had a serrated edge. Sharp enough for what he wanted. Blood beaded on a fingertip.

He reached around, ready to etch his new name on the shiny metal wall. The little glowing box below poked him in the ribs so he slithered on his belly like a worm, away from it.

Pressing metal to metal, he hesitated. He wasn't sure how to write his new name. M—he knew that letter, and he knew his numbers. In the end he just scratched M8 on the wall. Blood from his finger smeared over the markings, settling into the grooves.

M8te placed the disc beneath his name. Then he carefully drew out the last page of his comic book and laid it on top, smoothing the paper. He sat his only can next to it, pressing it into the soft earth. Then he lay back down.

The air was heavier now. His eyes drooped. He blinked, trying to settle but the green glow irritated his eyes. He rolled onto his back. The light was still bright enough to be annoying.

M8te wriggled his shoulders into the dirt, digging a hollow to lay in. A small tremor ran through him. He pushed dirt from his diggings over himself, snuggling down. It still wasn't enough to block out the light.

He smashed his heel down on the green box. It creaked, but nothing changed. He kicked it a few more times, and the light went out.

Familiar darkness spread over him like a blanket. Eyes closed, he settled his shoulders and feet sinking deeper, through the earth. The weight became part of his world, a heartbeat pulsing, rolling through him.

Breathing in was so hard now, and he was too tired to try again.

He sighed out a slow, long breath.

# AIR

# Moving in a Mysterious Way

*JA Henderson*

I'm only alive 'cause I was in Sunnyvale prison, visiting my cousin, Dave. I didn't want to talk to any other sad sacks, all turning up to show misplaced solidarity with dead-beat husbands or swoon over murderous pen pals, so I put on wraparound sunglasses and noise cancelling headphones. Distancing myself from the herd, if you like.

That's what saved me. It always does.

Nobody knows what happened to the air. All I'm sure is, on that day, human beings suffered an instant and complete sensory overload. Sunlight blinded people and burned their skin to a crisp. Every noise was amplified to a deafening roar. Each smell, sweet or sour, became an overpowering stench.

Like a disappointing screw, the end of the world came with a whimper masquerading as a bang.

I was in the canteen when Sunnyvale's sirens went off. Sirens are loud by definition but this was in a different league. Everyone began screaming, not the wisest course of action when you're caught up in a maelstrom of intolerable sound. Through a porthole to the communal room, I could see a stampede for the exits, including guys in leg irons—who had to hop. The light pouring through the upper windows turned swiftly and intolerably bright, as if a supernova had exploded in the atmosphere.

I threaded my way through visitors, who were bumping into each other in panic, eyes squeezed shut and hands over their ears. My head was throbbing, despite the headphones, so I darted into the kitchen. Prison food smells awful at the best of times but now the stink was stomach churning. There was a big walk in fridge at the back, so I got inside and pulled the door shut. I tried to eat a sausage roll but now it tasted of mouldy carpet. Instead, I waited in the dark until a blessed silence descended.

When I emerged, it was night and the place was deserted. No visitors. No warders. No prisoners. No Dave.

One of the guards must have opened the electronic cell doors as a last act of altruism, setting the inmates free. Or maybe he just pressed the wrong button in confusion. Either way, it's doubtful anyone got more than a hundred yards outside the main gate before they were toasted.

Everything happens for a reason, Mum used to say. Then again, she was electrocuted by faulty Christmas tree lights and obviously no expert on fate.

The survivors all have different theories, but shit happens and I don't see the point in dwelling on it. After all, Corinne's Bible has God creating the whole universe in seven days, without actually saying how he did it. And the whole shebang only takes up half a page.

But I've always been lucky, and it turned out jail was the best place for me. Sunnyvale's male and female wings were subterranean, joined by underground tunnels. Metal shutters could be brought down on any windows above ground. The place even had its own emergency generator and I'd say the end of humanity definitely counted as an emergency.

For a while, I thought I might be the last person on earth. Then, one by one, I came across Corrine Telford, Floyd Peterson, WTF Hartley, Div, and Doob. I still don't know Div and Doob's last names. Or their first names for that matter. There's no real need when your universe only contains six people.

We get along well enough. Each of us staked out a little bit of turf but it's important to chip in to keep things running. Like vampires, we only come out at night, emerging from solitary confinement cells on the lowest levels, where we sleep the day away without being assaulted by sounds and smells and piercing light.

All in all, it's not a bad existence, considering the circumstances. I've always been lucky, I suppose.

WTF Hartley and I are a couple. He isn't really called WTF, of course, but now he can have any name he wants. Personally, I would have gone for something like Dirk Manly or Rupert Hyphen Poshhouser. Still, it kind of suits him.

He also wears a dress most days. Not in a feminine way, because he has a shaved head and a face that looks like it vacuumed a gravel driveway. WTF just doesn't see any reason to conform to old stereotypes. Then again, he has a broad Scottish accent, so perhaps it's the closest thing he can find to a kilt.

WTF's theory is that the air is the same as always, it's us who have suddenly become intolerant to it. He says it's proof people can change.

He also has the most important and hazardous job in Sunnyvale, foraging for supplies in town twice a week.

We've developed a routine. I lather his face with sun cream, while he distracts us both from the dangers he faces with a stream of meaningless banter. He keeps his voice low, as everyone does, so it's no more than a murmur. I don't mind, as it sounds sexy.

'I ever tell you about going tae the wildlife Sanctuary in Lone Pine, Mo?' he says. 'I had mah picture taken with a Koala called Sally. Grabbed mah bare arms with claws that could open a safe door, then peed on me. Close up, I saw she had beady eyes and wuz incapable of any kind of expression. Like a psychopath.'

He puts on several prison uniforms, each bigger than the last. It's fortunate some of the inmates were built like garden sheds.

'In the gift shop were photographs of famous people holding Koalas. President Clinton. Pope John Paul II. Even Bono. If aliens landed, they'd probably think Monica wuz some kind of world leader.'

He sticks on a riot helmet, skiing goggles, rubber gloves, ear plugs and nose plugs.

'Koalas. The wee bastards have everybody fooled.'

I help him into a leather flying jacket and white silk scarf he found in a vintage store. He likes to be stylish, my man. When he first got it, I unbent a wire coat hanger and threaded it through the collar, so now it stands up and protects his neck. Looks pretty cool too.

Being civilized is all about keeping up appearances, WTF insists, and I agree.

'You take care out there,' I warn, as always.

'I am putting myself to the fullest possible use, which is all I think that any conscious entity can ever hope to do.' He gives me a thumbs up. 'That's the killer computer HAL, from the movie *2001*. Douglas Rain did the voice.'

WTF is a film buff.

I gently slap his butt and retreat, while he opens the door to the compound. In the distance are blocky silhouettes of redundant guard towers. Even with nose plugs in, a thousand natural odours assail me and I feel queasy. Thank god the sun has turned every corpse to dust, or we'd be eternally throwing up.

WTF blows me a kiss, steps into the night and is gone.

Time to do my rounds.

I'm officially head of security, prison nurse, health inspector and entertainment officer. I've always liked to keep busy. I'm also Mayor of Brisbane and Duchess of Queensland, though those are honorary titles. I've pushed to be addressed as Queen of Royal Britain Land and Its Associated Colonies, but nobody has taken me up on it.

First stop on my route is Corinne Telford.

Corinne is our cook, garbage collector and spiritual advisor. She's also a born again Christian and thinks what happened is God's punishment on the wicked—which completely fails to explain *anything*. Whatever floats your boat, I suppose.

She survived by hiding inside an empty coffin in the prison chapel and, out of gratitude, has made the building her domain. It once had beautiful stained glass windows, telling the story of Christ rising from his tomb and such like, but we've boarded them over. Now they're hidden behind cheap plywood facades, which would probably make a good parable if I could be bothered thinking one up.

Corinne spends most of her time reading the Bible and waiting in vain for the rest of us to come seeking guidance. I suggested she become a Jehovah's Witness so she could be more proactive and knock on doors. After all, we can't exactly pretend we're not home. She called me an unholy blasphemer, so I added that to my list of titles.

And she's obviously not too dogmatic, as she followed my advice. Everyone claimed to be out, but she said she could hear breathing as they hid under their bunks.

Since none of us rushed to be converted, I like to keep Corinne's holy spirits up. Each day, I present her with a theological question to ponder, hoping for a satisfying discussion.

'How's trick's, Coz?' I stick my head round the door.

'Please do come in. Mo.' She beckons to me. 'Would you like a Tim Tam?'

I accept a biscuit and sit on a pew. I imagine it's a bit like communion, not that I've ever been to one.

'Right, Corrine.' I launch straight in, as she isn't the type for idle chit chat. 'God is supposed to be all powerful, yeah?'

'That is what I believe, Mo. Certainly.'

Corinne has taken to speaking in a formal manner she probably considers saintly. It actually makes her sound a bit like HAL, which WTF finds hilarious. I don't know why she doesn't go the whole hog and throw in a few 'Thous' and 'Beholds'.

'Then here's my question, Coz. Is God able to build a wall so high, he can't jump over it?'

'Yes.' No hesitation there.

'But if he can't jump over it, he's not all powerful, is he?'

'He moves in mysterious ways, Mo.'

'There's nothing very mysterious about jumping.'

'It is not for me to question the Lord,' she replies serenely. 'We are simply here to serve.'

I bristle a little at this. As far as I'm concerned, the only people put on Earth to serve were waiters. But I know she'll think about my query. Maybe pause before that wall she's building round herself gets too high to jump over.

'You remember tomorrow is the big night?' I ask. 'You gotta do something for it.'

As entertainment officer, I have organised a talent show. In case that isn't enough of a challenge, I've given it a theme. *Air*.

Why not? I think it's funny and so does WTF.

'I've cleared my calendar.' Corinne licks chocolate from her fingers and I wonder if she just made a joke. 'I shall be there, never fear.'

'You're not going to give a sermon, are you?' I wince.

'Everyone has their own area of expertise,' she replies haughtily. 'It would be foolish not to use mine.'

'Of course.' I try to sound enthusiastic. 'Looking forward to it.'

I back out the door, crouched low and waving both hands in front of my face. Corrine looks suitably puzzled.

'What on Earth are you doing?'

'God's not the only one who can move in a mysterious way.'

Corrine sighs.

Next stop is Floyd Peterson. As always, he's in the prison education centre, lost in thought. On the wall is a whiteboard, where some unknown dead guy has written *You can't buy happiness, so steal it*, along with a drawing of a crab on a bike. Try as I might, I can't get the connection.

'Evening, professor.'

He appreciates it when I call him professor. In the old days he was a prison janitor, saved by being in the lowest level cleaning toilets when real shit hit the fan. He thinks our predicament is the result of mass quantum entanglement, set off by particles smashing in Switzerland.

I sit at a desk near the back of the room, like a naughty pupil, while he stands at the front.

Floyd Peterson tilts his head down whenever he looks at me. He must have worn glasses once, but nobody needs them any more, as our sight is crystal clear. The rest of us sport sunshades but I guess he was pretty myopic and relishes having 20/20 vision.

I think I understand why people lose their eyesight as they age. When they study themselves in the mirror they're pleasantly blurred and it hides the wrinkles. That's why, the older you get, the less inclined you are to have photographs taken. Nobody wants a portrait of their own Dorian Grey.

It makes me appreciate WTF even more. Though I'm getting on in years, he looks at me as if I'm the last ham sandwich at a Weight Watchers convention. Which, in metaphorical terms, I suppose I am.

'Whatcha pondering today, Prof?'

'I was thinking that there are billions of stars and planets out there.' He points in the direction of the roof. It is a mass of white splodges, made by bored inmates chewing paper and throwing them upwards 'til they stick. It reminds me of the night sky, but I don't think he's ever noticed.

Floyd Peterson is determined to live in his own head.

'In the good old days, we were unable to reach any of those myriad wonders. Didn't bother us in the slightest, did it?'

To be honest it always did, but I let the comment slide.

'Ever been to Venice?' he continues. 'Or Amsterdam? Moscow? Krakow? Munich? Edinburgh? Tokyo? Rhodes? Chicago?'

'I went to Bundaberg once,' I venture. 'But it was Sunday, so everything was shut.'

'All those fine places,' he says wistfully. 'Yet, when we had the opportunity to visit them, we never took it.' He spreads his hands. 'Why should we care, now that we can't?'

Actually, I *have* been to most of those places, Venice being my favourite. But that doesn't fit with his theory either, so I stay mum.

'It's simply a matter of adjustment. See, all experience is filtered through the prism of our own perceptions and feelings, so it doesn't really matter where we are.'

'The prison of our own perceptions and feelings?' I raise an eyebrow.

Floyd Peterson stares at me and I instinctively put a hand to my face. In the super clear air, a bit of food on my chin can most likely be spotted from a hundred yards.

'Prism, Mo,' he scolds. 'Don't take the piss.'

'Sorry.' But I still think my interpretation is more accurate.

'Thanks for the lecture, Prof.' I get up, careful not to scrape the chair on the tile floor. The noise would be teeth-jarring. 'You always give me a lot to think about.'

But mostly I am thinking Floyd Peterson needs a hobby. Try to live in your own head long enough and you stop being comfortable anywhere else.

'Ready for tomorrow night?' I change the subject. 'The big show?'

'Not really. But I'll give it a try.'

Next on my rounds are Div and Doob, who live in the gymnasium and keep the generator and other geegaws running. Small and wiry, they've shaved each other's heads and remind me of male and female salt 'n' pepper shakers. Once part of the maintenance crew, they were sleeping off massive hangovers in a disused basement boiler when Armageddon came along, and most likely didn't notice.

Their theory is some big conglomerate invented a formula to remove pollutants choking our atmosphere and it got out of control. Fair enough.

Both are in their early twenties and I suspect they're in love because the rest of us are too old to be of consequence to them. They quite like me, though. Most people do.

I believe they're suffering from SMWD or Social Media Withdrawal Symptom, a condition I completely made up, but sounds about right. They've even created a home-made Facebook page, writing post it notes and sticking them to the wall. Visitors can tick the ones they like with a red pen on a string.

When I slide in, they are opening a box of wine.

'G'day mates.' I plonk myself between them and give both a peck on the cheek. Even that small gesture tingles, as if I've rubbed my lips along sandpaper.

'Hi, Mo.' Div passes me a drink. 'Heard you coming, so we broke out the best glasses. The foggy ones with decorative soap rings.'

I take a slurp. It's like swallowing turpentine in this new atmosphere, but all booze tastes horrible until you get used to it. Ask any teenager.

'Hope you've been practising your act,' I splutter, trying not to cough.

Div and Doob regard my talent show as akin to a Victorian get together, singing psalms around the pianoforte. But they're also bored out of their minds and welcome any distraction.

'Don't you know it!' They grin at each other. 'We're gonna win for sure.'

'There are no winners or losers, you know.'

'Spoken like a true loser. We demand a prize.'

'I'll see what I can do.'

We shoot the breeze for a while and drink more wine, grimacing with each sip, until it's time for WTF to return. Then I make my excuses and leave.

I help WTF out of his clothes and he goes for a shower, which takes a long time. Anything more than a trickle of lukewarm water is painful. In the meantime, I take out the contents of his rucksack which, as usual, is mostly tinned food.

'Baked beans,' I say brightly. 'There's a surprise.'

'Aye, but these ones are low sodium.'

There are also two bottles of port, some cheese crackers and six pairs of oven gloves.

I look quizzically at him but he just taps his long nose.

I found WTF sitting calmly in a padded solitary confinement cell, with the door unlocked but closed. The only inmate smart enough not to make a run for it.

I don't know what he did, and I've never queried him about it. I'm not a curious type nor one for emotional sandblasting. We've all been given a second chance and he has made the most of his. I wish there was still a parole board around to witness it.

'Want me to make you dinner?' I ask. This is our little joke, as heating food would require an asbestos suit. We have to eat everything cold.

'When I originally came here,' WTF talks carefully over the noise of the water. 'I went tae a restaurant in Apollo Bay and ordered my first proper Aussie burger.'

He turns off the faucet and I hand him a towel.

'It took three members of staff to lift the plate ontae mah table. It had lettuce, tomato, pineapple, a fried egg, watercress, bacon, some kind of hairy plant I didnae recognise but might be cactus, a cigarette butt, ketchup, mayo, more pineapple, cotton, ice cream and a bush turkey sitting on top. There may have been meat in there as well, but I gave up the will tae live halfway through and had to be rolled back to mah car.'

He chuckles roguishly. But his eyes are sunken and his skin is puckered like a prune. 'How come you guys put pineapple on *everything*?'

That's why I like WTF. He makes me laugh. Or he tries, which is just as good.

'You go to your cell and get some rest,' I command sternly. 'Those trips outside are taking a real toll.'

'I've seen things you people wouldn't believe,' he quotes. 'That's Rutger Hauer as the killer replicant Roy Batty in *Blade Runner*.'

'Let me put everything away.' I hang up the towel. 'Need you on top form for tomorrow night, baby.'

'I won't let you down.' He smiles resignedly and plods off.

Though we are lovers, I don't sleep with WTF. The touch of flesh on flesh is too extreme to stand in more than small bursts. And if one of us started snoring, it would end in fisticuffs.

Instead, I go to my own cell, take a bottle of wine and a strip of Diazepam from under the mattress and down both.

We each cope in our way. This has always been mine.

The next night everyone files into the prison hall and sits in the back row. They are certainly dressed for the occasion, sporting finery WTF brought back from his last trip to the mall. Corrine has on a full length fur coat. Floyd Peterson is in a dinner suit and bow tie. Div and Doob have on pork pie hats and striped braces over white T shirts. WTF is resplendent in a red mini skirt and silver spangled halter top. He hands each of us a pair of oven gloves and I finally understand.

It's so we can clap without making too much noise.

The stage is basic, just a raised wooden platform with one metal flagpole at either side, minus the flag. Not exactly the Sydney Opera House but it'll suffice. I appear from the rear door, clutching a roll of loo paper covered in pen marks.

'Good evening ladies and gentlemen,' I announce. 'And welcome to the first annual Sunnyvale talent contest. I've prepared a small speech for the occasion.'

I let the roll unfurl and spill across the boards for several feet. The audience gives a stifled groan.

'Tough crowd, eh? And I thought you'd appreciate some toilet humour.'

There's a slight titter this time and WTF gives me the thumbs up.

'Without further ado,' I continue.' Let me introduce Div and Doob—the gruesome twosome.'

Div and Doob spring up and move along the line of bemused participants, shaking hands and patting them on the shoulders. Then they scramble on to the stage and stand at opposite ends.

'Check this out,' Div chuckles. 'I will now make some shit appear from thin... *air*.'

Going with the theme. Well done.

He runs one hand up his leg and produces a large piece of dried fruit, seemingly from nowhere. On his wrist is a small gold timepiece that wasn't there before.

'Hey! That's my snack,' Floyd Peterson frowns. 'It was in my pocket.'

'And he's wearing my watch,' Corinne adds. 'I shall be wanting that back, young man.'

Div puts the fruit on his head and stands perfectly still.

'Oooh, what a lovely pear,' Doob says appreciatively.

'You took the words right out of my mouth,' Div shoots back and the audience groans again. They *are* a tough crowd.

'That's fae the movie *Carry on Doctor*,' WTF stage whispers. 'Stop nicking jokes, you wee shits.'

Doob pulls a knife from her sleeve, twirls it round her fingers and grins at him. WTF pats his top, suitably impressed.

'You've got mah shiv,' he whistles appreciatively. 'Well played, lassie.'

Before anyone can object, Doob tosses it in the air, catches the blade and throws. It shoots across the stage, imbeds itself in the pear and tumbles into the wings.

Every jaw is open. Div and Doob take this as a positive sign, mime high-fiving each other and return to their seats. I begin to suspect they might not have been part of the maintenance crew after all. But the show must go on.

'Next up is that master of mirth and purveyor of puns, WTF Hartley.' I beckon to my partner, expecting him to do some sort of stand-up routine. Instead, he grabs a basket from his feet, bounces up the steps and opens it.

It is filled with balloons, long thin and multicoloured.

He blows them up, turning bright red in the process and everyone grabs their ear plugs. One pop will send us into a coma. But he begins to fold them expertly into each other. They have been lubricated with cooking spray so the rubber won't squeak—we can smell it, even at a distance. Within a few seconds, a sculpture begins to take shape, a donkey or perhaps an alligator. Either way I'm impressed that he's made an effort to stick with the subject matter. I should have known he'd try hard to please.

He lets go and the animal whizzes over our head, deflating as it twists, producing a seemingly endless wet fart. In the amplified atmosphere, the sound is exaggeratedly comical.

Everyone starts giggling.

'Thank you. I'll be here all week. Probably all year.' WTF holds up a trembling hand. 'Try the veal.'

He glances nervously at me as I regain the podium and my heart goes out to him.

'And now Professor Floyd Peterson,' I say. 'No idea what he's going to do but it's bound to be intellectual. Take it away, Prof.'

Floyd Peterson brings his folding chair to the stage and sits on it. Takes a home-made recorder from his jacket. He puts the instrument to his lips and blows as softly as he can. It is *The Lark Ascending* by Vaughn Williams.

He plays it perfectly.

The thin, reedy tune floats around us and up into the rafters. One by one, we remove our ear plugs. Amplified by the clear air, the sound becomes as full bodied and moving as any orchestra.

We are rapt. From my position in the wings I can see tears running down upturned faces. Floyd Peterson finishes and we wait until the last echoes have died away before clapping. He smiles gratefully and returns with his seat.

I wish I hadn't decided to let Corrine go last. Unless she can turn water into wine, she'll ruin the moment for sure. Unfortunately, it's too late now.

'Finally, we welcome Corrine Telford.' I try my best to sound keen. 'Who, I'm certain, is going to give us all something divine.'

Corrine makes her way hesitantly into the limelight. She takes a deep breath, and I wait for her to launch into some diatribe about the glory of God.

Instead she unfastens her fur coat and lets it fall. Underneath she is wearing nothing but a silver, two-piece bathing costume. Her body is lean and muscular, the kind of physique you only get after years of push ups and crunches.

What the hell?

Corrine grabs one of the metal poles at the side of the stage and effortlessly flips upside down. Begins to slowly revolve, her long blonde hair brushing the floor.

The silence is palpable.

She lets go with one hand and curls into the pole, spinning faster. What the sensation of cold metal is doing to her skin I can't imagine, but it makes my toes curl.

The audience's eyes are on stalks.

There's no way she can pull off what I think is coming next. Yet she does.

Corrine removes her other hand and draws up her knees, holding on with only her stomach muscles. I put a hand to my mouth and the others give a collective intake of breath.

Eventually, Corrine slows to a stop and pirouettes back onto the stage, as casually as if she were dismounting a bike. Her face is flushed but she is barely out of breath.

'There's moving in a fucking mysterious way for you, Mo,' she hisses.

The applause is thunderous. Or it would have been if we weren't wearing oven gloves.

'That is bloody art, that is!' Div removes his hat and salutes. 'Respect, woman.'

Corrine puts her coat back on, comes down and sits next to Floyd Peterson. She is shivering, so he puts his arm round her and she nestles into his shoulder.

This certainly is a night for surprises.

'I want to thank you all from the bottom of my heart.' I wrap things up with a curtsey. 'There's port and nibbles in the foyer. Well... that table at the back.' My voice is choked with pride. 'Tonight has been such a success that, next year, we're putting on a musical.'

'I vote for Godspell,' Corrine says and all of us laugh, loudly as we dare.

The cast party is a happy affair. We are all a bit in awe of each other and there is a sense of camaraderie that wasn't there before. Each of us knows it takes a long time to perfect tricks like these, not just a few days.

More like years surviving on the streets or rotting in a cell.

For the first time, they begin to talk about the future. Floyd Peterson floats the idea of irrigating our prison yard and planting vegetables under a home-made sail. Corinne offers to help, admitting she grew up on a farm. Div and Doob mention casually that they used to grow marijuana and know a lot about fertilizer.

When the rest have retired, WTF takes me onto the roof, because that's our place. The sky is damp with glittering stars and the world is silent, though occasionally we hear the chirp of an insect, far in the distance.

'Not everything is dead after all.' I cup my ear. 'There might even be other people out there.'

'Life, uh, finds a way.' WTF does a passable American accent. 'That's Jeff Goldblum in *Jurassic Park*.'

He opens a tin of peaches and the bottle of port he saved for us.

'I think you'll find this a cheeky wee number,' he deadpans. 'It has overpowering notes of barbecue sauce and a kick like a prostitute with epilepsy.'

I take a sip and wrinkle my nose.

'Well done tonight, Mo.' He hands me the can. 'But I was looking forward tae your effort. How come ye didnae do something?'

'I was the compere. Wouldn't have felt right, joining in.'

We each try to eat a slice of fruit, but the taste is so strong and sweet it stings our mouths. We spit them out, smirk at each other and I wait for him to launch into one of his funny stories.

Instead, WTF gazes out over the vista. 'Look at this view,' he remarks. 'It's beautiful but kind of sad and empty.'

He glances sideways at me. 'When I was younger, I used tae think the right person for me wuz someone who'd sit by my side and feel exactly the way I did about a scene like this.'

He frames me in a little box, shaped by his fingers. 'But no. The right person is really someone who fits *intae* that picture.'

He sighs and it reverberates loudly over the roof. The sound is unexpectedly heartbreaking.

'Thing is. Just cause someone is perfect for one scene, it doesnae mean they'll be right for the next, eh?'

I've underestimated WTF Hartley.

'Why exactly did you come to Australia?' I break my rule and finally ask him a question.

'Land built by convicts?' He hyuks. 'Maybe I thought I'd fit intae that picture.'

'I love you WTF.' I stroke his cheek.

'I love you too.' He tries to stifle a yawn. 'Why don't you come downstairs?

'I told Div and Doob the show wasn't a competition. Didn't say there weren't prizes. I want to leave them out while everyone is asleep.'

'You are most definitely the bee's knees.' He clasps his hands together in an imitation of the scene from the film he's quoting.

'Andy Garcia.' I pick up the thread. 'The killer turned hero from

*Things to do In Denver When You're Dead.*'

'Clever lassie. What am *I* getting, then?'

'Stay awake long enough?' I nudge him. 'You'll find out.'

'There's no way I'm nodding off now.'

He kisses the top of my head and leaves with a spring in his step.

I sit for a long time, wrapped in soft-skinned silence. Then I go downstairs, unlock the storage cupboard of level three and retrieve a stash of goodies.

Time to make my rounds.

I raided the prison library for the Quaran, the Tripitakas, and the Torah, which I stack outside the chapel door. Corinne may as well keep her options open.

Next, I go to the education centre and set down a telescope I took from the guard tower. Floyd Peterson can use it to look at the stars, though he'll finally have to put sunglasses on. It won't bring them any closer, but it might seem like they are.

For Div and Doob, I leave a couple of hazmat suits, which took me ages to find. They were once used for scrubbing cells if inmates smeared faecal matter on the walls. Floyd Peterson would have known they existed if he really had been a janitor.

WTF has done enough. It's time Div and Doob started putting their light-fingered talents to better use. Anyway, they need to get out more.

Then I enter WTF's cell and take off my clothes.

We have sex quietly and gently, because there's no other way to do it. It's very intense and also rather uncomfortable. Forced intimacy turning something that used to be fun into a bit of a chore.

Afterwards we lie, side by side, fingers entwined. It's all we can manage.

'You're the glue that keeps this lot together, Mo. Know that?' Though it is dark, I can see WTF has on a serious face. 'You've turned us intae a family.'

'Like the mafia?'

'Nah, I mean it.'

He closes his eyes and I wait until his breathing is deep and regular before getting dressed. Wisps of my white hair remain on the pillow, a painful reminder of how old I am.

I spot the basket in the corner and sigh. Making balloon animals is not something you learn in jail. More like the props a failed entertainer would use if he was performing for a bunch of convicts.

It's nice to know we have *something* in common

'You don't have to pretend any more.' I softly kiss his cheek. 'You're one of them.'

Me? I had a family once and sure as hell don't need another. I was bored enough with my last life. Besides, I've used up all the pills in the pharmacy, WTF has emptied the local bottle shop of wine and I can't stand spirits.

WTF will understand, I hope. He knows how exhausting it is, pretending to fit in.

I go upstairs and struggle into the prison outfits. Stick on the riot helmet and glasses. Insert the nose and ear plugs. Take the leather flying jacket and white silk scarf from a coat hanger and wrap them round myself. They smell strongly of WTF and, I imagine, always will. But, unlike him, my armour is for defence, not crusading.

Everyone will have their theory as to why I left. But, in the end, I put on a great show and that's what they'll remember.

I edge open the gates and step outside. I was hoping for a sense of freedom but, inside this get up, everything is muffled and dark.

I'll travel by night and hide in basements during the day, though the air could still get me in some unguarded moment. I console myself by imagining, for a fleeting second, it might feel like being born again.

I'd love to go to Venice, as I could afford to live there now, but

Sydney will have to do. I'll move into a suite on the top floor of the Waldorf Astoria with a balcony overlooking the opera house and thick curtains. Watch the stars, drink champagne and dine on tinned caviar, even if it tastes like crap.

There won't be anyone to share the view or feel the way I do about it. But I'm used to that. I'll survive, as usual.

To be honest, the end of the world hasn't really made much difference to me.

As I say, I've always been lucky.

# The Eye of the Storm

*Sam Brown*

'I had that dream again last night.'

Audra's voice stopped Brock in the doorway of their squat brick bungalow as he left for work. He gripped the doorhandle tighter, half wishing he could pretend he hadn't heard; just head on out to work. To his second job, deliveries for a bakery. An extra hundred bucks or so off the debts each week, but it meant he was up at 4.30am. No wonder he was knackered all the time.

'You know, the drowning one?' she added, as if he could forget. Brock stared out at the street, waiting. The sun spilled over the horizon, revealing the leaf-littered street. No real damage here, at least, although the radio said Cairns copped a flogging.

They'd hidden from the gales in the shelter Brock built under the house, curled up together on a foam mattress with Audra's bare feet and hands touching the damp earth. It helped calm her.

'It rained and rained and rained,' she said. 'And we were chained to the house. We climbed up on the roof, but the water kept rising. We tried to get each other free but we couldn't and the water went over our heads…' Panic rose in her voice.

'Hey, hey.' Brock turned back and pulled his wife into his arms so he didn't have to see her distress. They were both on edge. It could have been a bad one. The storm had even taken the Bureau of Meteorology by surprise. But Brock couldn't excuse himself easily. He should have known. Seen it in her skittishness when the barometer on the wall dropped into the red.

He rested his chin on Audra's head. The familiar scent of her kiwifruit shampoo mixed with that of wet earth—which reminded him of the puddle forming in the corner of the shelter. More problems. He closed his eyes.

'I was so scared,' she whispered. 'I knew I was dreaming and I tried to scream to wake myself up but I couldn't make a sound. The water went over our heads and it was crystal clear and all I could do was float on the chain and…and watch you die.'

Brock was pretty sure he knew what the dream was really about: they were one crisis from disaster. He was still paying back the poor buggers who lost money when his business went bust. And the mortgage. And the failed IVF treatments. And his work ute. And Audra's Hyundai. Second hand but on tick because everything was fucking on tick; robbing Peter to pay Paul. The embers of his shame flared. He'd vowed to protect her, and he failed, again and again. All he knew was to work hard and be honest. When did that start being enough?

'Don't go to work,' he said. One less worry, please? It was crazy, really, a woman with Audra's condition living in the storm-prone tropics, but Cairns was the only place either of them knew. The storms were more frequent now, more intense. Extreme weather events, they called them. Not a good combination for someone with *extreme air pressure sensitivity*—the bullshit name doctors called her condition to make it sound like they knew something.

'Paul and the Mayor are stranded. It's all hands on deck.'

'I have to go to work,' said Brock. If only he could just crawl into bed, or under a rock; never wake up.

'I know,' she said, unhooking her right hand from around his waist and sliding it into the pocket of her robe. Brock pretended he didn't know she was reaching for the bloody green notebook she obsessed over.

'I forgot to tell you!' Audra's voice was suddenly brighter. Her small, pale face shone. Brock couldn't help smiling.

'We got the passports.'

Brock could tell he was supposed to know what she meant. He often tuned her out when she rabbited on about getting away. He vaguely remembered her saying something about getting their EU passports. They both had ancestry; her through Ireland, him through Italy. He pulled out of the embrace, suddenly itching to move.

'That's great, Aud. Look, Benny will be waiting for me.' He kissed her. The uncomplicated love in her grey eyes made him feel small.

'Please don't go to work,' he said.

'I'll see what I can do,' she said.


Watching Brock drive away was a physical wrench, every time. After Audra's mother 'went away' no one could make Audra feel calm when the weather changed. Not until Brock came along. She owed him everything. But there was no way she was staying home alone. Whenever she and Brock were apart the flurries and gusts that swirled through her turned into fierce currents that threatened to tear her adrift and toss her away. She had to keep busy.

It was true that her boss was stranded. He and the Mayor were out with the federal member travelling the gigantic Far North electorate, shoring up votes ahead of the election. And, with half the region cut off by flash flooding, the police were asking people to stay off the roads. So, HR told all the Mayor's staff to work from home. But her boss—the Business Manager for the council—would be trying to reach her and she had crap reception at home. Paul was an important man. It was her public duty.

Ignoring the voice in her head that said stop, she went inside and dressed for work.


The city was a mess. Palm fronds littered the streets. Whole trees in some places, shallow roots torn out leaving red mud wounds in the rich green grass. The cheap signage that tempted tourists lay littered along the Esplanade. The destruction ratcheted up Audra's anxiety.

In the empty office, she found messages waiting on email and the phone system.

'See, Brock,' she said aloud. 'I'm needed.' She called her boss.

'Paul, sorry. We had no reception at home. I just got in. I haven't listened to all your messages.'

'Jesus, Audra, the Mayor and I are shitting ourselves here.'

'Yes, sir,' she said. You can mean 'eat shit' but so long as you say 'Yes, sir' they'll never know.

'We're stuck out here. In the middle of bum fuck nowhere. There's not even a fucking pub, there's a temperance society. You can imagine how the Mayor is taking it.'

'Yes, sir.'

'You can better fucking believe there'll be funds for the roads in the next budget, mate.'

Audra realised he wasn't addressing her. She waited.

'Look, you're going to have to authorise a few things on my behalf, or payroll won't go through. There's just no fucking way to get online out here for long enough! NBN my fucking arse. Yeah, mate, too fucking right.'

'Maybe you could go somewhere…quiet?'

Audra wondered if he would be so stupid as to read the authorisation codes for the council payroll aloud in a public place. Experience suggested, yes. The day he offered her the job was one of the proudest of her life. She'd worked hard since her traineeship, taken on some shitty jobs and, despite her condition, she'd learned everything about how council worked. But it turned out he just wanted someone to cover for his disinterest in all but the most glamourous aspects of the job.

'Yeah, good call,' Paul said. There was a rustling and background chatter while he moved. 'Right. I'm in the bathroom.'

Audra took down the details he dictated. His network ID and password. His FinSoft login. Same password, tut, tut. IT would not be pleased. The file path to where he kept his authorisation code cheat sheet.

While they talked, the sun broke through, filling her little office with golden light. The carpet of clouds parted to reveal endless azure. Audra responded to the glittering brilliance with a broad smile, and a sigh of relief.

'Of course, Paul. You can trust me,' she said. She wasted no time doing what he asked and rang to let him know when it was done.

'What?' he snapped by way of answer. Asshole. Yes Sir.

'I processed the payroll.'

'You'll be in trouble if you fucked it up.'

Audra stroked the little green notebook that held her hopes and dreams. 'Let me know if you need anything else.' She tried hard not to think the thought pressing against her consciousness. Tried not to think how that asshole would deserve it. How much they needed it.


'Brock, you know we've got to get away?'

'M-hmm,' he responded, still scraping his dinner plate clean. Audra had barely touched hers, as usual. She was staring up at him, bright-eyed and nervy.

'I'm serious, pay attention.'

'I'm paying,' he said, putting down his fork, and sitting back.

'What if we could get the money?'

He sat up again, touched the sides of his plate, wanting to get up and walk away, but staying put, always staying put.

'Well, we can't. I can't even drive for the bakery until the storm debris gets cleared up. They sent me home this morning.' Less money this week, dammit. He'd gone up to the bluff overlooking the river to work out what to do. He hadn't come up with anything, but at least the time alone had given him some breathing space.

Audra touched her small, pale hand to his solid brown one.

'If we could,' she insisted, 'we'd go, right?'

Her eyes beseeched. He could feel her energy. It was like holding a bird; feeling its heart race against your skin. Suddenly the bloody green notebook was in her hand. She'd started making escape plans, and recording them all in the little green book, after a bad storm two summers before. At first it seemed like a harmless distraction. Now it was an obsession. Brock closed his eyes. Had his father ever felt like this? Like it would be easier to be dead? He couldn't imagine it. He missed the old block, his solid presence, his unshakeable strength.

'Don't shut me out,' she snapped. Brock opened his eyes warily. 'I'm begging you, Brock. I have to believe there's a way out.'

How could he say no? And what did it matter? There was no money.

'Of course, babe. Of course, we'd go.'

It worked like magic. Suddenly she was clearing the dishes. She hummed as she went to the kitchen. Brock watched her, carefree like she hadn't been in an age. What's a white lie to someone you love, right?

The rain stayed away over the weekend, but the floodwaters didn't recede. Paul called constantly to bark instructions, never grateful, never kind. So, on Monday, Audra did a little experiment to see how much access she had to the council accounts. She called it an overtime payment. A thousand dollars. Since she was keeping the city running, she was worth a small gratuity.

On Tuesday Paul called with more instructions, zero gratitude and no mention of the money. She looked up how much he could authorise without further approval. Fifteen thousand. She transferred another fourteen.

She stood in Paul's sleek, glass-walled office and looked out at the storm-ravaged city. A careless man like Paul would probably use the same passwords elsewhere. With a little trial and error, she found her way into the safe in the cupboard. A Platinum American Express card and a bundle of cash. And the card for the account at the supermarket, which she used to buy big T-bone steaks. When she served them up for dinner that night, Brock questioned the expense. She kissed him and told him he deserved it.

'I'm going to get us out of here, Brock. We both deserve better. We'll have lobster. And champagne. And never buy bargain meat again.'

She barely touched her food, filling herself up with the spun sugar of her dreams as she talked. Brock nodded, intent on his steak.

The next day, she transferred another fourteen thousand. Feeling buoyant and full of light, she skipped through the deserted corridors of the council building and played party tunes up loud in the office. She could almost taste freedom, rich and airy as a soufflé.

That night the weatherman warned another major storm was forming to the south. The cyclone looked set to hit Cairns in the next day or two. Audra didn't need to be told. She'd felt it building inside her as the air pressure dropped. But, instead of the dark, malignant force she feared so much, this time it felt like power; a boost, a surge. She took that as a sign she was doing the right thing. If God didn't want her to have the money, Paul would have been able to get back.

She and Brock watched TV together, curled up on their soggy-bottomed sofa. She felt Brock's solid body tense against her as the weatherman droned the forecast.

'Don't worry, baby. It'll be okay,' she said.

'I'm just tired,' he said. 'So tired. So tired of being tired.' He slumped deeper into the couch. Audra leaned into him. No more, she decided. This was the chance, this storm.

'Don't go to the bakery in the morning.'

'It's too late, now. They can't replace me.'

'Well, from the next day then. No more killing yourself to pay off our debts, okay?' Audra's mind raced as she went over the plans she'd made, making a mental list, putting it in order.

'Sure.' Brock stared blankly at the television. Outside, the wind picked up, and the palm trees swayed.

Audra marvelled at how wide awake she felt. All her planning was paying off. She was going to save them. She could pay Brock back for all the sacrifices he made. They'd start again. They worked hard; they had just never been lucky. Not once. They would do better with a fresh start.

By morning, the winds were high. Audra was bouncing off the walls, but she had to drag Brock out of bed and push him out the door. Seeing him so down inspired her and she went to work as soon as he left. No need to wait until office hours. She literally had the keys to the city. The council would be shocked to discover how negligent Paul was.

She made all the bookings for their escape with council bank accounts and cards, using Paul's computer to put one extra step between her and discovery. The authorities would figure out it was her PDQ. But by the time they were certain, she and Brock would be far away, sipping vino in a piazza. She booked airfares and transfers. Two sets. Two destinations. One in their real names and one in the fake names on their real EU passports. Audra thrilled at how well things were coming together. Her mother would be proud of her.

Her mother was always there, just behind the veil, always screaming and kicking as the white-coated men carried her away. Whatever else Audra forgot about her mother, the screams never faded. Don't. Let me go. Don't let. Me go. Don'tLetMeGo.

Don't be like your mother. She got that message loud and clear. Everyone. Dad. Teachers at school. The creepy preacher at the church whose opinion Dad suddenly cared about. Other kids. *Are you mad, too?*

She opened her eyes and set her chin. Now she and Brock could be anything they wanted. In any city they wanted. Any city without cyclones.

'I'm Audra Daniels.' She practised the new name aloud. 'Who the fuck are you?'

Outside, the winds whipped at palm trees, tugged at laundry left on washing lines, churned the sea into surf. Galahs and cockatoos screeched, tumbling playfully on the currents. Audra felt the pressure dropping inside but she felt so good, she forgot her condition.

She printed off everything she needed—boarding passes, itineraries, and e-tickets—and slipped it all into a purple plastic wallet. Wouldn't want them to get wet.

She stopped by every ATM on the way home and withdrew cash until the machines refused. Easily another $10k. The wind inside her roared, smothering the tiny voice of doubt. She bought suitcases. Two sets. They'd need new clothes for their new identities, but she had to make their departure look real.

Brock arrived home to find Audra standing over four empty suitcases with her hands on her hips and piles of clothes everywhere. He had been so buggered that morning he hadn't really noticed the weather, and he was worried about her. She hadn't answered his texts. He'd expected to find her huddled on the floor of the shelter, trying to hold it together. What the hell?

She held up a Hawaiian-style shirt they'd got from Lowes for a Hottest 100 party, and the tuxedo shirt from his cousin's wedding.

'Will Brock Daniels wear Hawaiian shirts? Or tuxedos? Maybe Brock Daniels is the kind of guy who would wear a tuxedo shirt with jeans, you know, like that councillor does?'

She laughed, a carefree sound that made him so happy he laughed, too, even though he had no idea what was happening. Audra bounced up and kissed him. Moments later, the room filled with white light, and everything flashed in negative. They were still blinking when the thunder clapped and shook the house.

Brock watched his wife's face strobe on/off, on/off, her eyes and lips peeled back in manic glee. Deep inside he knew it was trouble. But when the lights came back on and she was still smiling and laughing, not quivering fearful in his arms, God help him, he didn't have the guts to question it. He laughed and swung her up for a playful kiss. The shared pleasure wrapped them in a cocoon of love that made everything seem okay, just for a moment.

When Brock put her down, Audra rubbed her hands together and clapped.

'Let's make it snappy, I want to get on the road in case there's more flash flooding.'

He wanted to make her happy, so he moved vaguely towards the wardrobe. 'Where are we going?'

Audra giggled.

'I don't get it,' said Brock.

Her expression softened, and she seemed to glow as if lit from within. 'Away, Brock. We're doing it. We're escaping.'

He must have still looked blank.

'We have the money, babe.' She was serious. Utter conviction.

He couldn't remember the last time he'd seen her like this. Audra pulled a passport wallet out of one of the bags. 'See? Cash. Legal amount. Plus a cash card.' She held them up. 'I've organised everything.'

She looked like a dog that knew it had been a Good Boy, so Brock reflexively praised her.

'You rock, babe,' he said. Audra gave a satisfied little nod and went back to packing.

'Babe?' said Brock.

'Uh-huh?'

'What's going on?'

Lightning flashed again; not as bright this time and not as close. Wind whined, and rain thrummed against the windows. Audra locked eyes with him. Don't deny me, hers said.

'We're escaping. Like we planned. We'll drive to Townsville and fly out of there.'

Brock inspected the tickets. Audra opened her mouth and closed it again.

'Where did you get this money?' Brock pulled out the Visa card, inspected it. Opened the passport.

'Audra, who is Brock Daniels?'

She gasped like the wind had been knocked out of her. But the shock quickly twisted into the sting of betrayal. She snarled. 'I discussed this with you. Months of planning. Don't you *listen* to me?'

Pain radiated from her. Fragments of half-heard conversations came back. She *had* told him.

'I didn't know you were serious,' he confessed.

Audra looked at him like he was a stranger. 'How could you not know?' she whispered. 'It's my life.'

'How could I not know you were serious about running away to Europe with false identities? False identities, Audra? What were you thinking? We're not criminals.'

'You agreed! You said rich people do it all the time, why shouldn't we? All I did was get someone to sign one extra form.'

Brock remembered. Drunken bravado after six tinnies. Impotent anger. He never thought she would do it. Never thought she could, if he was brutally honest.

'Jesus, Aud.'

They stared at each other. Outside, the wind took it up a notch. Audra started like a cat, every hair on end, her eyes darting about like she was looking for an escape route.

'We have to go,' she said. 'Please. Please let us go. Let me go.'

Brock wanted to give in to the undertow pulling him towards her, but he couldn't run from his responsibilities. 'Where did the money come from?'

Audra laughed, a brittle sound, and ducked his gaze. 'Such a funny story, I'll tell you in the car.'

'Aud.' He felt the way he did the first time they met, like it was his destiny to protect her.

'I told you.' She sounded defensive. 'Paul gave me access to some accounts.'

'So you—' Brock struggled with the word he knew was correct '—stole? From the council?'

'It's insured,' she whispered. 'We paid taxes. It's our money, really.'

She wouldn't look at him. She looked so vulnerable standing there, he forgot his anger and pulled her into his arms.

He breathed an apology into her hair. 'Oh babe, I had no idea. I am so, so sorry.' He'd failed her again. She was terribly unwell, and he hadn't even noticed. If he hadn't been holding her up, the knowledge would have knocked him down.

Audra shuddered a little and nuzzled against him. After a few moments, she smiled up at him.

'Shall we get going?'

The smile faded as her eyes skimmed his face. She wriggled, trying to get away from him. His grip tightened.

'Brock,' she complained.

'We can't go, Audra.'

She stopped wriggling. 'We have to.' Her bravado became begging. 'Please, Brock. We can't turn back now.'

'It'll be okay, Audra. We'll...give the money back. We'll explain you've been unwell. Paul will understand.'

Paul had been at school with Brock's older cousin. He'd testified that Brock was of good character in the bankruptcy court.

Audra gave an anguished wail. 'No! This is our chance. God wants us to take this money and start again. It's fate!'

'That's not how it works, Audra. We'll pay our debts honestly. All we have is our good name. We can't just run away and be someone else.'

'Why? Why can't we be the ones who eat caviar and drink champagne?'

'You hate fish.'

'That's not the point.'

'We can't just leave, Audra.'

'You mean you can't,' she spat at him.

'No,' he said, steadily. 'I can't.'

'You hate me, don't you?' Her face was distraught, pale skin flushed, eyes wild like a cornered cat. Knowing she was lashing out didn't make it hurt any less.

'You hate me, you want to hold me back. You want me to die here in this miserable shit-hole town. You lied to me. You said we'd go. LetMeGo!' She flailed at him, but it was her words that lacerated his weary flesh. He froze, heartbroken. Audra pulled away from him.

'I'll go without you, then. You don't think I can, do you? You think I'm stupid. Stupid sick Audra, just like everyone else. Watch me buddy. Fucking *watch* me.' She grabbed one of the carry-on bags she'd been packing. 'You know what? I hate you. You've always bought me down. I should never have married you. You promised to look after me and look, look at me! This is all your fault. I hate you.'

If she'd impaled Brock on a rusty fence post it wouldn't have hurt half as much. She hit him exactly where it hurt. He'd done his best. God knew, he had done his best, but—and he knew this now, as sure as his own name—his best would never be good enough, no matter how hard he tried. He let himself collapse onto the bed, unable to think, unable to breathe, unable to do anything but be swept away by the shame of his failure.

A loud crash sounded outside. Audra was sure every hair on her was standing on end. She sucked in oxygen to fuel the fight. Energy pulsated through her, stronger with every beat of her heart. She took one last deep breath, and bolted past her husband, expecting his hand to dart out to grab her, disappointed and relieved that it didn't. She pictured her mother; two men not enough to hold her. Her desperate words had new meaning. Not 'Don't let me go', but 'Don't stop me: Let me go'.

Audra ran to her car. The rain was sheeting, blinding. She was mad to go out but she had no reason to stay, now. She flicked the lights onto full beam and the wipers on high and she drove.

At first, she drove like the wind, carried along on exhilaration and adrenalin, too hard on the accelerator, navigating by habit more than vision. There were few cars on the road and the sky was black. It was hard work, seeing through the wipers, looking for hazards. By the time she was on the highway south the effort had worn the buzz off.

She flushed hot and cold as she thought of the cruel words she'd spat at Brock. Surely he knew it wasn't true? But his horror-struck face shimmered before her eyes.

A sign appeared warning of an exit up ahead. The last exit to go back to the city. Should she drive on, into the future? Her foot eased off the accelerator, but she made no move to turn. What about Brock? None of this was his fault, really.

She was almost past the exit. Almost free.

No. She couldn't go without Brock. She slammed on the brakes, reversed to the exit, then sped towards home. She could put the money back. Maybe no one would notice. What mattered was being with Brock. There was no point without him.

What had she been thinking? The storms must have screwed with her brain. How absurd her plan was. Running away to Europe? Who did she think she was? She pictured them joking about it together and laughed out loud at the thought. It sounded crazy in the confined space of the car, with the rain beating down. She drove faster.

His ute was still parked in front of their house, thank God. She ran inside calling his name. Why didn't he answer? She hurried from room to room, then down to the shelter.

'Brock, are you there?' Her voice sounded thin and fluttery. He would be there, surely. Except he wasn't. A puddle was forming in the corner from the leak in the wall. Her nightmare came back to her, and Brock drowned before her eyes again. She shuddered and looked away.

She called out to him, her voice breaking, heart racing. She searched the house again, breathless. On the kitchen table, a piece of paper, tucked neatly under Brock's iPhone in its Star Wars case. Hands trembling, she opened the note. His familiar handwriting was shaky.

*I made Audra steal, it was all my idea, don't blame her.*
*Let her be free.*
*I'm sorry.*
He'd signed his full name.

*Brock Andrew Keppell.*

She read it again. She recognised all the words, but they made no sense.

'No,' she said out loud, as if the sound made a difference. He wouldn't leave her, surely? Where could he be? Relief coursed through her, weakening her knees. He'd be up on the bluff. His favourite place to go and think.

She ran through the house and out the back door. Lightning cracked overhead, but it didn't slow her down. She shot out into the rain and sprinted, legs aching. Up the hill and across some stranger's yard into the park at the top of the street.

'Brock,' she screamed, her voice carried away on the wind. She chased it along the path to the top of the escarpment where the barrier fence started. Rainwater criss-crossed the muddy track. If Brock had come this way there was no sign. But Audra knew, she just knew.

She climbed outside the fence line and scrambled along, peering through the rain. Surely this was where he liked to sit? He would be here, somewhere. The cliff edge was softening in the torrent, and her feet slipped. She imagined herself tumbling, sliding, the rough stone bruising and cutting her flesh.

She pushed on, clinging as close to the tree line as possible. She came to another drop. Lightning flashed.

There, on the ledge below: a broken shape. Her heart stopped. She got down on all fours. The rain ran down her hair and onto her face, but she saw him. Wearing that ugly old Drizabone his dad gave him. Legs bent in impossible directions.

'Brock' she cried, but the wind snatched the plea from her cold lips. Her legs gave way and she collapsed onto the wet ground. She pressed her face into the gravel, welcoming the sting, mashing herself harder against it, trying to grind the anguish out of her body. She lay there in the leaf litter and the mud, oblivious to the howling fury overhead.

The rain drenched her, until it finally stopped when the eye of the storm passed over the city. Afternoon sunlight broke through, hot, brilliant. When she sat up, Brock still lay broken at the bottom of the cliff, never to be mended, a red halo around his head.

The winds had died down, but it was only calmer, not calm. The breeze tugged at her, still, and she was untethered; her tie-line gone.

Should she call the police? What if it was that awful bully from school? And what about Paul and the girls in the office? She couldn't do it, not without Brock.

She got to her feet. She was wet and dirty, and there was a leech on her leg, and Brock was never going to rescue her ever again. Dizziness swamped her. Vertigo pulled her closer to the edge, like she might just plunge over the edge after him. *Smash.* Her small body next to his large one, their heads touching. It would be so easy.

She backed up against a tree. A gust of wind raised goosebumps on her bare arms. She glanced at the patch of blue sky overhead. She could feel gusts and zephyrs whirling inside her. The storm would be back, any minute. She dropped to her knees and buried her hands in the wet earth. Think, Audra. Think!

The air tickets were still tucked into her bag in the house. The green notebook. The bookings. The bank accounts.

She looked down at Brock's body again. Suddenly certain, she stood, right on the cliff-edge, gazing up into the tumbling clouds. For the first time since she could remember, she felt completely calm.

What if she could fly?

# Something in the Air

*Susan Ruth*

'Lukas Jacobin Sunhalvar Fafnir, you are charged with wantonly disobeying lawful orders, and with fomenting dissent and mutiny within military ranks. How do you plead?'

Dragging his gaze away from a nearby window and a vista of parkland and blue sky, Fafnir considered these words. Were this a properly constituted court he might tell the honest truth, plead guilty, and hope for the best. Pleading guilty would not help him here, though. There was no hope to be had.

This was no trial by his peers: the court officials and judges were all civilians, there were no military personnel present. This was a show trial, designed to set an example, and the deck was stacked against him. He would be signing his own death warrant if he entered a guilty plea. Here, those fortunate gifts that usually stood him in good stead—social status, wealth, good looks, charm—were worthless.

'How do you plead?' The clerk of the court tried to engage Fafnir's gaze, while the chief of the three judges adjusted the spectacles on his nose as if to see the plaintiff better.

Fafnir stared into mid-air, still debating internally. He had often been called reckless by his fellow officers in the Flying Corps of the Army of the North, but recklessness had no place now. Nor did courage. This was a time to do what did not come naturally to him: to be cautious and to bide his time. More than anything he wanted to be up in the air, practicing aerobatics.

He felt the eyes of the judges upon him. They sat in the upper half of the big double room, through the archway and behind a wide, scuffed table. The chief judge, a man in his sixties, thin-faced and hard-eyed beneath his full-bottomed wig, made a brief note on a paper before him and then looked up, staring at Fafnir.

This was Messire Richaldis Halt. Widely reputed in Mercia as a hanging judge and a personal enemy of Fafnir's late father. Fafnir had no knowledge of the true reason for the disagreement between the two; his father had also been unsure. *It's as if Halt resents my very existence. I've no idea what I've done to put him so offside. Just keep out of his way, dear boy. That's all I can advise.*

But it was no longer possible for Fafnir to keep out of Messire Halt's way. Halt sat enthroned between the other two bewigged judges at the ill-polished table, alert and sceptical. With a cool stare, he turned to the clerk of the court and nodded.

'How do you plead?' said that individual in raised tones, as if to make certain of being heard.

Fafnir got to his feet, making his mind up. He had felt the orders he was given were unlawful, and he had argued against them in debate with his fellow flying officers, but they were still orders. However, he was not going to admit any guilt in this forum. There was no support for him here.

Fafnir resolutely looked away from the window and that beguiling patch of open air. 'I plead not guilty. The orders I was given were not—'

'That will do,' said Messire Halt coldly. 'You'll have the opportunity to state your case in due course.'

Fafnir remained silent and sat down behind his own small table near the archway between the rooms. He had no-one beside him to make his defence; no-one to advise him; no supporting counsel, despite the presence of a prosecuting attorney waiting just a few feet away amongst a knot of supporters. This was a show trial, Fafnir again thought. He did not rank his chances of an acquittal as very high.

With a quick glance around underneath his lashes, he calculated the odds of escape. A large country house set in extensive grounds, Chelmsford Park had been requisitioned by the government of the North at the outbreak of civil war in The Isles and handed over to the Ministry of War. It was now a centre for scientific research. This double room showed signs of its more gracious origins as well as the subsequent neglect, but not even its current shabbiness could undermine its earlier incarnation as an elegant drawing-room.

There appeared to be no security guards in the chamber, just court officials with the three judges in the adjoining room. And the window was close by. What were the chances of getting through it?

The clerk of the court was speaking once more. 'I call Master Tantaliss Seadrake of the Ministry of War.'

At this, Fafnir's heart sank further. Here was another enemy. Seadrake had married one of his father's cousins, a member of the extended Fafnir clan, and he was widely suspected within the family of having mistreated her. She was now sunk into mind sickness and had been a patient in a private asylum for some time. Fafnir and Seadrake were frequently in court over her legal status and the control of her fortune.

Seadrake was a tall, dark-haired man with a vigorous manner. He strode into the room and looked across at Fafnir, his handsome face hard to read. Despite this enigmatic glance, Fafnir knew full well that any testimony Seadrake gave would not work in his favour.

With the assistance of the clerk of the court, Seadrake swore his oath on the Book of Sol Invictus.

When the oath had been administered, the prosecuting counsel, a sharp-faced female with a shock of brown curls imperfectly concealed by her wig, rose in her place. Adjusting her dark robes about her, she faced the witness, who now stood behind a small table by the archway between the rooms, mid-way between Fafnir and the judges.

'Pray, good sir, detail the orders that were given to the Air Corps of the Army of Mercia, Scotia, and the Northern Marches. The orders that Captain Fafnir here disregarded.'

Hearing this, Fafnir wondered whether to object. That had not been established yet. Surely, he was innocent until proven guilty? But even as he thought this the moment passed. He glanced around, hoping someone might come to assist him, but there were no friendly faces.

'Certainly,' said Master Seadrake, his voice deep and compelling. 'They were orders to bomb a Southern battlefield with an experimental weapon.'

'And what is this weapon, gentle master?'

'I need to give a little background first.'

'Of course, sir,' said the prosecuting counsel invitingly, spreading her arms wide.

Seadrake spoke formally, in rolling sentences. 'At this stage of the Civil War—and taking into account the massive and unrelenting onslaught upon us by the South—it's been thought necessary to develop new weapons with which to defend ourselves. The scientists here at Chelmsford Park are at the forefront of this important research.' He glanced around, allowing himself a slight smile.

'And new weapons have been successfully developed?'

'Indeed. Chief amongst them in recent times has been a debilitating gas. A gas that's also been synthesised by the South, and as far afield as Frisia and Prussia, as our military intelligence indicates. It's called mustard gas, because it has the aroma of mustard and, when prepared for delivery, is yellowish in colour. As I say, the South has now formulated this gas. It's only a matter of time before our enemies use it against us on the battlefield. However, we have succeeded in making mustard gas deliverable ourselves. And just in time too, if our intelligence is accurate. The method of getting it to where we want it to go is to drop it from aircraft in the form of bombs.'

Flight machines were still something of a novelty in The Isles, but they had quickly been used in the conflict between North and South.

'Is this new weapon now operational, sir?'

The judges, led by Messire Halt, were listening intently, each of them taking notes of Seadrake's testimony.

Seadrake continued, standing straight and upright. 'The experimental work indicates that the gas is indeed operational, and we're ready to make the attempt to use it on the battlefield. We can't afford to delay, or have the South use this weapon first. Accordingly, there's been a very measured debate within the Ministry of War about the appropriate use of mustard gas, and we've deemed it necessary to issue orders for its deployment on the battlefield. Orders that Captain Lukas Fafnir has seen fit to flout.' Seadrake glanced coldly at Fafnir and brushed a speck from his dark coat sleeve, before turning to the prosecuting counsel and looking at her expectantly, his hard eyes intent.

'And these orders? They were quite legitimate?'

'Quite legitimate. The orders weren't issued lightly, and they were relayed to the military authorities in the proper, proscribed manner. There's no doubt about their appropriateness. No doubt whatsoever. We're at war, after all. We must do our duty, even if it's hard. Every second we delay costs us dearly. The South won't wait for us.'

The prosecuting attorney glanced at her notes and then faced Seadrake, her hands to the front opening of her robes. 'Gramercie, sir. I've no further questions for you.'

Seadrake bowed his head politely to the judges and then left the chamber, sparing an impassive glance in Fafnir's direction as he did so.

Fafnir looked about the courtroom. A few people now sat behind him, but this was a quiet Solday afternoon and Chelmsford Park's workers were on their day off. Again he could see no sign of security staff. He looked once more at the window and that tantalising glimpse of wide blue sky beyond.

Three more witnesses were called, each from the Ministry of War like Tantaliss Seadrake. All three testified on oath, saying that the orders issued by the department were quite legitimate, and that they had been relayed to the military authorities in the standard manner.

When the last of these had given her evidence, Messire Halt adjusted his spectacles, lined up his notes to his satisfaction on the table, and then cleared his throat before speaking in very precise tones. 'And you saw fit to disregard these orders, Captain Fafnir? Why?'

Fafnir knew this might be the only opportunity he had for stating his case. He got up, intending to do so succinctly and powerfully. 'I didn't disregard them, Messire Halt, your excellencies. I thought about them long and hard. In the end, I concluded that bombing an enemy battlefield with poison gas was an unlawful and unjust order. I couldn't do it. In consequence, I didn't feel it incumbent on me to obey such an order.'

'Didn't feel it incumbent...? Perhaps you could explain more clearly what you mean by that,' said the chief judge, looking towards his colleagues as if wanting recognition for his meticulous fairness.

'I can try,' replied Fafnir, hoping he would be listened to and believed. 'We're told, we fighters for the North, that we're fighting a just war, and that hostilities have been forced upon us by an aggressive and unreasonable South. In such a war—a just war—there are rules of conduct for both leaders and followers. We must all do what's right, and not go to extremes in our aggression. Certain acts are prohibited—killing prisoners, for example, breaking truces without notice, disproportionate responses—and individual soldiers have to think for themselves if they're asked to perform such acts. They have the right to refuse such an order.'

'But this order was not asking you to do anything prohibited. We have Master Seadrake's testimony to that effect. And the testimony of other witnesses from the Ministry of War. The order was the subject of proper consideration, of due process. And it was given to the military authorities in the normal way. Yet you took it upon yourself to disobey this order.' Messire Halt adjusted his spectacles once more and peered owlishly at Fafnir.

'As I said, messire, sometimes in war an individual soldier has to think for himself. Or herself. Women serve with distinction in both the North and the South.'

Messire Halt raised his hand. 'Captain Fafnir, you are straying from the point. Pray tell us why you have set yourself up in opposition to your superiors, and to the legitimate authorities in the Ministry of War.'

At this daunting request, Fafnir wondered if it was any use going on. But that was defeatist thinking. He must fight as long as he had the opportunity. This was his only chance. He glanced again at the window nearby, at the view of flower beds, parkland and trees, and at the patch of blue sky beyond. He would give anything to be up in the air on this beautiful afternoon. He wondered once more about the possibility of escape.

Then he turned to the court at large, and saw that there were now more onlookers and officials clustered in the seats behind him. He did not stand a chance of getting away: there were too many people here. But when he spoke it was to everyone in the double room. He would not go down without a fight.

'I felt that I had to think for myself about the validity of this particular order—to bomb a battlefield with mustard gas. And, in the end, I decided it was an invalid and unlawful order. As a soldier, and as a flyer, I've learnt how to kill in the last three years of the civil war. But this new weapon is different. I couldn't see my way to poisoning the very air on which we all depend. That was a step too far for me.' Fafnir glanced around, trying to make eye contact. People looked away, bowing their heads. He continued doggedly. 'The air is a common good, essential to every living creature. It should be left untouched, even in wartime. That's what I think.'

Messire Halt finished his notes in a leisurely manner, and then he started speaking once more, his voice resonant and carrying. 'That may indeed be what you think, Captain Fafnir, but you also sought to influence others to your way of thinking. You face another charge today, quite apart from that of disobeying orders. To wit, that you plotted dissent and mutiny amongst your colleagues. How do you answer that?'

And here it was, thought Fafnir, an even more serious charge. This time he had no option but to tell the truth. He faced the three judges, looking into the faces of each of them: Messire Halt, thin-lipped and hard-eyed in the middle; a bewigged and raddled woman with pince nez on his right; a bored-looking, bland-faced man to his left, his chin propped up on one hand.

'I didn't seek to influence anyone else, your excellencies. Certainly none of my colleagues. I realised the gravity of my actions and the risk I was running. I didn't want to bring anyone else down with me. I merely stated my case when my friends asked me why I was doing what I did. That's all.'

'Nevertheless, it seems to have been quite sufficient to land you in very serious trouble, Captain Fafnir,' said Messire Halt, dryly. He turned to his two colleagues. 'Do either of you have any questions of the plaintiff.'

The bored-looking man shook his head and stared down at his fingernails.

The female judge with the pince nez burst into speech, her voice high-pitched and urgent. 'Do you feel this way about orders in general, Captain Fafnir? I'm curious about the extent of your opposition to properly constituted orders. Do you object to bombing an enemy battlefield in general? Or is it only poison gases that you object to?'

Fafnir bowed. This judge was not on his side either. 'As I said, ma'am, I've learnt what it means to be a flyer in wartime. I flew flight machines before the civil war broke out, and when I was called up to military service, I asked to join the Air Corps. I don't much like the idea of bombing a battlefield and killing from the air, but I serve as a fighter pilot to protect the bombers that do so. I've managed to make my peace with myself in doing that. But I couldn't see my way clear to bombing our enemies with poison gases. That's a step too far for me.'

'Nevertheless, it's a decision that's likely to cost you very dearly,' said the woman, her face stern and unrelenting.

'Yes, it's likely to cost all I have to give,' replied Fafnir, knowing it was all up with him. There was no hope here. He glanced again at his window, studying the blue sky and the wide, open air. This might be the last time he saw such a view before the expected death penalty was pronounced. He wondered if he would have the heart to ask for a look at the sky as a last wish, and whether it would be a fine summer's day like this one.

Then, before he had managed to drag his gaze away from the vista, he heard a voice speaking from behind him, projecting clearly into the quiet courtroom.

'I think you're all forgetting something.'

At these words, Fafnir turned. The speaker stood quite close by. He was a nondescript man of average height and build, wearing a dark grey greatcoat over grey trousers and jacket, and a white shirt unbuttoned at the neck. He had long dark hair loosely tied at the nape of his neck, and light grey-green eyes. In one hand he held a rucksack that he had just taken from his back. In the other hand he held a gun.

Fafnir stared at him.

Messire Halt adjusted his spectacles as if he was not sure what he was seeing.

The stranger moved forward to the table behind which the witnesses from the Ministry of War had stood. 'As I said, I think you're forgetting something. Or perhaps you never knew it in the first place.' He raised the firearm, though pointing it at no-one in particular. 'This isn't like any court I've ever heard of. Where's the defence counsel? Where are the witnesses from the military? Where's the presumption of innocence?' With each *where*, the stranger visibly gathered power to himself, growing fierce and energised, and very certain. And far from nondescript.

Messire Halt stared at the gun. 'This is outrageous! You can't just walk in here like this! This is a duly constituted court of law.'

'Is it? That's what I'm asking.'

Messire Halt glanced briefly from the gun to the intent gaze of the stranger and then back again. The bland-faced judge, no longer bored, clasped and unclasped his hands. The third judge, the woman with pince nez, adjusted her full-bottomed wig, then tugged at her red robes. All three were silent.

The stranger sighed. 'I gather the firearm makes people uncomfortable. I'll put it down, but I warn you it's loaded.' True to his word, he set the gun down on the table before him, along with the rucksack. 'Oh, just in case anyone tries to jump me, I'm not alone.'

With that the stranger gestured to the back of the chamber.

Four followers—men and women both—arose from their places, drawing their own firearms as they did so.

The silence in the room spun out in the face of this wider threat. The people in the upper chamber—the clerk of the court, the prosecuting attorney, the other officials and retainers—peered about themselves, worried looks on their faces.

'I suggest everyone sits down quietly. I have some evidence to give which might help you make up your minds. There's really not much to worry about. I just want the chance to talk to you. And then a demonstration.' As he spoke, the stranger was unfastening the rucksack. 'Ah, there it is.' With a wide and charming smile, he took out a large metal canister and set it down on the table beside his gun.

Fafnir sat in his place, transfixed. He had recognised the stranger, but he was the last person he expected to see at Chelmsford Park. This was Felix Skryker, the maverick flyer. Or, to give him his true name, Thomas Felix Sheldon, Viscount Sheldon, son of the exiled Earl of Gresty, the longtime Prime Minister of The Isles and leader of the Free Peoples Party.

He had not used his given name or title, however, since the outbreak of the civil war, preferring to go as plain Felix Skryker. He took his surname from the *skryker* of Mercian legend, the mythical black dog that haunted the night-time countryside and could either be foul or fair depending on circumstance.

Catching Fafnir's eye across the room, Skryker gave a slight nod. Fafnir did likewise, and stayed in his place to await developments. He had no idea what mood Skryker might be in—whether foul or fair—or what he might say or do. Even so, this was a new departure. A temporary reprieve. He felt convinced that the judges had been about to pronounce the guilty verdict, and the subsequent death penalty.

Meanwhile, Messire Halt was attempting to reassert his

authority. He glared at Skryker. 'How dare you disrupt our proceedings in this way! I should have you arrested for contempt of court.'

Skryker smiled, but said nothing.

'Who are you? And what do you want?' Messire Halt shifted his papers on the table before him until they were lying in a perfect parallel, aligning his fountain pen just so, as if trying to master chaos. He peered at Skryker over his spectacles. 'Why are you here?'

'To discuss something I think you've forgotten. Or that you never knew, as I said earlier. And to give a demonstration. Oh, and as to who I am, I go by the name of Thomas Felix Sheldon, but I'm better known these days as Felix Skryker. It's possible you've heard of me.'

There was a chorus of gasps, but Messire Halt maintained a stony silence.

Fafnir knew the story; it was well known in the North. Felix Skryker, as the newcomer now called himself, had been heartbroken at the coming of the civil war, and he had not accepted the division of The Isles. He refused to fight for either side, but used his and his father's contacts in both North and South to maintain a precarious neutral position. Forming a small private air force, Skryker worked hard to support the warring states equally, taking medicines to besieged hospitals, repairing beacon lights, carrying back-channel messages, exchanging hostages. So far his maverick concern had succeeded.

'And what do you want?' Messire Halt repeated, his voice cold.

'I want to add to Captain Fafnir's evidence, messire. He hasn't called on anyone to speak on his behalf. It's only fair that someone does.'

Glancing again at the gun near Skryker's hand, and then at his four, armed supporters at the back of the adjoining room, Messire

Halt nodded his acquiescence. 'Very well. I do this under duress, however.'

'Shall I swear an oath on the Book of Sol? Although I rather think that Sol Invictus—should He exist, which I sometimes doubt—must be looking elsewhere at this time in the history of The Isles.'

'Oh, get on with it, pray!' snapped Messire Halt. 'Make your oath, give this evidence of yours, and then leave us in peace to our deliberations.'

Skryker smiled, and bowed his head.

The clerk of the court came up timidly with the Book of Sol, staying as far away as possible from the gun. In a low voice she asked Skryker to take the Book, and to repeat the words of truth-telling after her. When that was done Skryker looked questioningly at Fafnir.

Wondering what to say, Fafnir leapt to his feet. After a few moments silence, he found words he hoped would be suitable. 'You've something to tell us, sir. What is it, pray?'

'Gramercie. I want to talk a little more about the concept of a just war, and then about mustard gas. Finally, a demonstration. I promise I won't take up much of your time.' This last was directed with a deprecating smile to the courtroom at large.

Messire Halt cleared his throat and glared at Skryker again. 'Well I, for one, hope you don't. We're not finished for the day. Not by any means.'

Skryker bowed gracefully. 'I'll be quick.' He shifted the canister and the gun on the table, and tucked the rucksack down beside his feet before turning to face the three judges. 'I'm sure your excellencies are aware of the concept of a just war. Captain Fafnir referred to it earlier.'

The judges sat stony-faced.

'Pray explain to those who aren't clear on the matter,' said Fafnir, speaking into the tense silence.

'For centuries military experts, theologians, ethicists, and philosophers have worked on a theory of a just war. Such a notion lies behind the decisions our governments have made here in The Isles before committing troops to the battlefield. Basically, there are two aspects to such a war: the right conditions for going to war, and, if there's no alternative to military conflict, the right conduct of combatants. As we're already at war with Alba, I'll leave the first aspect aside.'

'Gramercie.' Fafnir was still on his feet.

Skryker continued. 'Down the years certain rules have grown up about the right and proper way to fight a just war. Civilians are to be targeted as little as possible. Prisoners are to be treated fairly. A military response should be proportionate. Then there are the weapons we use in warfare. We now have aircraft that can bring destruction from the sky. It's deemed acceptable to bomb a battlefield using flight machines, but not a residential suburb. And a weapon, any weapon, should be controllable and properly directed.'

'How does that apply to mustard gas?' Fafnir asked.

'Mustard gas is delivered in an aerosol form. That means it's put into some form of container under pressure, and then it's released into the air as a spray powered by propellant gases when the container is breached. On the battlefield, this happens when mustard gas is put into bomb casings and dropped from the air by flight machines.'

'Is mustard gas a controllable and properly directed weapon?'

'No, it's not. It'll be at the mercy of the air when it's dropped from a flight machine. Of currents of air. We can't be sure where it'll go. We might intend to bomb an enemy battlefield, but the wind could carry the gas to a civilian area. Or to a place where non-combatants gather—a hospital, for instance, or a school.'

'And the mustard gas? What does it do?'

'We know what it does from reports of accidents during the

discovery and development process. Mustard gas has been around for a while now, and there's quite a history. Basically, it produces large blisters—on the skin, and in the lungs, and in the eyes. A chemical burn, and very painful. Very debilitating. The gas can be fatal if given in strong enough doses. It's been fatal in the past. And it's persistent—surfaces on which the droplets land remain contaminated for days after release of the aerosol.'

'Gramercie,' said Fafnir faintly. 'And you spoke of a demonstration?'

'I did.' Skryker took the canister from the table and held it up at arm's length. 'Mustard gas is a new weapon. As we're thinking of using it so freely—and of taking the life of a man who refuses to—I thought we might have a little example of its effects.' He set his free hand to the lid of the canister.

The prosecuting counsel gasped. 'What's in there?'

'Just gas under pressure. I've not opened the container yet, so it's not got into the air.'

Messire Halt reared up in his place. 'You're insane! You can't open that thing here! This is a courtroom!'

Skryker twisted the lid. 'You won't feel any effects immediately. They'll come on slowly. But by tonight blistering will occur on those exposed, and the blisters will be big and very painful. It'll be difficult to breathe. You mightn't be able to see if the gas gets into your eyes.'

The people in the courtroom, including the judges, moved away from Skryker.

Messire Halt was trying to contain the situation. He glared at Skryker, and spoke in bracing tones to his colleagues. 'Disregard this madman! This is all a bluff!'

'Try me,' said Skryker softly, shaking the canister. 'You want to drop this on a battlefield, messire? Well, it's only fitting you have a little demonstration.' He whirled around. 'I've no idea where the gas will go when I open the container.' He moved further towards the archway into the upper room, towards the judges.

The bland-faced man clutched a handkerchief to his mouth and nose. The woman with the pince nez cowered against the wall, her head well down under her robe.

At that point, Messire Halt sniffed, and then again. 'I can smell something! Onions! There's something in the air!'

'Onions!'

'Mustard!'

'Something in the air!'

With that there was a great outcry, and a general stampede for the doorways.

Skryker waited. Then he turned to his supporters who still stood quietly at the back of the room. 'There's likely to be a bit of a panic now as the word gets out. You lot go and secure our escape route. Fafnir, you're with me. We'll just give their excellencies time to clear the building.'

Fafnir pulled himself together, and glanced at the window beside him. 'I've a fancy to go through here.' He moved across to open the casement.

'Excellent,' said Skryker, returning the canister to his rucksack, hoisting this onto his back, and picking up his gun. 'It'll be quieter that way.'

Even as he spoke there came the sounds of screams and shouts from the corridor outside.

With the window now open, Fafnir scrambled out, Skryker right behind him.

'This way,' said Skryker, pointing to the corner of the building. 'And run! We mightn't have too much time before people start coming to their senses. We're heading for the front drive.'

Chelmsford Park was a large mansion, and Fafnir rushed off after Skryker feeling a little lightheaded. He felt even more disoriented when he rounded the corner and saw a flight machine on the front lawn.

'That's our way out,' said Skryker, pointing to the aircraft. 'I hope my people can keep any bystanders away.'

Fafnir stared as he ran, not taking his eyes from the machine. He recognised her as a T4 transport, similar to those in service in the Northern Flying Corps: twin-engined, sleek egg-shaped fuselage tapering towards the back, forty-foot wingspan. But the markings were unfamiliar. 'How in the name of Sol Invictus did that get here?'

'That's *Sunlight*. She's mine. I flew her in this morning. Now we're ready to go!' Skryker, his firearm in his hand, was running towards the flight machine.

Four motorcyclists surrounded the craft. Skryker's supporters from the courtroom raced towards them, one to each vehicle. Others from the building hurried behind in an aimless, panic-stricken fashion. The motorcyclists began to herd them inexorably down the drive, and away from the flight machine.

Meanwhile, Skryker increased his pace. As he drew level with the aircraft, he thrust his gun into the holster at his waist and began to clamber up to the open hatch. 'This way!'

Fafnir followed without a word.

Soon they were both inside the flight machine, and the motorcyclists moved clear, the harried crowd with them.

Taking his rucksack from his back, Skryker sank into the pilot's seat, and gestured to the place beside him. 'Fafnir, I want you to act as co-pilot. Strap yourself in and get us started. I'll take over from there. We're going to my place at Woodhall for tonight, and then on to London in the morning.'

Getting himself into place, Fafnir glanced around. He had flown such a craft before, and he knew the layout of the dashboard. With a deep breath, he began to make the usual start-up checks, relishing the calming routine, and then he engaged the power. That done,

Skryker pushed the throttle levers gently and the flight machine moved forward across the smooth expanse of lawn.

As it gathered speed, Fafnir listened to the sweet sounds of the engines. Then, in a surprisingly short distance, the craft became light on her wheels, and they were in the last place that Fafnir had expected to be on this sunny afternoon — in the air.

The following evening, Fafnir sat in the library of Skryker's London townhouse, a glass of aqua vitae to hand. The room was furnished in the modern style, with comfortable leather chairs before the hearth. Books with mellow bindings and golden tracery on their spines were set in serried ranks on black bookshelves against primrose walls. Yellow roses stood in vases on low tables.

'So, it was all a bluff?'

'Of course. I had water vapour in that canister, with yellow colouring. It would have made a nice hissing sound if I'd finally opened it, and produced a yellow haze. Fortunately, I didn't get that far. Imagination did the trick for me. It seems fitting that that judge was the first one to break.' Skryker swirled his spirit in his glass, watching the play of light. 'Well, you're safe for now, my friend.'

'I can't thank you enough. I thought I was a dead man!'

'That was on the cards, wasn't it? The Ministry of War certainly had it in for you.'

'And you? What will happen to you now?'

'Oh, I'll spend some time in the South here. I've plenty of things to do.' Skryker paused and looked across at Fafnir, his grey-green eyes thoughtful. 'You can help if you want. I can always use another flyer.'

'If I want? I'd love to!'

'Then I'll be happy to have you.'

'But I hope you haven't burnt your boats in the North.'

Skryker shook his head. 'Not by any means. There's something of a standoff between the Ministry of War and the military at present. Oh, you'd have been punished for what you did, make no bones about it. But the military authorities would have gone for a prison term, or perhaps a demotion. They didn't want to make it a killing matter. I had General Crewe on my side, and the Archbishop of Deva, and your uncles on the Star Council. They knew what I was doing. I'll spend some time down here in Alba, as I said, then I'll go back up North and make myself useful there. There's always something for me to do. I imagine you can go back yourself in time and make your peace. This war can't go on forever.'

'It'll be good to fly again, anyway. I've that to look forward to.'

Skryker smiled, and got up to refill their glasses. 'Then there's a flight machine waiting for you.'

'Gramercie.'

'Let's drink.' Skryker raised his glass. 'To the open air.'

His heart light, Fafnir did the same. 'To the open air.'

# Finding Elliot Finch

*Ted Johnson*

*Friday*

The old woman watched him, from across the street. Boot-to-neck black dress. Gloved hands. Her eyes glinting from porch shadows, rocking slowly in her chair, she watched him.

Elliot's spine prickled.

Some said she was a witch.

He could almost feel her foul breath on the back of his neck.

He counted down the remaining steps to his tiny fibro home with its peeling white paint and drunken timber frame. Just fifty paces more, if he stretched his steps out, from where the old leopard tree rifted the footpath. Forty-nine, forty-eight, forty-seven. He couldn't wait to open the front gate and turn his back on the witch. Couldn't wait to turn the key. To step inside and hear the door click shut behind him.

He reached the gate, breathless. He glanced back at the trail of wet prints left on the concrete path by his rain-sodden socks. How stupid was he for wearing his new runners to school today? Mother's words would be loud; scathing. Her words didn't bother him. It was after she spoke that hurt. Her sigh, her slumped shoulders, her belief she'd somehow failed him. That twisted his stomach into knots.

Finally inside, he leaned against the door and gulped his first breath of safe air. The silence revealed his mother's whereabouts. Asleep. Probably surrounded by empty wine bottles and Twisties packets, as usual.

He lived in this house alone. With his mother, but alone.


Elliot sat quietly on their sagging, relic of a sofa while his mother fossicked through kitchen drawers. Karen Finch stole a sip of wine from her coffee cup. At least tonight she was trying to be her old, cheerful self. She hadn't even mentioned his missing shoes.

'So…is Sarah dropping by?' She winced, sucked at her fingertip and sipped her wine.

Elliot cringed. Even he pigeonholed Sarah as a fair-weather girlfriend. 'Ahh…finals next week. Practising tonight.'

'Ah huh.' She rechecked the second drawer. 'So…um…any of your other friends dropping by?'

'Hmmm…well…you know I posted about two million, bazillion invites.' Elliot rolled his eyes as he lied. 'No official RSVPs. Not yet, anyway. Maybe they'll all just swing by later.'

The screaming pitch of a fast-rising passenger jet, low over the house, made him duck instinctively. A glance at his watch brought a smile. QF758, Brisbane to Denpasar direct. He cranked his head to watch her lights disappear into the twilight.

Who was on that plane? Did they travel alone, or with someone?

Elliot returned to his quiet solitude. Maybe, one day, he might be someone who travelled. Or maybe, one day, he might be the someone they took with them.

Karen wrenched the third drawer off its runners and pounced. In amongst potato peelers and whisks, lay the red cigarette lighter. Cake plate in one hand, the other concealed, she flicked off the kitchen light with her chin and launched into an enthusiastic, off-key

'Happy Birthday'. She rattled the cake onto the coffee table. Elliot blew out every candle and smiled.

'So, beautiful boy,' she said. 'Any special birthday wishes this year?'

'Earth to Mum. Sharing my wish with anyone—including you—goes against the ancient and sacred rules of wish making. And you, of all people, should know this.'

'Oh, I do my amazing boy. Or, should I say, my amazing young man? Sixteen years old today.' She presented a shoebox.

Elliot shook his present close to his ear, as he always did. He hid a sigh as he opened the lid.

'I wrote your name on *these* ones. So…well…hopefully they'll last longer. You'll need a pair for the air show on Monday,' she said brightly. 'I know how much you've been looking forward to—'

'The school called, didn't they?'

Her gaze slid from his. 'That Simons boy…bullying you again.' She touched the shoes then snatched up her cup, downing the contents in one fierce swallow. 'I wish we could afford a better school.' She stood abruptly and stalked back to the kitchen.

Elliot hunched his shoulders. 'There'll always be another Dave Simons. He's just pissed 'cos he was the smartest kid in school until I showed up.' He smirked. 'Now he's just the best athlete—who gets all the girls.'

Karen called out from the kitchen as she refilled her cup. 'Well, I'll bet he's not the kindest, most sweetest, and most beautiful boy in the whole world.' She sauntered back to the lounge room, coffee cup held high. 'Happy birthday, my awesome boy.' Her eyes flickered across his face, searching for something. 'I know you, Elliot Finch. You are destined to right everyone's wrongs and make this world a better place.'

She hugged him close, like he was all that mattered to her. He hugged her closer, like he was losing her.

*Saturday*

The aroma of frying bacon lured Elliot downstairs.

'Welcome, young man, to your special, sweet sixteen birthday breakfast.' Karen kissed his forehead and beamed.

Elliot sat and rubbed his eyes. Fried eggs, toast, burnt sausages and soggy bacon. Perfect. He savoured every mouthful and leaned back in his chair. For the first time, in a long time, he felt good about being him.

After breakfast, he retrieved the morning junk mail, so his mother could sigh over new clothes and jewellery they could never afford. He braved a glance across the street. The witch wasn't there and he exhaled his relief.

His left foot knocked something, another shoebox. *Happy Birthday* scrawled on top. His mother was playing with him. He picked it up. Nah, too heavy to be another pair of running shoes. He shook it close to his ear. Nothing. Elliot opened the box and gasped.

This gift was not from his mother.

He left the box on the porch, raced to his bedroom and closed the curtains. It took him a few seconds to unravel the bubble wrap and find the ON switch. The high-pitched squeal made his fingers flitter. He adjusted the strap and fitted the night vision goggles over his eyes.

The room swam in a pasty sea of green. He raised his fingers. They sparkled silver and white. Strange. He used these things all the time in online gaming and they only ever showed shades of green.

He wiggled his fingers, laughing as they emitted white sparks. Awesome. He traced his name in the air. Every stroke sparkled and slowly dissolved into nothingness. He wrote Sarah's name, his fingers dancing. The letters glittered in the darkness and melted away.

He had to share this with her. With fists clenched and quick strides, he paced his room. He could do this. He had to do this. Elliot removed the googles, took out his phone and hit speed-dial.

She answered on the fourth ring. 'Hello?'

'Hi Sarah. It's Elliot. Well, you know this already cos I'm the name on your telephone machine.' He grinned.

Her reply was monotone, aloof. 'Yeah...Okay. What up?'

'Oh. Um. Just wanted to invite you over.' His tone pitched high and his fingers twirled in nervous circles. 'To check out the most amazing thing in the world. And the moon. And the universe! You're gonna love this so much. It really is so freaking amazing.'

'Hmmm. Please. Tell me you've just won lotto, and you want to give me half.'

'Um. Almost. Kinda?' His voice cracked. 'But this is super way cooler than any lotto win.'

'Cooler than a lotto win?' She paused. 'Don't tell me, you found another peacock feather? No. Wait. You've just discovered you're related to the Kardashians. Now *that*...would be cool.'

Elliot's fingers stilled. 'Who?'

'That's the thing about you, Elliot. No offence intended, but your social skills. Hmmm, seriously lacking. Always. You didn't even ask how I was. Isn't that what people do when they call?'

'But I thought—'

'You thought what? Sometimes, what you think just doesn't gel with what I think. Or what anyone else thinks. And what I'm thinking right now is that maybe it's time we took a break. I've got a lot going on here. Yeah. You know what? How about you do your thing and I'll just do mine.' She ended the call.

Elliot stared at his phone and threw it onto his bed. Social skills? He didn't need her to remind him people were incomprehensible shits.

He grabbed the goggles, lay on his bed and drew stick figures in the air above. Him and her, with downturned smiles. A love heart crossed out. White wisps sparked and flew from his fingers. Elliot flicked his index finger against his thumb. A string of white air sprouted. His body twitched, as though a tiny electric shock had jolted him. He sat up and watched the string slowly fade. Would different fingers do different things? Huh—same. But flicking harder made longer strings. Cool. He stood to watch himself in the wardrobe mirror. What about all five fingers at once? A white ball of air shot to the ceiling and rebounded off the wall. It brushed against his chest. The ball exploded into the carpet. Elliot tasted bile and doubled over.

'Fuck me,' he mused as he regained his stance and stared at his fingers. 'I'm an air bender.'

'Nonsense,' a dark voice came from behind. 'You're nothing of the sort.'

Elliot froze. Cool sweat beaded on his forehead.

'At best, boy, you're a neophyte aerokinetic. Like my grandson was.'

He removed the goggles and forced himself to turn around. He already knew there was nobody there. 'What? What does that mean?'

Silence. Just the deafening sound of his breathing. The room drew darker and colder, until his breath misted.

'It means your journey has begun,' she whispered from his right.

'My journey? What? Where am I going?' Elliot drew an icy breath. He held it and he waited.

'That's for you to discover.'

Cold perspiration drenched every pore. His fingers scrambled for the light switch. Impossible. Surely, there was a built-in speaker. He checked. No speaker. He couldn't have imagined what just happened. But he must have. That was the only explanation. The chill faded.

He examined the goggles again and found a button labelled

'Daylight'. Why hadn't he noticed that before? He pressed it and took the goggles outside, desperately in need of an escape. Head down, eyes shut, he put them on. He covered them with both hands. Then uncovered and squinted. The goggles refocussed; the image sharpened. The front yard, the fence, the path—all perfectly clear in shades of green. He could even see across the street. She wasn't there but he knew she was watching. Should he thank her for his present? Maybe when he saw her next. Maybe she wasn't a witch. After all, she'd given him the most amazing toy he'd ever—

'They're not a toy,' she snapped.

Elliot gulped. 'I—I'm sorry.'

'Don't be. Just show some respect for what you've received. Use your gifts wisely. Go find people. You're a smart boy. You'll work out the rest.'

'Gifts? There was more than one?' He must've missed something in the box. Had he brought it inside? Nope. Not at the front door. Damn. Admitting he'd overlooked a second gift was way too embarrassing. Elliot re-visited her instructions. *Use your gifts wisely.* Wisely? *Go find people.* But what people? Which particular people?

Elliot closed the gate behind him. Immersed in a world of green, he headed toward town.


The trees had an aura. As did birds, insects, dogs, birds, and people.

Mrs Banks waved a curious hello from her front garden as he passed, her aura shining bright yellow amongst a myriad of daffodils. Elliot grinned and waved back politely. Maybe his goggles were defective. A postie took a second look as he sped by on his motorbike, his blue aura trailing behind.

As Elliot neared the town square, the crowds thickened. He and his goggles drew sideways looks, he tried not to care. The crowds grew thicker. Dozens. Then hundreds of bustling people, starting their day. As their pace quickened, their glances lessened, until they seemed not to notice him at all.

Elliot slowed and stood still. His escape to this new world full of wonder made him smile. People flowed around him, in both directions. No judgement here. Just the colour of air. Reds, greens, purples. Every shade. The colour of hundreds of peoples' souls, like long clouds of smoke, enriching and tangling with others behind them.

He glanced behind. His aura was pure white and sparkled like no other. What did that mean? He shivered, spiky jolts of excitement fluttering low in his stomach. Was he…important? Special in some way? His shoulders slumped and the thrill faded. No. That was just stupid-people thinking. He was no-one and nothing. Never had been and definitely never would be.

The crowds dwindled. Elliot checked his watch. Mum would be wondering where he was. He turned and headed home.

A small green aura drifted about fifty metres ahead. Elliot recognised Mister Singh, an elderly Indian gentleman who ran the local newsagency. His aura was thin and shrinking. He hobbled forward, leaning on his walking stick, heading towards an intersection.

A dark shadow followed him, swallowing his aura, stalking the old man.

Elliot doubled his pace. Somehow, he knew the shadow meant death. Had to. He sprinted, dragging deep, painful breaths. The goggles distorted his vision. He tripped but regained his footing. He ran on, tore the goggles off and threw them aside.

Mr. Singh stepped onto the street. Elliot cried out but the old man didn't stop. A car engine revved high. Brakes locked and tyres screamed. Red metal flashed. The old man's eyes widened and his mouth gaped. His hands flew up to cover his head.

Elliot dove, reached out, and screamed, 'Stop!'

Face down, on the unforgiving concrete, Elliot groaned. How long had he been out? He opened his eyes and squinted against the light. The car had stopped. Sideways. Mid-intersection. Elliot struggled to rise. Head pounding, he lurched and vomited. Feet spread apart to steady himself, it took most of his remaining strength to remain standing.

Mr. Singh lay, sprawled and still, on the other side of the road. A rubbish bin had tipped on its side, papers tumbling away. A sidewalk tree's lower branches were snapped, its leaves floating back to earth.

Palms sweaty and cold, Elliot placed his left foot forward. He swallowed bitter nausea and willed his right leg to move. A car door slammed. 1960s Ford Mustang. Perfect condition. Bright red.

'You stupid old coot! What the hell were you thinking? I could've killed you!' the driver yelled.

Elliot's breath shortened. Could've? The old man moved an arm. Elliot checked the intersection before limping across. He helped Mr. Singh sit up and searched his eyes. 'Are you okay?'

Mr. Singh shook his head, then nodded and patted himself down. He plucked at his torn trousers. 'I think I grazed my knee'. He pointed. 'I think you might've grazed yours too.'

Elliot looked down at his own bloodied mess and laughed. 'I think you're right.' His elbows and chin stung too. A car engine turned over. Tyres squealed and the noise faded away. It didn't bother him that the driver didn't seem to care. The pain from his wounds didn't bother him either.

What bothered him was the old man was alive when he should be dead.

Mr. Singh gripped Elliot's hand with gnarled fingers. 'You saved my life.'

Elliot pulled him to his feet before responding. 'You're very welcome. I just did what anyone else would've done.' He shifted, uncomfortable with the undeserved praise. He hadn't touched Mr. Singh until now. They'd been on opposite sides of the street.

The old man squeezed Elliot's shoulder. 'You're a good kid. Thank you. I'll be okay from here.'

Elliot watched the old man limp away before returning to retrieve his goggles. He knew exactly where he'd thrown them. Probably broken. Idiot! A search of the footpath and fence-line produced nothing. Guilt crept into his stomach. He searched again, double checking gutters and drains. His guilt built to a panic. They were gone.

His watch ticked over to lunchtime. Mum would be worried by now. He had to get home, knowing he'd just lost the greatest gift he'd ever been given. Shoulders slumped, throat tight, he abandoned his search and limped home, too weak and sore to run.

How would he explain this to the old woman? What if she really *was* a witch? What would she do to him?


Elliot stopped at the old leopard tree and used a sleeve to clean the dried blood from his knees. He didn't want Mum to worry. The grazes weren't as bad as he'd first thought. He checked his arms, barely scratched, already scabbed over. Weird.

He imagined how amazed the other kids at school would be when he told them how he saved Mr. Singh. His pace found a new bounce and a smile curled his lips. He imagined how they would react when he showed them his special power. 'Wow! Elliot,' he could already hear them say. 'You really are some kinda super...' He thought it through and paused, his smile fading. Hands on knees, he stared at the concrete path. Only one word could finish that sentence. '...freak.'

He opened the front door and his mother's snoring filled the living room. He needn't have worried. He quietly retreated, closed the door and stared at the house across the street. He glanced down.

A fresh white shoebox sat on the porch landing. Elliot hugged it into his chest and hurried to his room.

Another set of night-vision goggles. Or the same ones? It didn't matter, they came with a folded note on top. *I expected you to be more careful with your gifts. Remember! Everything is a test.*

Guilt heated his cheeks as he pondered the note. Gifts?

Elliot searched the box properly this time. Nothing but bubble wrap, the goggles, and the note.

Gifts?

He pressed the on switch, selected 'Daylight' and ventured out the back door. With the goggles fitted, he surveyed his backyard. A small, galvanised iron shed, two bins, his mother's precious angel statues, an abundance of weeds, and an unruly garden hose, knotted and crimped.

A ball of white air sparkled from his fingers. He launched it forward and cheered when an angel statue fell sideways. The ball bounced and split his mother's favourite gardenia. He glanced around guiltily. Maybe he could tie it up later and she wouldn't notice.

A wave of dizziness hit and bile rose in his throat. Ignoring it, he made another, much larger ball and sent it at full speed. Another statue fell, beheaded. Elliot dropped to his knees and vomited. His head swam but he didn't care. He rose, stared at the shed, built a sphere of swirling air the size of a soccer ball and launched it. The shed toppled and ripped from its footings.

The world vanished into darkness and sparkling white lights…

It was near dusk when he came to. Elliot sat up and rubbed his head. Right. So, the bigger the object he tried to move, the more it drained him. He groped his way back inside and headed for bed. Content with his experiment, but weary and nauseated. He slept through most of Sunday, waking only to eat and pee, ignoring his mother's questions, and her complaints about vandals wrecking the back yard.

*Monday*

Elliot had set his alarm for an early wake-up. He ironed a shirt to a crisp military standard and slipped on the new running shoes. He checked his reflection in the mirror. Today was special and he wanted to look his best. The goggles lay on the desk behind him. Should he take them or not? Surely there would be someone at the air show who could tell him how old they were, or what was wrong with them. He emptied the contents of his backpack and buried the goggles at the bottom. That way they'd be safe from falling out—or from idiots like Dave Simons.

Walking to school, Elliot contained the urge to put them on. People would stare. OK—the other kids would stare. Instead, he imagined seeing the auras again. Did death stalk any of these people hurrying to work? He squinted, eyeing the half dozen people waiting at a bus stop, busy on their phones, ignoring each other. Were they doomed to die in a bus crash? His fingers itched to dig out the goggles. He sighed. Even if he saw death, they wouldn't believe him. They'd just laugh. He shifted his backpack and walked on. School was just around the next corner.

Miss Woodley stood at the front of the classroom, arms crossed. Grey, pinstriped pencil skirt, white blouse, brown rimmed spectacles, her long, auburn hair pulled into a neat bun. Even da Vinci could not have created something so geometrically perfect. Miss Woodley was his favourite teacher and history his favourite subject.

She tapped her biro against her sleeve and waited for the year eleven history class to find their seats. On the whiteboard behind her, in large blue letters: RAAF AMBERLEY AVIATION HERITAGE CENTRE—AIRSHOW. And directly below: BUS DEPARTS 9:30

SHARP. Underlined twice.

She spoke over the settling din. 'So, who can tell me something about today's excursion?' Elliot's hand shot up. She surveyed the class, then her eyes and smile centred on him. 'Yes, Elliot. Enlighten us.'

'It's a fully operational air force base and museum in one. The twenty-third squadron is based there. They have a Boston bomber, a Canberra bomber, a Caribou, F one elevens, Iroquois helicopters, Mirage fighter jets—'

'Yes. Thank you very much, Mister Finch.' Her interruption was delivered with a warm smile.

'And today's their seventy-fifth anniversary air show,' he added.

Her smile widened but her eyes begged his silence.

'Such a geek.' A low whisper from behind stirred a few smirks and sniggers.

Miss Woodley's frown tempered the murmurs. 'Please, pay attention. This is important. The bus will leave in exactly ten minutes. The air show will be well underway by the time you arrive. Mr. Jackson was to accompany you there, but he's called in sick. The bus driver knows where to drop you. I'll follow in my car, later. Until I arrive, please remain at your drop off point. I trust you'll be on your very best behaviour.' She adjusted her glasses and surveyed the room. 'Remember that you're representing yourselves and your families. But most of all, you're representing your school. Please make us all proud.' The class was silent. 'Any questions?'

Elliot was last to board the bus. As he reached the top step, he locked eyes with Sarah. She looked away. She cupped her hand and whispered to her girlfriend. Elliot tried to ignore their stares and smirks as he searched for a spare seat. Dave Simons sat in the back row with his mates. He looked Elliot up and down before making a comment that had them all sniggering.

Elliot chose an empty seat far from Sarah and Dave. He stared through the window, fingers still and tears welling. He wiped his cheek with a sleeve and stared into nothingness. Why should it matter to him what they thought? If only it didn't matter. If only they would just leave him alone. If only they were dead. He hated them. All of them.

'Careful what you wish for, boy,' her dark voice warned from the seat behind. Was that her reflection in the window? The bus lurched forward. He turned…

…and stared directly at Dave. She laughed. Dave eyeballed Elliot and flipped him the bird. Elliot returned to his window.

Cold breath prickled the hairs on his neck. His hands, his back, his neck were drenched in freezing sweat. He stiffened. It wasn't the witch's foul breath, but something far more sinister. Death stalked him. Maybe death stalked all of them on that bus.

Bus crash. He'd predicted one. Was that one of his gifts? Maybe they all would be dead soon. Maybe he should warn them. Or maybe not.

Elliot couldn't help the dark smile that curled his lips. And he couldn't help the tears that welled, because suddenly, all he wanted was to tell his mother he loved her.

He reached for the seatbelt but there wasn't one. His heart pounded and he gripped the bar on the seat in front with both hands. Cold perspiration stung his eyes. He squinted and blinked but maintained his brace position, ready.

The bus took the last turn and stopped. He raised his head, wiped his eyes with a sleeve, and waited for Dave and his friends to pass. Then he dug deep into his backpack, turned on the goggles and watched as each student disembarked. One by one, dark shadows rose with them and sucked at their vibrant life-halos.

He stiffened, sweat prickling. The hairs on the back of his neck rose. Classmates gone, he stood. Cold breath wafted the back of his neck. He didn't want to see, but he had to know for sure.

He turned and stared into the black abyss. It drew him in. Mesmerising. The rest of the world dissolved into white. He froze, mouth agape, feet cemented to the floor.

This. Was. The end.

Her voice broke through. Dark and menacing, from above. 'Stay on the bus, boy. And you will surely die.'

The echo of her laughter pierced through his stupor. He forced himself to move. Every step an effort—towards fate, towards uncertainty. He managed the three steps down to the tarmac. He looked ahead and stumbled. Death stalked everyone. Everywhere.

To his right, giggles and pointing from Sarah and her girlfriends spilled into laugher. Elliot's cheeks burned. More heads turned.

'Check out the freak. Must be blind. Has to wear his special glasses now.' Dave slapped his thigh and laughed so hard tears formed.

Elliot snatched off the goggles and shoved them inside his backpack.

Dave towered over him, poking Elliot's chest. 'Oh, no, no, no.' He smirked and pointed to the backpack. 'We want to see what you've got in there, freak.'

Elliot weighed up his options.

Option one: Hand over the goggles. Not even Dave Simons would disrespect such an incredible piece of technology. But would he ever get them back?

Option two: Run. But that would be short lived. Dave was on the track team.

He chose option three.

He looked up at Dave's sneering face and, in the calmest, clearest tone possible, said, 'You are going to die today, Dave Simons.' Dave took a step back, scowling. Elliot faced the crowd. 'You're all going to die today. Correction. *We* are all going to die.

Today.'

Dave stared Elliot down, a smirk replacing his bemusement. His foot pinned Elliot's to the dirt. Dave grinned a bulging white-toothed smile. 'And there you have it folks. You heard it here first, at freak central. We're all gonna die.' He glanced at his watch. 'Today.'

Their classmates erupted into laughter.

Elliot fought tears. They would never know what it was like to be him. And never care. Why should he care about them? Bunch of stupid, ignorant, knuckle-dragging Neanderthals. All of them. The world would be a better place without them.

He glared at his classmates. 'It's true…And… And I hope you *do* die. All of you.'

Their laughter dwindled into awkward, foot-shuffling silence.

The chilling breath on his neck told Elliot his time was close. He shuddered and a long-forgotten warmth filled his groin and his thighs. Dave's eyes followed the growing dark stain on Elliot's shorts and moved down to the yellow liquid that overflowed from his shoes. Dave stepped back.

'And now, ladies and gentlemen. The freak has pissed himself.'

The crowd exploded with howls of glee again. Sarah's eyes flashed sympathy, but she covered her mouth and looked away.

A voice broke through the noise. 'You'd better call your mummy, freak. She must've forgotten your nappy when she dressed you.'

This was his only chance. Elliot grabbed his backpack and sprinted away. He pulled out the goggles. A glance behind confirmed Dave had launched into pursuit. He threw the goggles up and high behind him. Maybe that would make him happy.

Dave locked onto the goggles. He altered course and caught them deftly. Elliot looked behind and slowed. Dave strode back towards the mob. He held the goggles high in the air, they cheered and clapped.

Elliot hid behind a building, panting, tears blurring the world. His stomach shrank and took the rest of him with it. He curled into a ball and buried his head in his knees; small, empty.

'What?' Her dark voice penetrated his melancholy. 'So, you're just giving up?'

'Yes. Piss off. Leave me alone.'

She said nothing.

'What's the point in having powers if I can't stop arseholes like that?' Elliot glared up at the clear blue sky and the planes zipping overhead. 'I hope he *does* die. I really do.'

'Just remember, young man. Everything…is a test.'

'Fuck your test.' He didn't want to talk about it. He didn't want to think about it. But her words had stirred a distant gust of wonder, from deep within him. A test for what? What was he supposed to do? He didn't even have the goggles anymore. Elliot scrubbed a sleeve across his nose, sniffled, and pushed the thought aside. Stupid old woman.

He found the men's washroom and tricked the hand dryer into blowing his pants dry. He dressed and sat stoic, on a toilet seat inside a locked cubicle. He didn't know how long he was there. Maybe two minutes. Maybe twenty. The breath on the back of his neck had found him once more but he desperately tried to convince himself he was safe in this place.

He hid, detached from the real world but connected with the droning buzz of planes flying in formation. His fingers danced as he celebrated the whizz and roar of aerial stunts. The crowd gasped at the unexpected *WHACK* as jets broke the sound barrier. He wished he could be there to watch. He wished he could just sit with his classmates. But he couldn't. Not now. Not ever.

Mostly though, Elliot wished the breath on his neck wasn't so close and wasn't so cold.

The thought of death consumed him. Would it hurt? His body ached for release. His heart thumped. Tears drowned his eyes and his world was reduced to the single awareness of impending doom. Like a mounting thunderstorm, clouds thick, black and heavy, wind like ice. He waited for the thunder to crack.

Sirens blared. Piercing into his small, dark world.

EVACUATE. EVACUATE. THIS IS NOT A DRILL. I REPEAT. *THIS IS NOT A DRILL.* EVERYBODY MOVE IN AN ORDERLY MANNER TO YOUR DESIGNATED MEETING AREA. EVACUATE. I REPEAT. EVACUATE. *EVACUATE.* THIS IS NOT A DRILL. AIRCRAFT MALFUNCTION. EVACUATE IMMEDIATELY.'

As echoes of the announcement faded, the words filtered into Elliot's silent madness. He stood and stepped forward. His hand reached and turned the latch. This hand did not belong to him but it was his. It moved ahead on its own and he followed. He left the cubicle and watched his hand wrench open the door to the outside.

He stepped into the sunlight, dazed but still trapped in his nightmare. Leaves scattered to his right and a warm breeze surrounded him. The chill on his neck was gone. Maybe he'd evaded death. He smiled. Maybe, somehow, they all had. In the distance the bus driver rushed from the coffee shop and ushered the other students back onto the bus.

A droning sounded, far away, approaching from the sky. Just a pinprick of darkness in the clear blue. A Lancaster bomber hurtled downwards. Three engines immobile. The last engine spluttered, about to seize. Thick, black smoke trailed behind.

The bus driver spotted Elliot and waved, urging him on. All eyes were on Elliot as the entire bus waited.

'Run,' they screamed. '*Run.*'

Elliot awoke from his stupor and sprinted. He looked up at the plane and back to the bus. No way could he make it. The driver cast a despairing look skyward and shook his head. Bus doors closed. A plume of exhaust smoke signalled Elliot's fate. All but one set of eyes fixed on the plane plummeting toward the slow-moving bus. The bus engine coughed and spluttered. Gears ground. It picked up speed, but not fast enough.

Elliot halted, hands on knees, panting, tasting bile.

Breathe.

He gasped as the warm breeze entered his lungs. He drew it deep within, lowered his head and begged forgiveness.

The dark voice came. 'No. You've not failed. Not yet. But you face your final test'.

'A test?' He squinted at the crippled plane. 'My final?'

'Everything is a test. Everything every human does. Every moment of every day. From their very first breath...' The air around him stilled as she consumed it. All of it... a vacuum of black silence swallowed every sound.

Her words returned with a squall. 'To their very last.'

Elliot stood, transfixed by her words; by the plane. The bus would never make it away in time. But what if...

'You cannot stop the plane, boy,' her dark voice cautioned. 'You're not powerful enough. And you will perish trying.'

He struggled to move forward. His legs were stuck fast. The breeze inside him built into a gale.

'Why would you even try?' she hissed. 'Think about how they've treated you. They wouldn't risk their lives for you.'

A timid voice rose from deep within him. 'Some people...' The voice was familiar. His own? He had no time, but he chose to block out the world and let this voice grow stronger. 'Some people...only ever truly live...when they're faced with death.'

It was all he needed. Frustration fuelled his rage. The gale inside became a tempest.

He closed his eyes, let it grow, then opened them. He tore

himself from her grip and moved toward the gut curdling screams of those trapped on the bus. He smiled with anticipation as the icy chill on his neck returned.

And he ran toward his doom.

The tornado inside him exploded through his outstretched arms.

Forty tonnes of airplane slammed into the parking lot.

The screaming faded and death reached for his prize.

Elliot lay still, spent.

The breath on his neck was warm; soft and familiar. Mingled with cheap wine and the scent of antiseptic. Each sobbing breath was punctuated by the beep of machines. His mother curled beside him in the hospital bed. Trapped by death, he couldn't tell her how much he loved her. Maybe she could visit in his dreams. She wept quietly and held his hand in hers.

Gentle voices spoke to her of turning off his life support.

She held him close against her breast. He struggled to open his eyes, heavy with eternity. To reassure her that he didn't mind dying. He would miss her more than he could ever tell her. But he'd failed his test. Failed to save the bus. His death was justice.

'It is time, Mrs Finch,' said a soft voice.

Her fingers wrapped tighter around his limp ones. Her cool tears on his cheek; her warm breath on his neck sparked all that was left of that tiny zephyr within, conjuring a memory of majestic purpose.

She held him and whispered low, 'I love you, sweet boy. And I'm so proud of you. Your friends from your history class sent flowers, see? They're safe. Please don't go'.

The machines stopped.

Elliot squeezed her fingers.

Two weeks later he walked the school corridors once more, doing his best to remain invisible. Miraculous, the doctors had called his recovery, nothing less than a miracle. Elliot grimaced and hunched his shoulders. Just another word for—

'Hey, Freak!'

He slumped with a sigh and glanced sideways. Dave Simons stood at his locker. No crowd this time, though. Elliot straightened and walked over. May as well get it over with.

'Hey, Freak. I've got something for you.' Dave pulled out his phone. He paused and locked eyes with Elliot. His stare pensive. He swiped at his phone. 'I knew I was going to die. We all did. I'm not telling you I was scared...I was fucking terrified. But you...' he shook his head. 'You seemed so calm and certain running towards us. I watched you when everyone else panicked'.

Elliot blinked. 'Er...'

Dave hit play on a video. The audio made Elliot's stomach churn. Screaming and panic. The roar of the approaching plane. But the video was clear. Zoomed in on him at the moment he was tested. He saw his hands extend. Watched as he dove forward. A cloud of dust and air slammed into the bus and the video changed to chaos, tumbling images of the roof, windows, seats, falling bodies. Dave stopped it.

'Huh.' Elliot couldn't hide the satisfied grin that twitched at his lips. He knew they'd survived but had no recollection of how.

Dave's eyes searched his. 'You saved us. All of us. How? Why? Why would you do that?'

Elliot's fingers flittered as he shifted his feet. 'I dunno. I just. Um.' He shifted again. 'There...There was a voice.'

'A voice? Now you're sounding like a...' Dave hesitated. He stared down at his phone and back to Elliot. 'No. Tell me. What did it say?'

Elliot looked up. 'Who am I to judge? When I can give them a second chance to be better.' He dropped his gaze and hunched his shoulders, waiting.

'Maybe you're right. Maybe we could all do with a second chance.' Dave gripped his arm and smiled. 'What's your name, Freak?'

Elliot stood tall. 'Elliot Finch'.

'Well…That's just way too hard. Let's just leave it as Freak. Only cos this all proves you really are one.' Dave tousled his hair. 'I'm glad you're alright.'

Elliot nodded. 'But,' he said, eyeing Dave's phone. 'You won't tell?'

Dave shook his head. 'Not a word to anyone. Oh. Just one more thing.' He reached into his locker and produced the night vision goggles. 'I thought you might be missing these.'

That night, in the anonymity of his bedroom, Elliot removed the goggles and placed them on his bedside table, disappointed. They seemed to be working just like any other night vision goggles. He closed his eyes and let sleep take him. He dreamed of yesterday and tomorrow, and of her. He spoke aloud to her in his dream. She was listening.

'Hear me witch. I'm not afraid of you anymore!'

'Why?' she responded, her tone curious.

'I don't know. You…just have no power over me now. I'm stronger now, than you might think.'

'You are stronger, Elliot, than *you* might think.' Her tone hinted at a wry smile. 'You always have been.'

A year later, almost to the day, Elliot stepped outside to collect the junk mail.

His right foot connected with something. A white, cardboard, shoe box. *Happy Birthday* scribbled on the lid in black. He looked across the street. There she sat, rocking in the shadows, watching him. He waved, but he knew he didn't need to. He gathered the box to his chest and grinned with anticipation as he turned because he also knew…everything…is a test.

# FIRE

# A Happy Place

*Barry Townsend*

The first year had its challenges, but no major calamities had befallen them.

'Well, not yet,' Jack Telford muttered to his chestnut mare as he stroked her neck. 'Winton might be smack bang in the middle of nowhere, like everybody said, but that's just fine with me. No blasted busy-bodies out here.' The horse lowered her head to pick at a tuft of grass.

He dismounted, stretched out the stiffness from a day in the saddle, and closed the wire gate that marked his cousin, Bob's, Cooinda property boundary. He turned up the collar of his oilskin coat and pulled his hat down as the chilly early winter breeze found his neck.

'Poor blighters.' Jack gazed at the 1000 head of freshly shorn Merinos returning from the neighbouring property, Wynora. 'Stark bloody naked through the coldest part of the year just so you can grow a better fleece.'

He swung back into the saddle and rode over to join Bob, who watched the tail end of his stock run down to Cooinda creek. Jack whistled and three crossbred dogs ran back from the flanks of the mob. Between the two men and the three mongrels—worth a half a dozen stockmen—most of the woolly blighters were still alive after the five months it took to drive from Goondiwindi to Cooinda and the following six months while the sheep grew wool and fattened.

The two men sat astride their horses and surveyed the rich, knee-high Mitchell Grass covering the surrounding countryside.

'This country's everything I dreamed of, Jack,' Bob said. 'Still can't believe it's been a year since I won that land ballot. And, if what Murray Hamilton at Wynora said about current wool prices is true, we can start on the house earlier than I hoped. All going well, I can marry Sandra as soon as it's done.'

'Reckon her father'll come around, Bob? He's dead set against having you as a son-in-law.'

'We aren't worried about the old man.' Bob shrugged in his easy-going way. 'But we do want her family's consent. That's why we agreed to wait until you and I make something of this place. If he still objects, then I'll just have to wait until she's twenty-one and she can marry whoever she damned-well pleases.' He grinned.

They headed across country towards the one room slab hut that would be their only protection from the cold nights ahead. The sun set behind the Werna Creek tree line in a fiery glory of reds and pinks that softened the dry landscape.

'It'll be dark soon,' Bob said. 'I'll ride ahead and get a fire started. I know you'd be just as happy without one, but I'm not about to freeze my arse off just for your benefit.'

Jack shuddered and nodded gratefully. In two minds, he watched his cousin ride ahead. Once Sandra came, he might have to move on and give the couple space. Bob was on the verge of fulfilling his dreams and Jack couldn't be happier for him, but he also couldn't help but feel a little despondent. He had accepted a long time ago that no woman would see the ugly scarring to his upper torso and still care for him. Being alone wasn't what he wanted, but what choice did he have?

Bob hadn't gone far when Tess, the only bitch among the three dogs and Jack's favourite, gave a single bark and ran ahead ten yards, then waited for a command.

'Come behind,' Jack called to her as he saw what had caught her attention. 'Bob! What the hell is that?'

'No bloody idea, mate. Let's take a gander.' Both men kicked their horses into a trot.

They soon made out a large, ox-drawn wagon with an elderly Chinese man shuffling along, leading the big animal. A woman of similar age sat on the cart's front bench seat while two younger men and a young woman walked alongside.

'What are you doing here? You lost or something?' Bob dismounted and stood in front of the old man.

The oriental fidgeted with the bullock's lead rope. 'Jing Guòlái zhèlǐ.'

Jack also dismounted. The young woman trotted forward, patting at her long dark hair pulled into a bun at the base of her neck. She wore a handwoven grey woollen jacket and long black pants. She stood with her head lowered, listening to the Chinese man's words before turning to face Bob.

'My name is Zhang Jing.' She bowed. 'My father has asked me to explain. We are looking for a place to camp near water so we can grow vegetables and spices to sell in Winton. In exchange we will do some work for you.' She bowed again.

'I'm sorry, but we don't need any help. It's best if you just move on.' Bob's tone carried a note of sympathy.

The old man whispered to his daughter, his face impassive.

Jack watched narrowly. The father was playing his cards pretty close to his chest. The girl on the other hand intrigued him. In the middle of a point she was making for her father and between her consistent head bobbing she looked directly at Jack. Catching him staring, she blushed then returned her focus to Bob.

'My father's is called Zhang Yong,' she said softly. 'Before coming to Australia, he built bridges; many bridges. He says if you allow us to stay, he will build one for you out of stones.'

Bob nodded and cast a swift glance at the nearby creek. Jack looked as well. It was true that the flood season caused all kinds of problems getting into town.

The old man knelt down and drew a twisting line in the earth and said, 'Werna Creek.' He drew two lines across it and pointed.

'That is where Father would build the crossing.' The girl said as she bowed once more. She took several long paces away, scratched a line in the dirt and returned. 'It would be this wide.'

What he proposed would not only provide a stone culvert capable of getting even the largest wool wagon across in the wet season, but also back the water upstream for half a mile, increasing the holding capacity in this one spot, twenty-fold. He had also picked out the perfect location for his preferred camp, half a mile from the proposed crossing.

Jack drew Bob to one side. 'There's more to this than meets the eye. The old bugger must have been out here before to know exactly the right place to build an overshot. Not to mention that nobody in their right mind would drag an old woman and a girl around the countryside unless he had something to hide.'

'Take it easy, Jack.' Bob slapped his cousin's shoulder and grinned. 'Everybody deserves a chance, mate. I'll listen to what he wants. If it doesn't cost me the Earth, I just may give it a go.' Bob turned his back and continued his negotiations. Zhang Yong looked nervously at Jack and then placed himself in front of his daughter keeping her out of sight.

'What does your father want for doing this work?' Bob asked Zhang Jing, who stood with her head lowered, avoiding eye contact.

After talking quietly to Zhang Yong, the girl replied. 'We would like five pounds of rice and a sheep to butcher each month. We would also like permission to build a shelter for cooking and sleeping. In return, we will have the work completed in six months. If, at the end of any month, you find our work unsatisfactory, we will move on.'

'But how much do you want to be paid?' Jack couldn't contain himself and pushed forward.

The cold look Jack received from Bob stopped him short.

Zhang Jing moved behind her father, her eyes wide and arms wrapped around her body. 'No money. Only supplies, we will grow vegetables to sell in Winton. The soil here is very good,' she responded meekly.

Bob nodded. 'Okay let's give it a shot and see how it goes.'

They left the Chinese to make their own way to where they planned to set up camp.

As soon as they were out of earshot Jack grabbed Bob's arm.

'Sorry, mate. I behaved like a total jackass, but there's something not right about them and it got under my skin.'

Bob merely grunted. 'Don't worry about it, Jack.'

Jack glanced back. Zhang Jing looked up and met his gaze for a split second and then turned away. He grimaced.

'You're a fucking idiot,' he muttered to himself.


At the end of the first thirty days, even Jack was impressed. Bob was more than pleased. The overshot's base was far wider than he had originally imagined—at least twenty yards across—and the stonework was perfect. The rocks had been gathered from miles away and carted back to the site in the old wagon by the two younger men so the old man could lay them in place. Mother and daughter were kept busy cultivating a large garden that was already a mass of green. A few plants were recognizable, but most were completely foreign to Jack.

Late in November, Jack saddled his horse and headed out to the fishing hole where he hoped to catch a few yellowbelly. Bob had ridden into Winton to pick up his wool cheques and would join him on his way back.

The fishing wasn't going well, so Jack set his line and lay back on the hard earth, with his hat shading his face, and daydreamed. The possibility of seeing Zhang Jing was foremost in his thoughts and his stomach turned with exhilaration, expectation, and sick fear, all at once. He swore at himself and pushed the thought of her aside. Lulled by the warm afternoon and the twittering of birds, he dozed off.

'Are you alright, Mister Jack?' Zhang Jing's timid voice stirred him from his rest.

Jack shot upright and gulped. She stood just a yard away with a concerned look on her face. This was the closest they had ever been. Her delicate features were enchanting. He gaped and opened his mouth, but no words emerged.

Finally, he managed to croak out a reply, 'I was just... taking a nap. The fish aren't biting.'

'That's good.' Her smile disarmed him. 'I thought you had fallen from your horse. I came down to get some freshwater mussels for Mother and saw you lying there and feared you might be hurt.'

'No, I'm good.' The words came out bluntly and her smile vanished.

'I'll go then. My mother will worry.'

'Have you got your mussels?'

'No, but my parents wouldn't like it if I stayed.'

Jack cleared his throat. 'Er...why don't you get what you came for? I'll go back to having my nap and we can pretend we didn't see each other.'

The smile returned and she hurried to the other end of the billabong where she waded into the water and began searching the mud with her feet. Jack watched her from under his hat and cursed himself for letting her get away so easily.

He stayed at the same spot until Bob arrived, hours after Zhang Jing had left. Bob didn't dismount. He jerked his head east, towards the Zhang's camp. 'Going to stop by the Zhang's. Want to come?'

'What for?' The possibility of seeing Zhang Jing again warred with the fear of compromising her if she hadn't told her family they'd met.

'The payment from Grazcos was better than I'd hoped. Most of our wool was graded as AAA. So, I'm going to offer the Zhangs ten pounds as a bonus. You said yourself they've done a bloody good job.'

'You're the boss, but I think you're crazy. They made a deal and seem happy enough with it. You'd be better off putting the money into Sandra's house.'

'Probably,' Bob said, shrugging. 'But I feel like this arrangement is a little one sided.'

'Okay. I know better than to try and change your mind.' Jack scratched at his chin and tipped his hat back. 'But can you do me a favour? Don't mention I've been at the waterhole all day. Might cause a problem.'

'What's going on, mate?' Bob's brows rose.

Jack told about his accidental meeting with Zhang Jing and what he'd suggested to her.

Bob grinned. 'Okay, no problem. Are you getting a little sweet on her Jack? She's a fine-looking woman.'

Jack mounted his horse and didn't comment, but the stupid smirk on Bob's face riled him.

The overshot was completed ahead of schedule, in December, just prior to the wet season. It stood ten feet high and ten feet wide across the top, tapering down to the broad base. The overall length was just short of forty yards. Now, with each stone placed to perfection, they could see the design's intricate structural integrity. Bob complimented the family and said they'd built him a masterpiece. Zhang Yong grinned and bowed deeply. The Zhang family agreed to stay for another six months at the same campsite and build a similar crossing, three miles from where they camped.

Jack wasn't certain what to think. He was glad the overshot added value to Bob's land, but every time he passed the Zhang's camp, he looked for Zhang Jing.

He was an idiot.


Two weeks after the Zhang family began work on the second overshot, Jack and Bob saw their neighbour, Murray Hamilton, with four of his men. They were digging up bushes in Cooinda Creek on Wynora's side of the boundary.

'Murray,' Bob said, nodding and leaning forward in his saddle. 'What's all this?'

'Noogoora Burr, Bob. The bloody shit's a wool growers frigging nightmare.' Murray wiped the sweat from his brow with his sleeve and disturbed dozens of flies resting on his shoulders. 'Surprised you're not already onto it, yourself. The bloody stuff will be all along Werna Creek as well.'

'Shit, Murray, I've never heard of it. What's it do?'

Murray looked at them with raised brows and shook his head. 'Well, mate, you better get stuck into it pretty damn quick. You let those bloody seed pods get into the wool and you're going to have one hell of a time getting any shearing team to touch them. Even if you do, your clip'll be worth squat.'

'How much time do you reckon we have to get rid of it?' Bob asked, thoughtfully.

Murray looked down along the creek and then studied the Noogoora Burr he and his men had gathered before giving his reply.

'Six weeks. Maybe, if you're lucky.'

'Fucking hell, I've got close to twenty mile of water ways. We've got no chance in hell of getting on top of it in that time.' Bob yanked off his hat and slapped his leg with it.

'Sorry, I can't help you, Bob. We're flat out clearing away what we've got on our side of the fence. Don't bother looking in Winton, either. I was there yesterday and there's not a bloody soul available.' Murray sighed. 'Come on I'll show you what you're in for. You've got to dig it out roots and all then burn every damn skerrick.'

That night, as they ate, Jack was silent, staring moodily into the hut's small cooking fire.

Bob, as he always did, came straight to the point. 'I know this is going to be hard for you, mate, but I'll be totally fucked without you. We could lose everything if we can't work our way through this.' Looking Jack square in the eye from across the rough timber table, he asked, 'Are you up to it?'

Jack forced a chuckle. 'You know I will be. I'll do my bit. Just keep me right away from any bloody fires you have to light.'

'I had to ask.' Bob shook his head. 'You shouldn't have to face this, mate. But if you're sure you can handle it. We'll use the small wagon to collect the burr as we dig it out. Then I can do the burn off each night, using kerosene and any dry timber we can find.'

Jack didn't object. He wasn't keen but he knew Bob would do everything in his power to make sure Jack never had to be within cooee of any naked flames.

'What about the Chinese? They'd probably help and they're bloody good workers,' Jack suggested. He still didn't fully trust the Orientals, but their skill set and work ethic had more than impressed him.

'You don't miss a trick, do you Jack? I knew I dragged you along for a reason. We'll leave before the sun comes up and try to catch them before they head off to the new overshot.' Bob's grin turned mischievous. 'And it'll give you a chance to see Zhang Jing again.'

Jack pursed his lips and focused on scraping mutton stew from his plate. 'What are you talking about Bob?'

'Come on, mate, you know bloody well what I mean.'

'Give it a rest, Bob. Even if I was interested, I doubt very much if she would be.' Jack shot him a glare.

'Don't sell yourself short, mate. You're nobody's fool. I've seen how she looks at you and it's my bet that she sees what sort of a bloke you really are.

'Maybe, but there's a lot she hasn't seen.' Jack put a hand to his chest feeling the huge welts beneath his shirt.

'True enough, but I reckon it wouldn't bother her as much as you think.'

Jack went back to his meal without replying.

They rode out before dawn flushed the sky pink. Werna Creek was the longer of the two channels. They would start there and get the worst of it done, first. It wasn't until they neared the Zhang family camp that they discussed what to pay Zhang Yong's two nephews, Zhang Bai and Zhang Wie for their help.

Jack gave a suggestion. 'Offer them the going rate. You couldn't get better workers even if they were available. But don't let on how desperate we are or Zhang Yong'll charge you like a wounded bull.'

Bob laughed and shook his head. 'You're a cynic, you know that?'

By the time they arrived at the camp the two younger men and the wagon had already left to fetch a load of the stones. Fortunately, Zhang Jing was there to interpret.

Bob had dug up some Noogoora Burr to show Zhang Yong. He drew a mud map showing the full lengths of the two creeks. Looking hopefully at Zhang Jing, he reiterated that he was willing to pay for their assistance to help with the monstrous task.

Zhang Yong listened as his daughter translated. He seemed to give it a great deal of thought before answering, shaking his head in the negative. 'Méiyǒu.'

'My father says no.'

Bob and Jack exchanged appalled glances.

Bob cleared his throat. 'Er…Zhang Jing, can you please ask your father again? Tell him it's really important that we get help with this?'

Zhang Jing went into a deep discussion with Zhang Yong, who listened intently then started to chuckle.

Jack whispered to his cousin. 'I told you. The crafty old bastard's about to screw you.'

Bob cut him off as the girl swung her attention back to the grazier. She, too, was smiling.

'My father apologises for any misunderstanding. He doesn't want any money for helping you. But if you let us have a sheep to kill every two weeks, instead of every month, our family would be grateful. He said that if that arrangement is acceptable, we will start tomorrow when my cousins have returned.'

Bob let out a sigh, grinned, bowed awkwardly and then offered his hand to seal the deal.


Jack and Bob worked alone the first day and barely cleared a hundred yards of the mongrel weed. Dejected and exhausted, they ate bully beef and beans and then rolled straight into their swags.

At daybreak the second day the entire Zhang family arrived. On one side of the waterway the mother led the oxen drawing the cumbersome old wagon. Zhang Yong, his daughter, and one of his nephews chipped out the burr with garden hoes that were much lighter and far more effective than the mattocks that Jack and Bob used. Zhang Wie, the elder of the two young men, worked with the Australians. By the end of the day they had almost covered a mile.

The next morning Zhang Yong took the mattocks from Jack and Bob and replaced them with tools similar to those the Chinese family used.

Jing shyly told Jack, 'Father fashioned the handles from saplings and attached two spare metal heads he carries in his wagon.'

'When did he find the time to do that?' Jack asked.

She giggled. 'This morning, early, while you slept.'

Once the two stockmen became used to handling the longer device, they removed the bushes faster and with less effort.

A week later they were making great headway and Jack had come up with a routine that solved the problem of being near the fires. He would help the others gather the dry wood. Then he took the horse and bullock to a distant spot to give them feed and water. Next, he sharpened the hoes, not returning to the campsite until the flames had subsided. Jack also set his swag up away from the campfire where everybody else slept.

Even so, when the flames were at their peak, the flickering light, scent of smoke, and distant crackling caused him to tremble like a terrified seven-year-old again.

One afternoon, as Jack led the horse and bullock away to be fed, Zhang Jing approached him.

'Mister Jack, my family are worried. Every night you stay right away from us. Have we done something wrong?'

Jack hesitated. But the hurt in Zhang Jing's face melted his usual resolve to stay silent.

He stared down at his feet and scuffed the dry earth with one foot. 'It's nothing against you or your family, Zhang Jing.' He shrugged one shoulder. 'I copped some pretty bad burns when I was a kid. Can't stand to be near any open fire. Please tell your family

I'm sorry if I've upset them.'

Jing looked into Jack's face, her eyes wide. 'What happened?'

Jack choked back an irrational surge of dread. He clenched his fists. 'It doesn't matter. Just leave me be and don't ask again.' He turned his back and didn't look around until her soft footsteps had faded. His stomach knotted and he cursed himself for an idiot. Of course she wouldn't stick around.

The following evening, Jack finished carting the wood for the day's burn off. He was collecting fodder for the horse and bullock when he saw Zhang Jing also gathering hay.

'I can do that, Zhang Jing,' he said, embarrassed over his outburst the previous day.

'Our bull, I'll help,' she replied politely.

'It's not a bull. It's a bullock.'

'What is the difference?'

Jack flushed and cleared his throat. 'Er…It's not important'

She chuckled. 'Do you find it difficult to explain to me that he has been castrated?'

Jack laughed. 'Well, I won't make that mistake again, will I?'

'We'll see, Mister Jack. But you should smile more. It looks nice on you.' As an afterthought she added. 'And please, I would like it if you called me Jing.'

'Okay. I can do that. But only if you call me Jack.'

'Jack is nice,' she said, bowing. 'Even if you don't wish to tell me what frightens you, I intend to come here every day and feed my bull.'

Jack stood in silence, hiding a secret smile. 'It's a bloody bullock.'


That became the new ritual each afternoon and Jack soon wanted to know more about Jing and her family.

'Why did you leave China? To be honest I know very little about the place.'

'My father was a senior official in charge of building a naval base,' she said. 'His work brought him into conflict with a radical group called the Society of the Righteous and Harmonious Fists. The English called them the Boxers. Bai and Wie were involved in some of the demonstrations and learnt of a plot to kidnap a Chinese official's daughter to use as leverage to disrupt the building of the port.' Jing wrapped her arms around herself, lowered her head for a moment, then continued. 'The intended victim was me. My cousins risked their lives to warn us. Even though the kidnapping plot failed, our family remained under threat. So we made our way to Australia.'

Jack blew a breath and shook his head. 'I can understand why, but it's a tough life out here. Pretty isolated.'

She nodded. 'We had a big house and servants in China.' She sighed. 'I feel like it's my fault we are so poor, now.'

'That's mad,' Jack said. 'It's not your fault some bastard threatened your family.'

She sent him a quick, grateful smile, but the anxious look didn't fade from her eyes.

Jack frowned. 'You're not worried about them, are you? Surely no one from your country would think to look for you here.'

'No, perhaps not. But that isn't the only reasons why Father keeps us moving around.' Jing looked away and the colour rose in her face. She quickly added, 'We are happy living here on Cooinda and we find it really peaceful.'

'Cooinda is Aboriginal for a Happy Place and you're right it is peaceful.' Jack said. 'I'm...um...sure Bob isn't in a hurry for your family to move on. You could probably stay here for as long as you like.'

'That would be nice, but soon we'll leave to find somewhere permanent. Mother is frail and finding it more difficult to live as we do. Father says we have to settle shortly if he's to find me a husband.'

'Is that what you want, Jing, a husband?' Jack blinked and his heart stuttered.

'Perhaps, one day.' Jing looked into Jack's eyes. 'What about you, Jack? Would you like to find a wife and have children someday?'

Jack fidgeted with the halter. 'I haven't thought about it much,' he lied. 'Look, I'd better finish up.' He stalked to where he had placed the hoes that required sharpening.


By the time they had only a few miles of Cooinda Creek left to strip clear, seed buds were practically bursting off the bushes. So, Bob made sure the fires were large enough to destroy every bit of the plant they tossed into the flames. Without rain, the surrounding grasslands became dryer so they were extra vigilant when they burnt off. The hot dry conditions also brought small whirly-winds that whipped up dust and dry grass high into the scorching blue sky.

The last stretch seemed to be the worst. Barren clay pans ran for miles on both sides of Cooinda Creek. But the soil on the banks of the creeks was deep and rich, clogged with the thickest grass and Noogoora Burr they had encountered. With both wagons full of the weed by early afternoon. With only a half a mile left to clear the following day, Bob decided to stop early and burn off.

Jack laid out a great pile of dry wood on a claypan and then helped the Chinese brothers heap the burr from the wagons on top.

He smiled at Jing. 'Come on, let's feed those animals.'

The temperature was over 100 degrees. Jack mopped his forehead and looked over his shoulder as Bob lit the fire. The initial blaze was immense as dry stalks and leaves ignited. The stack roared into leaping flames that licked the hot blue sky. The old fear returned. Jack started to tremble and sweat. Jing slipped her hand into his and kept him walking.

Zhang Yong called out. A whirly wind danced across the claypan, heading straight to where Bob was burning off. Jack groaned. The mini tornado hit the fire at full speed. Small particles of burning wood soared a hundred feet into the air. It raced towards Cooinda Creek dropping flaming embers into the dry grass.

'Oh, Christ. No!' Jack yelled. He and Jing ran towards the channel where clumps of dead grass had already burst into flames. Bob, Bai, and Wie were well ahead of them, carrying whatever they could to beat out the fires.

Jack's pulse raced and his mouth dried into desert sand. He heard Zhang Yong call out but paid no heed until Jing grabbed his arm.

'Father says wait.'

Jack's stomach churned. The crackling, hungry flames urged him to run. But if the grass caught now, they'd have nothing to feed the stock. They'd worked too hard to lose it all.

He shook off her grip. 'I have to help, Jing. I can't just stay here.'

Zhang Yong caught up to them and stood in front of Jack, putting his hands on the younger man's arms. 'Tíngzhǐ, Jack Tíngzhǐ.' He spoke rapidly to his daughter.

'Father says to stop. The fire is heading downstream. We can build a firebreak there.' She pointed to a section of the creek where it was flanked on both sides with barren claypans.

Jack nodded, both guilty and relieved. He and the old man ran back to the camp for their digging implements, while Jing went to fetch Bob and her two cousins.

The blazing front was less than a hundred yards away and their bodies were covered in soot blown by the hot winds. Jack struggled against the urge to run from the intense heat. Sweat poured out of him. The smell of the smoke brought bile to the back of his throat and the crackle of burning leaves made him want to scream like a kid. He caught sight of Jing looking helplessly at him. He swallowed, forced a smile and continued digging.

With a ten-yard fire break cleared across the channel, Jack and Jing stayed on its downside while the others started back burning. Using wet sacks, Jack and Jing extinguished a few jump-overs and Jack dared to hope the worst was past. Then, on the edge of the gully nearest to Jing, a fresh fire ignited in a section thick with dry vegetation. Jack hesitated as she worked at the edges. All her efforts made little impact and the flames intensified.

'Fuck!' He ground his teeth and swallowed down terror. He yelled at the fire and ran in, swinging the wet sack like a madman, beating the flames into submission.

They were winning. He grinned fiercely. Then Bob yelled. Another small cell had started in thick grass.

'Jing.' He pointed. 'Another one. Go. I'll take care of this.'

Jing hesitated, fear in her eyes. Fear for him.

'Jing, you have to go now, or it will get away on us.'

She nodded and ran, looking back twice.

Jack's heart raced as he grimly beat the flames with his scorched corn sack. A high-pitched screeching from the tall burning grass made him jump. A mob of wild piglets appeared, running in all directions, squealing loudly. Jack forced a chuckle and swung the sack again.

The sow thundered out of the fire and ploughed him into the smouldering grass.

Jack scrambled shakily to his feet. Flames licked up his arm. He screamed his throat raw. His shirt was burning. Heat seared his skin. The stink of burning flesh made him retch. He'd set the shed on fire. But Kathy was in there. Where was she? Where was his sister?

'Kathy!' he cried. 'Kathy, where are you?' He collapsed to the ground, sobbing.

Something cold and wet slapped at his body and Bob's big

hands held him firm.

'Mate, it's ok. You're ok.'

'Jack?' Jing's anxious voice recalled him to some rationality. 'Jack, it's alright. The fire is out. You're alright.' She led him away from the smoke and sat him in the shade of a tree.

He sat with his head bent to his chest. The pain on his back and shoulders was too much; too much like before; too much to hide any longer. Tears scalded his cheeks.

'I need to cut off your shirt so I can tend to your burns.' Jing said quietly and proceeded.

'No,' he snapped. 'Get Bob.'

She took his hand and gazed at him with steady dark eyes. 'Don't worry. Bob said that you wouldn't want me to see your scars. It won't matter. I intend to care for you like my mother does for my father when he ails. Now let me get on with what I have to do.'

He froze, a new kind of fear crushing the breath in his lungs. He choked back resistance and nodded, allowing her to peel away his shirt, revealing the old, unsightly welts that covered most of his torso and upper arms. Jing showed no sign of repulsion. He relaxed as she gently applied her mother's salve to the new burns.

She touched one of the old scars. 'How did this happen?'

He hesitated, and then made his choice. 'When I was just a kid, I started a fire that almost killed my sister, Kathy. Out of pure dumb luck she got out safely. I can't forget what I did. Especially when I see myself without a shirt on...'

Jing squeezed his hand. 'You are a good man, Jack.'

The following day, when the final stretch of burr was cleared, the Zhang family returned to their campsite and Bob and Jack made their way steadily back to Cooinda's temporary homestead. Jacks burns were painful but not severe enough to keep him bedridden. With the use of Zhang Li's salve, he quickly healed.

A few days after the fire, Jack headed down to the Zhang's camp. He rode a little slower than usual. His plan to ask Jing's father for her hand in marriage had seemed a lot more practical the previous night when he had discussed it with Bob. Now, doubt undermined his resolve. What if he'd misread her feelings? After all, she hadn't said she loved him, only that he was a good man. What did that mean?

He checked his mount. He was a fool. He should turn back. Then the memory of how Jing had tended his burns and stayed with him afterwards gave him renewed confidence. He patted the mare's neck and said aloud, 'Come on Jack, don't be a bloody squib.'

Having bolstered his courage, Jack rode into the camp. As he dismounted and unsaddled his horse Jing ran out to greet him, but she wasn't smiling. Tears streaked her face and her eyes were red.

'What's the matter, Jing?'

'We're leaving tomorrow.' Her voice broke.

'What do you mean you're leaving?' The words came out harsher than he intended.

Jing dropped her hands to her sides and looked at the ground. 'We have to go. Father was in Winton yesterday and there are people looking for us.'

Jack placed a finger under her chin, lifting her head. 'Who's looking for you? Surely the people who threatened you in China haven't followed you out here?'

'No, it's the police.' Fresh tears ran down her cheeks.

Jack's heart pounded, but he managed to keep his voice calm. 'Why would the police be chasing you? That doesn't make any sense.'

Jing told Jack everything. When she had finished, she stood with her hands by her sides and shame in her flushed face.

'It doesn't matter, Jing.' Jack took hold of her hands. 'Marry me and stay here. They're after your father, not you.'

Jing pulled away and hung her head. 'I have to go. Mother is ailing. Until we get her properly settled, she needs me. It would be wrong to abandon her.'

Jack's heart stopped, all that he'd dare to hope for was slipping away. He took her hands again. 'I can't just let you go, Jing. I love you. There has to be a way we can be together.'

Jing lifted her gaze, her fingers clinging to his. 'My father trusts you and believes you are a good man. If you tell him you wish to marry me, perhaps he will tell you where we are going.'

Jack was so mesmerized by the tender look in Jing's eyes and her shy smile that it took a second for what she had just said to register. He took her in his arms. Her tiny hands encased his face and she kissed him gently.


The following day Jack rode with them to the boundary and watched until they were well out of sight.


Bob discovered they had left when the police arrived on horseback a few days later. Zhang Yong was wanted for selling opium in Ballarat and had been eluding the law for a number of years.

'You boys have any idea where they might be headed?' the senior constable asked.

Jack pulled off his hat and shook his head. 'Not really. But they seemed to think there would be plenty of work building overshots down in the Channel Country.'

Bob hesitated, then cleared his throat and added, 'That's right. I had an old map of Queensland that I gave him. He asked me to pinpoint the major water ways in the southwest.'

With nothing more to go on the lawmen left, saying they would pass on the information to their counterparts in the south.

As the two officers rode away Jack said, 'Thanks, Bob.'

'Welcome. But you should have let me know.'

'Yeah, well.' Jack scratched at his chin. 'Didn't want to put you on the spot, mate.'

'Fair enough.' There was a long silence, and then Bob grinned. 'When are you leaving?'

'How long will it take to finish Sandra's house?'

Bob pondered a few seconds and shrugged. 'Probably ten weeks. It depends a bit on the weather.'

'Well, I guess I'll be going as soon as that's done.'

They stood quietly for a while then Bob said, 'Do I get an invite to the wedding?'

Jack smiled. 'Of course, mate. Best man.'

# One Hell of a Trip

*Georgia Willis*

The phone rang. I snatched it up. 'Hello?'

'Hi, Lizzy, it's me,' Marg murmured, her words slurred like she was barely conscious. 'He's not on Earth.'

'What the Hell?' I sank onto the worn blue velvet couch, my heart pounding.

'Exactly,' she whispered.

'What?'

Marg wasn't making sense. Had scrying for Bruce caused her some sort of brain injury?

'He's not on this plane anymore. He's somewhere demonic. I'm sorry, I have to go throw up,' she said and hung up.

I stared at the phone. Marg had found him. Just like she said she would. Having a witch friend was sometimes helpful. I owed her big time. Scrying was exhausting work. I just wished she'd had better news.

I looked at the three remaining elemental dogs who'd gathered around me, their eyes wide and tongues dangling. I hesitated.

'Well?' Harold asked, wagging his brown speckled tail. A strong breeze broke open a latch on the closest window and swirled around the room, whipping my frizzy blonde hair into my eyes.

'She found him—' I said.

Lilly yipped, spinning around on the spot, her shaggy chocolate brown labrador fur dripping with water. A miniature rain cloud formed over her shoulders, leaving a puddle at her feet.

'Can you *not* destroy the house before we get Bruce back,' Iris snapped at her sister and lifted a paw to avoid the growing puddle.

But it was the least damage my threadbare purple carpet and dilapidated two-bedroom cottage had suffered since their brother had gone missing. Elementals out of balance were a dangerous thing, and something that would concern a whole lot more people than just my neighbours if this went on much longer. Just ask the people of Pompeii.

Even my unconscious ability to Null magic around me had no effect on Elemental dogs. They were a force of nature.

'Where is he?' Iris asked, turning to me.

I took a deep breath. 'He's in Hell.'

Harold raised his brown and white beagle head and glared. 'We have to go get him!' More window latches exploded. The windows slammed open and a gale force wind swept around the room. I braced against the couch. This was why everything that wasn't nailed down was stored away.

'I...' What could I possibly say to fix this?

Lilly's eyes poured small creeks of water, that were swept up and thrown around the room until I was half-blinded in my own private hurricane. I wiped my face and squinted at Iris. She stood perfectly still. Damn! Had she turned herself to stone again? She was like that for almost a month last time.

The house shook. Its wooden beams groaned in protest. The plastered walls cracked and covered the floor in white powder. That was enough to scare her siblings out of their power displays. Lilly's bottom lip trembled. Harold buzzed around the room anxiously.

'We're going now!' Iris said, glowering at me. For an earth elemental, she sure had a lot of fire in her eyes.

'None of you can go.' I cringed, waiting for the house to collapse. When it didn't, I continued, 'Harold, you can barely survive the hot sun. Lilly wouldn't make it a few feet in before she evaporated. And Iris...'

She eyed me defiantly.

'Iris, you'll melt,' I finished. She growled, her hackles standing up.

'Lizzy's right, Iris.' Lilly sighed. 'Us getting killed in Hell won't help bring Bruce back.' She nuzzled Harold, whose face was wet with tears.

'I'll get him back.' I said, trying to reassure them. How, I didn't know. But I knew someone who would. I had never been—and never wanted to go—to Hell. But what choice did I have?

I sent them all to bed. There was nothing any of us could do that night. They reluctantly went. Then I rang my mother.

'Hello?' came the stern, familiar voice.

'Hi, Mother,' I said, trying to hide my exhaustion.

'Oh. Hello, Elizabeth. To what do I owe this unexpected pleasure?' she purred.

'My Hell hound has been nabbed by a demon. I need your help to get him out.'

She was silent for a few seconds. 'Let me get this straight. You want to get a Hell hound out of Hell?'

'That's what I said. And not just any hound, *my* hound.' You could never be too careful. Making a deal with my mother was like making one with a devil. You always had to read the fine print and check your soul when you left.

'You aren't asking *me* to go get it, are you?' she asked. 'I mean, you know I'd do almost anything for those little darlings of yours, but...'

Her honeyed tone made me want to vomit. Apart from being a very powerful mage, she was also a fanatical collector of all things magical. She'd wanted my dogs ever since she found out I had them. Elemental animals were incredibly rare and, apparently, very collectable.

'But,' she continued, 'I'm afraid Hell is a little…inconvenient for me at the moment.'

I grinned at her sudden airiness. 'You mean because there's a bounty on your head for the Lazarus amulet you stole?'

'I did not steal it. I recovered it. But…well, alright, yes,' she snapped. 'The demon-king, Leraje, put a bounty on me. Happy?'

'Maybe a little. But I just want your help. I'll go get Bruce myself,' I replied, trying not to snigger.

'Hmm…' she said, a hint of excitement in her voice. 'I think I could probably help you manage that, but—'

'What do you want?'

'I want your dogs to come and visit me from time to time,' she said, breathless, like a five-year-old who's just been promised an icecream and a polymorphing sabretooth kitten.

'How long would these visits last?' I knew my mother. She would try to make this 'visit' a lot more permanent. But that was a problem for another day. I needed to get Bruce back and save what was left of my house—and the city—first.

'A few days, nothing more,' she said.

'I'll ask them. But, if they agree, they get full discretion on when and how long for,' I said. 'And I'd suggest you look at the fine print on your house insurance policy.'

There was a long silence. I could almost see her tapping perfect, red-painted lips with her perfect, red-painted nails as she tried to work out if it was worth it.

'But,' I grated, 'if you don't help me, they won't last the next couple days, and then where will you be?' I clenched the phone and the plastic flexed and creaked.

'Fine,' she said flatly. 'I'll have the stuff you need ready in the morning.'

'Good. See you then.' I finished. I didn't say goodbye, I just hung up. Mother had never been one for goodbyes, and she didn't deserve one.

Breakfast was quiet the next morning. Iris, Harold, and Lilly had agreed to visit my mother, and we'd deal with that problem later. When I found them, they'd been 'collected' and locked in cages in a dank basement. They wouldn't go back to that life willingly. But, if agreeing to see her was the only way to get Bruce back, then we'd all play along.

'Ok, I'm going now.' I rose from the table. All three dogs looked at me with fear and hope. I smiled to reassure them. 'It'll all be fine,' I said, stroking Lilly's ears—more for my comfort than hers. I exhaled slowly, trying to calm my nerves. Going to Hell had never been on my bucket list, so ticking it off seemed a hollow victory.

'Define "fine",' Iris snapped.

'Er...alive and back with Bruce?'

'You'd better,' she growled. 'Or I'll kill you both, myself.'

Without another word I walked out of the house and got into my car. It groaned to life, rattling and clunking. At least it still worked. The thirty-year-old piece of junk had been the only car I could get that had pretty much no magic I could Nullify.

I drove to my mother's. She opened the door, smiling, her eyes darting around me into the car. She frowned.

'Where are they?'

'Once, and *only* once, we have Bruce back, will you get anywhere near them,' I said, keeping my cool. I still needed her help.

- 199 -

She rolled her eyes and gestured me inside. 'Don't touch anything *please*. I don't need any more items turned to junk or worse.'

She waved a hand at the door, but it stayed open behind me. She glared over her shoulder and huffed. I shut the door the old-fashioned way. My parents were both mages and hated that I turned out to be a Null. I always messed up their magic.

I stepped into the house I grew up in and crinkled my nose. Just as I remembered it. A sterile, bleach-soaked, white-washed space, with the bare minimum of decoration and furniture. I shivered. I took a few steps forward, but it was like walking through jelly filled with needles. The air shimmered around me.

'Stop it with the protection wards,' I snapped.

Mother smiled sweetly, as if she had no idea what I was talking about.

I looked pointedly at the hideous, abstract sculpture of an eight-legged spider-unicorn on a side bureau. 'I'll touch it. I know that's where you hid the Lazarus amulet, and everyone'll see it when I kill the glamour.' When I continued to glare at her she rolled her eyes again.

'You can't begrudge your poor mother some fun, now can you?' she drawled.

'Yes, actually I think I'm entitled to some begrudging.' I had spent a lifetime putting up with my parents so-called fun. Sometimes ending up in hospital because of it.

'They were my strongest wards. I wanted to see if they'd work on a Null. Not bad.'

'What did your last guinea pig die of?' The pain was beyond a joke now, and I gritted my teeth.

She sniffed and walked into another room. The wards vanished. Grumbling, I followed her. That room hadn't changed, either. Pristine white walls with deep burgundy couches and a dark wooden coffee table. You wouldn't even know someone lived there—except for the lack of dust.

But today the usually-empty coffee table had three items upon it. A floppy, straw sun hat with a fake daisy in the pink ribbon brim, a large purple and white polka dot umbrella, and a multi-coloured plastic children's gun.

'Well? Sit.' She gestured to a couch and sat on the opposite one, chic in her tailored blue pantsuit with its discreet pattern of mage-symbols woven into the fabric. My mother had all the grace and poise of a cat. Maybe that was why my dogs didn't like her.

I plonked myself down and stared at the items.

'Marvellous, aren't they,' she purred.

'If you're a three-year-old kid going to a pool party,' I said, trying to keep a lid on it. I failed. 'How the Hell are these things going to get me into—and out of—Hell!'

Mother pursed her lips. The vein on her right temple pulsed. She took a deep breath and let it out, but the walls changed from stark white to beige. That only ever happened when she was angry at me.

'Now look what you made me do, Lizzy. Honestly,' she grumbled, eyeing off the sickly wall colour. 'All you ever do is complain. These items were the only things I had. It's not as if you gave me much time!'

I glowered.

'Do you want them or not?' she asked, sitting up straight.

'Fine. What are they?'

She grinned like a Cheshire cat. 'This,' she began, taking the hat and walking around the table, 'is how you'll get to Hell and back. Just firmly tap your head.'

She shoved the hat on my head, not trying to make it fit. It flopped to one side, threatening to fall off. My head was too big.

'If it comes off, am I going to get stuck there?' I asked.

She frowned and shrugged. 'Most likely. Oh, and it's got enough energy to open 3 portals.'

I scowled and pushed it on more firmly. Hopefully I'd only need two.

'What about the umbrella?' I picked it up. It would almost shelter a toddler from a very light rain shower.

She tilted her head and gave a smug smile. 'What do you think it's for?'

'I don't know, protecting me from the heat?'

Her smile faltered and she sat back down, sniffing. 'Don't be silly. That's what the water gun is for.'

I collected the toy gun, which was a size too small for my hand. My finger barely fit into the trigger. 'Are you telling me that I have to shoot the rivers of brimstone and fire with *this*?'

She smiled triumphantly. 'Exactly! And if you need to defend yourself just open and close the umbrella in the direction of your target.' She relaxed back on her couch, beaming like she was expecting a pat on the head and a treat.

I stared for a long time at the toys. 'So,' I said, rage bubbling just below my calm, 'you just happened to have these things to hand?'

She nodded, plucked eyebrows raised.

I glanced around the stark room. 'In *your* house? This house?'

She waved an airy hand. 'Well, of course not. They're from the toy store down the road. As if I'd have anything like this here.'

I closed my eyes. 'That would be the toy store right next to the hardware store full of useful things, like fire blankets, chainsaws, and hard hats, wouldn't it?

I was going to die. I was going to go to Hell and die trying to save Bruce. The other dogs would be left defenceless. Then again, maybe that's what she wanted.

Her eyes were wide. 'A hardware store? Really?'

There was no point in playing her game, so I inspected the water gun. 'Please tell me the water gun has an unlimited supply of water?'.

'Oh, like I could get an unlimited supply in that tiny thing!' she scoffed.

'Of course.' I rubbed at my face. 'What about my powers? I won't Nullify the magic of these…these…*things,* will I? You protected them, right?'

'In a manner of speaking… yes.'

'What does that mean?' I groaned

'Well, nothing can really protect against your Null effect.' She grimaced. 'Believe me, I tried for years to find something. But as long as you don't take too long everything will work just fine.'

My mouth fell open. My Null magic was going to play havoc with them.

'And remember,' she said, wagging a finger, 'don't lose any of these. Who knows what would happen if a demon got hold of—'

'The dogs aren't property. They don't go to you if I don't survive this,' I said.

The smile faded from her face. 'What?'

'You don't get them if I die or disappear. I made sure of that. In my will.' I sat back on the lounge.

Mother looked at the three object each in turn. Her face went pale. 'They're the best I can do on such short notice.'

'Right.' I stood and walked into the hallway. If I was going it had better be now. She'd never let me go if she thought she'd lose access to those dogs.

'What are you doing? If you wait a few more days, I can probably do a bit better a job.' She scrambled up and ran after me, reaching for my hat.

I bopped my head, thinking hard of fire, brimstone, and Bruce. A shimmering purple portal tore open in front of me. The magic rippled around me.

'Wait!' Mother cried.

I stepped through the portal.

I hit the worst wave of heat imaginable. It was like being caught in a rip out to sea; I was drowning, but in molten air. I gasped and spluttered as the heat burned my lungs, threatening to melt them. I squeezed the little trigger on my water gun. A small trickle of water shot out. The air around me cooled. I took a deep breath and grimaced. Pain radiated through my chest. My lungs were burnt. Hopefully not too badly.

Taking shallow breaths, I took in my surroundings. I was definitely in Hell, but exactly where was anyone's guess. Marg had once told me portals were a very unreliable way to travel.

I had landed on top of a small, black-sand hill. Behind me towered giant rocky formations, made of black glass. To my left snaked a bright yellow river with vivid blue flames licking the banks. To my right lay endless, rolling hills of black sand. Mother must have hated the colour palette here when she came for the amulet. So gothic.

In front of me, in the distance, stood an obsidian citadel. Gleaming black columns and arches spanned the entrance to a high-walled city. I could just make out twisted beings shuffling, limping and scurrying through the lane ways. That must be where Bruce was being kept.

The daisy on my head vibrated—the hat losing some of its power. I had to move. I hurried towards the city, the tiny figures getting bigger as I went. Pity there were no discarded demon costumes lying about for me to use as a disguise. I wasn't exactly inconspicuous.

The demons spotted me when I was about twenty meters away. Truly poor lookouts. They eyed me with both bewilderment and amusement. Maybe they'd just die laughing and I wouldn't have to try flapping the umbrella like a demented chicken.

The first demon stepped in my way.

'Move!' I tried to look fierce.

He crossed his four arms and bared black fangs at me. He looked sort of like a giant sloth and didn't so much as snigger. Time for the demented chicken. I flapped the umbrella and sent him flying. He hit a pillar and crashed to the ground. Black glass fragments fell from above and impaled him. Blue blood oozed out of his twitching body. I pointed the umbrella at the remaining five demons.

'Anyone else?' I snarled. My path cleared. I passed the demon's body quickly, before the others decided to try their luck. The body groaned. I flinched and scurried inside the city.

Once in, I moved along the walls trying to keep out of sight. The demons at the gate screamed, an echoing sound that vibrated the black glass city. Now everyone knew there was an intruder. Oh, yay.

I crept around a corner, and almost ran into a demon the size of a gorilla. It bared fangs dripping with saliva. I flapped the umbrella, which gave a small cough. The demon grinned and growled. I flapped the umbrella wildly. If it didn't work, I was dead. The gorilla stalked forward, not in any rush. The umbrella wheezed but I could feel the magic building up again. The demon unhinged its mouth like a snake and gusted a breath of pure sulphur. The umbrella caught. A giant blast of air exploded straight into the demon's mouth and sent it careering away—into a group of red, bull-like demons who had just rounded the corner.

Demons are not known for their patience. The group turned on the gorilla and on one another. More demons soon came to join the fight. I'd started a brawl.

Excellent.

I slunk towards the centre of the city and the largest building. Surely, that would be Bruce's prison. By keeping to the shadows, I was able to hide from several demons. They were all heading the way I had come.

It took a few more minutes to get to the tower. I stood in the shadow of a large building and examined the tower. Tall and cylindrical, the smooth black walls were broken only by a steel door at the front, and small windows spiralling up from the ground. Towards the top protruded a small balcony.

A demon stood on the balcony. It looked different to the others. Where the demons on the ground looked animalistic, this one looked almost human. Except for the extra arms, claws and skin so white it could blend in with snow. A small flying creature—probably an imp—launched from the demon's shoulder, heading in the direction of the commotion I had caused. The demon walked back inside.

When the imp was out of sight. I ran for the tower door. Bruce *had* to be inside.

The door stood almost twice as tall as me and was immensely heavy. I pushed and pulled but couldn't get it open. Footsteps tap-tapped around the side of the tower. Desperate, I lifted the umbrella and gave it half a flap. The door groaned and shifted backward, just enough for me to squeeze through. I gave myself a second to calm down. The footsteps passed the slightly opened door and continued away. I was surprised the demons couldn't hear my heartbeat, it was so loud.

The inside of the tower matched the outside for stunning architectural features. Blank black walls, with a large wooden spiral staircase, leading up through the tower. Smaller wooden doors lined the walls. Black glass furniture decorated edges of the room. The place smelt of putrefying flesh. I gagged, managed not to vomit, and wrapped my free arm over my nose and mouth, trying to block the smell.

I tiptoed to each door and carefully peered in. Some rooms were lit, drenched in wet blue and dried red blood; others totally black. None were occupied. Again, I managed not to vomit. My mother had never mentioned this part from her descriptions of her visit to Hell. Then again, she had a stronger stomach than me for this sort of thing.

I crept up the stairs to the next landing. Almost identical to the floor below.

Sweat soaked my clothing and dripped off my nose. I squirted the water gun, a few drops trickled out, cooling my environment to something akin with a very hot sauna. I needed to hurry. Looking in the rest of the rooms revealed nothing important. No Bruce. I headed up to the next floor.

The landing only contained one door. I cracked it open a fraction and peeked inside. The demon I had seen on the balcony sat at a large obsidian table. He was examining a tattered scroll of some thick, leathery substance I suspected was probably human skin—or something equally demonic. The room was tastefully decorated with books, comfortable-looking leather lounges, a small coffee table made of bones, and an assortment of chains, torture devices, and weapons. I began carefully closing the door. I didn't want to confront that demon. Maybe I had missed something in one of the other rooms.

'What do you think, dog?' the demon said.

I froze—impressive when I was, literally, melting.

'I think you should let me go,' Bruce snarled.

My heart skipped a beat. I couldn't see him. A bookshelf full of locked and chained books stood in the way

The demon laughed and shook its head.

The imp landed on the balcony and squawked. 'Lord Leraje, there's a riot. Something about an intruder.'

The demon sighed and put the scroll down. He walked out onto the balcony. I pushed the door open more and ran inside. Behind the bookcase, Bruce was stuck in a cage. His eyes widened. His expression flickered between hope and absolute terror.

I didn't have much time, if the imp spotted me, or the demon came back in we were doomed.

The cage was locked, Bruce pointed towards the bone coffee table. A key lay there. I crept over, staying out of sight of the balcony, snatched the key, and hurried back to Bruce.

'Hide!' he hissed, and I scurried behind a wingback chair.

Leraje's long-clawed feet tapped on the obsidian. I peeked around the chair. The demon had stopped at the partially opened door. My vision blurred as the heat increased. I just hoped he didn't see the trail of sweat evaporating off the floor. Leraje walked out the door and the rhythmic scritch-clacking of his claws faded down the stairs.

I stumbled back over to the cage and unlocked the door. Bruce pushed it open.

'How are you even here?' he whispered.

I shook my head. Explanations later. Besides, my mouth was so dry I could hardly swallow, let alone speak. I touched his fur, and he was able to suck some of the heat from around me, giving me some relief. I tried the water gun again, but nothing came out.

'How are we going to get out of here?' Bruce asked.

I tapped my head. Magic swirled, then dissipated. No portal appeared. I tried again. Same thing happened. Panic set in.

'You can't use magic up here,' Bruce whispered. 'He has some sort of blocking device, only his magic works.'

I groaned. 'Outside.'

We headed for the open door. Leraje stood, arms crossed, on the landing. I gasped and backpedalled inside. He followed, grinning. I tried flapping the umbrella, but it gave off a wheeze and stayed silent. Bruce growled and stood between us, hackles raised.

'Well, well, well,' Leraje said flatly. 'What do we have here?'

I shuffled backward, heading for the balcony. Bruce followed. Leraje lunged, knocking Bruce out of the way and into the bookcase.

A dozen thick old tomes fell out, half-burying Bruce. I floundered, but Leraje grabbed me, his claws digging into my arms as he lifted me into the air. I cried out. His hot skin burned mine.

'I'm going to enjoy eating you,' he mused.

He slammed me down on the obsidian table and locked my arms in place with a pair of manacles. Bruce was out cold. I screamed out to him and he stirred but didn't wake. Leraje leered at me. His foul breath made me choke. I struggled in the manacles, the chains rattling.

'Don't bother trying to escape, that's elemental steel. I had them put it in after another unwanted guest came here to rob me.' He snarled, baring sharp white fangs. 'I hate mages and their trickster magics.'

He picked up a butcher's knife from a rack of torture instruments and sat down. 'Now, how am I going to cut you up?' He laughed, positioning the knife above my stomach.

'Wait!' I cried.

He paused, scowling.

'I can give you information on the Lazarus amulet,' I muttered thickly. My tongue was practically stuck to the roof of my mouth.

The demon eyed me for a long second. 'And what makes you think I can't get this information by just torturing you?'

'Because...' My body ached and burned. The words were hard to form, from a throat dry and scorched.

He clicked his fingers, magicked a jug and tipped the contents on my head. I gasped and spluttered. Whatever had died in that water was now firmly up my nose.

'More?' He clicked his fingers, but this time nothing happened. He frowned and clicked again.

'What is this?' He grabbed me by the throat. His skin sizzled against mine. He howled and leapt up, cradling his scalded hand.

'What are you?' he growled.

'I'm a Null,' I said, laughing with relief. 'Your magic won't work around me, and if you even come near me, I'll destroy you.' I was bluffing, but hopefully he wouldn't realise. It was a pretty shaky bluff because clearly my Null effect didn't work all the time on him.

He eyed me suspiciously.

'Now,' I said, trying to sound confident. 'I have information on where the Lazarus amulet is. You agree to release us both. We get to leave here without any interference. And I'll give you the address of the mage who stole from you.' I needed to make this deal before he realised that non-magical implements could hurt me just fine.

Leraje looked at Bruce, who was staggering to his feet.

'Agreed,' the demon snapped.

I told him my mother's address. She'd tried to get me killed, now I was returning the favour. Leraje stalked to the balcony and left me shackled on the table.

'Hey! You made a deal. You need to let me go!'

The demon snorted. 'You said no interference, so I'm doing as we agreed.' He grinned and turned away.

'Bruce!' I yelled.

He stumbled towards me. But the locks needed a key. He jumped up on the table, a key in his mouth He put the key in the lock on my right arm and turned. The cuff popped open, but the key snapped. Bruce looked at me, horrified.

'Seriously? Can this day get any worse?' I asked, panic rising. Without the key I was stuck here. I sat up and tugged on the chain. Bruce put his paw on my wrist, stopping me.

'This is going to hurt, I'm sorry.' He grimaced and shifted his paw to the chain connecting the cuff to the table. The metal warmed, glowing red, burning into my flesh. I screamed. Bruce yanked the chain, it broke easily. I was free, but the metal cuff was still wrapped around my wrist. I couldn't feel my hand anymore.

'Let's go,' Bruce whined.

He helped me off the table and we stumbled down the two flights of stairs. The big front door was still partially ajar. We squeezed out and limped for the entrance to the city. Demons began filing out of the alleyways, cutting off our escape. They grinned manically, snarling and snapping at us. I swore. I'd forgotten to include them in our deal. I hit my head. Magic buzzed around me. Purple sparks sprayed, but the portal didn't open. The demons ran towards us.

I hit my head again, and again. More and more sparks appeared. I kept hitting my head. The demons were almost upon us. Bruce snarled, ready to fight.

The sparks caught. A purple portal opened. I grabbed Bruce with my good hand and we fell through.

We landed on the hill where I'd first arrived. I fell to the ground. Barely conscious. The heat was roasting me alive.

Bruce barked and yelled at me, but I couldn't make out the words.

Between long blinks I saw demons running out of the citadel, like black little ants, teleporting closer.

'Home,' Bruce yelled. Or at least that was the only word I could hear.

Home wasn't this hot. It was warm, sure, but the floor was wood and carpet, not sand. There were bright pictures on the walls and soft couches and beds. Home smelt like lavender because of the plants under the large bay window in the dining room. Home was where my other dogs were, waiting for us to come back to them. I thought of Lilly, and Harold, Iris, and Bruce. They were what made the house a home.

Something hit my head. I whimpered, and my vision was filled with purple. It was too much, and I closed my eyes. Something tugged on my good arm, dragging me somewhere.

Suddenly the oppressive, killing heat was gone. The sand turned to wet purple carpet, and the sulphur smell turned flowery. I opened my eyes. Furry noses snuffled at me.

Was I dead? I breathed in cool air and choked. My lungs hurt so much, but the pain was fading. Something landed on my hand. It was smooth and solid but had rubbery things on it. I pressed one and it made a small beep. Overwhelming tiredness took over my limbs. I couldn't move.

My eyelids felt like steel doors, closing never to be opened again. I breathed in the cool air, wanting to cough, lacking the energy to do so. Voices, familiar and scared chatted around me. Then a screeching noise pierced my ears, and I escaped gratefully into the darkness.


Noise. A gentle beeping, heavy breathing, clip-clop of shoes on hard surfaces. Smells. Chemicals, laundry soap, and musty dogs. Then the pain. Enough pain to make me scream and cry and beg. But I didn't, I didn't have the energy. I pried my heavy lids open. I was wrapped almost head to toe in bandages, a heart rate monitor beeping at my side. My dogs lay sleeping around the room. A hospital room.

I coughed, and Harold leapt up beside me.

'Are you ok?' he asked worried, licking my face. I groaned.

'Now, now, Harold,' a familiar voice said. 'Let the girl recover.'

I lolled my head to the side. Marg's friendly face smiled back at me.

'What...' I asked, coughing and wheezing.

'Easy.' She pressed a button to call a nurse.

'You want to know what happened?' she asked. I nodded.

'Well, Bruce dragged you back through the portal into your living room. But you were in a very bad way,' she said, petting Lilly on the head. 'They couldn't even get you to call an ambulance. So, Bruce set off the fire alarm. Help got to you soon enough.'

Bruce leapt up, snuffled my hand and whined. 'I might have

burned the house a bit, though,' he said.

'How much,' I croaked.

Marg and Bruce exchanged looks. 'You'll need a new house,' Marg said.

I groaned.

A nurse came in and held a small vial to my mouth.

'Drink this, it'll make talking easier.' She said. It tasted like strawberries.

'Is Bruce ok? Am I ok?' I managed.

'Yes, you're both fine,' Marg said. 'Well, Bruce is, and you will be. They put Burn-Go bandages on you, so there shouldn't even be a scar. But they haven't been able to get that cuff off.'

'Burn-Go bandages won't work on me, though' I protested. It felt like my whole body was covered in them.

'Actually, it seems that cuff has some interesting magic attached to it. It's doing something to your powers. The burn bandages are working just fine,' she said, and smiled at me when I gaped. 'Something that Nulls the Null. Weird, huh? We'll work it out when you're better.'

'Don't tell my mother,' I whispered.

'Ah,' Marg said. 'About your mother. She was in earlier. She's a bit annoyed at you, apparently. You—'

A knock fell on the door and a burly man in a grey suit walked into the room, barely glancing at me as he pulled out a note pad.

'Are you Elizabeth Sycamore?' he asked.

'Yes,' I replied.

'I'm Inspector Rodgers, Dimensional Border Enforcement department. I'm here to ask you a few questions about your mother's house and the demon incident.'

# Rise from the Ashes

*Rebecca Nolan*

'I said, no!' Jack's hand smacked against the rickety wooden motel-room table.

'Why?' I said. 'You used my connection to Van-al to find him and now I'm not allowed to go? Talk about rude.'

'He's dangerous, Morgana.'

'Well, duh.' I threw my hands up. 'Like I don't understand, Jack. He murdered my family, stole my father's sword and drained me of magic. I haven't forgotten. I'll never forget.' Some days I wished he had killed me. The thought sent a shiver down my spine.

Jack pulled at his raven hair. 'Another crucial reason why you shouldn't come.'

I puffed out my chest, determined to win. 'I'm coming. Besides, without me you won't even be able to see the sword. When it's not in the hands of my bloodline, it's invisible to other humans.'

He grimaced, hesitated, then shook his head. 'What if I can't protect you? I can't...' His voice held an unfamiliar wobble. Did Jack

Barrons, the good-looking, rogue fae hunter and third level mage, care for me? Or was his concern because his sister had died by Van-al's hand? Only fifteen when she met her gruesome fate—a few years younger than me.

'I'm not like Abby.' I rubbed his shoulder. 'I can protect myself.'

He patted my hand. 'You don't have magic anymore, luv.'

I shrugged. He repeatedly brought that up when he didn't want me to tag along. 'I don't need magic. Father taught me how to wield a sword and daggers. But, with your magic, I probably won't even need them.'

'I'm not going to win, am I, luv?'

'No way. I'm coming and that's that.'

Jack sighed, tossing me a helmet, dagger, and thick leather motorbike jacket. 'Fine, but out there you listen to me. You can't go off and do something stupid. I'm serious, Mor. I've been chasing fae for centuries.' He frowned. 'This particular one you don't want to mess with. You're a rookie.'

I produced an innocent smile. 'Of course. You're the boss, Boss.'

Jack shook his head and yanked open the motel room door. 'Don't make me regret this.'

I slapped on the helmet after securing the dagger in the sheath on my hip.

In the sweltering heat of summer, air rose in shimmering waves from the bitumen outside. Jack swung a leg over the bike and looked back at me.

'Ready?'

I nodded, my arms wrapped tight around his waist. The engine roared, thrumming through my chest and legs. The sensation spelled danger, adventure, and all the things I wanted.

Using a charm created from my aura, Jack followed Van-al's

magical essence to the outskirts of town, where we found a deep-rutted dirt path. One used by traders who didn't own motorised vehicles. Since the revolution, most folk hated technology and shunned the use of anything modern.

In some ways, the loss of tech was for the best. People like Jack and I—mages, witches and other magic users—were again embraced by the common people. Employing us for our abilities, like in the old days. Paying good money for potions and spells. If you were powerful, you were respected and earned the king's favour. Something unheard of since Merlin's time with King Arthur.

My father's impressive magic had granted him favours from the aristocrat class. His skills had been unique. The King had gifted him a grand estate in the country when he retired to marry my mother and raise me. But even my father's magic hadn't saved him and my mother from Van-al's inexplicable attack. I grimaced, glad Jack couldn't see my face.

Jack eased the bike off the road, into a grove of trees. Crisp, earthy air filled my lungs as I placed my helmet on the back of the motorbike.

'Wait here,' Jack said, pointing to a bush near a river. 'The charm indicates that your father's magic is near and so Van-al must be close.'

'You think he has Father's sword? Here?' My heart quickened. Van-al stole my family's sword and my mother's fire-crystal necklace the night he killed them. Retrieving those items was my mission. I needed them back so Van-al could be brought before the Mage Council tribunal; punished for his crimes. Then he would be forced to return my magic, as well.

'Yes.'

'So, what are you going to do?'

His eyes lit up. 'I'm going to lay a trap.'

I hid behind the bush, peeking out the side to watch. Jack

bespelled a length of rope that he pulled from his jacket. With the click of his fingers, he vanished. Advanced level magic. Impressive.

Ten minutes passed.

Why did he have to go invisible? Damn him! If I had my elemental magic, we would be equals. I could even be the stronger one. But I hadn't, so Jack regarded me as fragile and helpless.

A bloodcurdling scream pierced the silence. I ran, weaving between the trees and bushes. Twigs lacerated my legs as I passed. The mud along the riverbank slowed me, clinging to my feet. My lungs burned as I ran on, struggling to locate the source of the scream.

'Please, don't hurt me.' That sounded like a young girl. What was Jack doing? Or could Van-al be slaughtering more girls and drinking their blood? I shivered, racing on.

'No!' she screamed, shrill and agonized.

Where the hell had Jack disappeared to? How could he not hear the commotion? I skidded to a halt just outside a small clearing by the river.

Jack had two water nymphs backed up against a massive tree trunk. He'd managed to prevent them from returning to the water, binding them with the ensorcelled rope. One of them cradled an arm bent at a peculiar angle. I crept forward.

Tears shimmered in the nymphs' eyes. They reminded me of children. No older than twelve. Until I saw their naked bodies. Those were not childlike at all. My cheeks flushed.

'How dare you torture us, blood hunter.' The smallest nymph said as the other sobbed on her shoulder.

'Tell me where the sword is and I'll grant you freedom,' Jack said.

'No,' she said. 'You won't keep your word.'

Jack's hand rose. 'You little piece of shit. I dare you to defy me.' He struck the nymph across the face. Her head lolled to the side.

'Tell me or your friend here will pay with her life.' Jack removed his iron and crystal *athame* from his jacket and held the two-edged blade against the injured nymph's skin. Her flesh sizzled and popped. She screamed, a high, piercing noise, like the sound of a train's wheels scraping along the tracks. The kind of sound that runs through you. I covered my ears. Jack's eyes never left the other nymph's face. He stared right at her while torturing her friend.

My stomach knotted. Dad always said, *torture is a fool's way of getting information.* Real magic users found other ways to obtain knowledge.

'Jack!' I shrieked.

He jumped back. 'I thought I told you to stay back there?'

I marched into the clearing. 'What are you doing?'

'Leave us.' He slid the *athame* back into his pocket.

'Not leaving. Not until you tell me what the Hell you're doing.'

'My job. They were with him, Mor. They helped Van-al.'

'You speak his name, magic thief. You are begging for death,' said the injured nymph, her head held high.

I arched a brow. 'So, you do recognize him. Where's my father's cursed sword? It must be close by. Tell me where and we'll free you.'

'There are hundreds of cursed swords,' the other nymph said.

Anger stirred. 'This sword is unlike any other. Crafted from the black stone of the underworld, it has the ability to consume souls and gives its owner power. You must have heard of it. *Soulfire.*'

They exchanged glances before shaking their heads.

Jack laughed. 'Of course they lie. I had to break her arm to retrieve this from her.' He held up my mother's charm necklace that Dad gave to her on their wedding day. Tiny flames danced in the crystals. The magic it processed was hard to identify but, knowing my dad, probably potent.

'Give it to me.' I attempted to snatch the jewel from his grasp.

He pulled away, wagging his finger. His eyes danced with amusement.

'Now, luv, snatching isn't nice.' He studied the trinket with renewed curiosity.

Heat ascended to my cheeks. 'Jack.' I said, icy. 'That necklace belonged to my mother and if you keep it from me—' I thrust a finger into his chest '—not even the Goddess will be able to help you. Magic or not.'

He stepped back, chin jutting. My foot tapped on the ground. Our eyes locked. A brief frown flitted over his face. Was he scared? No. Not Jack. He wasn't scared of anything, let alone me.

'Jack.' I held out my palm, pressing my lips together. He handed it over. I let out a sigh and placed the gems around my neck. A gentle warmth caressed my skin, causing me to shiver.

A piece of magic, returned. I glanced back at Jack and beamed.

The wail of Jack's magic alarm system rose to a high-pitched peak then ebbed before rising again. We spun towards the sound. Both nymphs were escaping. The rope which held the pair had disappeared. The small nymph lunged at Jack. The injured nymph dashed into the forest.

'Go get her,' Jack ordered.

The nymph shrieked and clawed at his face. Jack wrestled with her, but she was preternaturally strong. Did he need help? Jack pulled his *athame* and pressed the blade against the nymph's neck, ensuring her co-operation.

'Don't worry about me, Mor. Just get the other one.'

I took off after the injured nymph, glad she hadn't retreated to the river. At least she couldn't have gone far. There were no footprints on the ground to follow but Jack had taught me a clever trick. I opened my third eye. Waves of magic floated like gold dust. Faint, but enough to see which direction she'd gone.

I followed the dust, dodging trees. A *pop* sounded in the

distance and her magic trail shimmered then dissipated. I halted. She'd escaped. I knew it.

And the only way a fae's magic could vanish so entirely was if they crossed into the other realm. Ley lines must be nearby. Jack had forgotten to tell me. The nymph must've used them to create a portal to slip back to the fae realm.

I stood still, trembling. If I used magic, the portal might consume me also. Father had warned me about the dangers of ley-lines. Awful, twisted bedtime stories of how they trapped our kind. My neck grew warm where my mother's necklace touched my skin.

'Mor?' Jack called. 'Where are you?'

'Jack!'

A rush of footsteps. Jack seized my shoulders, shaking them. 'You silly girl. You let her escape.'

'Jack,' I said, trying to keep tears at bay. 'She crossed over. She must have created a portal.'

'Bloody Hell.' His eyes gave a swift search of the area before he groaned. 'We have to go. I know where to find Van-al. But that nymph might warn him we are coming.'

He grabbed my hand and dragged me back towards the bike. Silver liquid ran like delicate rivers down his jacket sleeve and grazed the bare skin of my wrist. The liquid burned like ice. But Jack wouldn't release my hand, so I couldn't wipe it off.

He hauled me along so fast I could barely keep up and stumbled over a root.

'Can we slow down?'

'Slow down?' Jack paused. 'Morgana, Van-al is going to pay for what he did to me. To us. Do you want to lose our only chance of finding him, after searching this past year?'

'No!'

'Well, let's go.'

Jack released my hand and sprinted off. I hesitated, wiped the liquid off on my jeans, then took off after him. For a second, I thought he might leave me behind. My lungs and legs burned in an effort to keep pace. When I arrived at the motorbike, Jack was already seated, helmet on and ready to go. I jumped on behind him, wrapping my arms around his waist.

It was still early morning when we arrived back at the motel. Jack darted around the room collecting weapons along with magical items. When he appeared satisfied with his arsenal, he spread a map on the table.

'We can find Van-al in this village. The nymph told me that much.' He indicated a small speck on the map. The air crackled around us, my skin prickling as his arm brushed mine. His aura tasted of anger, bloodlust, and vengeance. Nausea swept over me. The necklace flared against my neck once more.

'What happened back there?' I asked. 'To the other nymph?'.

Jack's head snapped towards me. 'Nothing. Why?'

'Did you let her go?'

'Seriously?' He gritted his teeth. 'Now is not the time.'

'Jack. Please.'

'We are done with this conversation. We have better things to do.' He cracked his knuckles, returning to the map.

'Fine, but first tell me.' I sucked in a deep breath. 'Did you cast dark magic? Did you kill the nymph?'

Jack's eyes darkened and his jaw clenched. 'Dark magic is not only dangerous but also forbidden, Mor. Even talk of dark magic could cost you dearly.'

I turned away, incapable of meeting his gaze. 'I'm sorry if I offended you. Honest.'

He placed a hand on my back. I felt nothing.

'Let's forget this and concentrate on finding the real monster— Van-al,' he said.

'Of course.'

Using a ruler, Jack drew red lines on the map.

'Why are you doing that?' I asked.

'Ley-lines. So, we aren't caught out again.'

He pinched the bridge of his nose.

'What's wrong?' I examined the lines. Two red lines crossed right outside the village's border. My heart dropped. We would have to go close to the ley-lines or miss our opportunity to catch Van-al.

'What are we going to do?'

'I don't know.' He took a deep breath.

'Promise I won't be sucked into the ley-line. I won't survive the fae realm. You know what they do to human magic-users.'

Jack cupped my chin, forcing me to stare into his eyes. 'Mor, I can't promise you because it's impossible to control the ley-lines. If I could, Van-al would never have taken Abby.'

I pulled away. 'Then promise you'll never let anything bad happen to me.'

'I would do anything to protect you from them. That, I promise.'

'Thanks.' I brushed away a single tear.

He smiled, reached into his bag and pulled out two crystal balls. 'These are for you.'

I gaped. Jack had created two fireballs for me to use. Orange and yellow flames danced inside them, just like the ones my father used to make. It warmed my heart. I picked one up, studying the flickering flames.

'Be careful,' he warned.

'I'm not stupid. I know how to handle fireballs. They're a part of my element. Used to be.'

I tossed the ball into the air, to prove my point. Fire magic was often seen as a destructive element. Other elemental magic users feared fire, even if they tried to not show it. But fire was passion and life. It kept you from freezing and brought light into darkness. Fire steamed up water, heated the earth and danced with the wind. It was my favourite element. It hurt knowing my magic had been stolen. I tucked the balls into my pocket.

'Mor, are you listening to me?'

'Yeah, you told me to be careful.'

'That was over a minute ago.'

I shifted my gaze to meet his. 'Sorry. What'd you say?'

'You need to concentrate,' he said. 'We're ready to go.'

My jaw dropped. 'Now?'

'Definitely,' he said. 'Time to catch Van-al.'


The midday sun heated my thick jacket as I moulded my body to Jack's back. Sweat ran down my back and pooled where my butt rested on the leather seat.

Jack pulled over to the side of the road. 'Come on.'

I jumped off, handing him my helmet. He pushed the motorbike behind a row of shrubs. 'Help me cover the bike before we head off.'

'Wait, do we have to walk?' The village was still a good distance away.

'Well, yeah. I must glamour us, and I doubt it will work if we are riding.'

I pushed my bottom lip out. 'You sure. My legs still hurt from this morning.'

'Yes. And a *surprise* attack works better when two strangers don't roll up on a motorbike, considering how few are around these days.' He smirked.

I surveyed his face. 'What are you planning?'

'You're going to be a sixty-year-old man.' He backed away, hands held up in surrender.

I glared. 'An old man. Tell me you're kidding.'

Jack's cheeks reddened. 'It's the only glamour I can perform.'

Full body glamour was a hard spell to cast. I sighed. 'Can I please be an attractive old man, then?'

He didn't reply. Instead, his hands waved about like he conducted an orchestra. He cast the spell. The magic coated me like a second layer of skin. I couldn't detect any difference in my appearance, but Jack had disappeared. An elderly, balding man stood in his stead. The guy winked at me. I let out a deep breath and smiled. Those eyes were Jack's.

'Do I look like you?' I dreaded the answer. I didn't want to have a weathered face with thinning, grey hair. Or a rounded belly.

Jack took a swig of a potion he pulled from his jacket. 'You are beautiful.' He passed me the bottle. 'Drink this.'

I drank. The liquid burned down my throat. I coughed, doubling over. The foul flavour tingled in my belly. I glared at Jack... and gasped. The old man was gone. Jack's youthful body stood before me once more. I rubbed my eyes.

'What happened? Did the glamour wear off?'

'Nothing's wrong, luv.' He grinned. 'The potion is to help see through glamour. We're hunting fae and they use glamour.'

'Isn't that elixir banned? My father told me it contained something.' I tried to think of the ingredient. 'I can't recall what, but it was bad.'

Jack shook his head. 'If the elixir was banned, would I really give it to you?'

Jack had never done anything to make me doubt him. The High Council showered him with their favour. So why would he give me a forbidden potion?

'Maybe I'm mistaken.'

'Your faith in me is outstanding.' He stalked down the dirt road towards the village.

'Jack,' I cried.

He turned, a finger placed against his lips. I scuttled up beside him. He looked around before setting off again. I followed in silence.

The trees appeared to be closing in. Or was the road narrowing? The sun began its descent and shadows lengthened. As we neared the village, the ley-line's power grew intense, calling out to any magic. My father had described it like a magnet, feeding off magic to create portals. I could feel it now because of my father's magic within the necklace. Most magic-users could feel it, but only a handful of humans could cross realms and come back.

Jack and my father were the only two I knew.

We walked faster. A sharp crack sounded in the distance. A branch snapping. We froze. The necklace heated my skin. Painfully hot. We glanced at one another, not daring to move.

'Do you feel like something is watching us?' I asked. Jack nodded.

From out of the dense forest, a Fir Darrig appeared. I wanted to scream but gulped it down. The Fir Darrig looked like an old, dirty man, whose lower jaw protruded from its squished-up face, like an ape's. Enormous fangs jutted up towards its flat nose, like tusks. At the end of its over-long arms were two clawed fists.

'What you staring at?' the Fir Darrig said in a gruff tone.

'Nothing, sir,' Jack replied. 'Only two weary travellers looking for a place to rest their heads before moving on.'

The Fir Darrig beady eyes examined us. I thought about the pull of the ley-line. Had he just crossed over from the fae realm? The creature inched closer.

'What's wrong with him?' He pointed a long, taloned finger towards me. I held my breath, lowering my eyes.

'He is a simple, sir.' Jack moved in front of me. 'The poor man is my twin and hasn't uttered a word since our Ma died all them years ago.'

The creature glanced over Jack's shoulder at me, catching my gaze. My necklace flared once more.

The Fir Darrig backhanded Jack and leapt towards me. His

hands gripped my throat, claws digging into my skin. I choked and scratched at its arms.

'Tell me who you are!' he spat, his breath hot against my skin and stinking of rotting flesh.

I tried prying his hands apart. Darkness threatened my vision. My mother's necklace sprang to life. Flames engulfed the Fir Darrig's hands. He recoiled. I dropped to my knees, sucking in gulps of air. Jack rose and whacked him in the head with a fallen branch. The fae collapsed.

My body shook and my throat ached. I could hear the repeated thwack of skin against skin. I staggered to my feet. To find the Fir Darrig with a bloodied face. His eyes were shut, and silver liquid pooled on the ground. Jack held his athame in his right hand. He began carving into the creature's chest.

'Don't!' I shrieked, pushing Jack off the Fir Darrig's limp body. Jack's fierce dark eyes peered up at me. His lips curled in a snarl. I took a step back.

'What are you doing? That's not right.'

Jack bared his teeth, feral. 'He was going to kill you, Mor.'

'How do you know?'

'Yeah, those hands around your neck were just a friendly greeting. I bet he does that to all his friends.'

I stood my ground. 'Why not kill him? Why do that?' I nodded towards the Fir Darrig's almost lifeless body. He could have quickly killed the fae. Hacking it up seemed less about eliminating the threat and more about ritual and violence. Bile stung the back of my throat.

'You were the one that wanted me to promise to never let them take you. To do whatever I had to do to save you.' Jack waved the blood-stained blade around. 'So, don't blame me, if you don't like the methods.'

I shuddered. 'Jack…'

He hesitated and lowered his head. 'I'm so, so very sorry, luv. I lost my mind when he grabbed you like that. It brought up memories of Abby. I didn't mean to frighten you. Just the thought of that vile creature taking you from me was enough to make me snap. Please, forgive me.'

His eyes lifted, damp with unshed tears. I gnawed my bottom lip.

'Mor.' He said, his voice soft. His body trembled. 'Tell me you forgive me.' He opened his arms.

I nodded, holding him tight for a few seconds before letting go. 'We should find Van-al.'

The sky was a mixture of pink and orange swirls when the first thatched and stone cottages emerged from the shadows of the forest. We walked past neat picket fences which kept bountiful cottage gardens from spilling on the path. The moon was now above the horizon. Soon it would be dark, and we did *not* want to be in a village full of fae at night.

Once more, Jack used my aura to track Van-al. If he had my father's sword then my aura would lead us right to him. Then I'd be able to see the sword, even if Jack couldn't. Jack's eyes glistened in the moonlight as we snuck through town. We arrived outside a modest cottage at the remote end of town.

The corners of Jack's lips rose. 'We've found him.'

My heart began to pound. 'What now?'

Jack's smirk widened. 'We make him pay.' He took another potion from his jacket and drank quickly. Beneath the moon-lit glow, beads of sweat glistened along his forehead as he cast a spell around the cottage.

'Throw your fireball at the door,' he instructed. He wiped his brow with one hand. The other held his *athame*.

I threw. The door shattered like glass. We rushed through the gaping hole. A seven-foot tall man with golden skin leapt out from a side door in the wide hallway. His amber slit eyes glared at us and he flicked aside a braid of orange hair. Jack let out a cry and charged towards the creature.

'You!' Van-al cursed. 'I should've known.' One giant hand yanked Jack off his feet and hurled him at the kitchen wall. I drew my dagger, charging at my family's murderer. Van-al evaded, knocking my blade to the ground. In his hand, the sword. My father's sword: *Soulfire*. I scrambled to pick up the dagger. My fingertips brushed the hilt. But Van-al grabbed me, his forearm pinning me to the wall opposite where Jack lay unconscious.

'You dare to enter my home and attack me, little magic thief?' Van-al hissed. He bared yellow, jagged teeth and his nails dug into my flesh.

'You killed my father. You took his blade,' I snarled. 'Tonight, you die.'

Van-al threw his head back and laughed. 'His blade? It was never his blade. Your father was a thief. He stole our magic and deserved to die. Humans do not possess elemental magic. It is too pure for their fiendish hearts. I'm surprised you can even see it. The sword doesn't reveal its true self to humans.'

'It does to my bloodline. It's ours.' I thrashed about in his arms, a kick striking his knee. 'And my father was not a thief.'

The necklace grew hot against my skin. Van-al fingers caressed the jewels. His brow arched as the chain scorched my neck. I yelped in pain.

'Fire magic.' Van-al sneered, his hand wrapping around the gems. 'This doesn't belong to—'

Jack slammed into Van-al, driving the *athame* into his shoulder. Van-al stumbled backward, growling. Jack slapped a pair of iron cuffs on the fae and shoved him to the floor.

'Miscreant... May you suffer a thousand deaths for breaking our deal,' Van-al said while he writhed on the floor. My father's sword lay beside his injured arm.

'Shut it.' Jack hit the sidhe in the jaw with the butt of his dagger.

I stood still, trembling. What should I do next?

'You think you can silence me. You are vile. A monster among humans,' Van-al said.

Jack ignored the comments. He stalked around the room, tossing objects aside as Van-al lay on the floor laughing. What was he looking for? My father's sword was the only thing in the room of value. The glistening black stone blade stood out from the oak wood floor.

But of course, he couldn't see it. I opened my mouth to tell him where it was.

Van-al sneered and jerked his chin at Jack. 'Tell me, blood hunter, is she aware of how you sold your sister to us for a few drops of—'

Jack's fists pounded his face.

Not again. I hissed, lunged at the pair.

'Jack.' I shoved him off Van-al. 'What was he going to say? Did you sell Abby?'

Jack snarled at me, eyes wild.

Van-al scoffed. 'You really don't know do you, little magic thief?'

Jack tried to charge at Van-al. I snatched up my dagger from the floor, pointing it at him. Jack's dark eyes narrowed, and he crouched lower.

'What does he mean, Jack?' I stood between him and the fae.

'Nothing. Lies. All lies.' He began to circle us.

Jack was lying. It was written on his face. Still crouched, he darted closer. I stumbled backward. My back smacked into the wall.

'He sold me his sister for a thimbleful of my blood and the power it gives,' Van-al said. 'The poor mage craves power more than he cares about anything else. Who do you think told me where your—'

Jack's blade pierced his throat. My mouth dropped open. Jack hadn't even looked when he threw the *athame*.

'What have you done?' I asked as he strolled over to Van-al's corpse.

Jack picked up his blade and licked it clean. His body quivered. 'I did you a favour. Van-al was a murderer and a liar.' He smiled and looked at me beneath his lashes. 'We need to get out of here, fast. Do me a favour, luv, find your father's sword?' He placed a small jar under the fae's wound and collected the blood. Like nothing had happened between us. My legs trembled. I slid down the wall until I hit the floor.

'This is wrong. Dark magic is wrong.' I had been working with a monster. Waves of nausea struck me. I beat them down, trying to get a grip.

'Stop telling me I'm wrong. This is what I do. Who I am.' He cast me a contemptuous look.

'But it's forbidden. Punishable by death.' I struggled to my feet.

'Only because the Council doesn't understand what's needed to keep these fae scum in check. You can only fight power with power.' He smiled and held out the jar of silvery blood. 'One little sip and you will understand. Just like the old days. Just like what your father did.'

I almost laughed. He thought I was talking about the fae blood. Did he think I was that stupid? That I couldn't understand what Van-al was saying. I knocked the jar from his hand. 'I won't do it. Not now. Not ever.'

Jack laughed. 'Oh luv, you've already had a drop. That anti-glamour elixir had nymph blood in it.'

I recoiled. Another reason to punish him. My face burned. My hands curled into fists. 'You're disgusting.'

'Sorry luv, but you're tainted too. No going back now, so why don't you join me and we can move forward?' He shrugged and collected the jar, holding it under the fae's wound again. 'Together we can wipe out these bastards. Where's the sword?'

Dagger in hand, I leapt forward. The cold metal slid smoothly into Jack's side. Frozen, I let go of the blade, leaving it protruding from his body.

'You bitch.' The back of his hand struck me across the face. 'You witches are the same. You think you're better than me.' He pulled the blade from his side. Blood streamed from his wound. Coppery-silver liquid, shimmering in the light. He flicked his wrist.

A sharp pain in my chest. The taste of blood in my throat. Air gurgling in my lungs. I touched where the pain was, warm wetness smeared my fingertips. My own blade stuck out from my chest. I gaped at it.

He grinned and strolled closer. The necklace acted once more. Flames licked out at Jack, but he was ready for them. Like light hitting a mirror the flames bounced off him and engulfed my body.

'How does it feel, luv? Do you like it when someone you trust turns on you?' He prowled around me, sneering, watching me burn. 'Tell me where your father's sword is, and I'll save you.'

'I curse you, Jack Barrons,' I cried. 'I curse your life so that all your fears will become reality. I may die this night, but you will never know peace.'

The flames leapt, eating at my clothes and skin; excruciating. Without my magic I had no protection against my own element. I fell backward, crashing to the floor.

I couldn't move or speak. Even when Jack ripped the necklace from my throat. He stood over me and laughed. Then he pocketed my mother's necklace and strode out, leaving me to burn.

Molten lava scorched through my veins. Death flirted with me. Tempting me to lie in her arms. Still, I would not welcome the embrace. Not yet, though I wished for it. Somehow magic—the purest form of magic—now flowed through my body. As the flames rose, a phoenix appeared before me. Its wings of red, orange and yellow wrapped around me, encased me in magic, unmade me, then remade me anew.

When the pain stopped, I broke through the magic shell. I was different. Reborn from the ash of my corpse I, too, rose like a phoenix. My hair now the colour of a phoenix's tail, My body the gold of a phoenix's eye. I was no longer a witch. I was pure Magic.

Father's sword sang to me. Demanding that I collect it. The sword still lay next to Van-al's corpse. I plucked it from the floor. The black stone handle melded with my hand. The blade sliced the air, effortless; an extension of myself. Remembering what my father had told me, I pricked my finger with the tip. A single drop sizzled into the blade.

I chanted. 'With this blood, my will becomes your will. Strike true the hearts of those I choose. Trap the souls of those who wronged me and never draw my blood again.' The sword sprouted delicate red veins amongst the shiny blackness. It understood what I wanted. Whose soul I wished it to devour.

I stalked past the sleeping cottages until I came to the local tavern. The pull of the ley-line was strongest here. Magic. Strong magic called it. Did Jack even realize he was feeding a ley-line portal?

The stench of death and fae blood lingered in the atmosphere. I stood before the doors of the tavern and commanded them to open. They parted to reveal Jack Barrons, seated at a table, surrounded by several dead fae.

I strutted inside. The sword's power sang in my hand. 'Jack Barrons, you have committed forbidden crimes. Tonight, you face your punishment…Death.'

'Shall I buy you a drink first?' He reclined in his seat, kicking a chair out for me. I ignored his arrogance.

'I'll drink when you're dead.'

Jack scoffed. 'You think you can kill me? Do you know who I am? Look around you.' He gestured at the dead bodies. 'They weren't able to kill me.'

I took a step closer, my eyes never leaving his. Jack's eyes widened. He rose and withdrew two blades from one of the dead bodies.

'That sword...' He frowned. 'Where did you get it?'

Ah. He could see *Soulfire* now? I looked at the blade in my hand. Flames danced, blue and purple, along the edges. Interesting.

'Do not move any closer,' he commanded. The magic in his voice brushed over me with nil effect.

But I did not move. Let him believe in his own delusions. Let him think of me as prey, just like before. He had no advantage now.

Jack sauntered towards me. 'What a pretty little fae. Oh, the things I'd like to do, luv.' He let his *athame* trace the curve of my neck. 'And I'll take that pretty black sword, too.'

'You're a fool, Jack' I whispered. 'You have the blood of many on your hands, including my father's—' I swept my hand and he flew into the wall. It was like swatting a fly '—and mine.'

Jack's eyes bulged. I could hear his quickening pulse in the silence. He tried to summon magic but only I could command it.

'Morgana?' His voice shook.

'Not anymore, thanks to you.' I strode over to him.

'How?' He eyed me up and down. 'Impossible. You're lying.'

'I was reborn and now I come to seek justice.'

His eyes darted around the room, looking for an escape. There was none. My magic held him against the wall. The panic in his expression told me he knew it. Then, I felt him reach out to the ley-line with dimensional magic—a form I couldn't control. He called it near. The ley-line responded. Was he going to jump? Was that his plan? I let out a strident laugh. What a fool.

'You think you can escape? That I would let you jump realms?' I asked. A ley-line portal grew in the corner of the room. I tried to destroy it, but my magic was too new and wild. It only fed the portal. Its magic called to mine. Seductive. Frightening. I fought to remain calm.

'Stop the portal Jack!' I commanded. 'Or I'll kill you.'

'You're not a killer, luv. You want to close that portal then you will have to plunge that blade into my heart. But know this… if you do then I will be with you forever, is that what you want?'

Jack studied me intently. We both knew the power the sword wielded: to capture the souls of those who lost their life by its blade.

Was I really prepared to do that to anyone? Even him?

The ley-line portal was visible now; a shuddering distortion in the fabric of the world. Reality-twisting. Terrifying. Irresistible. And nearing full strength. It consumed the bodies of the slaughtered fae. Each one vanished into the eye-warping shimmer in the corner of the tavern with a faint *pop*.

It was too late to close the portal. And too late to escape its pull.

'Give me the necklace and I'll be merciful.' I tried to hide the fear in my voice.

Jack's eyes lit up. He glanced at the portal and grinned. 'Sure thing, luv. We can fight the fae in their own dimension. Together. You with the necklace, me with the sword. Give it to me.'

'Of course,' I said. 'Hand over the necklace.'

I eased off the magic holding him still. He reached into his pocket and pulled out the fire-crystals. I seized the gems.

I shortened my arm to thrust the sword he so desperately wanted through his black heart.

'Bitch!' he swore, and threw himself sideways. The portal's chaos of light and power sucked him into the other realm. As his feet vanished, the portal began to collapse.

I ground my teeth. I couldn't let him get away. Not after all he'd done. So, I squared my shoulders and tightened my grip on *Soulfire*.

'Right. You want a war, Jack Barrons, you've got one.'

And I leapt through after him.

# Too Much Whisky is Barely Enough

*'Too much of anything is bad,*
*but too much good whisky is barely enough.'*
*Mark Twain*

*By Cass Cooper*

As I stand on the cobblestones, my entire body aches with desolation and with the bitter cold. My feet burn in uncomfortable black heels as we wait for the horse and carriage to make its way up to us. My unruly brown hair is pulled and primped into a perfect bun at the nape of my neck. I'm wearing simple pearl earrings, minimal make up and a simple black shift dress with stockings and simple black shoes.

I wear black often, but today I hate it. Everything about this day feels...simple. Like all the life has been sucked out of it.

I look to my mother. Her dark hair is perfectly coiffed to her nape. Her black dress more elegant than simple, pearls—not in her ears—around her neck. She's holding her hands together in front of her waist, and her eyes are set on the street ahead as we wait in painful silence.

The ever-dutiful mother and daughter.

If only everyone knew I am far from dutiful. If only they knew I'd not even seen my parents in eight months, and not spoken in four. And now this.

The carriage draws closer. The mourners' weighted silence pulls me into grief that I can't escape. The horses' hooves echo, matching my pounding heart. I want to turn and run.

Last night I dreamt of fire. I dreamt of flames that were wild; flames that consumed me; flames so high they fenced me in. Yet, I did not fear them. They were not my enemy. They were something else entirely. A barrier, maybe?

But I have no barrier today. Nothing to shield me against this heavy fog of misery.

For I don't know how to grieve for someone who tore me apart every chance he got. Who made it clear I was a dark cloud of scandal over the family. Someone who—like all the men around me—never bothered to ask what I wanted. Never noticed me unless I stepped out of line or didn't do as they desired.

And yet, to everyone else, he was the epitome of grandeur; of gentlemanly charm and charisma. If only that was the man I knew. If only that was the man I could stand here and mourn.

Yet I must find courage. Because, while the rest of the world farewells the British Prime Minister, Anderson Henley, I farewell my father.


After what feels like the longest service in history—with all eyes peering at me, judging my every reaction, documenting them—we finally return to Downing Street.

Number 10 hasn't changed. It stands proud in all its Georgian history and grandeur. The clean, short street leads to the famous black door. A sad and gloomy building, with its dark bricks and plain, white sash windows. To so many it is an icon. To me it's a barrier and a bubble. One I wish I could burst.

My mother leads the way to a reception room, its Victorian candy-striped wallpaper and antique furniture as heavy and solemn as the occasion.

'The service was everything I knew it would be, dear Mia,' Sir Thomas says. He is…was my father's right-hand man. He grips my shoulder with large, stubby fingers. He probably means to show support, but I want to shake him off. He's no comfort to me. He knows everything that's gone on these last few years.

But, as always, I hold my tongue and smile my reply.

'Thank you, Sir Thomas,'

I'm shuffled around as another cabinet member slinks over. Bradley what's-his-face; greasy hair and false smile. 'Yes. Lovely service, Mia'

I smile meekly in return.

'Mia, dear.' Bradley's wife kisses my cheeks with her pale and over-rouged ones. 'He will be sadly missed, my dear.' She pats my shoulder. 'But, at least you're home for summer. You can help your mother find a new home. I expect you need to get on that soon, dear. It would be inappropriate if you lingered here.'

I stand there, stunned, clenching my fists. 'Yes, thank you for that kind reminder, Ethel.'

Her name's not Ethel. She knows I know that.

'Edith, dear. Edith,' she grits.

'Oh, of course. So sorry.' I grin and move away.

More people murmur polite lies, throw in a false smile and look at me with false sympathy. Amongst people such as these I must play the game. I've learnt to be smart. To be tactful. Usually. No point running my mouth off or reacting to their bad behavior. I realised a long time ago that I don't respect the majority. So, I smile and nod. Then walk away.

I spot a tray with glasses of wine and what looks to be whisky, and have the sudden urge to down a whole bloody bottle. Then take another to my designated rooms and drink that while washing this day away in the tub.

When I turn from the waiter holding my wine, my best friend, Jess, is there.

Thank God.

She's my saviour. The only person in this room I have anything in common with. If I could, I'd take her and the bottle of whisky and we could drown our sorrows together. We've been friends for eight years. She's practically part of the family. I think my parents like her... liked her better than me, which is fine by me.

She kisses my cheek, genuinely, and fiddles with her bizarre necklace of tiny silver skull charms. That will make it into tomorrow's papers. And she won't care. Her eyes are puffy from crying and I give her a hug.

'He's here,' she murmurs, glancing over her shoulder.

I freeze and try to mask my emotions. Then I raise my glass to my lips, and my eyes to hers.

'Who's here?' is my stupid question, because I know.

'He who shall not be named. Now—' she leans in closer to whisper '—are you going to keep it together? Or are you going lose your shit and need me to create a diversion? And do not bullshit me.'

Before I get a chance to respond, I look up and my eyes collide with his. I turn away. My heart kicks up a beat...or ten, and my stomach drops.

Jess looks to him and back to me. 'Diversion it is. Say the word and I'll trip and spill booze on some uptight arse. Even better if it's someone I can knee in the balls because they voted for that other chap.'

I try to chug my wine without being too obvious.

'Don't look now,' Jess mutters, tossing back her wine, 'but here comes our favorite little secretary, Adele.'

'Oh, there you are, Mia.' Adele's saccharine tone doesn't fool me.

I turn mid swallow and freeze with my glass still pressed to my lips. All breath is knocked out of me and my heart threatens to jump from my chest. I stare into whisky-coloured eyes, flecked with green, and try to regain my façade of gracious calm.

'You remember Curtis Harrington, I'm sure.' Adele smiles like a cat and adds, 'You two knew each other quite well, didn't you?' She pats his arm. 'He's set to fill your father's shoes. Youngest PM in history.'

'Jesus, Adele, a little sensitivity for Christ's sake.' The deep timbre of his voice rocks me to the core.

Adele at least has the decency to look sheepish. 'Of course. Forgive me, Mia'

I slice my gaze back to Curtis and Adele quietly shuffles away.

For a moment, we stare at each other. I've really no clue what to say. What do I say to the man I fell madly in love with four years prior? The man who destroyed me.

'Mia...' He grimaces. 'God, Mia. I'm more sorry than I can say.' He tilts his head.

I loved it when he used to do that. I drink him in. All six-foot-with-pristine-black-suit-and-charcoal-tie. And those warm-whisky eyes, and messy deep brown hair. If I look to his shoes I know I'll find them perfectly shined. Impeccable and divine doesn't even begin to describe him.

'There you are, Curtis darling,' a woman's voice purrs behind me.

I turn to see my absolute opposite. Straight blonde hair, blue eyes, pale skin. She grabs his forearm. Almost spills his tumbler filled with what will be whisky. Her intention is clear—to show me they're together.

I can't do it. I can't stand here and play nice. Not today. I must escape, before I lose myself completely.

'If you'll excuse me? Curtis, it was nice to see you again.' I dart away, my heart thudding and tears stinging my eyes. I head down the corridor, past the winding stairs and down another corridor. With cameras outside the front door, I can only hide, deep in the house. I slip into one of the many sitting rooms and shut the door, embracing the silence.

But being here, alone, for the first time in nearly five days, the grief and loneliness shrouds me in its dark weight.

I kick off my shoes relishing the comfort of the soft carpet. On an antique French sideboard stands a drinks tray with decanter and cut-crystal glasses. I don't usually drink whisky, but my frayed nerves need something. I shouldn't be surprised he's here. As Adele said, he's set to take my father's place. Move into this house. I scoff out loud at the irony.

The door clicks. I spin to find I'm no longer alone. Curtis stands with his back against the closed door, looking like he's just stepped off a red carpet.

We stare at each other again, in silence. My heart falters as all the air is sucked from my lungs. The room is too small and my senses are overcome with all that is Curtis.

'She's no one,' he says.

I freeze, not knowing how to respond to that unexpected statement.

He shrugs. 'I didn't want you to think I bought a girlfriend to your father's funeral.'

Oh. I nod. 'It's fine. But thanks.' He always was a good man. Raised by a single mother, not to privilege like so many others here today. And it shows in how he treats people. Most people.

His stare intensifies. 'How are you holding up?'

I turn back to the decanter and pour my drink. My hands shake.

'I'm not even sure how to answer that, to be honest.'

I pour him a drink, too. When I turn to hand it to him, he's right in front of me. I jump and barely keep the whisky in the glasses. I remember that, too. His confidence and charisma—and how he moves with purpose and stealth.

I take a step back and shove the glass into his hand. 'Listen here, Romeo, seeing as how your priorities have never been on anything but yourself. You can drop the little white knight act and run back to your minions.'

His mouth curves into smirk. 'Is that bitterness I hear? It really doesn't suit you.'

His fingers brush mine as he accepts the glass and I snatch my hand away.

'No. Not bitterness, a little thing called attention to detail,' is my pathetic comeback.

'You've missed one very important detail.' He moves in closer and I retreat further, until the backs of my thighs hit the solid oak desk.

'That is?' I try to keep my breathing under control and fail.

'I always go after what I want, and I always win.' He grins, his eyes gleaming in the dim light. He plucks the glass from my slack fingers and places both tumblers on the desk.

I lean away and glare. 'Ah. So, this is about winning. I'm some little trophy to get you in good with the rest of your party?'

'That's bullshit and you know it.'

His hot breath sends goose bumps across my skin. His scent, all masculine and strong, is all I can absorb and nothing else exists. He overpowers my senses and renders me useless. He is my Achilles heel.

But I can't be his toy or a pawn in his political game. I've been trapped by these people for nearly eight years. I've been pulled and pushed in every direction they required. No more.

'Step back,' I whisper without looking at him.

'Is that what you really want?' he murmurs, and holds my hand against his chest. His heart is thundering, too. The warmth of his hand on mine, the strength in that touch, overwhelms me. He draws me in, drags me back into the depths of both my desire and my need.

I've missed him every second of every day.

'I don't want you to walk away again, Mia,' he says. His head lowers and our lips are just a breath apart.

'What about what I want?' I ask as I lift my eyes to meet his. Oh, God how I want him. But I'll be lost in the gravity of his ambitions.

His hand slides to the back of my neck and his lips capture mine. With one scorching touch from him, everything falls away. The pressure, the expectations, the constant judgement. All that remains is him and me. His hard body presses against mine, our mouths duelling, desperate to go deeper, to fuse, to rediscover us, to absorb each other.

There's a knock on the door. We both snap out of our haze and turn to look.

'Curtis, you in there, mate?' comes a muffled voice from behind the door.

And I take the opportunity to push free. I snatch up my shoes, rush to the other door and dash out. I make it around the corner and lean against the wall, attempting to find my breath. And my head.

'What was that about, mate?'

Sounds like Gareth, Curtis' best friend.

'Nothing,' is Curtis' short response.

'She ran out of here like you'd lit a fire, mate. Didn't seem like nothing.'

'Just drop it.'

And my heart sinks.

I make it to the bedroom on the fourth level. I lock the door, unzip my dress and flick on the light to the cavernous marble bathroom. I don't dare look in the mirror because I know I'll only see the shadows of lies. Instead, I turn on the shower and slide to the shower floor, allowing myself and my sorrows to be washed away by the water.

I sob so deeply my breaths are gasps and my limbs shake with lack of air, and I finally release grief so heavy that I can no longer stand under its weight. How did things get so painful and out of hand? How do lies and deceit creep up so slowly that people think it's acceptable? That a small lie and then another lie aren't a big deal. Until those lies come tumbling out so frequently it seems normal?

Once out of the shower, I drag on yoga pants, socks, and a t-shirt then climb into the giant bed and settle for the first time today. Trying to watch the telly to distract myself fails when the funeral is all over the news. I switch it off.

My phone chimes. Jess has texted me.

Jess: *You ok? Curtis came back in and drank two straight whiskys. Now that blond bimbo is hanging off his arm.*

Me: *Fine. He was being all compelling. I just couldn't face it. Coffee tomorrow?*

Jess: *Done. Give me the details then. Sleep good.*

My phone chimes again. A number I don't recognise. But I know who it is.

Curtis: *Come back downstairs.*

Me: *You don't need me there. You've got my mother and your lady-friend. She can fill in for me.*

Curtis: *I told you. She's no one.*

I sigh and type back: *What you do is none of my business.*

My phone rings. My finger lingers over the slide button but I'm so achingly tired I don't have the strength.

Curtis: *Answer your phone!*

Me: *No.*

Curtis: *Fine. You want to act like a child? Go for it. But pay attention, sweetheart.*

Curtis: *I made a mistake. I should have fought harder. You may be the daughter everyone knows. But to me you're the one I never should have let go. And never will, again!*

I sit up, suddenly awake. And confused. I don't respond. I don't know how to. I turn off my phone, slide it under the pillow and burrow under the covers. I can't give in to the hope. Because I know I will not survive the crushing reality.

Fire.

Fire is all around me. But somehow the heat isn't suffocating me. I don't feel trapped or scared. The flames are protecting me. Forming a shield. Against what, I don't know. But, for the first time, I feel secure.

I wake with a start from the dream, and stare at the ornate, plastered ceiling. Wondering if yesterday was all a horrible dream.

Someone bashes and bangs in the hallway. The peaceful moment shatters. I press a pillow over my face and scream into it, resisting the urge to get up and investigate. Probably none of my business. There's always something going on.

I used to love that this house was filled with noises and chatter and a flurry of activity. That some of the most incredible decisions had been made under this roof—both good and bad. I got a thrill from being around some of the greatest minds in the country and knowing that so much information passed through these walls.

Then the walls closed in on me, and my parent's obsession with power and public image took over. They chose country over their own daughter—a painful daily fact of life. I was trapped. A liability and part of the 'image'.

More thumping outside. I make my way to the door and swing it open, only to find two sets of eyes on me. One pair whisky-warm.

'What are you doing here?' I snap.

'Morning.' He smirks. 'Nice socks.'

I look down. My feet are covered in unicorns. I shrug, pretending I don't care.

He, of course, is perfect and polished. He's wearing tailored dark blue trousers, a matching vest and white shirt with rolled-up sleeves displaying muscled arms.

'What are you doing here?' I repeat and fold my arms. His gaze dips to my chest then returns to my eyes.

'Moving in.' He gives a one-shouldered shrug. 'I know it's fast after the funeral. Sorry. Parliament insisted.'

I shut my gaping mouth. 'What do you mean, moving in?'

'I mean I'm moving in.' He holds up both hands in the surrender position. 'Like I said: not my choice. If it were up to me I'd wait a couple of weeks to give you and your mother time, but...'

'That's preposterous. You can't do that. I don't care what Parliament says.'

His expression turns gentle. 'Sweetheart, I just did.'

'Right. Well I'm moving out, then.' I jam my hands on my hips. 'Today.'

'Ah, no.' His fabulous mouth twists into a wry smile. 'You don't want to do that.'

'Oh, really? And why is that?'

He walks towards me and looks down, deep into my eyes. 'Because you've got nowhere to go. Now you've finished your work contract, I mean.'

My heart sinks. Because he's right.

I huff. 'What? You've been checking up on me?'

He grins. The cheeky sod.

I turn and stomp back into my rooms, my stomach knotted and

hands trembling. Bloody control-freak men. I fling the door shut but it doesn't slam.

I look back.

He stands in the middle of my room and places his hands on his hips. He's not intending to go anywhere, by the looks of it.

'Let's do this, shall we?' he says.

I swallow, trying to maintain anger when all I can look at are his hands on those narrow hips. And all I can think about is what he used to do with those long fingers.

I throw my hands out. 'Do what? Seriously, what the hell do you want from me, Curtis?'

He shuts the door gently, folds his arms and plants his feet wide.

'The truth,' is his blunt response.

I fold my arms, too, and lift my chin. 'What truth?'

'Don't play games with me, Mia. Let's go. The whole truth.'

And that's it. I don't know if its exhaustion, grief, or just that I've had it with the façade, and the games, and the lies. I relax my arms and look straight at him.

'Fine. I wanted you. I wanted you more than anything in this entire world.' My voice cracks with each word.

He rocks back on his heels a little, eyebrows raised. I don't know if it's from my words or he's surprised I'm telling him the truth.

I swipe a hand over my face and continue, 'And he took you away from me.'

His brow furrows. 'Meaning?'

'My father.'

Curtis' frown deepens. 'What are you saying?'

I sigh and look away. 'It was him and his men. Not me, never me. They gave me a choice.' I curl a lip. 'Because it would never sit well in the press if the PM's daughter was flouncing around under the same roof with a man five years older. A man with political ambition.'

I turn to the window. Outside, the cameras are still there. Always there. Waiting. Waiting to pounce. Waiting to see weakness, or any crack in the armour.

One points at my window and I let the curtain drop. 'Father knew how strong a candidate you were. He knew if he taught you, then when his time as PM was up, he wouldn't lose control. Because he'd tie you so close to him, politically, that you'd need him.'

I laugh bitterly. 'But dating me would have been a disaster, apparently. So, I was told to end it—simply and without dramatics.' Now I look over my shoulder at him. 'Or they'd ruin your career.'

Curtis' jaw is set to stone and a muscle tics in his cheek. He stares blankly past me, his face hard.

But I don't allow myself to be deterred. Maybe, if I get this all out, we can finally move on.

'I told them where they could stick their pipes and smoke them.' I say on a half-laugh. One of my favourite memories is the look on my father's face when I said that. 'I stormed out and found you. We went for lunch. Do you remember that day?'

Curtis nods, his jaw remains tense.

I shake my head, my throat tight. 'You'd had a big promotion that morning. Which I knew was them pulling you in deeper. You were lit up with excitement.' I remember the crushing disappointment that look on his face afforded me. 'You said, *Baby, this is so great. I'm getting away from the shithole of my family's bad choices. Everyone doubted me, but I'm going to make something of myself and prove them all wrong.*'

When he frowns again, I continue, 'Yeah. You remember.' I nod and spread my hands. 'So, I came back here and agreed. The rest, you know. I went away to work at the other end of the country and you all immersed yourselves in politics. It was the most important thing to you. To both of you,' I finish, not hiding the bitterness.

I don't tell him the rest. There's no point. He'd only deny it.

Curtis glares down at me, pinning me in place. 'So, you just…decided for me, huh?' He grabs a handful of his hair then begins to pace. 'Christ, Mia! Why the Hell didn't you just tell me? Why didn't you ask me what *I* wanted?'

He looks at me and softly continues, 'I would have given it up for you. I would have fought for everything we had. My career is not what makes me the man I am. My choices are. And I would have chosen *you*!' He jabs a finger at me. 'You were always more important than this.' He waves a hand at the house.

And this time I'm the one to take a step back. Because I never thought that would be the case. It never even crossed my mind. I open my mouth, then close it again.

Gareth opens the door and looks at us both, warily. 'There's been a development.'

Curtis turns a glare on him. 'What?'

Gareth hesitates and takes a breath. 'Why don't you both come with me?' He turns and walks away, giving us no choice but to follow.

'Gareth,' I call, 'I'll just get changed.' I'd rather not go downstairs in yoga pants and unicorn socks.

Gareth sticks his head back through the door and Curtis walks around behind me.

'No,' they say, together. Curtis' hand gently pushes me forward.

I glare at Curtis but follow Gareth, anyway. Not like the staff haven't seen me like this before. Hopefully there are no dignitaries wandering about the House today.

Gareth's waiting at the bottom of the stairs and he points down the hall. 'We're in the yellow room.'

We walk in. The yellow room is oddly warm and inviting. Yellow walls. Parquetry flooring, a huge walnut table and deep grey high back chairs.

Gareth motions. 'Take a seat.' He smiles at me. How much I've missed the gentle giant. I lost a good friend in Gareth when I split with Curtis.

Curtis pulls the seat out for me. I can't tell anything from the look on his face. He's always been good at hiding his reactions in public. Always had an amazing poker face which, I guess, is one of the reasons he's so successful in politics. I used to love that he never used his poker face around me.

Gareth clears his throat and tosses a manila folder onto the polished table top. 'This arrived this morning. Courtesy of our team.'

Curtis pulls the chair out next to me, sits down and throws the folder open, revealing photos inside. My heart freezes and I grip the chair arms so tightly my fingers ache.

Photos of him and I, taken when we dated. Curtis flips them over. Us eating in a restaurant. Walking through Regent's Park. Curtis' arm flung over my shoulders. In profile, laughing. I remember that day. We'd been to the portrait gallery and walked through for hours admiring all the artwork in silence, except when he'd reach for me. Or when he stood behind me, slid my hair aside and kissed my neck.

He flips that one over to reveal another. Us in the park. Summer, and I was lying on him as he held my hips and laughed.

'What the hell is this? What, we had a bloody stalker or something?' He glares across to Gareth.

'Keep looking,' is Gareth's only response.

Curtis flips through more of the photos.

Then comes the one I've been dreading. It's Curtis, in bed with a woman. Not me. And there's a date stamp. Showing the same summer as the photos before.

My stomach drops and I fear I might be sick. The photo is a little grainy. Taken by some dodgy paparazzi bastard spying through the windows of wherever they were.

'You can't be bloody serious?' Curtis roars, shooting out of his chair so fast it topples back. His poker face is gone, all that remains is rage.

I can't take any more. I throw myself from the room and tear up the stairs. Heavy footsteps thump after me. But I must get away. I can't do this. I've seen those photos before. They ripped me apart then and have the same power to do so now.

I barrel into my rooms and run to the wardrobe. I yank down my suitcase and throw it on the bed. Curtis storms in with Gareth close behind. They both look like they're about to punch something.

I ignore them and start throwing clothes randomly into the suitcase. My chest is yet again cracked open and I am raw and gutted. My throat is so tight I can't speak even if I wanted to.

Gareth shuts the door. Curtis takes one look at me, hesitates, then addresses Gareth. 'Talk to me. What do we know?'

'Set up,' is Gareth's clipped reply. 'Photos are definitely doctored'

Doctored? I pause mid-pack and stare at Gareth.

'I could have told you that, G,' Curtis says. 'Can it be proved, though?'

My heart stutters and I crush a shirt in my hands waiting for the answer.

'Yep.' Gareth brings out the photo and taps the image. 'Our boys say it's obvious. There's a tiny tattoo on this guy's right arm. Dickheads who did the work missed that. Sloppy.' Gareth looks to me and I see the honesty in his eyes.

A tattoo? Fake? How had I missed that last time? My legs give way and I lean against the wall.

'Steps to find out who?' is Curtis' next question.

But Gareth cocks his head and eyes me narrowly.

'What?' Curtis says, frowning.

Gareth draws in breath and points at me. 'You've seen these before.'

It's not a question. And Curtis swings around to face me.

'Have you?' he snaps.

I jump and look away. What am I supposed to say? That I have and it almost destroyed me? That, after that lunch—his excitement about his career—I realised I would never be as important as this house, and his career, and those photos were just the final nail.

But that had all been a lie, apparently.

When I don't respond, Curtis returns to Gareth. 'Explain, G. Who?'

Gareth watches me closely 'Her father...and Jess. They set it up. The woman is Jess in a wig. The man some actor they hired.'

I hear a keening sound. It's coming from me.

'My father and my best friend?' I whisper. I fold over because someone has sucker-punched me in the stomach. I want to vomit, or cry, or scream. I don't know which.

Curtis grabs me, pulling me against his chest. And I let him and absorb his heat. His strength.

Gareth clears his throat. 'Adele, Sir Thomas' secretary, knew. Came clean. They set it up. Wanted to bring you both down. The PM so he could keep you on track, Curt. Jess...' He pauses and I look up from Curtis' chest, waiting. Wanting to know but not wanting to at the same time.

Curtis nods. 'What is it, mate? I think we've suffered at the lies long enough. Don't you?'

Gareth grimaces. 'They were having an affair.'

My mouth drops open.

Curtis curses, 'Jesus Christ.'

But my only reaction is, 'Ewwwww. Seriously? Eeeeeww!'

Curtis and Gareth both look at me and burst out laughing.

I push away from Curtis and scowl. 'It's not funny. This is some seriously crazy dramatic soap opera crap.' Then I can't stay still. I start pacing. 'I mean, seriously? She ate dinner with us at the country house. She used to go—' I gasp and close my eyes '—swimming with my father. Eeeeewww! They were hooking up in the pool house!' Now I really want to vomit.

The boys are still laughing, and I glare at them.

Curtis sobers and shakes his head. 'Oh, baby. I know this is messed up. But the joke's on them. They were hooking up and worked hard to derail us, but here we are.'

His expression gentles and he touches my cheek. 'Don't let them win.'

I look at him doubtfully. We've got a long way to go. 'But I don't understand why they wanted to succeed in the first place.' I lift my eyes to him. 'Why was I so wrong for you, anyway?' My voice is small and needy. I hate that, but the hurt hasn't gone. Curtis might not have done what they said, but he hadn't fought very hard for me, either. And my father and best friend betrayed me.

Gareth smiles wryly and slips out of the room.

Curtis shrugs, his mouth twisting. 'Jealousy of both of us, maybe? You're one of the smartest people I know. And way classier and kinder than Jess.'

I flush. No one ever compliments me. Ever.

He catches my chin and turns my face so I must look at him. 'Sometimes people can't handle it. They try to bring people down. Like your father always belittled others.' He shrugged. 'And they might succeed, initially, but long term it doesn't work. Their colours always shine through. People see who they are, decide they don't like it and get jack of them.'

He moves closer and tucks my hair behind my ear. 'The worst part, though, is the collateral damage done to someone undeserving—like you.' His lips brush my forehead. 'People like that are so self-absorbed they can't see past the jealousy, or the need to keep up with the Joneses. But that's what makes us better. Because we want more but not at the expense of others. We don't need to pull people down.'

'No.' I shake my head and look him in the eyes 'I don't think I can do this again. I can't be here, live here. This house, the politics, these people, they almost ate me up. It could destroy us.'

He moves his arms around my waist and my fears dissolve.

'People are the same no matter where you go, or where you live, baby. It's not about the house or any other house or place. It's about the people in it.' He pulls back to look at me with those warm eyes.

'You can't change them. You can only work at becoming a better person, yourself, and not buying into their bullshit. Now we get to choose who's in this house. So, let's choose the right people.'

I chew on my lip and slide my gaze away. 'I can't, Curtis. I can't be a dutiful decoration again. I can't put what I want on hold and be the PM's...what?'

He pulls back and frowns. 'I'm not your father, Mia. I won't treat you like he treated your mother. And I'll support your career, or anything else you want to do.' He kisses my cheek and I shiver. 'We can be happy here. And I will tear myself up making sure that happens. Let's do this together, create our life and make a difference along the way. I will put you first. Always. But I need you to trust me.'

Tears blur his face and the room, spilling onto my cheeks. And I can't stop them.

Curtis picks me up and carries me to the bathroom. He sits me on the marble bench, wets a cloth, accidentally soaking his shirt. He shrugs and gently wipes the tears from my face. I touch his chest. Feeling all the warmth and comfort radiating off him.

'Now it's just you and me,' he murmurs. 'You should have shared all of this with me, though. Saved us the heartache.'

'I'm sorry,' is all I can manage.

His lips quirk. 'I'll take that.'

I stare at my hands, twisting in my lap. 'You make it all seem so simple. I'm just not sure it is.'

He cups my face and says with certainty, 'It's only hard if we make it that way.' He kisses me briefly. Too briefly. Then pulls back and plucks at his wet shirt and vest. He turns away and yanks off first the vest then the white shirt.

I gasp.

Curtis pauses and glances back over his shoulder. 'What's wrong?'

I swallow, shake my head and point. Stretched across his back is a curving bundle of flames. And, in the middle of his back, across the sculpted muscle is one word.

FIRE.

'Fire. Fire on your back,' I whisper.

He grins. 'Yeah, got that about a year ago. That was my nickname when I raced. The support crew said I burned around the track like a wall of fire.' He shrugs and gives me his trademark cheeky grin that warms my heart every single time.

I stare into his eyes and I'm absorbed by his strength.

He is my firewall. My shield.

Maybe he always was.

# WATER

# Water Music

*Megan Badger*

When the work bell rang, Terjei rushed to leave. His father called out, but Terjei ran, pretending not to hear. If he could only put off learning the business for a while longer. Nothing could be more tedious than keeping the accounting books for Father's mill. Stuck here forever in this tiny, boring village. Dead before he even got to live.

Terjei followed the mill stream as it wended its way through the undergrowth. Birds twittered and flitted in the branches and small creatures rustled in the thickets. He envied their freedom.

A breeze caressed his cheek and carried with it the faintest hint of music; a light and joyful dance tune. The notes were clear as birdcalls, and as bright.

Who played so well? The stream led him to where the forest became wild and tangled. The music grew louder. He quickened his pace, excited as a child who hears the festival pipes and knows joy is close at hand. He fought his way through a last thorny thicket and emerged to a rocky riverbank below a waterfall.

A beautiful, fair-haired youth in an elegant red wool coat sat perched on one of the dark rocks. The youth's copper-coloured skin glowed with a tinge of green. He held, of all things, a fiddle.

Oh, what sweet music poured from his bow. Cascading like falling water, resounding from the rocks, dancing on the wind. Terjei stood, entranced, and the hair lifted on his neck. The water skipped and the trees swayed as though the music moved them.

And it moved Terjei. Pulled by his heart strings, Terjei followed where the music led, out from the cover of trees. A fine mist from the waterfall dampened his cheeks—or was it tears?

The youth turned toward him with a grin. 'Hello, boy. I'm Hemming. And you are?' The youth held out a hand. Terjei's mouth popped open and he stared.

'Do you talk, boy? Or are you content to stand there gaping like a trout?' Hemming took a small tin of rosin from inside his coat and rubbed it on the bow hairs.

'Pardon, sir. I'm Terjei.' He moved forward to shake hands. 'You play so well, I couldn't help but stop to listen.'

'There's no harm done.' The youth tucked the rosin away and turned to go.

'Wait!' Terjei grabbed his arm. The youth glared and Terjei swore his eyes flashed green. He let go. 'Sorry.'

Hemming tapped his foot. 'Well? What do you want?'

'I love music.' Terjei gazed at Hemming's instrument. A Hardanger fiddle, with a scene painted on it depicting a woman with a fish's tail, holding a happy baby.

Hemming looked down at it smiling. 'As do I.' Silence stretched out and the youth plucked idly at the strings, one fine brow raised and a faint smile on his lips.

'My father won't let me play.' Terjei's voice cracked. 'He has the most beautiful fiddle. It calls to me and I just know I could play it and I wouldn't torture the strings as he does.'

'Ah.' Hemming's mouth pulled into a tight line and his brow furrowed.

The words came rushing out. 'And I so long to learn. You could teach me?' Terjei turned his eyes to the youth.

Hemming's eyebrows shot up. 'I'm sure I could, if I were asked.'

Terjei's mouth dropped open again. 'My apologies. Hemming, will you teach me?' He held his breath.

'For a price.'

'But I haven't any money.' Terjei scrambled to think of what he could offer.

'I have no need of money. What I have a particular fondness for is brännvin.'

'Brännvin? The liquor?'

'Yes. If you bring some brännvin every day I will give you lessons.'

'Oh, thank you.' He shook Hemming's hand which was uncommonly damp. 'I won't let you down.'

'I believe you, Terjei.' Hemming chuckled. 'I'll see you tomorrow.'


Terjei approached home slowly, holding on to delicious excitement as long as he could. The house was a squat little cabin, nestled on a green bank by the creek. A heron nested in the corner where the chimney met the roof. The roof itself was covered in a thick blanket of moss which edged the stones of the walls like a boy's first beard.

The aroma of fresh bread and a rich meaty stew wafted from the open window. Inside, his mother bustled backward and forward past the window, her thick hourglass body more gnomish than anyone's he'd ever met. He smiled and walked around to the main door.

'Terjei.' She kissed his cheeks. 'You're sprouting up like a weed. You'll not fit through the door if you keep growing.' She wiped her hands on a white apron.

'Tish, Mother.' Terjei brushed a strand of greying hair from her face and tucked it behind her ear. 'Father will be home just past dusk. He's finishing accounts.'

'That man will find an early grave, working so.' She looked past him into the orange afternoon and closed the door. 'Go wash up for supper.'

'Yes, Mother.'

The kitchen was warm, the hearth fire reduced to a blanket of red embers for cooking. The square, scrubbed-wooden table was bordered by three carved wooden chairs. Terjei paused on his way to the pump. His father's Hardanger fiddle stood in pride of place, on a shelf behind Father's chair.

Its small, tubby body extended into a long swan-like neck that ended in the carved head of a beautiful woman. Her siren's call burned, deep in Terjei's bones. The fiddle's body was inlaid with mother-of-pearl in an intricate design of half circles like waning moons, and the pegs were made of bone.

Father liked to frighten him, when he was a child, by saying the pegs were made from the bones of children. He had told Terjei that a witch ate the hearts of naughty boys who played music.

Terjei's chest hurt to look at the fiddle. His body itched to hold it. He had been beaten many times for touching it. Every night he stared over his father's shoulder at the fiddle. It taunted him with the promise of freedom and joy and the music that pulsed in his blood. He would offer his heart to the witch for that.

He hid a smile and turned away.

Terjei and his mother were seated at the table when his father entered. Terjei's mother let out a breath and her shoulders relaxed.

'What time do you call this? And us just sitting to wait like a pair of barn owls for the mice,' she said, and rose to bring the food.

'And swooping on me the same.' He sat at the table, his dark hair peppered with grey like a wolf, his steel eyes piercing his son.

'Terjei, you're working hard. But you ran off fast today. I was hoping we could get started on teaching you the books.'

Terjei's throat tightened.

'You should get to know the business. It'll be yours one day after all. Tomorrow, then? What say you?'

Terjei's eyes darted to the fiddle and back to meet his father's. There was no escape from this.

'Thank you. Father. Of course, I would be honoured.' His voice shook but he held his father's gaze.

'Good.' His father smiled and took a swig from the mug of Brännvin that Mother had poured for him.

Terjei's skin prickled and a shiver ran down his back. Mother placed a bowl of stew in front of him and his stomach lurched, his appetite gone.

After dinner, his Father picked up the fiddle and played, as he had every evening that Terjei could remember. The first nasal notes picked up a scale and transitioned into a jaunty tune. Small puffs of dust rose where his father's foot tapped the floor.

His mother embroidered a length of cloth, her head nodding in time to the music. Terjei stared at the fiddle. The bow and instrument danced together and light winked from the polished wood.

He longed to reach out to it, to hold it, to make it sing. Occasional discordant notes cried out as his father's hands grew clumsy with drinking, his rough playing causing the strings to squeal.

Terjei couldn't take any more. He stood and kissed his mother's cheek. The music followed him down the hall and seemed to sob outside his door as he fell asleep.

Tomorrow the music would be his. The fiddle and her magic in his hands. Even if just for a little while. And Father need never know.

At the first stirrings of the dawn birds, Terjei rose to do his chores, unable to spend another minute in bed.

'Terjei, what's gotten into you?' His mother smiled as he brought in the milk pail and sat it beside the door.

'Nothing, Mother. I woke early and thought I'd get a start.'

'More likely you're possessed by the *nisse*.' She tousled his hair.

At breakfast Terjei watched his father fork each mouthful, watched his father's jaw move as he chewed. By the time the plates were cleared Terjei was jittery.

While his parents said their goodbyes for the day Terjei crept into the kitchen. There was the Hardanger fiddle, its polished wood glinting in the dim light. He sucked in a breath and held it for a long tense minute. Before his mother could return, he grabbed the fiddle and dashed away.

The air of the forest was close and every creak of branches or scurrying of small creature made him jump. He took a more direct route to the waterfall this time and, on stepping through the trees, saw Hemming, in the same elegant red coat, sitting by the water and playing. Birds dipped and swooped over the water. Frogs from the reeds croaked the beat in a harmonious chorus.

'Did you bring it?' The youth continued to play and didn't look up. Terjei took the corked bottle from his coat pocket.

'Three drops; in the water, if you please.'

A strange request but Terjei obeyed. The drops sat like oil on the surface and drifted with the current into the foamy maelstrom where the water fell. The music stopped.

'Show me. How do you hold a fiddle in your hands?'

Terjei looked down at his father's fiddle. It was truly the most beautiful thing the family owned. He traced the rosing pattern on the body. The woman's face carved into the scroll was so lifelike that he wondered if she would one day awaken and speak to him.

'Come along now,' Hemming interrupted, 'let me see it.'

Hemming held out his hand, snapping his fingers impatiently. Terjei hugged the fiddle to his chest. What if this stranger stole the fiddle? His father would know he had taken it; how much Terjei coveted the forbidden music. He trembled at the thought of his father's rage, and then took a breath. But there was no-one else to learn from, and the music wouldn't be denied.

Terjei passed the fiddle to Hemming who started to tune it. The discordant notes were twisted into submission until they too flowed like water.

'There now. That should make things better.' Hemming passed the fiddle back to Terjei. 'Show me what you know.'

Terjei lifted the fiddle to his chin and played the few scales he had practised in secret. The screeching notes made the hair prickle at the back of his neck.

'Enough!' Hemming grimaced. 'Show me your hands.'

Terjei held out his hands. Hemming turned them over and scoffed as he slapped them away.

'You have hands like a baby, all soft and pink and new. The instrument will never sing for you unless you're willing to bleed for the music. Are you willing to bleed?'

Terjei thought about the music Hemming played.

'If I do, will I be able to enchant the water and the trees the way you do?'

'In time, perhaps,'

'Then yes, I'm willing to bleed.'

Hemming grabbed Terjei's wrist. With his other hand he grabbed the fiddle. Terjei pulled back but the willowy youth was stronger than he appeared. Hemming crushed Terjei's hand and pushed his splayed fingers across the strings, backward and forward until blood came, and pain with it.

And Terjei was free. He wrapped his hand in a handkerchief and scowled at the boy, who stared intently at the strings. The blood glowed faintly and seemed to be absorbed.

'Yes,' said Hemming, 'you see?' He held out the fiddle. 'You must season the strings with your blood before the music will come.'

Terjei stared from the strings to Hemming. 'Are you a witch?' His heart jumped.

The youth looked into Terjei's eyes and Terjei saw himself reflected in deep pools full of dancing lights and shadowy nooks where lovers might meet in secret.

'I'm no witch, but there is magic in music. I am merely a vessel for that particular enchantment. Go, now. Come back tomorrow and we'll begin.'

Work became even more of a chore. Terjei was moved from the mill storehouse to learn the accounts. Four whitewashed walls and a large wooden desk. Books of lines and columns and numbers. And a ticking clock counting each second like a whip lashing his brain.

Beside the mill, the stream ran, gurgling and sparkling, into the woods and he longed to run with it.

Each morning he left home early, fiddle in hand, heart thumping. Each lesson began with the payment of three drops of brännvin into the clear pool. Then Terjei sat with Hemming and listened.

'You cannot play the wilds until you hear them with your body.' Hemming raised his face to the sky and closed his eyes.

So Terjei sat, his body quivering with concentration. The wind rustled the trees and a gnat buzzed by his ear. Salmon plopped and splashed in the water and the reeds and rushes whispered. But it made no sense. It was just noise. Distractions. Terjei wriggled on the damp sand and scratched his ear.

'Sit still, for goodness sake,' Hemming said.

For weeks the lessons were sitting and listening. Surely, it was all a trick? One day his father would discover the fiddle gone and Terjei would have nothing to show for the punishment. He stared down at the fiddle in his lap, still and silent, and sighed.

Then, one soft autumn morning when mist hung low over the stream, the discordant notes of nature began to blend. An elusive pattern to their sounds emerged. Melodies of water, wind, and reed.

'There! You hear it, don't you?' said Hemming, eyeing him intently. 'Now, pick up your bow.'

And the music came, slowly at first and haltingly.

Hemming gripped his shoulder. 'Not all at once, try the water'

Terjei played the soft lulling of rippling pools. Trios of notes and a soft back chord. Then the babbling of a brook over stones, quick and light, bow tripping on the strings.

Hemming touched Terjei's cheek. 'You have it in you; the water-music. It's in your blood.' And Terjei blushed to the roots of his hair.

'Hmm.' Hemming tapped a finger to his lips. 'Now that we have progressed to more complex lessons the payment will need to increase.'

'But I can't take any more, he'll notice,' Terjei said, then clasped his hand over his mouth as Hemming's eyebrow rose.

'The acceptable payment will now be a pinch of damp snuff.'

'But—'

'Good day, Terjei. Until next time.' The youth walked into the mist of the waterfall and disappeared.

Where could he get snuff? He had only ever seen people partake it at weddings where his father played the fiddle.

That evening after dinner Terjei remained at the table.

'Father, when are you playing again? At a wedding?' he clarified.

'Why, Terjei, are you looking to find a young lass to dance

with?'

Terjei grinned. 'Well, maybe it's time I started thinking about settling down.' He blushed at the lie.

His father smiled. 'Hmm, there's a young couple tying the knot on the eve of tomorrow. I can bring you along,'

'Thank you, Father,'

'All right, now.' His father took down the fiddle and began to practice some celebration songs.

But the music was missing something. It had rhythm, and melody, but no soul. No…connection to the Earth. Terjei fled the room, unable to bear it.


The bride and groom arrived, with hands bound together, laughing. A cheer went up from the crowd. His father took this cue to begin playing and the wedded pair turned in circles to the music.

Terjei's eyes passed over the guests until he saw an older gentleman open a small wooden box and pinch some snuff between his fingers. The room was warm and the man took off his coat and hung it over the back of a chair.

Terjei inched closer to the chair, watching the dancers as his nimble fingers reached into the coat pocket for the box. His hand wrapped around it. He secreted the box into his own pocket and untucked his shirt to cover the lump.

As they walked home, the evening air was misty and soft with the moon's cool light.

'So, what did you think Terjei?' his father asked.

'Father, why can't I play your fiddle?' Terjei asked. Father held the fiddle slung under one arm. The woman's face was turned away from him.

'It's not for you,' he snapped, his brow darkening.

'But why—?'

His father's free hand whipped out and slapped Terjei hard

across his cheek.

'This is not for discussion. Are we in agreement?'

Terjei pressed his cold fingers to his cheek, his eyes watering. 'Yes, Father,' he choked.

His father nodded and turned away. 'Come now, let's get home. Mother will worry.'

The pinch of snuff spun down under the water, releasing a fine stream of bubbles. Terjei took up his bow and played the water. Hemming stood by him.

'Yes, yes. Now find the mood. Feel the playfulness and play it.'

The bow skittered on the strings in melodic runs. The music skipped and played in Terjei's ears.

'Good, now listen for the grief.'

Terjei stopped. How could water grieve? But as he stood there the mist from the waterfall wet his cheeks. Chill and thin like an abandoned child's hopeless tears. Shadows deepened against the rocks. The falling water echoed. It cried out but there was no answer. Deep and hollow, the sound tore at Terjei's heart. He drew the bow across the strings; low, slow deep notes; discordant minor notes with no melodic reprieve. His heart was breaking. The loss in the music echoed in his chest.

'Yes, now—'

'No,' Terjei said. 'That's enough.' And he walked away.

He couldn't bear to go back. A week passed, then another. But the ache in his chest lingered. The sunlight hurt his eyes and he hid in the dim lit house. Mother tried to break his melancholy. She filled the house with candlelight to brighten it for him, but his smile was empty. Worry creased her face and added to his pain. He couldn't bear to distress her.

He took the instrument, which now felt cold to his touch and stirred up fear in his stomach.

Hemming was pacing the shore when Terjei pushed through the undergrowth.

'Well, there you are. Where have you been?'

'What did you do to me?' Terjei stomped forward and shoved Hemming who fell with a thud to the ground.

'I did nothing.' The youth stood and brushed dirt from his pants.

'Liar!' Terjei punched him. Hemming staggered back and looked up with narrowed eyes.

'It was the music, you mooncalf. Music speaks to the soul. You'd be better to ask what you did to yourself.'

Terjei paused. 'How do I make it stop?'

'How do you feel now? Angry?'

Terjei looked at Hemming and felt the hot snake rear its head in his stomach. He wanted nothing more than to punch that ridiculous too-perfect face. He swallowed. 'Yes.'

'So, play it. Listen to it and play it.' Hemming folded his arms. 'Don't try to stop it, *use* it. Make me feel what you feel. You wanted to make the world dance to your tune? This is how you do it.'

Punching sounded easier, and more immediate, but Terjei listened. The water pounded the rocks. It roared and boomed. And he played it, the strings screeching and the bow furiously sawing. His fingers blurred.

'Stop, stop!' Hemming grabbed Terjei's arms and pulled them forward. Terjei's breath was ragged. He felt full of energy. He could play forever.

'Look at the bow.'

Terjei looked. One single hair remained unbroken. He shuddered. There was no way he could hide this from his father. Hemming let him go and reached into a pouch at his side. Terjei thought he saw a flicker of light there. Out from the pouch, Hemming pulled a lock of fine cream horsehair.

'You'd best restring it,' he said, handing the hair to Terjei.

Terjei took his time, letting his heart settle. When he was done, he turned the bow in his hand to feel the balance. The hair glowed gold in the light.

'Thank you,' he said. There was no answer. Terjei looked up and Hemming was gone. He sat for a while by the water and let the peace of the afternoon wash over him.

The lessons followed the moods of the natural world, one damp pinch of snuff for each. Terjei played the moods of the water then moved on to the air. He played howling winds searching for lost love, cheeky breezes that flirted with the hair around his face.

He played sombre storms rolling their slow grumbling way over vast distances, and sudden gusts that tricked and tripped and stole hats and scarves. He played the critters of the woods, the rustling whispers of leaves, and the creak of branches.

'When will we learn to play fire?' Terjei asked one day in early winter when his fingers were almost numb with cold.

'We don't play fire.'

'But, why—'

'Fire takes. It consumes life to live. We don't play it.' Hemming paced beside the water's edge. Terjei said nothing, but ground his teeth and glared. Hemming's steps were fluid, his pants wet to an inch above the hem. His sleeves, too, seemed wet at the tips and drips of water splashed out in arcs when he turned to pace back again.

'What's left for us to play, then?' Terjei said.

Hemming snarled and Terjei cringed.

'There is one final lesson but it has a price you cannot pay.'

'What is it?' Power thrummed through Terjei's body. He was so close to being good enough. So close.

'The eleventh lay. Only night spirits may play it. It has more power than a mortal man can wield.' As he spoke, the shadows in the glade seemed to lengthen, reaching for them. All warmth was sucked from the air and Terjei shivered.

'The eleventh lay is an enchantment,' Hemming murmured, grim. 'When it is played table and bench, grey-beard and grandmother, baby and bairn will be moved to dance. It is pure power. Pure control.' His voice echoed, hollow, and his eyes stared, blank. The shadows wrapped around his legs.

'Stop.' Terjei stepped further into the light. He put up his fiddle and played. He played the light through the leaves, sunlight warm on his face. He played joy. And the shadows receded. Hemming sagged like a puppet released from its strings. He blinked and looked at Terjei.

'You can't afford the cost.'

With the shadows gone, all that remained was a brilliant vision. 'But,' Terjai whispered, 'can you imagine… dancing tables and chairs. And the fortune it would bring. Everyone would know my name. It would be spoken through the ages—'

'Is that what you want? Fame and fortune. Is the music not enough?'

'Of course, but my father would be so proud, and my mother—'

Hemming hissed, 'You have no idea what you ask.'

'I haven't asked anything.' Terjei's blood pulsed with heat and behind his eyelids he saw red. He had to know. He must. His mouth curled in a manic smile. 'You can teach me. Can't you?'

'No.'

'I don't believe you.' Terjei stepped forward, his hands balled into fists.

'No.' Hemming stood his ground. 'I won't do it.'

Tears sprang into Terjei's eyes and rolled down his cheek, cold against his hot flesh. 'Please?' He fell to his knees. 'Please? I've always done as you asked. I'm a good student. Please, give me this last lesson?'

'You fool.' Hemming spat at him, the spittle hitting Terjei's neck and running under his collar before he could wipe it away. 'What of your soul, your mortal heart? Will you give it so willingly?'

Terjei's breath caught in his throat. 'What do you mean? Will I die for it? I don't understand.'

Hemming touched Terjei's wet cheek and looked hard into his eyes. 'You must give of life and forfeit your soul. The cost is the blood of your father.'

Terjei laughed. 'Is that all? What, a drop? A thimbleful?'

'No.' Hemming smiled coldly. 'All of it.'

Terjei tossed in his bed and sat up, punching the blankets off. He had to learn the eleventh lay. Visions of dancing objects spun in his head and he stood in the centre, his bow a wizard's wand, his music magic. But his father's life was not a price he would pay.

There must be some other way.

In the morning, Terjei took an empty milk pail and hid in the far corner of the barn behind the hay pile. He pulled off his trousers and cut a nick in his thigh—he couldn't risk injury to his arms—and bled into the pail. When the blood flow slowed, he wrapped the cut, pulled on his pants and went about his day. His blood was partly his father's, after all.

It took days to fill the pail. As the days went on Terjei grew wan and grey. His skin took on a sickly sheen. But by the fifth day the pail was almost full. For some strange reason, the blood didn't congeal. One more day; one more cut, and it was finished.

Terjei carried the lidded milk pail through the woods to the waterfall. The sloshing of the blood made his stomach lurch. It was a relief to hear the sound of rushing water through the trees.

Hemming sat on a rock in the spray of the falling water playing a haunting tune on the fiddle. His head snapped up when Terjei entered the glade.

'I was sure I'd seen the last of you,' he said. 'You came alone?' The youth craned his neck to look behind Terjei.

'Yes.' Terjei gulped. 'I brought your payment.' He removed the lid and tipped it over. Blood gushed into the water with a sickly glug, glug, glug. The two liquids stayed separate and the rim of the pool swirled with red until it caught in the current of the waterfall which churned it into pink and foaming bubbles. Several small clots were trapped on the shore near the mouth of the can. Terjei vomited onto the stones.

'You did it. I can't believe it!' Hemming rushed to Terjei and threw his arms around the boy, lifting him in the air and spinning him. He kissed Terjei's forehead and skipped toward the edge of the clearing.

But his footsteps slowed. Hemming shook his head and looked to the water, then back towards the cool shadow of the trees. He took another halting half step and stopped. His brow furrowed, then the skin smoothed and his eyes blazed at Terjei.

Hemming roared and charged.

The lithe form grew, a foot or more. The hair writhed down, serpentine, to his hips; her hips. Terjei's mouth dropped open. He stumbled back as Hemming reached him, her arm raised. Her hand swung and struck his cheek. The crack from the blow echoed off the wet stones, across the water. Then another blow, then another. Hemming squeezed Terjei's shoulders, shaking him with each shouted word.

'What did you do, you fiend? What. Did. You. Do?'

Hemming—the woman—held him at arm's length. Her brown hair hung in wild ropes of knots tangled with water weeds. Her pale, green-tinged skin dripped with water. Her eyes glowed green.

'Oh, Terjei, what did you do?' Her shoulders slumped. She reached towards his cheek and he recoiled.

'What's happening? What are you?' He backed away, stumbling, sweating, swallowing.

'Terjei—'

'What are you?' he screamed. A warm, wet trail of urine ran down his leg.

The woman put down her hands and looked into his eyes.

'Please, don't hurt me,' he whimpered.

'Of course, I won't hurt you.' The woman stepped forward but Terjei backed further towards the woods.

'Stay back, witch.' He picked up a stone.

'Terjei, please?'

'I trusted you. Monster. What do you want from me?' Terjei looked left and right for help. His eyes settled on the milk pail. 'My father's blood. Is that what you wanted, all along?'

'It was the only way—'

'For what? What did he ever do to you?'

The woman clenched her fists. 'He trapped me here.' Her voice broke. 'He kept me from you.'

'Wha…?'

She paced in front of him, water spraying from her hems as she turned to face him. 'I am Audun, the deserted. The desolate.' She looked from under her lids at him. 'I'm your mother, Terjei.'

'No.' He squeezed his eyes shut. It was a dream. He would wake up and it would have all been a dream. Cold, damp hands pressed against his cheeks.

'Terjei, look at me.'

He peeked through the cage of his lashes. Her blurred form became clear. Her face was wet with tears. He pulled away from her hands and ran. Branches whipped his body, punishment for making his mother cry. No! His vision blurred. It was a lie. It had to be.

His house crouched in the meadow. Light glinted from the kitchen window like a winking eye, the open door like welcoming arms.

'Terjei? Goodness, child, what in the world happened to you?' Mother took a cloth and wiped at his snotty, tear-stained face.

'Are you my mother?'

'What are you talking about?' She wouldn't meet his eyes.

'I met a woman who says she's my mother. But you're my mother.' Of course, she was. She would wrap him in her warm, familiar hug and everything would be right again.

'Terjei, sit down.' She sighed and pulled out a stool.

Terjei stood where he was.

So, she sat down instead, age and sadness pulling at her beloved face. 'This isn't right. You shouldn't have found out like this. Your father should be here.'

'My father—'

'He never meant it to go so far.' She wrung her apron in white-knuckled hands. 'He loved her so much—'

'Who?' But he already knew. The truth settled in his stomach like a stone.

'Terjei, I'm sorry.'

'I have to go.'

'Terjei, I love you. I always loved you like a son.'

'I love you, too.'

'Wait for your father. Please—'


He walked into the clearing by the pool. His mother sat on a stone, weeping.

'How did he do it? How did he trap you here?' He didn't mean to sound so cold. 'What are you?' Then, old childhood tales whispered in his mind and his breath caught. The fiddle. The water. The unearthly music. 'You're a fossegrim.'

His mother rose in a sweeping motion. Her voice rang in the clearing, 'I am keeper of the waters and pools of this land. I am a fossegrim. A nymph. And a fool for loving your father.' Her form diminished.

'He asked me to teach him to play. So eager. So caring. I fell in love. But he didn't have the soul for the music. His playing...' She shuddered. 'So, he trapped me here with a curse, sealed with silver. His wedding band. It lies in the deep hollow under the waterfall. I can't touch it.' She gestured helplessly at the water.

Terjei removed his coat and stalked into the pool.

His mother raised her head. 'What are you doing?'

'Getting you your freedom'

Terjei dove in. Light glittered on the stones and water weeds danced. He pulled himself along the bed of stones, searching. Twice he came up for air but he wouldn't give up. A deep hollow had formed beneath the pounding waterfall. Terjei allowed the water to push him down. The very bottom was sandy. Small bones and scattered stones nestled there, and a silver ring.

Terjei grabbed it and tried to swim up. The hollow was too narrow to turn in and the water forced him down. He fought to the surface as his throat burned for breath.

He emerged panting and shaking and lay on the stony shore. He put the ring on his finger and sat up.

'I'm ready for my final lesson, Mother.' He walked toward where the fiddle lay.

'I can't.' Audun wrung her hands and shifted from foot to foot.

'But I got the ring.' Terjei hesitated.

'The curse will only break with your father's death.' Her voice sank in a monotone.

Terjei stopped short. 'I don't believe you.'

'Believe what you want, you'll have no more lessons until I am free.' She spun on her heel and disappeared into the waterfall.

Terjei grew hot, rage warming him in his wet clothes. He left the fiddle and stormed back into the woods. His anger billowed out before him like a storm. The birds were silent. No creatures rustled. He marched to the mill. The wind rustled his hair, whispering. He waited until the last worker was gone and his father was alone.

'Father!' His voice cut the cool evening air. A shadow moved in the doorway.

'Terjei, where have you been?' His father stepped through the door, frowning.

'What did you do?' The words shot like arrows at his father.

'What's wrong?' His father glared at him. 'Has something happened to your mother?'

'My mother...' Terjei charged forward and grabbed his father, shaking him. 'Which one?' he screamed.

His father's eyes widened. 'How—'

'I met her. She told me.'

'What did she tell you?' Father's eyes flashed with anger and his muscles tightened under Terjei's grip as he fought to free himself. 'What did that bitch tell you? That she broke my heart? That she abandoned me? That not even binding her could keep her from running away from me? What?'

Terjei had never seen his father so angry.

'Did she tell you I wasn't good enough?' Spittle formed at the corners of his father's mouth. The veins in his temple throbbed. 'That the water called her? That she couldn't fight it? She didn't love me enough to fight it. But I showed her.' His father sneered.

Terjei stumbled back burned by his father's rage. 'You did this.'

'Bitch had it coming.'

'You kept us apart.' Terjei trembled.

'It was for your own good.' His father looked down his nose at Terjei.

'No. You did this for your own good, not mine.' Terjei saw his father clearly for the first time. A bitter old man, his dreams crushed by the mill.

'You hate her because she plays so much better than you. That's why you didn't want me to play the fiddle—because I'm half her child and would play like her. And I might get out of this place, but you never could.'

'Terjei, listen—'

Terjei roared and fell on his father like a waterfall. The old man slipped and his head slammed into a rock by the pool. Blood gushed into the water. Terjei's ears rang. His father moaned.

'Father!' Terjei rushed to the old man's side. What had he done?

His father's eyes blinked open and focused on Terjei. His lip curled back.

'You think you know everything, you little piss-ant. But you're just like her. Not even human. Half-breed. You're nothing. Never have been, never will be.'

Terjei's ears filled with a sound like rushing water. He grasped his father's head. He slammed it again and again into the stone.

'I'm not nothing,' he growled. 'I am not nothing! I am not nothing!'

Blood poured freely into the stream, now. All the blood.

All of his father's blood.

The old man lay under the twilight sky, his face ragged in death. Terjei lifted his father's hand to feel for a pulse but there was none. The calloused fingers were so like his own. He looked back to his father. They had both bled for the music. But only one of them was good enough to own the music.

He rose and strode towards the woods for his final lesson.

# Swept

*Nicola Buzan*

A few weeks after Arlo drowned, Jenny reopened the nursery. Scowling, she tore the sign off the door. The faded print read: *Closed until further notice due to family emergency.*

She crushed the brittle paper and lobbed it into the bin.

The place was neglected, the air stale and choking. She walked the aisles, earmarking the dry, crisp plants. Too many were now unsaleable. With a good drink and some pruning she might be able to save two thirds of them. Jenny switched on the sprinklers until the air thickened, tinged with the green smell that called her back to the past.

Jenny flung the dead plants into a wheelbarrow. There were more than she first thought. She frowned. The displays would be patchy when she was done.

After she finished watering, she pushed the barrow out to the skip in the carpark. Behind the skip, the ground sloped away to the river. The water sang to her; it always had. But she resisted the call. She hadn't been there since Arlo—

Gravel crunched in the carpark and she turned her business smile on the large, red-faced woman who bustled into the nursery. The woman had a small denim backpack slung over one shoulder. She swept through the aisles examining the wilted native plants, before pausing at the display of homewares and small succulents. She ran her fingers along a deer ornament, frozen in mid-prance.

'Nice.' She perused the little succulents and cacti. 'Are these easy to manage?'

'Oh yes,' replied Jenny dredging up enthusiasm. 'They're the last ones, too. We won't restock the bitsers and homeware stuff. It's a good time for a bargain.'

The woman selected a star-shaped succulent. She glanced around and wrinkled her nose. 'If you don't mind me saying so, your other plants look a little worse for wear.'

Jenny did mind, but swallowed a sharp retort and shrugged. 'They're just a bit thirsty. We had other things to concentrate on while the nursery was closed for a bit.'

The woman dropped her voice to a conspiratorial whisper. 'Ooh yes, I know. I know all about that poor wee boy drowning. That bloody river. Accident waiting to happen with so many people living nearby. Council should have dammed it up ages ago.'

Jenny tightened her lips and bagged up the woman's plant. 'The river's important. Lots of birds and animals rely on it. There's even platypus and turtles down there.' Her mouth was dry. She hadn't anticipated talking about the river so soon.

'That right? Well, no dice, you won't catch me going anywhere near it. Especially now.' The woman sniffed and patted the little plant. 'This is the closest I get to nature, thanks very much. I like my creature comforts. I love all the new shops and so on. Bring it on, I say.'

Jenny wrinkled her brow. 'Right. I'm guessing you live next door in one of the new townhouses?'

The woman extended a hand. 'That's right. Tracey.' She paused. 'Actually, I know your stepmother, Mary, quite well. Wondered how long it would take you.'

That's why the woman looked so familiar. She must be the 'Tracey' Mary had forever been lunching with while Jenny ran the nursery. 'Ah, yes. I remember Mary mentioning you.'

Tracey leaned forward. Her breath was hot, and sour with the faint whiff of pickles. She lowered her voice to that awful stage whisper. 'That's why I'm here, love. Mary wanted to know you were okay—'

'Really?' It wasn't like her stepmother to care about her welfare.

'She didn't mean to leave so suddenly.' Tracey tutted, shaking her head. 'Arlo's death crushed her, it's hard enough for a mother to lose her son—but to have all the mystery and suspicion around what happened. Well, it would do your head in.'

Her buttery face folded up into a frown. 'I mean, I know there were issues, and Arlo wasn't quite right in the head and all, and Mary and your father found him to be a bit of a handful. But still, such a cherub.' Her thin eyebrows leapt up her forehead. 'And you having to drag his body out! Goodness me.'

'Dad pulled him out. Arlo... fell in, and Dad was the one who got him out.' Jenny spoke through gritted teeth as the heat rose in her cheeks.

'Of course, of course,' soothed Tracey. 'How is your father?' She sighed. 'That's partly why Mary left, of course. Mary said it wasn't the first time he'd used his hands on her.'

Jenny froze as the woman droned on.

'I mean, I don't want to get into your family stuff. Maybe that's the way he handles grief. Anyway, Mary wants you to report him if he's ever rough with you, too. It just might help... maybe solidify what she's been trying to say.'

'Right. I get it.' Jenny didn't bother hiding her icy tone. 'She wants me to tell on Dad?'

Tracey looked wounded. She patted Jenny's hand. 'She's just

worried, love. No need to get a bee in your bonnet about it. Just if there's anything that he's done, anything abusive, or wrong at all...' She sucked in a breath. 'Well. Mary just thinks you should be telling someone if he continues to lose his marbles or lash out—'

Jenny freed her hand and crossed her arms. 'I'm fine. We're fine. We don't need Mary, or anyone else poking into our business. We had enough of that after Arlo.'

Tracey rushed on as if Jenny hadn't spoken.

'Look, I don't want to rock the boat. But I didn't just pop in to buy plants... although I do like supporting you rather than Madrigal's hardware—'

Jenny nodded at the mention of their new competitor. 'Thank you. And you popped in, why?'

Tracey retrieved an envelope from her backpack and placed it on the counter. 'I should speak to your father. Is he around, or...?'

Jenny pressed her palms into the counter and leaned forward, her chin jutting. 'He's out doing deliveries. I'm curious. Why didn't Mary come herself?'

Tracey held her steady gaze and lowered her voice. 'She won't come back if he's here. Worried he'll fly off the handle again. She asked me to see if I could try to talk some sense into him.'

She paused and pushed the envelope into Jenny's hands. 'Tell him to sign it, Jenny. If not for Mary's sake, and her poor wee Arlo—God rest his soul—then for you and your father. So you can pick up what's left and move on. This place is a bloody white elephant. My advice is, sell up and get out while you still can.'

Jenny took the papers out of the envelope. She cast her eye over them quickly and dropped them to the counter, shaking her head. 'He won't sell the place to these guys. They've been trying since the first townhouses went in. The developer calls every day. But the river, the wildlife, this place—this is my father's dream. It's his place and he'll hold onto it. If Mary thinks she's getting any cash out of him, she can think again.'

'You're missing the point. She's just worried about you, that's all.' Tracey's smile didn't quite reach her eyes. 'Though, Lord knows, she'd be within her rights. You can't just discount three years of living together—three challenging years, I might add. And, even if Arlo wasn't your blood brother, he died here and she deserves something for that at least, don't you think?'

Jenny didn't answer. Her fingers flexed and curled into claws under the counter.

Tracey snorted. 'Besides, he's crazy not to sell! Times have changed. People want ornaments and pot plants.'

Jenny bunched up her fists. 'Dad knows what he's doing.' Her voice was high like a whistle.

'Look, give him the documents. Try to talk some sense into him. One more thing—' Tracey overrode Jenny's protests. 'Mary wants you to bag up Arlo's clothes, and that photo she kept by the bed. She's desperate to have some of his things back. Anyway. You can drop it off to me.' She wrote out her details and passed the paper to Jenny.

Once she made sure Tracey had gone, Jenny took another wheelbarrow full of dead plants out to the skip. Snapping the tinder dry branches and hurling the vegetation into the skip gave a raw sense of satisfaction. She didn't give a second look at the bags of clothes, the box of toys, and the photo of the dimpled blond boy—which were soon buried by the plant carcasses.

Once she had finished, Jenny booked the contractor to empty the skip later that day.

When her father returned, she related Tracey's visit, and gave him the developer's documents.

Jenny put the counter between her and her father. She feigned tidying up receipts while she surreptitiously monitored his reaction.

The last time he received a contract offer, he had virtually chased the developer out of the nursery. He had kicked over a stand of displays and punched a wall. Jenny had spent the whole afternoon tidying up.

This time he dropped the papers in the bin and reached out to her. She steeled herself to avoid flinching as his hand patted her shoulder awkwardly.

His eyes bored into hers. 'It's just Mary out for what she can get, like you say. Moneygrubbing. She wants to punish us. She always blamed you. Said you had the chance to save Arlo.' He latched onto her shoulder hard and lowered his voice.

She bit her lip to stifle a cry.

'I know you did what you thought was right. We're on the same team. I'll always stand up for you, and I'm sure you'll do the same.'

He raised his eyebrows. She nodded sharply and he released her.

That night Jenny dreamt Arlo called to her, even as the river swallowed him up, silencing him. And she saw a malevolent muddy thing rear up in the water. It dragged itself from the bowels of the river and she dashed up the slope to safety, not daring to look back.

She woke, her ears ringing with his scream.

An owl. God, it was just an owl.

The next morning, Jenny and her father took their coffee down by the river and sat on the bank. Her father stared intently at the water taking loud slurps from his drink. They were seated side by side, but a chasm yawned between them.

'It's good, you getting the nursery going again,' he said. 'It helps. Even before—you know—Mary was forever shutting the shop in the middle of the day while she had coffee with God-knows-who.'

'Tracey,' said Jenny, automatically.

'Who?'

'The neighbour that dropped in the developer's papers. I told you about her?'

Her father paused, frowning slightly and rubbing his forehead. 'Right. So, you did.'

Jenny scuffed her sneaker in the damp soil and blinked away tears. She plucked a feather from the ground. Sulphur-crested cockatoo. The pinging echo of a whipbird rang out. She shaded her eyes and scanned the canopy for signs of the small green bird with the oversized voice.

Her father neither stirred nor mentioned the birds. His shoulders were hunched forward, and his face was blank and grey. She sighed softly and released the feather to flutter to the ground.

A few days later, Jenny suggested he take over her nursery shift, so she could clean out the truck. Dealing with customers might be just what he needed.

She clambered into the cab and her nostrils were assaulted by the rotting food smell. It stunk like something had died behind the bench seat. She tugged the seat down and held her breath as she gingerly collected oozing bags and plastic wrap dripping with putrefied food. Maggots, too. The remains of the lunches and snacks she had spent umpteen mornings carefully preparing. She retched, the sour tang of vomit in her throat.

She cleaned up as best she could, spritzing the cab with citrus spray. The ghost of an underlying mouldy odour lingered.

Her father was the last person she wanted to see right now. Instead, she walked down to the river. She washed her hands in the cool water, then sat quietly, enjoying the fresh air, and rolling her stiff shoulders to loosen them up. The meditative movement of the river calmed her, as it always had.

She would have to monitor his eating more closely, but it wasn't worth bringing up the mess in the car and getting in a big argument.

Back in the nursery, her father had removed all the succulents and homewares from their shelving.

'What are you doing, Dad?' she wailed.

'Helping. I saw you pulled this out. You finally going to get rid of Mary's fancy stuff now she's gone, eh?'

Jenny spoke through clenched teeth. 'Erm, no. Moving it up front, actually. I thought it might tempt some of the people from the townhouses to spend a bit more time in here.'

Her father's face slackened. His skin had the sheen of rubber.

'Well, just a thought,' she rushed on. 'I did sell a bit of this stuff online lately. Maybe Mary had a point?' Her voice squeaked and broke.

He silently stared into space. Jenny licked her lips, and hesitated. The phone rang and she scampered to the office to take the call. A customer had called to change a planting order. Jenny ran through all the individual items with him.

She pressed a hand over her ear to block out the jarring crashes coming from the nursery and asked the customer to repeat himself. Her skin was taut, her forehead throbbing with a dull ache.

She finished the call and closed her eyes, mustering strength to return to the nursery. Her father had disappeared. She stood with her hands on her hips, surveying the damage. The shelves she had shifted were reduced to piles of splintered wood, sprinkled with dollops of dirt. An axe lay abandoned in the midst of the debris.

She found more shelving remains dumped in the skip along with the plants and ornaments. Her father sat slumped in a chair by the river's edge. She pressed her lips together in a thin line, lowered her head, and picked the salvageable plants out of the rubbish, pausing every so often to swipe away tears.

When he returned to the nursery, she looked up from sweeping the floor. Would he apologise? Or had he already forgotten about the smashing and the violence. He walked right up to her without saying a thing. His eyes were filmy and unfocussed. She dropped the broom, and instinctively reached out to him. He took a quick step back. His feet tangled and his arms pinwheeled as he lost balance and tumbled to the floor with a crash.

He blinked, rubbed his head and frowned. 'What happened?'

Jenny knelt, slinging his arm around her shoulders to help him to his feet. It took all her energy to prop up his dead weight.

'Don't be scared. I'm here,' she whispered.

She managed to steer him and half propel, half tip him into a chair.

'Tomorrow you're going to the doctor. No arguments.'


'Dementia, I'm afraid. Too advanced. Incurable.' The doctor spoke fast, efficiently delivering the follow-up punch without leaving space for them to digest the first wallop.

The diagnosis explained so much of his past behaviour. All the things that weren't quite right. Oh God. Why hadn't she brought him in sooner? Jenny gulped and sniffed back sobs.

'What I can do is help to ensure your father is comfortable and safe.' Dr Venkateswaran said.

'Incurable?' Jenny whispered the word. 'You're certain?'

Dr Venkateswaran gave a curt nod and arched an eyebrow. 'When your father and stepmother were here last year, they made certain decisions—'

She clenched her fist. 'What? They were here?' Mary had been meddling again! 'What decisions?'

He shook his head gently and examined his square, scrupulously-clean fingernails. 'I understand your stepmother left your father, and you're looking after him now. But it's an ethical grey area. I urge you to speak to your stepmother about future arrangements—'

'And if we don't speak anymore?'

The doctor pressed his fingertips together and regarded her

solemnly. 'Jenny. You would have only been—what—sixteen at the time? A minor. You'll need to get power of attorney to take over your father's care in a more formal sense. I'm sorry. But it would be best if you discussed these issues with a lawyer.'

'Right.' She frowned at her father. His head bowed as he intently studied his hands. Was he taking this all in? 'Dad, are you alright?' She exhaled sharply through pursed lips and waited. 'Do you have any questions for the doctor? About treatment, or anything else?'

He lurched backward, bouncing a little off the chair spine. He folded his hands over his chest and closed his eyes.

Jenny shot a look at the doctor, whose expression remained neutral. 'Dad? Any questions?'

With his eyes still closed, her father shook his head. She grimaced and asked the doctor what next.

They left the clinic armed with a stack of brochures providing bullet pointed tips, hotlines, support groups, and funding assistance forms.

The mood of the weather had changed. A storm lashed the sky. Jenny gripped her father's hand and they walked with short fast steps through the rain. Her father moved slower than she would have liked, but she resisted the urge to yank on his hand. They would get soaked anyway.

Once in the car, she passed the bag of soggy pamphlets to her father who promptly opened the door and dumped them outside. She huffed a sigh and started the engine. What the Hell. She wasn't going out in that rain again.

She tapped the steering wheel. 'Dad? Can you tell me about the last appointment you had with the doctor? When Mary was there?'

Her father didn't respond, but slowly opened the window. Jenny bit back a rebuke about rain and upholstery. He craned his head out and pointed his face skyward. His eyes were closed and his mouth open with tongue out. The rain streamed down his face, into his mouth, and soaked his t-shirt.

Jenny gripped the steering wheel, blinked furiously to choke back the tears, and willed herself to just concentrate on the road.

A few days later the rain cleared. Jenny and her father went down to the river, Jenny with the chairs slung over her shoulder, her father hobbling along after.

She sorted out her father's chair, then parked in her favourite spot. The familiar river landscape meandered along before vanishing around a bend where the bush and trees were thick and dipped low over the water. If you followed the river down, you came to a little footbridge. One of her father's old favourite places to watch birds.

She chewed her lip. The water was a turgid, frothing mess. Sometimes that happened after rain, but it should be clear now. Not this awful silty, brownish-cream hue.

On a hunch, she picked her way upstream. The discolouration continued to a sediment fence and sandbag barrier, enclosing a long, tarped area. Behind was a construction site. Dirty clay run-off oozed down the tarp and fed into the water turning it brown, in stark contrast to the clear water upstream.

She glared at the huge crane and its menagerie of digging implements clustered at the construction site and set about taking photos with her phone.

That afternoon she detailed a complaint to the Council about the history of the wildlife in the area, the problems with the run-off, and the failing sediment trap.

A response arrived the next week. She tore it open and her frown deepened as she scanned through the letter. Unbelievable! The Council mostly seemed to agree with her, although they disagreed with her allegations of wildlife endangerment.

They gave the developer a week to fix the sandbags and sediment fence. If the issues weren't fixed, the Council would consider issuing a stop work notice. Consider! She could have punched something. She ripped the letter up, letting the pieces flutter to the bin. Useless.

Jenny opened the next envelope, revealing the developer's familiar, thick paper stock and flashy logo. She tapped a finger on her lips, frowning. The developers had raised their offer considerably.

Perhaps she should speak to someone who could give her some advice. The trouble was, a lawyer would cost a fortune. There was always Tracey. She shook her head. She didn't trust her. Not with the association with Mary. She smooshed the letter, then reconsidered, and flattened it on the countertop, under a paperweight.

Jenny's phone chirped. She scanned the text and checked her father. He was slumped in his chair, a flop of thick greying hair shielding his eyes. Still asleep. She smiled fondly. She should get him in for a haircut this week.

Tentatively, she retrieved the keys from their hiding place behind the owl ornament on the mantelpiece. Although she handled them carefully, the keys jangled. Her father jerked awake and stared around the room, a wild look in his eyes.

'What are you doing with my keys?' he demanded.

She gasped and took several steps back towards the door. 'Just groceries, Dad. Back soon.'

He got up, tucking half his shirt in and sweeping his hair back, lurching forward like a mad conductor preparing to lift the baton. He surprised her by springing at her and snatching at the keys, missing them by a fraction.

She shoved the keys into her pocket. She took his arm and gave him a gentle push, encouraged by his burst of energy.

'Dad? Dad, are you feeling better?' Hope surged in her chest, but his face slackened and went blank. She dropped his arm and sighed as he wobbled back to collapse in his chair.

Her phone trilled again.

The buyer met her in the carpark. He encircled the truck like he was stalking prey. 'She go alright?'

Jenny nodded, handing over the mechanic's report. He actually kicked one of the tyres and she choked back a brittle laugh.

The man poked his head into the cab and wrinkled his nose slightly. 'Still a bit stinky.' He paused, but she didn't respond. 'All good. Shall we say $2300? That right?'

She considered her position. The man had already test driven the truck last week, and she didn't have anyone else lined up. It was crunch time. They'd agreed on $2,500. It didn't seem worthwhile digging her heels in. They needed the money.

'Yeah, alright,' she said, through clenched teeth.

In the nursery, she ran her eyes down the list of her father's delivery customers. She sighed and checked off the first name as she dialled the number. 'Hello? Mrs Fong? It's Jenny Kenn, calling about the gardening delivery service my father was providing...'

Jenny had the bills spread out on the kitchen table. She tapped on a small calculator and tallied up numbers on a jotter pad in her scratchy handwriting.

Her father shuffled in. He moved clumsily, but with a single-minded purpose, across to the door. She paused as he planted his palms on the door and stood on teetering tiptoes. He shoved the panel and rattled at the doorknob. She never knew whether to step in or let him be.

She kept the door locked since he had begun going walkabout. It was a comfort to know he was safely shut inside the house. He rattled the door again. She sighed and rose to let him out. He scooted past, making a beeline for freedom. At the veranda stairs he gingerly navigated down each step, gripping the banister with white knuckled hands.

Jenny followed him to the river. The sour chocolate colour of the water and the dead surrounding growth made the river look sick.

Her father landed heavily in his chair. The chair wobbled but somehow he stayed on dry land. Her body sang with tension, ready to pounce if he slipped or lost his balance. She frowned, rubbing at the sharp pain in her temples. What if he fell in? Would he even know he was in trouble? She shook her head violently, alarmed at the track she had gone down.

He looked oddly nonchalant. His gaze swept up and down the river but didn't appear to fix on anything. But maybe he had been captured by the undulations of the swift current. His head dipped and jerked back. Jenny caught his arm, levering him out of the chair. He wobbled, and she tightened her grip.

'I've got you. Time to go back to the house, Dad.'

His eyes were bloodshot and glassy, but he held her gaze and spoke with a forgotten clarity. 'Let me go on, Jen.'

Her mouth dropped open. She searched his face for recognition, but the curtain had fallen. Her head pounded as she led the stranger up the slope to safety.

The developer left another phone message, which Jenny immediately deleted. She squeezed her eyes shut and massaged her temples. She still had the crumpled papers. She hadn't decided what to do with them.

Dr Venkateswaran had left the next voicemail. 'Jenny? Ravi Venkateswaran from the Dementia Clinic. I got your message. Deterioration isn't unusual for people at the same stage as your father. It's a lot of pressure on you. I hope you've been able to get some legal advice on the situation.' He paused.

'You could work on moving him out of the home and to assisted living, like we discussed. Much safer for him with the security of round the clock care. Anyway, I look forward to talking through options with you both. Give the clinic a call and we'll see you soon. Thank you.'

Jenny fiddled with the edges of the crumpled papers. The door rattled in the background. She scowled and deleted the doctor's voicemail too.


Jenny ran up to the tall dark-stained door and pounded the wood. She rang the doorbell and thumped again. And again, harder, louder. Her knuckles flared with pain. What if no one answered?

The door flew open and Tracey stood there, her cheeks flushed.

'He's gone!' Jenny shouted. 'I went to the nursery for a moment, then back to the house, and he was gone...' Her nose dribbled, and she swiped at it with her sleeve. She snatched panting breaths, her chest tight. She ignored the throb in her forehead and scrabbled at the older woman's sleeve. 'We have to go! We have to find him. I don't know where he is.' She hurled the words before lapsing into bubbling tears.

'Okay. It's okay. Take some deep breaths.' Tracey patted her shoulder and slid on sneakers.

Jenny ran ahead and Tracey followed. They reached the house and Jenny pointed out the door to the balcony before taking the stairs two at a time. 'He would have gone out here, he's always fiddling around with the door.'

At the bottom of the stairs, Jenny pointed down the slope. 'The river, it's the only place left. I thought he was inside! I did the house and the nursery. You take the river down to the footbridge, and I'll go up the development side.'

Tracey nodded and they ran down the hill before peeling off in opposite directions. Jenny had got only a few metres up the river when she heard her name shouted in a long, anguished yell.

Tracey stood near the river, fifty metres or so downstream, pale and trembling. She pressed her phone against her ear and spoke loudly. When she noticed Jenny, she motioned her to stay back.

'You don't want to see this, Jenny.' Tracey turned away and spoke again into the phone. 'The daughter, yes. Just arrived. I found him.'

Jenny edged closer and Tracey swatted again at her and shifted her weight to block something. Jenny stepped around her. Tracey grimaced, her words running together, eyes wide and panicked.

Jenny stood with slack arms as she took in the scene.

Tracey rang off and put her hand on Jenny's arm. 'I told you, love. I just spoke to the police. We need to keep back. You might slip.'

She cleared her throat. 'The police need to look at the slip marks, and him too. It's a crime scene. They said we have to stay away. Which means you can't touch him, I'm afraid. Sorry.' She spoke gently. 'Though I daresay he slipped further up, where the chair is, and floated here.'

Jenny didn't respond. The bedraggled body mostly submerged in the water transfixed her, as did the ghostly white arm stretched with a clawed hand halfway up the bank. She cocked her head. Had he tried to pull himself out?

She was so close… close enough to step forward and give him a little nudge with her foot, just enough so he would slip under the water. So she didn't have to look. Or perhaps she could grasp the hand and drag him out. Tracey's grip on her arm tightened, as if the woman sensed the terrible thoughts.

His hair fell over his face in straggly strands. Oh, God, she hadn't taken him for that haircut after all. She began to sob. Her body shook uncontrollably. Tracey enveloped her in a firm clasp, and Jenny sagged against her bulk.

'Sorry, love. You've been through the wringer. Just hold on. The police will sort everything out now. How about a cup of tea?'

The summer rains had been persistent, and the river flooded again. Jenny stood at the barricade, where white and red police tape sealed off the area, and a sign slapped backward and forward in the rain, the edges fluttering:

*Warning - danger! Do not enter! By order of the police.*

She slipped easily under the tape and stood at the place they used to sit, stepping down carefully on the slick ground. The river had breached its banks and mercifully covered the spot where her father's body had lain.

The rain streamed over her face and tiny rivulets ran down her neck, saturating her clothes. The river was no longer meek and long-suffering. The ferocious brown water greedily swallowed plants and slashed notches from the bank, as it burst out of its course.

Jenny took a cautious step back. Her boots skidded on the slick ground.

In the river a huge tree branch and part of an office chair surged past. Dams of debris and branches built up, only to be swept clear by the roaring water.

She turned her back on the mesmerising power of the river. Deep shadows shrouded her house, the last Queenslander standing. The townhouses hunched around it, low and uniform as boxes. The black finger of a crane jutted up from the embrace of earthmovers and stood silhouetted against the roiling sky.

Once the developers got the signed papers she'd posted after the funeral, the crane would swing its arm towards her place and smash her father's dreams into dust.

Jenny turned back to the river. The water had crept up and showed no sign of dropping back. Tiny fingers of water caressed her boots. Hair lashed her face and stung her cheeks and water seeped into the cuffs of her jeans.

A devastating crack rang out and she spun to trace the sound. A sheet of water doused her, blinding. She screamed, a long, primal howl. The thunderous water swallowed up the roaring answer of the river as it surged forward, unstoppable.

# Hide the Moon

*Annie Bucknall*

It's strange. When Amy was little, my biggest fear was of something happening to her. I must have imagined losing her a thousand different ways, keenly aware of her tiny, porcelain-fragile body. If I thought about it too hard, my throat closed up, my heart pounded and I had to fight to recover a sense of perspective and calm. I loved that little girl so much I couldn't fathom the hurt, the gut-twisting sorrow I'd experience if ever I lost her. If ever I had to bury her.

Not once, did I consider the grief I'd feel if she were the one choosing coffins and headstones with her father. Yet, as the three of us sat, crammed into that oven of a doctor's office, I knew that was exactly how things would play out.

I didn't need the test results to tell me my bones were liquifying. Like dawn raids from the enemy, every day now, a symptom intensified or a new one appeared. I'd already lost this battle. The stench of decay was the latest. It clung to my skin. I'd overcompensate, spritzing myself with perfume but the floral notes in my signature scent only made me feel like a funeral bouquet.

Frank picked up my hand, stroking his thumb over my palm as

Dr Adams scowled at the numbers on a file labelled 'Josephine Willoughby'. A stranger's file. My file.

Amy fidgeted, squirming in her chair like a child instead of the confident young woman she'd become. The doctor cleared his throat and set down the papers. He took issue with my daughter attending these meetings. 'Indelicate', he put it. But he couldn't dissuade her and it was just easier having her here. This way she could ask him questions, directly. I no longer had the energy to be the only source of her information and her father had proved useless with this stuff.

'I'm afraid it's not good news, Mrs Willoughby.'

Amy and Frank took a collective breath.

The doctor continued, 'The latest results show the disease has stopped responding to treatment. Things are...accelerating.' He paused, closing his eyes for an almost undetectable moment. 'The time has come to begin making your end-of-life arrangements.'

Frank's hand fell open, as though he were letting go of me already. A stubborn optimist, he lived by the maxim that *'Good things happen to good people'*. I'd always loved that about him. But lately, it had shut him off from reality. He refused to listen to my complaints, didn't want to know things were worse. So, as much as possible, I played pretend.

Only Amy saw the gritted teeth underneath my smile or caught my wince as I stood from a chair. For Frank, goodness would prevail. And, in some ways, his worldview wasn't all that naïve.

His real mistake? He considered me amongst the virtuous. Someone worthy of a divine pardon...if such a thing existed.

He stood abruptly, excusing himself to fetch a glass of water, leaving Amy and I to deal with the doctor. She started in with her questions before the door had even clicked shut behind him.

'How long does she have?'

'Three months at best. Maybe less.'

'Is there anything else we can try? Any other trials we can get her on?'

'We've exhausted all options—experimental and otherwise.'

'How much longer will she be able to stay at home?'

'It's hard to say. My best guess is that she'll be with you, with some support, for another month at most. But as soon as she starts to deteriorate, she'll be back here.'

And on it went. With Amy cross-examining Dr Adams as though she were already a barrister and Dr Adams evading specifics like a slippery criminal. I sat silent, clasping my hands in my lap.

Not that I ever paid too much attention to what Dr Adams said. From the first moment I became ill, I'd known, even when he hadn't.

For six months the disease had been building momentum—a freak wave towering over my peaceful life in the shallows. I saw it coming, and I'd swum, desperately kicking against the current, for Amy and Frank's sake. But I was tired, now. And, as I looked over my shoulder into the barrel of the monster, I was sure. When it broke, it would drown me.

Amy? She'd never seen a wave that big before in her life and she was still young enough to believe she'd get the lifeboat to me in time. But, as the conversation continued, her posture changed—the line of her mouth softening and her shoulders sagging.

When she'd exhausted her questions, she leant back in the chair and folded her hands in her lap. She'd laid down her oars. Dr Adams must have sensed it, and his voice lowered into compassion as he gathered pamphlets and scrawled down hospice recommendations.

It was coming. The inevitable falling apart. Any minute. Any day now. That's how it happened when people died slow like this. I'd seen it before when my friends had lost their parents. You fell apart first, then you had to put yourself back together to get through the rest. I was under no delusions. The end would be horrific…worse for them than me. They'd carry their suffering with them long after my relief had come.

In many families, the mother was the steadfast thread that held the well-worn patches of the family quilt. Not so, in ours. We were three mismatched pieces, and I'd weaved us together with a yarn of deception. I needed to unpick the stitches before it was too late. Before they mourned a woman who didn't exist.

We left the room and found Frank pacing the hall sheepishly outside. I held his shoulders, making him look me in the eye so he'd see I was okay. That I was still here. We were still here.

'Take me to the sea,' I said.

As we pulled into the driveway of the old beach house, the sunshine yellow front door greeted me, vivid against a backdrop of royal blue weatherboard. The bold colour palette was Aunt Gloria's signature, and I'd never been able to bring myself to change it. As though painting it any other hue might somehow vanquish her essence from the place. Instead, every few years, when the harsh ocean air scrubbed the colour back to timber, we'd crack open the paint cans and give the grand old lady back her pride.

I opened the car door to the playful sprite of the sea breeze on my face. It tousled my hair, jangled the wind chimes on the porch and lifted my tired spirits. I would gladly spend my final days here—laid out on a lounger on the beach—my last breath slipping salty and cool over my tongue. The gaudy cottage had always been home for me.

But if I ended things that way, I'd take something important from Frank and Amy. Instead of walking in the front door and seeing happy memories play out, they'd only see loss. I'd take something that was *ours* and make it only *mine*. I couldn't do that to them.

Leaving the rest of the luggage for Frank, I grabbed my handbag and headed up the rickety porch. Amy stood behind me as I clicked the lock and pushed the heavy door open. Even though we'd left the house shut up for well over six months, it was still so alive. No matter how long it remained unoccupied, it never had that musty, dead smell.

Light filtered into the living room through colourful stained glass windows patterned with mermaids and tropical fish. Amy, Gloria and I had made them when I'd turned up the summer Frank was deployed overseas. I'd been frantic, desperate. But she'd put me to work, insisting making pictures out of sea glass would keep five-year-old Amy occupied and me sane. As always, she'd been right. The windows—and those long summer days on the sand—had been her parting gift. Our final project.

Kaleidoscope rays illuminated the eclectic mix of Gloria's handmade trinkets and my modern furniture. 'Make it your own,' was one of the last things she'd said to me. And I had…mostly. But every corner still held something she had made.

A painting, a blanket, a piece of pottery. By keeping those things, I kept moments of her life. Pieces of her more real than a photograph would ever be. Once Frank and Amy had worn the furniture beyond repair, would anything remain of me?

'I wish I'd been older when she died. I hardly remember her,' Amy rested her chin on my shoulder and wrapped an arm around me.

'She adored you,' I said.

'She was a remarkable woman, wasn't she?'

'Yes.' And soon she'd realise just how remarkable Glory was. I couldn't allow nostalgia to carry me away. We weren't here to reminisce. We were here to make sure Amy's story didn't die with me. To give them both the opportunity to part ways with me and say their goodbyes now if they wished. If nothing else, I'd go to my death an honest woman. Before the weekend was out, they'd understand.

I sighed. 'Come on, let's get these beds made.'

We went slow, working our way through freshening the rooms.

Amy tried to take over, tried to force me to sit down, but I shooed her away. It's a wonderful arrogance of the young and healthy, that they don't realise the pleasure in being able to do simple things for yourself.

One day soon, I wouldn't make a bed or cook a meal. Pain would dissolve every part of my identity; reduce me to bed-ridden anonymity. I wouldn't be 'Josie who cooks the world's most amazing apple pie' or even 'house-proud Josie'. Soon, far too soon, I'd only be 'Josie who is dying,'.

Josie the liar.

By the time we made it downstairs, Frank had opened up the house. We followed the tune of the radio to the back porch where he sat, cradling a beer. Two glasses of crisp white wine waited for us on the table. A hundred metres away, the long waves rolled and thundered against the smooth white sand, sending spray and seagulls whirling into the tumbled grey sky.

Property like this—with private access to the beach—was almost impossible to find now. This place was an heirloom. Something special. Our oasis nestled in the dunes. We had neighbours but they were so far out of sight, I only remembered their existence when we headed to the shore and spotted them bobbing in the surf.

I closed my eyes. Would Amy's children, her grandchildren and theirs bound through the yellow door to run, laughing and splashing into the wild ocean? Would they, too, fall exhausted and sun-kissed into bed and drift off to the lullaby of crashing waves? Would their sticky fingers touch the glass mermaids we'd etched into the windows so long ago? Would a part of me still exist to see it?

'You'll hold on to Aunt Gloria's house, won't you? When I'm gone?'

Frank put his beer down with more force than necessary and moved to get up. I put my hand on his arm.

'Stay.'

He sighed and looked down at me for the briefest second. My heart near-broke at the sorrow in his eyes.

'I can't. I can't hear this talk.' His voice was hoarse with repressed emotion. I gripped him tighter, anchoring him to the spot.

'You have to, Frankie. It's time.'

'They don't know everything!' He wrenched free. 'How can they know it won't be long now? Doctors still don't know shit about cancer.'

This was all I ever got when I tried to get him to open up. Exploded emotion; his rage like shrapnel bursting through his outer shell every time I trod on a pressure point.

'Dad!' Amy stood and gripped Frank's shoulders. 'She's dying, Dad. This is it.'

He looked away and I swear she wanted to shake him.

'Amy…' His voice was quiet; controlled temper.

She dropped her hands but before he could walk off, she lowered her voice.

'I can't do this alone, Dad.'

He grabbed his beer and slammed the door closed, retreating to the quiet of the house. Amy slumped to the floor in front of me, her head on my knees as she sobbed. I shushed her and stroked her hair, just like I'd done when she was a girl.

My poor, brave baby. She'd always seemed like the strongest of us all. Indestructible Amy we called her. Unshaken by a skinned knee, a disappointing grade or even a broken heart. She was so much like her Dad. To outsiders they were stoic and resolute. But to love them was to see through the veneer to the terrifying vulnerability that lay underneath.

She lifted her head from my knee, her eyes red. 'When you're gone, it's just going to be me and him. What if he never lets me talk about you? What if it's like you never existed?'

And what if she didn't want to? I pushed the sandy blonde hair back from her face.

'No matter what happens with your father, honey, I will always be with you. When he's being a real pain, trust me, I'll be standing right beside you, rolling my eyes at him.'

She gave a little laugh. 'Can you do more than that? Like slap him on the back of the head or something?'

'Oh, you bet. I'll haunt the hell out of him if he gives you grief. We're talking light switches, temperature dropping, furniture flying around the room. Some real poltergeist stuff.'

She grinned. 'Good. I don't think he'll even believe you're dead until that happens.'

I kissed the top of her head. 'Probably not. He's always been a difficult man. But he adores you Amy. He's loved you from the moment he met you.'

She stiffened. The air around me shifted, and a distant rumble of thunder heralded an incoming storm.

'Why do you always say it like that?' she asked. 'From the moment he met me?'

'Because he did.'

'Yeah, but how come you don't say from the moment I was born?'

'I don't know. It's just a turn of phrase.'

'So, he did then?'

'Did what?'

'Love me from the moment I was born?'

I paused. It was infinitesimal, but it was there, and she noticed it too. Secrets presented themselves like signposts on a highway. If you didn't take the exit when it turned up, you had to continue with the lie, never knowing how long it would be before you could change course. My insides constricted as I steeled myself.

This was my moment.

The truth bubbled in the back of my throat, ready for release.

Something shattered in the kitchen. Frank swore.

'Are you okay?' I called out.

'Fine. Just a plate.' He was brusque. Amy's earlier words reverberated around my head. *What if he never lets me talk about you?* If Frank knew how I'd really come to raise Amy, would he shut her out completely? Would it leave her with no one?

I smiled, and the lie came easy. Just as it had her whole life. 'Yes, of course. He loved you from the moment you were born.'

Amy nodded and stood. I couldn't tell if I'd assuaged her concerns. Her law student persona had clicked back into place and she'd shut me out.

'I'll get us a refill, Mum. You stay here while I sort out the old man.'

I handed her my glass, then picked the blanket up off the chair and wrapped it tight against the sudden chill.


The storm didn't come. Instead, the atmosphere hung heavy over the house, and every clang of cutlery against dinner plates felt as though it might burst the clouds and release the deluge. Frank and Amy sat at opposite ends of the table, barely speaking, while I sat in the middle, too tired to carry the charade of a pleasant family dinner alone.

I cursed myself for missing my opportunity but I couldn't do it when the two of them were on opposing sides. Widening the divide between them would break us all. Frank was coping as best he could. I had to be patient.

I pushed a mouthful of ocean-fresh snapper onto my fork and forced a smile. He sent messages with food. Snapper was my favourite and his least; it was Frank for 'sorry'. Over the years, he'd learnt to cook fish to perfection so that the lemon-buttered flakes practically melted on my tongue. If I reached the end of the meal and I was still mad, sticky-date pudding sometimes appeared an hour later. Char-grilled steak, though? When he served that, I knew to keep my distance.

I ate as much as I could, knowing he would take offense if I didn't at least attempt a few mouthfuls.

I was grateful they both ended the charade early. Frank grabbed his beer and excused himself while Amy stood to clear the table as soon as he'd left the room. The back door slammed shut and he headed towards the beach.

'I thought you said you were going to sort things out with the old man?' I said.

Amy scraped a knife along the plate a little too forcefully.

'It's a bit hard when he won't talk.' She put down the dishes. 'I can't keep doing this, Mum. I can't keep living in this fantasy world where we all pretend you aren't dying. It's dishonest and it's not helping any of us.'

My heartbeat quickened. She was right. I'd have to sort Frank out...help him face the situation.

'I'll talk to him, Ames. Promise.'

'Good, 'cause I'm sick of it.'

I sat up in the armchair past nine o'clock, keeping vigil in case the clouds burst and we had to go find the stubborn old dolt. Years of experience had taught me not to bother trying to stop him. When the storm dissolved into clear skies, I climbed the stairs one at a time— my aching bones craving the feather-soft mattress of Aunt Gloria's four-poster bed.

I shivered as I entered the room. The chill sea-breeze made it feel like the inside of a refrigerator. Glory's white-lace bed curtains fluttered about, casting floral shadows on the walls as they danced a ballet to the night air.

I walked over to close the windows and end their performance but the full moon caught me. The whitecaps were molten silver and I stood transfixed, following the waves as they whooshed to the shore.

How many more times would the ocean rock me to sleep? How many more moons did I have left? I left the window open, enjoying a thrill of recklessness. Slipping on a pair of socks, I climbed into bed and pulled the thin coverlet up to my chin. It didn't take long for the ocean's hypnotic opera to send me to sleep.


Hours later, the bedroom door creaked open and Frank's familiar footfall entered the room. As his movements stirred me to wakefulness, I realised how foolish I'd been. In the time I'd been asleep, the refrigerator had become an icebox.

'Can you close the window and bring an extra blanket, please?' I called in the semi-dark.

He yanked the pane shut and the curtains fell back into position, lifeless once more. He'd stripped down to his singlet and underwear and, when he slipped into bed, his skin was cool to the touch. I rolled over, breathing in the salty smell of him. I wanted to imprint that smell into my soul so that wherever I was going next, I'd still be able to inhale him.

'Frank...'

'Mmm...'

'What do you think will happen to me? When I die?'

His body stiffened and I snuggled in deeper to his chest. He wasn't going anywhere. I wouldn't let him.

'I don't believe in an afterlife, Josie. You know that.'

'What happens then? To my memories? To the love I had?'

He took a deep breath and stroked my hair. My husband shared his heart the way some lovers shared trysts—under the cover of nightfall, riding the border of sleep and consciousness. His feelings were a clandestine affair and over the years I'd had to create the opportunities that would bring us closer.

'I think they live on, Jose. But with us.'

I swallowed. 'What about my secrets?'

His hand stopped its stroking. 'That one dies with me, love.'

Of course, it did. He'd never wanted Amy to know the truth.

'Does it matter, do you think? Going to your death with a lie that big trapped inside of you?'

'Not if the keeping of it protects your daughter.'

'You're not going to tell her?' I asked, my voice trembling. 'You're going to take this to your grave, too? Don't you feel burdened?'

He sat up in bed, pushing his hands through his spun-silver hair. When he turned to face me, I could see the intensity of his expression.

'No, I don't feel burdened. Amy is my daughter. I raised her. I saw her take her first steps, taught her how to ride a bike, scared off her first boyfriend. She's mine, Josie. That's my truth. The only truth I allow myself to dwell on.'

'She needs you, Frank. She needs you now and she's going to need you when I'm gone.'

He exhaled slowly. 'I know.'

I sat up and touched his leg. 'Well, you can't keep hiding from this. You can't keep leaving the room every time someone mentions my illness…or my death.'

His voice was tight. 'I will be there for her when the time comes, I swear it. But you're all so busy living in the future—a future where you're not in it. A future where…' His voice cracked. '…you've died a painful death and it's just the two of us left. I don't want to live there until I have to, Josephine. I can't. Right now, you're still here.' He cupped my face in his calloused hands. 'This. This is where I want to live. In the moments when I still have you.'

He kissed me then and as our mouths came together I tasted salt on his lips. Was it sea spray or tears?

I dreamt I had a panther inside me. A dark, velvet beast enraged by the cage of my body. He clawed and gnashed his teeth on my insides as I fought to contain him in my skin. But I was being shredded, eaten alive from the inside out.

I awoke writhing and moaning in pain, unable to focus on Frank's face hovering above me.

'What do I do?' His voice was small, boyish.

'Get Amy...' I rasped. She handled all my medication. I was vaguely aware of Frank's heavy footsteps as he rushed from the room and Amy's as they returned together.

'Oh, Mum...'

I heard the medicine bag unzip as she rifled through it for the worst of the drugs...the ones that would leave me woozy and comatose for most of tomorrow. I usually hated them and refused them at all costs. But, if I'd been capable, I would have got on my knees and begged for them, now.

'I'll do it. Show me.' It was Frank's voice.

'Are you sure, Dad? You'll have to inject her?'

'She's going to have more nights like this now, isn't she?'

'Yeah, Dad, she is.'

'Show me. I need to know what to do.'

Amy gave gentle instructions. Frank fumbled with my nightgown and the needle pricked into my thigh. I balled myself up in the center of the bed, praying for relief. The sheet underneath me was damp with my tears, the pain leaching from my body in any way it could.

Warm arms circled my waist, embracing me and slowing my pulse. I tried to focus on steadying the jagged rhythm of my breath as my consciousness slipped further away. Just before I succumbed, I opened my eyes. Frank's arms wrapped around me from behind and Amy's from the front. Their hands clasped together across my torso in a prayer I didn't deserve.

The sun was fading from the room by the time I roused the next afternoon. I tried to sit up in bed, but my muscles were still too weak. Amy appeared, adjusting my pillows and helping me up.

'Are you okay?' I asked.

She gave me an indulgent smile. 'I wasn't the one in agony last night. How are you feeling?'

I took a long swallow from the water glass beside my bed. 'Groggy. Stiffer than usual. I just hate to be a bother.'

She kissed my forehead. 'You're not a bother, Mum.'

*Mum.* The word made me avert my eyes and train them on the corner of the room. A tear slid down my face and caught in my hair. Amy didn't miss it. She sat on the edge of the bed and clasped my hand in hers.

'Oh, Mum. It'll be okay.'

But it wouldn't, would it? Last night had just been a preview of the main performance. I was asking them both to watch the character I'd been playing all these years wither away and die. The real Josie didn't deserve their sympathy, their restless nights. I'd clung steadfast to the lie, convincing even myself, but life had eroded my façade.

'Amy...can you get your father? I need to talk to you both.'

She left and the room fell to silence save for the ticking of Aunt Gloria's mantle clock. It used to comfort me, that sound. I'd lie here at night, timing my breathing to the steady pendulum, feeling as though she were still with me. Now, though, it served as a reminder of the promise I'd made. The promise I was about to break. I could almost feel her reach out to stop me.

Frank and Amy entered the room and I turned away, pushing the memory of Glory from my head. I braced myself. Amy sat on the end of the bed and Frank pulled up a chair, leaving barely a hands width between them.

'What is it, love?' He furrowed his brow. 'You've had a bad night.'

I nodded. 'The first of many, I assume. But it's not that. I need to talk to you both about something else.' I looked heavenward, taking in the crack in the ceiling. 'Promise you'll hear me out, Frank.'

Amy squeezed his arm. Something had passed between them. They'd gone to bed foes and woken up allies. At least they'd have that. Frank gave me a nod to continue.

'Amy, this mostly concerns you. There are things about me...about yourself, that you need to know. Things I've kept from you over the years.'

'No, Josephine,' Frank's voice was firm. 'No.'

'It's time, Frank. There are things you need to hear too.'

His chair made a muted screech on the carpet as he scraped it back. 'You *swore.* You swore on our marriage vows.'

'I made those vows as another person. An imposter,' I said.

I looked at Amy, expecting shock and confusion. But instead, her features remained calm, a steady mask. When Frank reached the door, she spoke.

'Dad, I already know.'

He stopped, his hand gripping the door frame and my guts flipped.

She continued, 'I found your marriage certificate in the back of a drawer when I was fourteen.' She turned to me. 'I was three when you married. Frank's not my biological father, is he?'

I shook my head. She slipped from the bed and embraced him.

'It doesn't matter, Dad.' There were no words after that—and if there were, Frank's shuddering sobs muffled them.

My throat tightened. All this time and his only fear had been that she would reject him. Yet she'd known for years and tried to protect his feelings the same way he'd protected her.

She was stronger than me, my daughter.

*My little sister.*

I'd always believed I was acting, playing the part of Amy's mother—a spell Gloria had forced me to weave around myself until I, too, was convinced by its glamour. I'd given up my life, my identity, *everything,* to protect Amy; to keep her safe. But—somewhere among the nappy changes, the sleepless nights, the homework lessons, and the break-up tears—the enchantment had come true. I had mothered this child the best I could. The way our own mother couldn't.

I'd come here wanting her memory of me to be real, convincing myself that telling her the truth was the right thing to do. That I was giving her the chance to leave before things got too bad. I wanted her to know I'd only been the understudy, pretending to be the lead part of Mum.

But as I looked at Frank and Amy, arm-in-arm, making their way back to my bedside, I knew. I'd only been trying to free myself.

I finally understood what Gloria had tried to teach me. Amy needed a Mum. Deserved one. I wiped my eyes as they took a seat.

'Do you have any questions?' I asked.

She pursed her lips and darted a look at Frank. 'One. Did you love him? My biological father?'

*Broken glass. A clenched fist. Bellowing shouts. My mother's stifled screams. The light fading from her eyes.*

'I was afraid of him. He wasn't a good man.'

She nodded. 'Is he still alive?'

*My trembling hands. My voice, clear and strong. The retort of a shotgun.*

I shook my head.

'Good. I've seen enough scumbags in my court observations to know the type. That's all I want to know,' she said.

'It's as much as I ever wanted to know,' Frank echoed.

And it was as much as I would ever tell.

That night I feigned sleep, knowing it wouldn't take Frank long to drop off from exhaustion. When they both slept, I slipped downstairs. I lit a pillar candle and sat outside on the porch—Aunt Gloria's old writing pad and pen tucked under the crook of my arm.

There was something divine about the sea at night. The full moon perched above the ocean like a conductor, pulling the waves into shore to a tune only she could hear. I shivered and pulled my cardigan closer around my shoulders.

'The full moon is for letting things go,' my mother had told me, wistful after Dan had been in one of his remorse-cycles. 'You think of something you want to release from your life, write it down on a piece of paper and Selene—the Goddess of the Moon—will take care of it for you.' Her voice had been lyrical, full of longing.

'Do you ever think of things you'd like to let go?' I'd asked her.

'Mostly I wait for the new moon and I wish for things I want to bring in. Like your sister. That's where she got her name.' She'd kissed Selene's soft cheek. 'I met Dan on the night of the new moon, when I wished for love.'

I'd bunched my fists in my dress to keep myself from screaming. She was blind to him. That night I'd written Dan's name over and over on the paper, praying to the goddess of the moon to take my stepfather away. And she had. She'd taken him from my life, from our lives. But his spectre had never left.

Now, by the full moon's fey light, I picked up the pen and addressed the letter.

*My Dearest Selene.*

I scrawled and scratched, purging the story from me, simultaneously reliving and rejecting the horror of my history. I wrote till my fingers cramped; the ink blotted in places, punctuated by my tears. When I finished, the secret no longer resided in me. It weighed down the paper in my hands, but I had evicted the black, venomous truth from my lungs. For the first time in my adult life, I could breathe to my full capacity.

From the kitchen, I retrieved an empty wine bottle. Rolling my letter like a scroll, I tied it with kitchen twine and popped it inside the sea-green glass. I put a cork in and sealed it tight with candle wax. The grandfather clock in the sitting room chimed, announcing midnight and a shiver ran over me. I could feel Gloria's disapproving gaze on my shoulders.

'Oh, stop fussing, Glory. We can't all be bank vaults.'

I made my way down the back-porch steps, eased off my slippers and wriggled my toes in the cool sand, pausing for a moment to savour the sensation. Did they have sand in the afterlife? Or would I keep only the memory of it underfoot?

I made my way along the deserted beach, silent save for the rhythmic rolling of the waves. By the water's edge, I glanced around then removed my nightgown and underwear, cladding my tired old body only in moonbeams.

My skin prickled with goosebumps as I picked up the bottle and splashed my way into the open mouth of the ocean. Why, in all this time, had I never swum naked in the sea? A fear of sharks, maybe? Modesty? But then, as the shock of the cold water hit my shins, I realised the truth—it had never occurred to me that I could be this daring. That I could be this free.

I waded further in until the waves caressed my waist. If I could throw the bottle far enough, the current would catch it and carry it far from here. The pearlescent moon gazed down, watching with curiosity as I lifted my arm.

Tonight, I offered Selene my biggest sacrifice yet—my confession. I sent a silent prayer that she'd help me find peace in all I'd done to protect my little girl. A prayer that if Amy ever found out, somehow she'd understand.

I'd loved her from the moment I'd met her.

It was time to lay our past to rest.

I propelled the bottle through the air, yelling to give force to my throw. There was a distant splash and a lone gull cried out. The hairs on my arms stood up. The goddess had granted my wish. She had taken my sister. I waded forward and plunged through the cool skin of the water, into the black womb below me, keeping myself submerged until my lungs burnt. When I resurfaced, I gulped at the air.

Transformed. Reborn.

I turned around to make my way back in and there she was. The moonlit figure of my daughter watching me from the shore.

# Heart of the River

*Caitlyn McPherson*


The scents of rain and ozone, drifting in from Chang'an, are not welcome. Guzzling down the fish in my mouth, I raise my head towards the sky searching for the intruder. Scales of deep emerald catch the light and twinkle like stars against a burnt copper sky. It is Yangzi—dragon of the Chang Liang River. Although we are kin, his presence unsettles me. He shouldn't be in my domain.

Yangzi weaves through the clouds, fluid as a silk ribbon. He circles overhead twice and descends, landing with a loud thud. The cranes amongst the reeds panic and take flight with a ruckus of honking cries.

Of all our kind, my brother Yangzi is the most tremendous in size. Though I'm far from being the smallest, I must stretch out my neck to hold his gaze. Our eyes connect and the air turns heavy with the promise of rain and the pulsing energy of rivers and storms.

'Brother Huang He.' He greets me with the slightest incline of his head.

I return the gesture, albeit stiffly, my eyes never leaving his. 'Brother Yangzi. What brings you here?'

Yangzi's moonlight silver eyes trace my face with mild interest as he idly scratches his jaw. 'I've come to check on you, brother. The winds from the north have been whispering strange things. I wanted to see if they were true.'

I cock my head. 'What are you talking about?'

Yangzi's eyes roam my river bank with slow deliberation, taking in every detail before returning to me. 'I see things are well cared for here, but what of your domain further to the north? It's not like you to neglect your duties and remain in one region for so long.' He lets the weight of the words hang in the air between us.

My tail flicks and nostrils flare. 'I have not been neglecting my duties, brother. Just slower these last few seasons to attend each region. Nothing you need concern yourself with.'

Yangzi gives a half-hearted shrug of his neck. 'If you say so. But don't say I didn't try.'

I frown. 'Try what? Spit it out, already. I have no time for your ambiguity.'

Amusement flickers in Yangzi's eyes. He takes a purposeful step towards me, dorsal spines rippling with the movement. I refrain from backtracking but regret the decision when Yangzi sniffs the air around me.

His face twists in unveiled disgust and dread swells inside me.

'Yes, I can see you don't have time for me. Your *human* pet is waiting isn't it?' he growls.

I open my jaw to protest—to explain—but snap my mouth shut before I make a fool of myself and feed anymore rumours floating in the breeze. Yangzi looks at me with disappointment and concern.

'So, the rumours are true. Tread carefully brother. Spending too much time around the humans will unbalance you. They're chaotic creatures. Arrogant, small-minded and only concerned with their own self-importance. Too much Yin.' He eyes me steadily, allowing the words to sink in like silt on a riverbed. My claws dig into the dirt but I remain silent.

Yangzi's warning rings with truth. Humans are more trouble than good. It's why I've always avoided interactions with them...but this is different. *She* is different.

I remain silent and Yangzi frowns.

With another lazy shrug, he sighs. 'Suit yourself, brother. I tried.'

My tail flicks with impatience. 'Duly noted.'

With a curt nod and a lithe leap, Yangzi takes his leave and disappears along the horizon.

The tense pressure of building storms eases back into a refreshing breeze and I withdraw into the river with a weary sigh.

I close my eyes and let my awareness drift. The running water always helps to clear my mind. The flow of each tributary is the blood in my veins; the ebb and pulse of the currents, my heartbeat. This is where I belong, where I'm supposed to be. Yet I find myself drawn more and more to the surface. To the world of the humans.

'Huang He? Huang He? Where are you?' Her voice wakes me from my meditation. A shiver ripples through my body. With a simple command, the dark depths swell and push me up above the surface on a loud gush of water.

The fading sunlight catches on gold embroidery and layers of scarlet and lilac silks. Braids of ebony are woven into intricate loops, held together by chrysanthemums and a white-jade hairpin.

Princess Xiu-ling.

Xiu-ling's kohl-lined eyes catch mine and her soft lips part in a radiant smile. I unfurl from the water and step onto the river bank. With a quick shake I dispel the water from my body. Xiu-ling rushes towards me, arms outstretched. She barely comes to my chest and her arms don't come close to holding me, but her embrace warms my whole body. I inhale deeply, breathing in the sweet fragrance of mandarin and jasmine that I've come to associate with her.

Xiu-ling pulls away and smiles at me, child-like with simple joy. Her wide eyes reflect my image; pearlescent white against midnight black. Yin and Yang in perfect harmony.

'I missed you,' she murmurs.

I nuzzle her head. 'As did I. How was your journey?'

'Long.' She sighs, 'But it was good to see how things are outside the capital and see for myself that the empire is prospering.'

Xiu-ling had been concerned about the welfare of the country prior to leaving. With rumours of civil unrest to the north, it's no surprise.

'And the festival?' I ask, eager to hear her melodic voice recount her journey.

Xiu-ling's eyes sparkle. 'It was so beautiful. Everything was alive with the glow of spring. The streets, the people, the flowers...I wish you could have been there with me.' Her words echo my own sentiments. But my responsibility over the Huang River prevented me from going.

Xiu-ling draws her hands from behind her back. 'I have a gift for you.' A small scroll, neatly rolled and tied with silk thread rests in her delicate fingers.

A smile creeps onto my face, although it's not quite the same as a human's. Xiu-ling laughs and I chuckle in response.

'Shall I read it for you?' she offers.

I dip my head in a nod and Xiu-ling unfurls the scroll with practiced ease.

> *'You ask why I live*
> *alone in the mountain forest,*
> *and I smile and am silent*
> *until even my soul grows quiet.*
> *The peach trees blossom.*
> *The water continues to flow.*

*I live in the other world,*
*one that lies beyond the human.'*

She finishes reading, closing her eyes and holding the parchment to her chest.

'Beautiful.' I exhale. 'Who wrote it?'

'Li Po. I like it because it reminds me of you.'

Tilting my head to the side I eye her. 'Oh? How so?'

She lightly traces the mother of pearl pendant strung around her throat. 'Well...you are rather mysterious and quiet and you are from the Celestial Realm.'

The sun has long since taken its leave. The birds hush as crickets begin their moonlit song. Bamboo grass rustles gently in the breeze. Xiu-ling shivers so I wrap myself around her, coiling against her small form. She snuggles closer, resting her head against my shoulder. We fit together like a tangram puzzle. Each breath in perfect unity and harmony.

Xiu-ling breaks the quiet and points to the heavens where a twinkle of silver falls in a graceful arc. 'Look, a falling star!' She scrunches her eyes closed, lips pursed in concentration. I stare at her curiously.

'Xiu-ling?'

'Shh!' She swats a hand against my shoulder. 'Hurry and make a wish!'

A wish? Why would I make a wish on a dying star? It doesn't make sense to me, but if it makes Xiu-ling happy I shall try. I close my eyes and ponder, but I'm unable to think of anything I want except to dwell in this moment with Xiu-ling a little longer.

Peaking one eye open, I glance sideways at Xiu-ling.

Her lashes flutter open and she catches my eye and smiles knowingly.

'I hope our wishes come true,' she whispers. But her smile

wanes, the edges of her lips turning downwards. Even after years of practice I still find it a challenge to understand the variety of complex gestures humans use to express their thoughts and feelings, but I recognize this one. It's all too familiar. Sadness.

She glances away, biting her lip. 'All I want is for things to stay the way they are. Is that so selfish?'

I blink, unsure what she means.

Her shoulders sag and her head bows. 'I guess it must be, since destiny seems to have other plans.' Her voice is distant.

My stomach clenches uncomfortably to hear her speak in such a way.

'What is wrong, dear one?' I ask.

Xiu-ling is quiet for a moment before she replies on a shaky breath, 'Father is worried about a rebellion. He believes marrying me off to a general will gain him more support. You know I would do anything to ensure the continued peace and prosperity of the empire, but I...' Her voice cracks. She swallows, takes a breath and continues, 'I don't want to marry someone I don't love!'

She buries her face into the ruby folds of her sleeves. Crickets chirp softly in the heavy silence.

'I wish I had been born a man,' she mumbles.

I affectionately nudge her shoulder. 'I am glad you were not.'

Xiu-ling peeks above the embroidered silk. 'Why?'

I tilt my head. 'Isn't it obvious? Your male-kin are not nearly as agreeable, nor nearly as lovely. Also, I could not imagine you with a beard.'

A giggle escapes from beneath her sleeve. It's beautiful and a pleasant warmth spreads through my chest.

'Besides,' I continue, 'it is the Emperor's loss if he does not see you are a treasure to be kept, not given away. You humans are such funny creatures. The only species where one of your kind believes itself superior to the other. Why, if you'd been born a spider you would devour your male companions.'

Xiu-ling's face contorts, nose scrunching. 'I am glad I'm not a spider. They're so scary.'

I snort. 'A dragon—with the power over the river and rains; to give or take life—does not scare you, but a tiny spider does?'

Xiu-ling shakes her head and laughs. 'When you put it like that it sounds silly, but yes.'

Her eyes warm as she reaches out and cups my cheek, 'You know, you're more to me than a dragon of the river. More than the power and responsibilities you bear. You are the one who saved me when I was drowning. The one who gave me a life and gave me hope. You're the only one in this world who truly cares for me. To me you're...' A mixture of expressions dance across her face, too fast for me to catch their meaning. '...my most precious friend.'

So this is what the feeling is? The concept of friendship is very human. A pack thing, safety in numbers. Dragons are solitary beings. Yangzi had called Xiu-ling my pet, but that sounded wrong. It's nice to have a name for the yearning for her company; the desire to see her smile and laugh, to give her the sun and moon if she'd but ask.

'Friend?' I test the word. It sits better on my tongue than pet.

She nods, wrapping her arms around my neck and nuzzling her face against my mane. 'My one and only,' she whispers.

I wake from slumber at the call of my name.

'Xiu-ling?' I ask, voice croaky, the fog of sleep still heavy in my mind.

'Huang He! I need to speak with you. Please...it's urgent.' She's using a *jìnghuā shuǐyuè*—a water mirror. Xiu-ling's reflection glimmers dimly, overpowered by the moonlight upon the river's surface. It's hard even for my sharp eyes to focus on her soft features as they shift and move with the water's flow.

'Xiu-ling, what's wrong?'

'I need to see you, but Father has me under lock and key. Can you come to my bedchamber, like you have before?'

I give a quick nod. 'Of course.'

Sinking beneath the water's surface, I prepare for my transition. It's hard to explain the sensation of changing forms, whether it be from solid to liquid or from hard scale to soft flesh. I melt and expand within the water, becoming nothing, yet everything; existing nowhere, yet everywhere all at once. As I rise out of the water, I become heavy and my body condenses into a smaller flesh form. It's stifling at first. Taking shape as a human is always uncomfortable but it's the only way I can fit within the palace walls.

I emerge from the warm waters of a large wooden bathtub in Xiu-ling's private bathroom chamber. Water sloshes against the wooden frame but, as I step out, not a single bead of water clings to me.

The tiled floor is cold and hard against my bare feet. Human bodies are so soft and sensitive. With a wave of my hand, soft silk robes of pearl and cerulean appear and wrap themselves about me. I make my way to the door leading to Xiu-ling's bedchamber.

The lanterns flicker, sending light and shadow dancing around the room while the perfume of expensive oils and incense fills the vast space. Xiu-ling turns and stares at me, her eyes puffy and shadowed, turmoil glistening in them...or is it tears? Her painted lips part to speak but the words don't come. She frowns, mouth pressing into a hard line, and returns to pacing the length of the room. I trace Xiu-ling's anxious footsteps in silence as I wait for her to speak.

She stops again, turns back to me, and takes a shaky breath. 'Father says I'm to be married by the end of the month.'

The news has a strange effect on my body. My insides quiver, as if the fish I ate earlier are trying to escape. Ridiculous. They are long dead. But it's unsettling and I pause a moment before answering.

'You knew this was coming.' The words taste bitter in my

mouth.

Xiu-ling plays with the seam of her sleeve, picking at a rosy thread. 'Yes, but I didn't think it would be so soon.' She ceases her thread-pulling and flails her arms against her side with an exasperated sigh. 'General Zhang is old enough to be my father. The idea of marrying him is repulsive!' She storms away, silk robes trailing behind her.

I'm left in confusion and frustration. Centuries of wisdom fall beyond my reach like fingers through smoke. What can I say?

Xiu-ling moves towards the lavish bed structure in the centre of the chamber. She throws aside a gossamer curtain and collapses onto the bed. She's swallowed up by the sea of silk cushions and fur rugs.

I follow, sweeping back the fine curtain to hover by her bedside.

'If the proposal repulses you so much, why not refuse?' I ask.

Her snort takes me by surprise. 'The Emperor's word is absolute. To refuse would mean death, even if I am his daughter...' She plays idly with a cushion before shoving it away, 'All this luxury is nothing more than a gilded cage!' Xiu-ling sits up again and gives me a pleading stare. 'Take me with you when you leave.'

I would give her anything within my power to give, but I cannot grant her this. Yangzi's warning swims in the back of my mind. I couldn't whisk her away to the Celestial Realm. Not when many of the gods and spirits, like Yangzi, look down upon humans with contempt. Some are even vengeful, spiteful towards humans. I shiver at the thought of what they could do to my Xiu-ling.

And if we remained in the Mortal Realm, I couldn't offer the life of freedom that she sought. My duty restricts me to the rivers and tributaries within my domain—all within her father's empire. She would never truly be safe or free.

My fingers curl into fists at my side, but my voice is smooth as I speak.

'Your place is here among the rest of your kind. I can't give you what you ask.'

'But you don't understand! If I marry General Zhang, I won't be able to see you…maybe never again.' She stares at me with a new resolve, 'I…I don't want to be with anyone else…only you.'

She looks so vulnerable. Like the day we first met. A child-ling lost in my river currents with no hope of escaping on her own. She's crying out to me to save her once again and my heart sinks. I can't help her. Not this time. For all my powers, I am powerless here.

The words catch in my throat before they come out as a sorrow-filled murmur, 'I can't.'

Xiu-ling's lip quivers and tears pool in her eyes but she blinks them away before they can fall. Something pulls uncomfortably in my chest, a kind of gnawing sensation I can't explain. I don't want to see her cry. I want to wash away her fears and worries, but I can't.

With a hesitant hand I reach out and draw her against my chest. Xiu-ling's arms wrap tight around my waist, fingers splaying against my back. Like that night by the river our breathing finds harmony. I press my cheek against her head breathing in the sweet citrus and jasmine scent. My fingers brush through her hair and gently tuck the silken strands behind her ear. It's so soft against my fingers it gives me a new appreciation for this human form.

Xiu-ling pulls away just enough to look up at me. Something in my stomach flutters. The way her eyes glimmer as if they shine only for me. But she swiftly turns, burying her face back into my chest. My hands twitch. I want to see it again. That look in her eyes.

Running a finger along her jaw I cup her chin and tilt her face back towards mine. Her skin is so soft, like fresh petals on a flower.

'Huang He…' she breathes, cheeks flushing.

Like coals in a fire her dark eyes are burning with something that I can't quite place. Once again, I catch my reflection in them. Not the dragon but a man. Soft flesh and warm blood.

Xiu-ling places a hand on my chest where my heart pounds like a *tanggu* drum. My gaze flickers to her scarlet painted lips, slightly parted and glistening in the lantern light. Something dark and carnal stirs within me as Xiu-ling leans closer.

Balancing on tiptoes she tilts her face towards mine, achingly slow. Everything about her beckons me. Like a moth to a flame. What I would do to dive into that blaze and burn.

My body shivers, pale skin glistening briefly like scales before returning to a normal skin tone. It's enough to break the spell. I might look human, but I'm not. I'm a dragon, bound to the river. She's a princess, bound to her duty.

My blood cools. The flame Xiu-ling had sparked, snuffed out by cold reality. Before our lips can touch, I turn aside.

Her body stiffens. 'Huang He?'

There is confusion in her voice. I want to explain but there is nothing I can say to make this right. More than my own selfish desire, I want her to have a long and full life; to experience all of life's joys and wonders as only a mortal can.

She pulls away and the loss leaves me hollow and cold.

'Huang He, look at me.'

Even if she wasn't the emperor's daughter I couldn't disobey her. Turning back I see the hurt. She frames my face with her delicate fingers. Soft and warm and gentle, everything she is.

'Do you not feel the same as I? Do you not love me as I love you?'

I should have realised this was more than simple companionship, but love? Was this really love? How can I have fallen so blindly for her?

The answer is strangely simple, like I've known deep down all along.

She is the sunlight that warms me, the air in my lungs, the blood in my veins. She has carved herself into the very marrow of my bones. This wonderful human girl who laughs and smiles at me, when others flee in terror. Who picks up her skirts and dances in the breeze like a sparrow. Who loves to read me poetry and plait braids in my hair. I would give anything for her health and happiness. Anything.

As certain as the sun rising in the east and setting in the west, I swear I love her...but I...I love her enough to do what's right, to let her go. The words fail me as I try to express the turmoil within me.

'Xiu-ling, I...'

'It's fine, you don't need to explain. I was a fool to hope.' Xiu-ling says, letting her hands drop away. She smiles but the warmth does not reach her eyes. The fire in them is gone, and they're startlingly cold in its absence.

I've hurt her. The knowledge twists a blade in my chest. But removing myself from her life is the best thing I can do for her. She will have no reason to be chased down by the Emperor. No angry gods or spirits will seek vengeance on her soul. She'll be forced to marry the general, but she will be safe in the care of a warrior. She might even find happiness in the offspring they will one day share.

It's not really a comforting thought, but it's one I can live with.

I sigh. 'The only fool here is me. Forgive me, dear one.'

Her smile becomes bitter. 'Fate makes fools of us all...'

I can see the cracking and crumbling pieces of her heart as if it is my own. She *is* my heart.

'Well, fate can have tomorrow,' she says. 'If all we have left is this moment, then will you stay? Just one night where I can fall asleep in your arms. That's all I ask.'

How can I say no?

I gently draw her into my chest and curl up with her in the plush bedcovers. For hours we lie wrapped up together as Xiu-ling recounts every memory of every moment we've ever shared together. The lanterns eventually flicker and die, and in the darkest hours of pre-dawn, Xiu-ling finally drifts to sleep, lips slightly parted as her chest rises and falls in steady rhythm. I reach down and brush my lips against her cheek in a ghost of a kiss.

'I'm sorry my love, this is goodbye.'

The day of the wedding comes and goes. The seasons change. Spring becomes summer, summer becomes autumn, autumn becomes winter. And so it goes for two cycles around the sun. But, despite the time apart, the loneliness inside my heart doesn't ease. The fields dry and the mud of the riverbanks crack from neglect as I half-heartedly attend to my duties.

I shouldn't be surprised when I catch the scent of ash and smoke in the air, yet I am. It's too early in the season for fires, even if it has been dryer than usual. A tall plume of smoke rises to taint the blue sky an awful hazy grey. My heart skips a beat and my stomach drops. It's coming from Chang'an. The fields might be dry but there is no reason a fire should be coming from the city.

There is no way for me to know if Xiu-ling is there, but I can't sit back and watch if there's even the slightest chance she is in danger.

I sink into the river...melt into the currents...and rise in my human form, out of the carp pond within the palace courtyard.

Like geese spooked by a fox, people rush about frantically in all directions. Their screams are drowned out by the clamour of clashing steel and shouts of soldiers. The putrid odour of burning hair and flesh mingles with the smoke and ash. My eyes sting in the smoke-reddened afternoon light. Armed imperial guards battle against rebel soldiers marked by their darker armour and banners of deep violet. The emperor's guards are outnumbered. The rebel soldiers cut them down and kill every servant in their path. All the while, the blaze engulfing the palace grows.

'Xiu-ling? Xiu-ling?'

An ember flicks up, catching my cheek and I flinch away. The fire is beyond tempering. Not even my powers would be enough to snuff it out. What if I can't find her in time? Cold terror seeps into my veins. No. I have to find her. I swear to the Jade Emperor himself; I will not give up until she's in my arms.

I'm about to run into the main entrance when I catch her voice across the courtyard.

'Zhang? Anyone? Please help!' Xiu-ling emerges from the burning structure, her face smattered with blood and ash, her vermillion robes in tatters. She clutches a small child-ling to her breast as she stumbles out of the curtain of smoke. A nearby soldier wearing the polished armour of a general spots her and approaches in confident strides.

Xiu-ling's face lights with hope and she reaches a shaky hand towards him.

'Zhang! What's happening? We have to get—'

General Zhang backhands her cheek and sends her stumbling to her knees. Despite the blow, Xiu-ling's grip on the child-ling doesn't falter. Her eyes are wide as she gazes up at her husband.

My feet are moving before her name tears out of me. Several soldiers turn their attention and weapons towards me. Zhang barely acknowledges my presence save for a wave of his hand.

"Deal with him while I finish this once and for all," he commands.

I barely register the soldiers marching towards me as my eyes connect with Xiu-ling's. The rest of the world fades away. Emotion dances across her face. She turns her gaze back towards Zhang, face now a mask of fiery resolve.

Zhang lets out a mocking laugh as he steps forward, blade raised.

My skin bubbles, flesh bursting and tearing as pearlescent scales, claws and horns rip through the human façade mid-run. The band of soldiers blocking my way yell and stumble backward as I close on the general.

Zhang brushes the tip of his sword just below Xiu-ling's collarbone. 'You've outlived your use to me, wife.'

Time slows. The world falls silent. I cannot reach her. I watch in helpless horror as general Zhang drives his sword through Xiu-ling's chest.

A strangled sob escapes my throat as she slumps to the ground. The sound draws Zhang's attention and his gloating sneer disappears. He yanks the blade from Xiu-ling and directs it at me. Blood trickles down the polished steel.

The world turns red. Fire and blood and fury. Then I'm upon him. I snare Zhang between my jaws, digging deeper and deeper into his flesh. He screams and thrashes, but it's the rancid taste of his blood that makes me spit him out. Zhang struggles on the ground, moaning. Blood oozes from his wounds. I fight the bile rising in my throat. Too much Yin in my system.

'General Zhang!' a soldier cries.

An arrow whistles through the air and pain explodes in my shoulder. I recoil with a roar. An archer several paces away lowers the bow, hands trembling. The colour drains from his face.

The air pressure around me intensifies. Static charges flicker and storm clouds roll in, crashing together like waves. Lightning strikes the archer and scatters the rest of the troop around him.

But even amidst the chaos I've created, some still dare to fight. A soldier directs his *qiáng* spear towards me and charges. More men, brandishing polearms and *hu-cha* follow his lead.

I dodge a spear and swing my tail, smashing the man-ling into the palace's stone wall. He smacks against it with a wet crunch and sags to the ground.

A polearm drives towards my chest, but I'm faster and stronger.

I slash and tear, claws and teeth ripping through armour, flesh and bone alike. I will send them all to the deepest pits of *Diyu.*

Lightning cracks across the heavens and thunder drowns out the soldiers' screams. One sinks to his knees, deep puncture wounds in his chest. Another fumbles to keep the soft pink folds of intestine caged behind trembling fingers.

As their bodies fall, the smell of their urine and blood taints the air. It's sickening. I want to gag and turn away, but I will have vengeance for what they've done.

The rest of the soldiers run, even as their injured general barks out an order, 'Do something!'. Zhang's movements are slow but determined as he drags himself away, armour scraping against stone.

My eyes narrow into slits. Nostrils flaring and tail twitching. A flurry of violent images flitter through my mind. All the ways that I wish I could kill this man-ling before me. The one responsible for all this bloodshed. The one I'd entrusted Xiu-ling's life to. I've been such a fool.

I stalk towards him, talons clacking against the bloodstained stone. With a moaned curse Zhang grasps his sword and twists towards me. I bat away the weapon and it clatters to the ground.

'N-no, please!' he screams.

I dig my claws into his leg and drag him towards me. He squirms and shrieks beneath my grip and I find myself tired of the sound. With a swift tear and a jerk, Zhang's head rolls away, smearing a dark trail behind it.

I turn away from the bloodshed, my focus returning to Xiu-ling still lying where she fell with the child-ling resting beside her. Her chest flutters and lips quiver as she gasps for breath, but she's still alive.

I rush towards her, changing into my human form, scales and claws receding like smoke. I drop to my knees. The crimson flower of her life-blood blossoms from her wound, visible even against the scarlet silk of her robe. There is nothing that I can do to save her.

Hands trembling, I cradle her in my lap.

'Huang He...You're hurt...' Her voice is husky and raw.

'Hush, now,' I murmur, brushing stray strands of hair from her face.

'I'm so happy to see you. I've missed you so much...Every day.' Tears stain her pale cheeks.

'I know, dear one. I...' My voice breaks, the lump in my throat making it hard to talk. 'I'm so sorry!'

Xiu-ling reaches out, cupping my face. Soft, gentle, warm...just like her. I press my cheek into her hand and brace it with my own.

She tugs me closer and this time there is no hesitation. I close the distance between us. Her lips are soft and warm and, for a moment, nothing else matters. There is nothing but the warmth and tenderness of her love.

Her hand falls away and the moment ends. Her dark eyes burn.

'You are my one and only love,' she says.

'You're my everything,' I tell her.

A smile's shadow pulls at her lips and my heart aches. Never again will I see her smile. With a ragged breath she turns aside, looking at the still form of the child-ling beside her. Her daughter.

'Huang He...Look after Meng-Mei for me. Please?'

I give her hand a gentle squeeze. 'I promise.'

'I...I wish to hold her one last time.'

I gather up the child-ling, unconscious nearby. Its small chubby form fits so easily in my arms that I pause for a moment in wonder. Meng-Mei stirs briefly but does not wake. She's so much smaller than Xiu-ling was when I first met her, yet the resemblance is unmistakable.

Carefully, I move Meng-Mei into her mother's arms. There is no smile, or flicker of emotion in Xiu-ling's face as she holds her offspring. Her body is too weak for such things. But there's no doubt of her love. It's almost tangible—an overwhelming force.

And, in that moment, I see the life that Xiu-ling had begged me for. A life of tears and joy, of pain and hope…a future…a family.

I blink back the stinging in my eyes and try to ignore the icy claws digging into my chest. I was such a fool to have let her go. My throat tightens painfully as my vision blurs, hot liquid pooling and spilling.

Tears. How human I've become.

Rubbing my eyes on my silken sleeve, I gaze back at Xiu-ling. Her expression is soft and peaceful, all signs of pain gone. An empty cocoon of a butterfly now flown. The cold claws twisting in my heart release, leaving a hollow emptiness in their place.

Gone. It's all gone.

Tears cascade and rain plummets to the earth in reflection of my grief. My life-giving water soaks the death-stained palace grounds. I pull Xiu-ling's body closer and bury my face in her hair. The scent of jasmine and citrus still lingers under the ash. I choke back a sob and fight to keep talons from ripping through my fingers and shredding everything apart.

A muffled gurgle pulls me from my anguish and I turn to the child-ling by Xiu-ling's side. Meng-Mei.

The child-ling stirs again, crying now as the bitter-cold rain soaks her tiny body. I wrap her within the folds of my robes and her crying ceases but not her shivering. She cannot stay here, even if I wish to stay in the biting cold until I die. I promised Xiu-ling that I'd look after her daughter.

Holding Meng-Mei closer I stand. There is nothing left for her here. Nothing left for me. I look up, past the stormy clouds to the heavens beyond—where sparkling lights flicker against the darkness—and I straighten my shoulders.

'I will not make the same mistakes twice.'

A promise.

And, without a glance back at Xiu-ling, the smouldering palace, or the countless bodies strewn about the courtyard, I grip Meng-Mei closer and walk away.

'What about your responsibilities? Who will manage the river and rains if not you?' Yangzi asks as we watch Meng-Mei from the riverbank.

She dances through the grass, pudgy arms outstretched as she chases after a butterfly. She looks just like her mother. Eyes sparkling with joy, lips parted in a radiant smile. A feeling of warmth spreads through me at the reminder of Xiu-ling. Though the memories are accompanied by a deep pain, it is lessened by the presence of Meng-Mei. She's like sunlight in dark waters. My precious child.

My eyes never leave her as I reply to Yangzi's question. 'I no longer care for keeping the balance. It is wasted on the humans. They are changing. Fewer and fewer of them believe in the old ways. Soon there will come a time when their arrogance and disbelief will force us back to the Celestial Realm forever. I'd rather stay and look after what's truly important. Let the river flow as it will. I will stay here. With her.'

I don't need to look at him to sense his disapproval.

His curt voice cuts in, 'There will be repercussions if you choose this path. You know they'll strip away your immortality and powers. Is she worth it?'

I glance down at my human hands, now marred with cuts and callouses from long days of toil. It won't be easy. My celestial duty still beckons me back to the river and living amongst the humans will test my resolve, but as I look at young Meng-Mei, the answer is simple.

'Yes, she is.'

# About the Authors

*The Springfield Writers Group.* Established in 2016, the Springfield Writers Group (SWG) is based in Brisbane, Australia. This group of emerging and established writers meet monthly over coffee and too many muffins to support each other's work and efforts towards becoming better writers. There is probably too much time spent laughing and enjoying each other's company, but we do get some work done as well. This anthology represents many months of work, learning, frustration, and joy.

Anyone wishing to contact the SWG can connect through the Queensland Writers Centre, who will forward information.

*Our Authors…*

*Megan Badger* is a Brisbane-based author of speculative fiction. She has been published in Sirens Call magazine and Veronica Literary magazine. Nicknamed *macabre Meg* by her friends she has a fascination with the dark and mysterious sides of human experience. Megan has a BFA in creative and professional writing.

*Sam Brown* writes crime fiction and sci-fi in smoky back-room bars and gin joints, splitting infinitives and spitting tobacco. Her stories are populated with scoundrels, hustlers, whores, and grifters…and those are the goodguys.
Find her online at **www.sirenofbrixton.wordpress.com**

*Annie Bucknall* is a freelance writer whose work has featured in some of Australia's most popular magazines. She writes stories that reach into the heart of human experience and relationships, using her pen to try and understand this crazy world. Follow her and her gorgeous labradoodles here:

Facebook or Instagram: @AnnieBucknall

*Nicola Buzan* a purveyor of dark and disturbing stories from the lush green Waitakere Ranges of New Zealand. When she's not imagining up speculative and domestic noir tales, she can usually be found reading pretty much anything she can get her hands on, polishing off a tricky crossword, or enjoying good food and wine with friends and family. Facebook - Nicola Buzan, Author or Twitter @opinionistas

*Cass Cooper* comes from a Film and Television background and writes children's stories and contemporary romance. She has a long-standing love of the written word, all things creative, and a desire to get a message across in her writing. She firmly believes that coffee is a food group, admits to eating far too much chocolate, and loves to get absorbed in a good book.

*Aiki Flinthart* has 11 published novels, including the popular YA fantasy series *80AD,* plus two fantasy/urban fantasy trilogies *(The Kalima Chronicles; Shadows).* And a non-fiction book *Fight like a Girl—writing fight scenes for female characters.* She has been shortlisted in the Aurealis awards and top-8 listed in the USA Writers of the Future competition. She practices martial arts, archery, knife-throwing, and musical instruments.

Website: **https://www.aikiflinthart.com/**    Twitter: @aikiflinthart

Facebook: **https://www.facebook.com/aiki.flinthart**

Instagram: AikiFlinthart

*Jan-Andrew Henderson (J.A. Henderson)* is the author of 24 teenage, YA and adult fiction and non-fiction books, published in the

UK, USA, Germany and the Czech Republic He has been shortlisted for thirteen literary awards and is the winner of the Doncaster Book Prize and Royal Mail Award. He recently moved to Brisbane from Scotland, to see what the sun looked like.
Website: **https://www.janandrewhenderson.com/**

*Ted Johnson* writes mostly non-fiction, amusing anecdotal stories about family, plus the occasional foray into fiction. Every year or so, God tries to destroy Brisbane. Her persecution results in extended power outages. And there's not much to do by candle-light except dig in and write. Just write.

*DA Kelly* is a writer and delighter in all things magic. Her stories are relentless, spellbinding mysteries stuffed full of quirky characters, wicked humour and delicious murder. She is writing the first book in her Arabella Black cosy paranormal mystery series, *Brooms Away*. If you like more magic with your murders then watch out for her upcoming novels.
Website: **http://dakellyfantasybooks.com**
Facebook: **https://www.facebook.com/grimsmead/**
Twitter: @dakellyauthor
Instagram: **https://www.instagram.com/dakellyauthor/**

*Lynne Lumsden Green* has bachelor degrees in both Science and the Arts, giving her the balance between rationality and creativity. She spent fifteen years as the Science Queen for HarperCollins Voyager Online. These days, she captains the Writing Race for the Australian Writers Marketplace on Facebook and volunteers at the Queensland Writers Centre, when not writing. You can find her blog at: **https://cogpunksteamscribe.wordpress.com/**

*Caitlyn McPherson* is an emerging author who lives in Brisbane with her feline overlord and pet fish. She has studied Creative Writing and Children's Picture Book Writing through the Australian and Queensland Writers Centres. In her spare time she dabbles in art, studies Japanese and is a student of Batojutsu.

Facebook and Instagram under the handle _CaitlynMcPherson_

Website at https://caitlynmcpherson.wixsite.com/authorartist

*Rebecca Nolan* is an internationally-published anthology author who loves to write all things paranormal, horror and romance. When she's not writing, you can almost guarantee she's scouring the shelves of her local bookstore, trying to find a book she doesn't own. To keep up to date with her latest releases, follow her on Twitter @RNolanauthor or Instagram @msrnol. You can also head to Wattpad to read some of her earlier stories - for free!

*Susan Ruth* loves to tell stories. She writes historical fiction set in England in the seventeenth and eighteenth centuries. She is also the author of the *Chronicles of Deva,* a fantasy sequence set in an alternative Britain in the early years of the twentieth century during a time of civil war. Her new novels, *Minister of State Security and Flight of the Queen,* will be available in 2020.

*Jo Seysener* is an emerging author who's always loved to write. She prefers to pen dystopian and YA fiction, but has recently published her first illustrated children's book. She lives in Brisbane with her family, two dogs and nine chickens.

Facebook: **https://www.facebook.com/joseysener/**

*Barry Townsend* is Brisbane-born emerging author. He spent many years working on cattle properties and writes stories steeped in Australian history and heart. He has two published novels *Werna Creek,* and *Where the Penny Falls.*

*Georgia Willis* is an avid reader, and emerging author writing in the fantasy genre. Born and bred in Brisbane, she lives with her crazy dog and numerous fish. She has had short stories published in two anthologies and plans on writing more.


Keep an eye out for future anthologies from the Springfield Writers Group.
If you enjoyed this one, you can also find the 2017 anthology, RETURN at your favourite retailer.

www.ingramcontent.com/pod-product-compliance
Lightning Source LLC
Chambersburg PA
CBHW031133120726
47905CB00006B/1679